EXACT REVENGE

Also by Tim Green
in Large Print:

The Fourth Perimeter

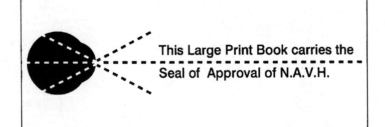

This Large Print Book carries the
Seal of Approval of N.A.V.H.

EXACT REVENGE

Tim Green

Thorndike Press • Waterville, Maine

Published in 2005 by arrangement with
Warner Books, Inc.

Thorndike Press® Large Print Basic.

The tree indicium is a trademark of Thorndike Press.

The text of this Large Print edition is unabridged.
Other aspects of the book may vary from the original edition.

Set in 16 pt. Plantin by Minnie B. Raven.

Printed in the United States on permanent paper.

Library of Congress Cataloging-in-Publication Data

Green, Tim, 1963–
    Exact revenge / by Tim Green.
       p. cm. — (Thorndike Press large print basic)
   ISBN 0-7862-7815-3 (lg. print : hc : alk. paper)
   1. Political candidates — Crimes against — Fiction.
  2. False testimony — Fiction.   3. Prisoners — Fiction.
  4. Revenge — Fiction.   5. Escapes — Fiction.
  6. Psychological fiction.   7. Large type books. I. Title.
  II. Thorndike Press large print basic series.
PS3557.R37562E93 2005b
  813'.54—dc22   2005010528

For Illyssa, because the brilliant light of your life warms even the deepest shadows of ours.

As the Founder/CEO of NAVH, the only national health agency solely devoted to those who, although not totally blind, have an eye disease which could lead to serious visual impairment, I am pleased to recognize Thorndike Press★ as one of the leading publishers in the large print field.

Founded in 1954 in San Francisco to prepare large print textbooks for partially seeing children, NAVH became the pioneer and standard setting agency in the preparation of large type.

Today, those publishers who meet our standards carry the prestigious "Seal of Approval" indicating high quality large print. We are delighted that Thorndike Press is one of the publishers whose titles meet these standards. We are also pleased to recognize the significant contribution Thorndike Press is making in this important and growing field.

Lorraine H. Marchi, L.H.D.
Founder/CEO
NAVH

★ Thorndike Press encompasses the following imprints: Thorndike, Wheeler, Walker and Large Print Press.

ACKNOWLEDGMENTS

As with every book I have written, there are people throughout the process who are invaluable. Each contribution, whether great or small, helps make the whole and for that I thank you all: Esther Newberg, my agent and friend, whose honesty exceeds all things. Ace Atkins, a brilliant writer and my good friend. Jamie Raab, my publisher, who spent her valuable time, creativity, and mental energy to make this book shine. The other people at Warner Books who have made me a part of their family, starting with our fearless leader, Larry Kirshbaum, and my editor, Rick Wolff, along with Maureen Egen, Chris Barba, Ivan Held, Tina Andreadis, Dan Ambrosio, Paul Kirschner, Jason Pinter, Jim Spivey and designer Ralph Fowler, and the special editorial assistance I received from Frances Jalet-Miller, Mari Okuda, and Roland Ottewell.

My parents, Dick and Judy Green, who not only taught me a love for books but for their inexhaustible reading of my manuscripts to give them their final polish.

Besides being the best lacrosse coach in the country, Ron Doctor was my expert on Native American lore, and I thank him for his many hours talking patiently to me. Dick Madigan was my expert on my characters' financial maneuvering.

Probably the most fascinating aspect of writing this book was spending time in and around Auburn Prison, and I could never have done that without the generous time of Captain John "Hoddie" Rourke and his wife Debbie, Lieutenant Mike Vazquez, and my expert up on the wall who took my calls day and night, Officer Clarence Van Ostrand.

BOOK ONE

BETRAYAL

A bitter laugh burst from the count's lips; as in a dream, he had just seen his father being taken to the grave, and Mercedes walking to the altar.

The Count of Monte Cristo

1

There was a time when people wished that they were me. The only boundaries I had were the limits of my imagination.

Now my world is six feet wide, eight feet long, and eight and a half feet high. It's less than you think. The only thing between the concrete floor and me is a narrow three-inch mattress. I don't need blankets or sheets because it's always warm. My shirt and pants were once gray. Now they are the color of oatmeal. They are no longer stiff with sweat and I can't smell them even though the guards angle their faces away whenever they try to let me out.

My days are full. They last one hour. It is the hour that they give me light. There are pests to be hunted and killed. Cracks in the walls need to be filled with a mortar I compose from loose pebbles and sand. My body needs inspection. My nails need to be filed down against the block wall. An ingrown hair scraped clean. Small ways that bring some order to my life.

When my work is through, I allow myself to languish and think about the times when I was a boy. I like to tilt my face to the light and close my eyes. I can feel the heat of the sunlight then and hear the swish of waves lapping the stones and the trees whispering secrets. I can feel the planks of wood beneath my towel. I hang my arm over the edge of the dock and press just the tips of my fingers into the water's pliant skin without breaking its surface.

I can smell the woodsmoke from the cobblestone fireplace in our small cabin and an occasional whiff of balsam. I can hear the bang of aluminum against the dock and my father asking me to go for a canoe ride. I say yes so as not to disappoint him even though I don't want to leave my mother's side. Her fingertips slide down the back of her page and her thumb snaps its edge as she turns to the next. I can hear the rattle and clang of the dinner bell.

Then my day ends.

I begin by allowing myself to vent, having somehow latched on to the notion that it's good for me. I have screamed myself mute. I have cried myself dry. I have laughed until my stomach convulses in painful knots. I have jabbered insanely to myself, reasoning with, arguing, begging, scolding, and mocking God. Eventually, I grow tired and I am ready to behave. Then I'm like everyone else, struggling to stay busy enough with what I have so I won't think about all the things I don't.

I still take pride in the long hard muscles, taut beneath the bronze skin of my six-foot frame. I have more positions for push-ups than a sex manual has for copulation. Push-ups on my fingertips. Push-ups upside down. Push-ups with my feet braced halfway up the wall. There is a thin metal seam above the door casing. I have calluses on my fingertips that fit nicely into that groove. I do pull-ups four different ways. Frontward with a narrow grip. Frontward with a wide grip. Same thing backward.

I can do five thousand sit-ups. I can run in place. I can jump on one leg and jump on two. I can shuffle from side to side the length of my world six thousand times without stopping. I know eighteen katas from Okinawa and I can do them all, ten times in succession without stopping. Then I sleep.

When I wake up, it's still night. Always. If I can, I go back to sleep. If I can't, I exercise my mind to keep from thinking of her. The velvety handfuls of dark hair in a curtain over my bare chest. The smooth pencil-line scar on her hip.

I can multiply and divide seven-digit numbers in my head. I can integrate and differentiate formulas I make up at random. I can regurgitate the meaning behind every mnemonic device from Pieper's New York State Bar Review.

I need to be strong.

Every sixty days, they come for me. Sixty days is as long as they can put someone into solitary confinement without giving him the opportunity to show that he is ready to behave. When they come for me, I will attack the first person I can get my hands on. I will do as much damage to him as I can because I know I'll get it all back and then some whether I spit in someone's face or tear out an eyeball.

At first, they try to beat it out of you. One at a time, the meanest guards get a chance to claim you from the hole. Then, when they realize that you are strong and that you will never stop, they begin to send the rookies. They will watch from behind the bars and laugh until they've had enough or until they get nervous. It takes six years to work through the digestive system of a maximum-security prison in

New York. I am in my third different prison. After today, I believe they will send me to a fourth.

My life didn't used to be like this. There was a time when I had everything.

2

The mind is like a screen in a water pipe. It collects the impurities of the past in random ways, a fragment of conversation, a snippet of color. A smell. I smelled like money that day in the cab when I passed through the tunnel into New Jersey to see Congressman Williamson at Valley Hospital. He smelled like death, old copper pennies, and bleached bedsheets.

I was the youngest partner at Parsons & Trout, with a suite at Donald Trump's Plaza Hotel and on the verge of a multimillion-dollar deal that would save my firm. It was the height of the Reagan era. There was a war on drugs. Russia was still an evil nation, and there was no shame in wanting to be rich.

But Roger Williamson only wanted to talk about duck hunting. He talked about the first double he ever shot with those tubes coming out of his nose, coughing into the air, like somehow he was handing me a small wooden box filled with life's secrets.

Then, I knew how to nod my head, respect my elders. But I didn't listen. Only fragments remain.

Roger had come from Syracuse and attended Princeton like me, only about forty years earlier. He lettered in basketball. I lettered in soccer. After he graduated, he went to Albany to work for Nelson Rockefeller. I went to law school to try to be Nelson Rockefeller.

I remember looking at the lines in his face. Road maps for my own future. Yes, I saw them. I recognized them without a thought.

It took Roger thirty years of kissing other people's asses before he was elected to Congress. At twenty-five, I hadn't even patted an ass and people were talking about having me be his replacement. That must not have seemed fair to Roger. But that's only if he was aware of it.

I was surprised that none of Roger's family was there. Two men in three-piece suits were. They didn't talk to me and I didn't really care. Roger had other tubes besides the one coming out of his nose. There was one in his stomach and another down below, collecting his urine in a clear plastic bag that was hooked to the stainless steel rail of his bed. There was a heart monitor beeping pleasantly and clear liquid dripped from an IV bottle.

"You aren't smiling," Roger said. His voice was strained and it came from the far reaches of his throat. "Every day you have your health is a good day. You should smile."

His skin had a blue cast to it and was sunken around the eye sockets and into the other depressions of his skull. His hair was wispy and gray. Only the very tips were still dark from dye. I thought I smelled the contents of the plastic bag and I cleared my throat.

"I'm fine."

"They say you might be the one to replace me. I'm glad. I wish they asked me, but I'm glad anyway."

I nodded and reached out to touch the back of his hand. The veins were pale and green and riddled with scabbed-over needle holes. His skin was cool, but dry. I regretted touching him anyway. The men in suits were watching.

"Hey," I said, "this might be like the '82 election. Remember that bounce-back?"

He started to laugh, but it ended in a painful-sounding choke that set the monitor off like a small guard dog. When he recovered, he turned his hand over and clutched my fingers in his own with an awkward grip. His nails needed a trim.

"My family left me two days after the first time I was elected," he said. "That was my second wife."

I nodded.

"Why?"

I shook my head.

"Duck hunting," he said, again. "Standing in those cattails, remember? The sun not even up. The birds swarming in on us like insects. Clear your head, Raymond. As often as you can. You grow cobwebs inside you until you die. They only clear for those last few weeks? Why would He do that to us?"

His lips kept moving, but little sound came out. I leaned closer.

". . . promise . . ."

"You want me to promise?" I asked.

He nodded and I moved even closer.

"You take this," he said, squeezing tight. "Only you. I wrote it myself. Here. In New Jersey. Remember that. You give it to her. As soon as you get back. Right away, Raymond. No one else. You tell no one. Will you promise me that?"

In his other hand was a legal-size envelope. He held it out to me. A woman's name and address were scrawled on the front: Celeste Oliver. I looked into his milky green eyes, red-rimmed and brimming with moisture, and took it from him. His eyes closed and his head went back into the pillow. The men in suits seemed to be oblivious to our arrangement, so I said good-bye to Roger, even though he was already asleep.

3

At eleven in the morning on Friday, the directors from Iroquois National Bank signed a seven-year retainer agreement for Parsons & Trout to be both their national and regional counsel in twenty-two different states. I threw my suit coat over my arm and jogged back to the Plaza. I threw everything into a suitcase, checked out, and left New York City for the first time in over four weeks.

The drive home took me just over four hours with a stop for gas and a drive-thru burger. The door of my black wedge-shaped Celica Supra stayed open when I jumped out into the brick flagpole circle in front of Parsons & Trout. Sunshine glared down from between the clouds. The agreement was clutched between my fingers and it ruffled in the warm breeze. I skipped the steps, leaping right to the threshold between the thick soaring columns that supported the pediment of the old post office.

Parsons & Trout bought the building cheap in the late seventies, then renovated it as a historical site with tax-free dollars all through the coming years. Now it was the most impressive office space in the state outside New York City. Inside, as I climbed the marble steps to the second floor, I realized that the firm would be able to keep it now. The brass banisters. The oriental rugs. The Tiffany fixtures.

Dan Parsons was my mentor, and I loved him almost as much as my own dad. He was tall and husky with curly white hair and a round florid face that changed colors easily. Three years without a cigarette had left him with a small potbelly. His nose was bulbous, but not big, and his eyes had crow's feet from smiling so much. He was the kind of man who smiled even when he was raving mad. He had two kids my age whom he didn't speak to and a young son with his second wife. She was a former Miss New York with false breasts and eyelashes and great muscular legs. But she also laughed at Dan's jokes and stood by him in the worst of financial times.

Dan's office was just off the old courtroom. His secretary kept people out, but I sprinted right past. I made a hard left and pushed through the leather-upholstered doors into the old courtroom. Fluted columns rose twenty feet to the ceiling. Gilt molding shone down on the crystal chandeliers and the parquet floors. Dan sat at the head of the long burl wood table at the other end of the room, under the shadow of the old mahogany judge's bench. Next to Dan sat Bob Rangle, only twenty-seven but already the chairman of the Onondaga County Republican Party.

Rangle could be a twit, but he was so damn ingratiating that I couldn't bring myself to dislike him, even though a lot of other people did. He was a thin man with big beetle-black eyes set close to a sharp little nose and well below the receding brown hair that he liked to slick back. His fingers were long and narrow and he liked to grasp all four with his other hand and crank his hand back and forth as if he were throttling a motorcycle or winding himself up. When he smiled, the pointed tips of his small white teeth made him look even more like a weasel. He wore a dark suit with padded shoulders, an electric blue tie, and a white shirt with big silver cuff links. A conservative Huey Lewis.

The two of them looked up at me like I'd forgotten my pants.

"Hey," Rangle said, "Raymond."

"I got the deal," I said, waving the agreement in the air.

Dan jumped out of his seat and snatched

the papers from my hand, scrutinizing the signatures as if he suspected a fake. He wore yellow suspenders and his blue shirt-sleeves were unbuttoned and rolled up to his elbows. He plopped down into one of the leather swivel chairs, laughing, with his thumb and index finger spread across his forehead.

"He did it," Dan said to Rangle, looking up.

"You did it," Dan said again, this time to me.

The corners of my face were beginning to hurt.

"This is thirty million a year," Dan said, snapping his fingernails against the paper. "Minimum. Your bonus will be over two . . . closer to three if I get my way. How's that?"

"I'll take it," I said.

Dan stood and put his arms around me. He clapped me on the back before holding me at arm's length to grin some more. Rangle sat looking at us with his head bouncing around like it was attached by a spring. He said "Congratulations" with that toothy smile of his.

"Goddamn, you're cool. Cool under pressure. You know what I'm going to do?" Dan said. "Make you a congressman."

"I just saw Roger on Monday," I said, subduing my voice to a level I thought appropriate for a man who had just died.

I looked at Rangle. His smile thawed and he blinked at us.

"What about experience?" he said, cranking up his fingers.

"We were just talking about it," Dan said to me. "Bob thinks it should be him."

Rangle's face turned blotchy. He folded his arms across his chest and shifted in his seat.

"Experience is going to be crucial," he said. "Politics is my world. It was my father's world."

"That's what's perfect about Raymond," Dan said, raising his hands into the air like a five-year-old, palms up, fingers splayed. "People don't necessarily want insiders. They want an everyman. Like Jimmy Stewart . . . The governor agrees."

"The governor?" Rangle asked.

"I talked to him," Dan said. "You know how much money I've given him. He wants to announce it tomorrow night."

Rangle's mouth fell open and his head tilted at an odd angle.

"The committee will have to vote on it," Dan said. "That's why I wanted to see you. You'll have to call an emergency meeting."

"The governor?" Rangle asked, his eyes drifting off toward the beam of sunlight poking through the tall arched window by the old judge's bench. "Of course, and Raymond's an Indian . . ."

"Being part Native American isn't the reason," Dan said. "It doesn't hurt, but that's not why."

Rangle recovered his wits, rose, and walked down along the conference table. His breathing was shallow, but he extended his hand. I took it.

"Congratulations, Raymond," he said, wrapping those long fingers around my hand.

"Thank you."

The leather doors swung behind him. Dan picked up a Mont Blanc pen off the table and twisted it open and shut. He shook his head.

"What are you going to do?" he said. "His old man was an asshole."

"Dan," I said, "we like to do favors for people who help us, right?"

"The world is round," he said. "We both know that."

"Dan, you know me," I said. "Do I want this? Of course I do. It would be incredible. Part of me knows I don't even deserve it, but if I do it, I want to be careful."

"Careful? Of course."

"I mean, I can't just run around making decisions based on favors," I said. "I have to represent the area. Do what I think is best."

"Well, there are two sides to every issue," he said.

"Exactly," I said. "And I don't want to choose the wrong side just because someone did me a favor."

"You can't forget your friends," Dan said. His smile was big now, but in an angry way.

"I don't mean that," I said. "I just want to be my own man."

The smile stayed, but the scowl left.

"You'll be fine," he said. "We both will. Go see that girl and get her a new dress or something for tomorrow night, will you? I've got a conference call with the Chicago office, and if you don't mind, I want to be the one to tell them about Iroquois. Trout's been all over my ass for sending a kid. That's what he calls you. But I told him. The hotter it is, the cooler you get."

Outside, Rangle sat on the low wall by the entrance to the circle. His long legs were crossed and his arms were folded. A half-smoked cigarette dangled from his lips as he squinted at the fountain and the reflecting pool across the street. The fingers of his left hand were clutched in the right. I eased shut the door of my Supra and took Roger Williamson's letter out of the inside pocket of my blazer. Pretending to study it, I walked quickly for the front of the circle. If I could make it to the sidewalk, I could lose myself in the swarm of office workers milling their way toward the bars. Out of the corner of my eye, I saw Rangle jump up.

"Raymond," he said, pitching the cigarette to the ground and pumping his arms to catch up. "Wait up."

The light was against me. I had to wait. Rangle grinned and held out his hand again.

"I meant it," he said.

"What?"

"Congratulations."

"Thanks, Bob. I appreciate it."

The light changed and I started to walk, feigning interest in the envelope.

"Celeste Oliver?" Rangle said, his nose poking around my shoulder, his big close-set eyes blinking.

"It's for a friend," I said, stuffing the envelope back into my jacket. "Do you know what end of Lodi Street is 1870?"

"The wrong end," Rangle said. "I'm

meeting Paul Russo at the Tusk. Have a drink with us."

"Maybe later. I have someone I have to see first."

"Before the wrong end?"

I nodded.

He smiled back in that sharp-toothed smile.

4

The door that led up to the second-floor condo complex where Lexis lived was just down the wide brick alley that bordered one side of the Tusk. I stepped into the shadow of the alleyway, leaving Rangle to search the crowd that had spilled out from the bar and into the railed-off section of tables and chairs.

The condos were high-rent, and I had to punch in a code just to get into the common area. As I started up the steps, my heart began to thump. I hadn't seen Lexis in four weeks. We hadn't even spoken on the phone.

On New Year's Eve, she threw a drink in the face of a partner's wife. The next day we took a long walk and I tried to hint around that maybe she should get some help to stop drinking.

When she figured where it was I was going, she got hot and started to yell. I tried to keep cool, but pretty soon we both said some things we shouldn't have. Stupid things neither of us meant. Then I got tabbed to go down to the city and salvage the Iroquois deal and we agreed to take a break and see how we really felt about each other. A test.

I knew how I felt. I felt like shit. Going up those steps, I suddenly didn't care about the Iroquois deal. I didn't even care about the United States Congress.

I stood there thinking about how to say I was sorry. Then I heard a voice through the door, deep and rumbling. My gut knotted up. It was her old boyfriend. A guy I knew whose dad was head of the Patrolmen's Benevolent Association. No surprise he was the youngest detective in the department.

My hands clenched into fists and I hammered on the door.

"Son of a bitch," I said between my teeth.

There was a pause, then footsteps, and the door swung open.

"Raymond?"

It was Lexis. I wanted to punch my fist through the wall. My face burned and my stomach felt sick.

Her dark hair hung in long smooth sheets that only made her blue eyes more striking. Her skin was from another age, a Victorian painting. China skin with a straight nose and high cheekbones. The hair around the fringes of her face was damp.

She wore a white cotton dress with a blue flower print that matched those eyes. Her legs were long and lean. Her waist was narrow.

"What are you doing?" she said.

I said, "What are you doing?"

"I didn't even know you were back," she said. "Frank is here. His mother is sick."

"Right," I said. My hands were jammed in my pockets and I stood glowering at her with my attention fixed on the interior of the apartment.

Lexis stepped toward me. She put a hand on my cheek and kissed me lightly on the lips. Her lips were full and soft, she smelled of strawberries.

"Missed you," she said. Her voice was hushed, tender.

I didn't kiss her back.

She sighed as if to say it was nothing more than she expected out of me and said, "Come in here."

She turned and walked down a narrow hallway into the towering loft that served as both living room and studio. Frank was standing by the glass doors next to an unfinished canvas. Outside was a balcony overlooking the hickory trees that lined the street below. The sunlight streaming in through the leaves dappled the scarlet silk of his shirt. It hung loose around his waist, but I could still see the bulge of his police-issued Smith & Wesson.

I despised him. He was like a giant from a children's story, with a mop of dark curly hair, flaring nostrils, and hands like slabs of meat. Most women thought he was handsome. So did Frank. He had this shiny olive skin, small fat red lips, and pale blue eyes with lashes like a girl.

"Sorry to hear about your mom," I said. "What's wrong?"

"Heart attack," he said. "She'll be okay. She's pretty tough."

"Yeah," I said, "they say those aren't as serious as they used to be."

I circled toward the kitchen, keeping my body sideways to him the way I did when I was sparring.

"Still working on that kung-fu stuff, Big Chief?" he said.

"Some people might be offended by a stupid comment like that," I said. "But they might not understand about people who are mentally challenged."

Frank laughed.

"You gotta be careful out there," he said.

"It's a dangerous world."

"Same for you, Frank. Don't try to walk and chew gum at the same time."

"Tell your mom I send my best," Lexis said, taking Frank by the arm.

He looked up at me and, showing his teeth, said, "Make sure you treat this girl right."

I forced a smile.

When he was finally gone, Lexis closed the door and came back into the living room. Almost every flat surface was covered with photos of her and me in delicate silver and wood frames. Us at Disney in front of the castle. Her sister's wedding in L.A. Camping. Our first-anniversary dinner. She moved slowly across the room, stopping to straighten the picture frames as she came.

"Oh, Frank," I said. "I'm so glad you could console his delicate spirit."

"He's gone."

"But he'll be back," I said. "An asshole boomerang."

"He's nothing," she said. "Don't waste your time."

I smelled the musky sweetness of Oriental lilies and looked for the source. In a glass vase beside the couch was a fresh-cut flower arrangement. The paintings on the high brick walls were the same as they'd been a month ago. Surreal, with electric blue skies and inanimate objects with bloody teeth. No new work. Even the canvas on her easel had seen little progress. I couldn't help feeling glad.

Across the room was the door that led to her bedroom. I studied the big king-size sleigh bed in the middle of the wood floor. It was neatly made.

Lexis was in front of me now. In her hands was an inlaid mahogany frame that held a picture of just me. My neck, shoulders, and chest were bare and tan, the lines of muscle and bone clearly drawn. My hair was a dark tangle. My eyes were half shut, but you could still see the yellow slivers set deep in their brown.

"Remember when I took this?" she said, her voice barely above a whisper.

I did remember. A seaside cottage on Cape Cod. She said after sex was the only time I ever really relaxed. She said she liked me that way.

"Yes," I said in a raspy tone.

She traced a fingertip up the front of my thigh.

"I'm sorry," she said softly.

"Me too."

I could feel her touch through the leg of

my pants, up over my waist, then through my shirt, sharp and tingling, ascending my abdomen, over my chest and coming to rest just above my collarbone, where she moved it back and forth in a gentle rhythm. It got hard to breathe. I stepped toward her and let my hand slide down the muscular ridge along her spine to the shelf of her round bottom, where I took hold and pulled her close, pressing her hips against my own and kissing her.

Lexis stripped off my coat and frantically unbuttoned my shirt. They both slipped to the floor. The corner of the white envelope poked out from the inside pocket. I started to bend down to tuck it back in, but her dress fell to the floor — came up over her head and down over the top of it. We began to kiss again, holding it as we moved sideways toward the bedroom. One of my hands slipped beneath her bra, the other under the waistband of her lace underwear, finding the small smooth scar at her hip. My belt buckle jingled and came undone.

By the time we reached the bed, we were both naked. She pushed me onto my back, and then, everything stopped.

5

I started from my sleep and, for a moment, didn't know where I was. Then I saw the deep web of Lexis's hair spilled across the pillow next to me. I breathed deep the familiar hint of incense she sometimes burned. I felt refreshed, but less than a half-hour had gone by. Outside, the sun's beams were still thick, although slanted nearly flat. They drew long shadows from the windowsills of the building across the street. Out on the studio floor, my suit coat still lay beneath her dress, but the corner of the envelope jutted up into the thin material, casting a small shadow of its own.

I sat up, and the cotton sheets slid easily from my legs.

Lexis groaned and reached for me.

"Where are you going?" she said, her face still buried in the feather pillow.

"I'm sorry," I said, running my fingers through her hair. "I haven't even spoken to my father. His phone was disconnected last week. Crazy coot. I've got to stop by. I was thinking I could do that, go home and change, and then we could meet for dinner . . ."

I looked at my watch.

"It's almost seven-thirty," I said. "How about nine-thirty?"

Lexis rolled over and I kissed her lips.

"I wouldn't go if it wasn't him."

She touched my lips with her fingertip and said, "I like that you care about him like that."

When I left Lexis's apartment, I decided I was going to ask her to marry me. I already had the ring. I'd been waiting to be sure. Waiting to see what the break would do to us. Now I knew. This was it.

When I saw Rangle at his table on the corner of the sidewalk and the alleyway, I was too cheerful to dip my head and walk on by. He was on his feet, waving to me and calling my name. Besides, I thought I owed his buddy Paul Russo a favor. Not my favorite guy, but the vice president at a local bank, and before I left for New York City he had promised to put together that small business loan for my dad.

The world is round.

The Tusk boasts a glass storefront with over five hundred kinds of beer behind a bar decked out in brass. Its doors stay open in the summer so you can smell the yeasty richness even on the sidewalk, and above the bar in gold carved letters are the words: *Reality is an hallucination brought about by the lack of good beer.* On the wall, in old-world letters, is another sign: *Est. 1978.*

It was an after-work crowd of lawyers and accountants, along with a handful of skilled tradesmen whose rates were high enough to afford five dollars for a pint of beer. People sat on tapestry stools or stood leaning against the high oak tables. But the best seats were where my friends were, outside in the line of tables that ran down the sidewalk and halfway up the alley.

It wasn't until I was inside the railing that separated the patrons from the foot traffic, and halfway to their table, that I realized Frank was hiding behind the brick corner of the building. He ended his conversation around the corner and sat down with the other two before looking up at me. He set his mouth in a flat line, then forced a smile. I did the same.

"My man," Rangle called out in a slurred voice, holding up his hand for a high five. "You know Paul . . . and Frank I know you know. Hey, we're all friends here. The future movers and shakers . . ."

The two of them were dressed for success with glimmering silk ties, white shirts, and suit coats with sharp-angled padded shoulders. In a mean way Rangle did have style, but Russo was shorter and such a potato-head that the clothes just couldn't compensate. Everyone else sitting around was in shirtsleeves at best. The women wore big-shoulder tops and high moussed hair and we all listened to Wham! U.K. and the theme music to *St. Elmo's Fire*.

"Hey, Paul," I said. "Thanks for helping out my dad."

"God, I've been wicked swamped," Russo said. His shoulders were broad but thin, like a paper doll's. His big hooked nose and protruding ears jumped right out at you from a chinless face that was otherwise flat as a pie tin. Pale gray crescents hung beneath his dark, pink-rimmed eyes. His head was mostly bald except for the buzzed-down patches around his mushroom ears that matched the shadow on his chin and jaw. He had a confident spark to him. "He and I have been trading calls. But we'll get it done for sure."

"You need a beer, Raymond," Rangle said.

"That's okay I —"

"Just one," Rangle said, holding up his long hand. "Paul, how about another

40

round of Rogue Ales and whatever Raymond wants."

"Me?"

"Your name's Paul, right?"

He flipped Russo his credit card.

To me, he said, "You can't not have at least one with me. People will think I'm not happy for you. People will think I'm holding a grudge or something if we don't have a drink. You and I have to work together. We've got politics to talk. I've decided to run for mayor. Frank will be my chief of police, 'buckling down' on all the bad guys. Please . . . sit."

He grinned. "We're going to own this fucking town."

I did sit, as much as anything to spite Frank and his dark look. I winked at him. Best way to piss off an asshole is to ignore him.

"I'll have a Hefeweizen," I said to Russo, trying to sound glib. "A Franziskaner."

"And cigars, Paul," Rangle said, raising his finger. "They have some Montecristo No. 2s behind the bar. Just tell them it's for me . . ."

Russo, with sweat beaded on his round brow and pit stains bleeding through his suit coat, stood swaying for a moment, puffed his thin lips, and then hurried off.

"You'll have to start getting used to good cigars, Raymond," Rangle said, finishing off the pint in front of him and wiping his mouth on the back of his hand. "You've already got a fine woman."

I pressed my lips together and stared flatly at him.

"Lucky in life and lucky in love," Rangle said, his teeth glinting.

I cast a look at Frank to see if he was in on the fun.

"In today's politics, the first lady is essential," Rangle said, belching quietly and loosening his tie before he clutched his fingers. "That's insider information. The kind of stuff my father taught me. The kind of stuff I'm going to share with you during the campaign and even when you're in Washington . . ."

Russo returned, staggering like a goblin slave with a quartet of glasses and a pocketful of cigars stuffed in with the burgundy handkerchief that matched his tie. I passed on the Montecristo, but drank half of the Hefeweizen before setting the glass down on the metal mesh tabletop.

"I'll be fine," I said, looking at my watch. "But I've really got to get going."

"Oh, that's right," Rangle said with a wink, "that little secret errand to run, right? Secret's safe with me, that's for sure . . ."

Rangle started to chuckle. It infected Russo, who wheezed through that big nose. Frank just stared down at the pint glass between his thick hands.

"I guess you don't get to where you are without doing some favors, eh?" Rangle said, clipping the end off his cigar. One eyebrow crept upward and he narrowed his big dark eyes.

"Meaning?"

"Nothing bad," Rangle said, looking up from behind the flame and smoke. Puffing. "We all do favors for people. Look at us . . ."

He pointed the butt of his cigar around the table and said, "Four CBA grads. Did anyone think of that? You wore the purple and gold too. A little behind us, but a brother is a brother. The next generation . . . We have to stick together, no matter what our differences. That's what the Brothers taught us."

Christian Brothers Academy was a parochial high school. Almost every Italian American family in Syracuse, as well as others that could afford it, wanted their kids to go there. It was also a sports power and I attended on a soccer scholarship.

I drained my beer and stood up. The first half had already gone to my head.

"You're right. Thanks for the beer," I said.

"But we're just starting," Rangle said, rising up, reaching for my sleeve.

"No, I've got to."

"Leave it to Raymond," he said to the others, "to worry about keeping his promise to a guy who's already dead."

"Leave it to me," I said, forcing a smile as I backed away, wishing I hadn't asked Rangle about the address. "Keeping your word is an odd concept for some people."

I ducked between two parked cars and waited for a motorcycle to sputter by before crossing. One of the lawyers from my firm walked out of a bar across the street and I was forced to politely accept his congratulations on the Iroquois deal. When I got to the corner, I looked back at the sidewalk table where Rangle, Frank, and Russo still sat. They weren't looking at me anymore. Instead, the three of them held their glasses high and touched them together in a toast.

6

I know they think I'm crazy, and maybe that's true.

Sometimes they take the punishment I give them in order to subdue me. It takes five men. After a time, though, strong as I am, they are able to chain me up and fasten a leather mask over my face to keep me from biting. Then they'll carry me to a room and chain me down to a chair that's bolted to the floor.

The first time they did this, I thought they were going to torture me. But all they did was bring in a psychiatrist. I still have to fight them when they come for me with the mask, otherwise they might not keep me here. But the truth is, I enjoy talking to the doctors. Four other times they gave me to a priest.

My point is this: I may very well *be* crazy, and maybe it's just crazy for me to believe that I know what happened all those years ago when I wasn't even there. But there were scraps of things I later heard. Before the trial. And for the rest . . . Well, I've had plenty of time to think.

These things are never clear during the night. It's during my one hour of daylight that they come to me. I don't want to know them. They just come, intruders lurking in the woods around the cabin of my boyhood Adirondack vacations.

And when these intruders commandeer my thoughts, what really happened comes to me in a way that leaves me as certain of the truth as if I were there myself. Listening. Seeing . . .

"That was cute," Frank said, his bulk shifting forward, his olive skin reddening. "I hope you enjoyed yourself, asshole."

The smell of spilled beer and laughter and smoke whirled around them. Rangle leaned across the table with his cigar stuck deep into the corner of his mouth and said, "I mean, how does a guy like you lose that girl to a guy like him?"

"Yeah," Russo said.

"Shut up."

Russo scratched the stubble surrounding his bald head and looked away with his ears sticking out from the sides of his head like two hunks of cauliflower.

"Who understands pussy?" Frank asked. He upended the rest of his old pint and started in on the new one.

The shadow of the building had shifted with the sun. They were in darkness now and their metal table was cooling rapidly. Only the smoke from Rangle's cigar drifted toward the street and into the sunlight, a twisting shimmering cloud.

"Hey," Rangle said, raising his hands, palms up. A strand of slicked-back hair had fallen from its ranks, and it hung limp from his high hairline. "No problem. We're friends."

Frank's thick fingers were clamped around the glass. His knuckles pale. His cigar lay there in front of him, untouched. Russo held his between his thumb and forefinger, caressing the Montecristo between his upper lip and the overhang of his nose. Sniffing it. Rangle leaned forward again, his silver cuff links clinking against the metal tabletop.

"How much do you hate him?" he asked. "What does it feel like in your chest and in your crotch . . . when you think about him fucking her?"

Frank's jaw went taut. He shoved the glass away from him with waves of beer sloshing up and over its rim. He picked up the cigar, crushing and twisting it until small brown flecks of tobacco fell to the table like snowflakes.

"That could be you," he said. His mouth was pulled down at the corners and his pale eyes bored into Rangle. The veins in his bull neck bulged. "I'll buckle down all over your ass, mayor or not."

"Hold that thought," Rangle said, showing Frank his sharp teeth without the smile. "But now think Raymond. It's him, not me. What if we did something about him?"

"Someone could find his head in a Dumpster with three slugs in it," Frank said. He was leaning forward too, speaking barely above his breath.

"Arrogant bastard," Russo said. "Guy thinks I'm his personal fucking banker."

"No one asked you," Frank said.

Russo frowned and said he was sorry.

"What if you could do something even worse than that?" Rangle asked, slicking back his thin hair. His eyes glittered. "Would you?"

"What's worse?"

"What if it was Raymond that had to think about you fucking Lexis?"

Frank's hand darted across the table, latched on to Rangle's tie, and yanked him across the table until his face smashed into the cluster of empty glasses. Frank's thick

48

lips brushed up against Rangle's forehead.

Overhead, Bryan Adams sang "Cuts Like a Knife."

"You don't ever talk about her," Frank said in a throaty whisper. "Never ever again. Her name doesn't come out of your filthy mouth or I'll beat you to a fucking pulp and throw you in jail for assaulting an officer. You got that?"

"Yes," Rangle said, choking and blinking the fallen hair from his eyes.

Frank let him go and Rangle collapsed back into his seat, tugging at his tie, loosening the collar and sucking in his breath.

"Good," he said, slicking his hair again and clearing his throat. "I want you angry. I want you sick with fucking hatred. Now, you dumbass, think Raymond, not me. I know a secret, and we have a chance to change everything. All three of us . . ."

The three of them leaned close and spoke in whispers that no one could hear. Russo's pink-rimmed eyes shifted around the sidewalk and he gulped his beer. Frank wore a scowl. Rangle's eyebrows were knit tight, but his teeth shone in a jackal-like smile. It was a simple plan. Quick and easy. Effective.

In less than a minute, the three of them sat back in their chairs and raised their drinks. They brought the rims of the thick pint glasses together with a clink that rang out loud and clear.

I hear that clink. I can smell their smoke. And I see those arrogant smiles every day of my life.

7

My dad's place was in the opposite direction of mine, half an hour east of Syracuse. The home I had recently bought was half an hour to the west, out in Skaneateles. I don't like to think of myself as running from my roots as the son of a rock man and a displaced Native American mom. Yeah, I heard my share of red man jokes in school, but I had only two real fistfights in my life.

I prefer to think that I'm in Skaneateles not because it's the priciest real estate in upstate New York, but because I'm actually closer to nature there. I put out nest boxes for bluebirds, martins, and swallows, and usually fill half of them in a season. Lots of my neighbors are farmers. They let me roam their woods during hunting season, and I can throw a fishing line in the water about a hundred feet from my back door.

From the law office, it was easy for me to hop on the interstate and get out to my dad's spot of countryside between Fayetteville and Chittenango. I kept the windows down, inhaling the cool smell of cut hay and trees and the soil of farm fields that were buzzing with insects. The letter sat on the passenger seat beside me, jammed into the crack between the seat and the backrest. In my rearview mirror, I could see the oblong orange sun settling into a blanket of glowing clouds. By eight o'clock, the long shadows made the woods surrounding the driveway nearly dark.

My father lived alone in the house where I grew up, a small brown ranch nestled in the woods. I could see its lines, even through the trees. The place once belonged to my grandfather. Like my dad, he operated the small quarry out back his entire life, blasting stone from the backbone of the earth, constantly struggling to survive in a world ruled by international conglomerates.

As I pulled up alongside the house, I heard a blast rebound over the lip of the hill that loomed in the near distance. I shook my head and kept going along the gravel drive, past the house, out of the woods, around the towering escarpment of jagged stone, and up over the hill into the purple shadows of the quarry.

In the headlight beams of a faded old dump truck, my father stood talking with another man. Dust from the explosion swirled in the glow of the light. I pulled right up beside the battered dump truck and hopped out.

"Dad," I said, raising my voice to account for his loss of hearing. "It's practically dark out."

That was as far as my complaint about blasting after dark could go.

"I can see that," he said. He wore the faded jeans, white T-shirt, and the jean jacket of a teenager, but the skin on his hands as well as his face was craggy and weather-beaten.

I walked up with my back straight and shook his granite hand the way he taught me that real men do. A bat swooped down from the shadows, flitting softly into the beam of light.

"Tried calling you last week," I said, ducking. "What happened to the phone? They said it was disconnected."

"Don't need no damn phone," my father said.

"Everyone needs a phone, Dad."

"Money-sucking corporate monkeys."

"What about business?"

"You do yours, I'll do mine. A rock man don't need no phone," he said. "The trucks keep coming and I keep giving them their stone. Been at it for two weeks without a phone."

"It's summertime, Dad," I said. I doubted he could carry on like this when things got slow.

"You ain't said hello to Black Turtle."

I turned and said hello to the ancient Onondaga Native American who had worked on and off for my dad since I was a boy. We shook hands and I was jolted by a clap on the back from my dad. He asked me if I cared for a man's meal. He and Black Turtle had their sights set on some venison steaks and a game of nickel poker.

"I'm having dinner with Lexis, Dad," I said. "I just wanted to make sure you were okay and tell you that you've got to get a hold of that guy Paul Russo at the bank and get that loan set up. I saw him today. He said you were trading calls."

"I don't need a loan."

"Dad," I said, "your phone was turned off."

"I called that asshole anyway, and he never called me back," he said, as he worked on a quid of tobacco in the side of his cheek.

"Well, he probably couldn't get through, Dad."

"If he tried, why didn't he tell you that?"

he said. "I called him for two weeks before that phone got turned off. His secretary always told me he wasn't in. Bullshit."

"Well, you've got to try again, Dad," I said, thinking that Russo was a lot more likely to shake a stick now that he knew I was going to be a congressman. "I spoke to him today and he said it's all set."

"How about tomorrow night for venison steaks?" my father said, stroking his mustache. "Black Turtle and I can save 'em and go get us a plate of spaghetti and meatballs at Angotti's."

His drooping mustache and his blue Buffalo Bills cap were white with dust from blasted rock, making his dark blue eyes seem almost black.

"I've got a political thing tomorrow night, Dad," I said. "A fund-raiser. How about Sunday night?"

"Political shmitical," he said, taking off his hat and slapping it against his leg before putting it back on.

"They want me to be the next congressman."

"To Washington?"

"I've got to win a special election, but with the Republican endorsement . . ." I said. Everyone knew that in this district that's all you needed. "I imagine I could

help get you some good road con-
tracts . . ."

My father put his hand on my shoulder
and gave it a squeeze.

"I know you want to help," he said, his
voice sounding choked. "But I got all the
work I need. You just do like I taught you.
You don't take any favors, you don't owe
any . . ."

I turned to Black Turtle and said,
"Don't you two blast at night anymore,
will you?"

He shrugged at me the way he always
had, knowing as well as I did that my
words were meant for my father.

"I appreciate it," I said. "Otherwise, I
worry."

My father held up a small blue blasting
cap in the waning light. It was no bigger
than a cigarette.

"You wouldn't think a little thing like
this could destroy twenty tons of hard
rock," my father said, "but it does. The
well-placed little things are the ones that
can move mountains.

"All right, Black Turtle," he said, gripping my shoulder, then letting go. "We got
work to do. Sunday night it is."

My dad climbed up into the cab of the
dump truck. Black Turtle faded into the

darkness and fired up the cranky old payloader. The two monster machines rattled off, leaving me in a fresh swirl of dust, the blue-white lights of the Supra, and a low rumble that continued on like thunder.

I got into my car and wound my way through the rocks, past the stone crusher and the sagging office trailer, and back to the main road. My hands turned the wheel without thinking, taking me back to deliver the envelope that sat beside me. In the scheme of everything that was happening in my world of business, love, and politics, it was undoubtedly a very little thing.

8

The orange sky in the west had faded to russet. It was after eight-thirty by the time I got back to the city and the north end of Lodi Street. Pinpoints of light, stars, planets, and airplanes winked overhead as I rolled down the dusty street with my windows open. People in broken porch chairs and others who slouched in rusty cars along the curb craned their necks for a better look at my gleaming car and its sparkling silver rims.

The homes were crammed together and in need of repair. Screens, bent and torn, hung loose from open windows. Roofs sagged. The leprosy of peeling paint and rotted gray wood had stricken every post, step, and shingle. The broken driveways and crumbling sidewalks were peppered with weeds, and the hush of dusk was disrupted by the thumping of boom boxes.

House numbers were a luxury and only a few had them. Celeste Oliver's place was missing the first two, but I could still see the faded images of where the one and the eight had once been. I pulled up into the driveway behind a red Honda Civic with a crushed rear quarter panel and got out. The envelope was in my hand. In the fading light, I saw the curtain drop and a face disappear.

I climbed the steps and knocked.

The door opened almost immediately and she stood there, pouting. I had to take a breath. She was tall enough so that even in bare feet she was almost eye-level with me. She wore tight stonewashed jeans and an aqua blue halter top that showed off breasts that were neither too big nor too small. Her midriff was honey-colored and molded with curves. Her lipstick was pink. Delicate eyebrows matched her straight blonde hair. Her eyes were powder blue.

"I'm a friend of Roger's," I said, when I could speak.

She moved aside and I stepped in. When she turned and walked into the small living room, my eyes followed a perfect bottom. The hammering in my chest and the current running through my center triggered a pang of guilt.

"You can sit down," she said, plopping down on the couch and picking up a pack of Newports off the glass coffee table. She slipped one into her mouth.

I laid the envelope down on the table in front of her.

"That's from Roger," I said, straightening. Unable to sit, but unable to get my feet moving toward the door.

"Did he tell you about me?" she asked, squinting up from the flame of her Bic.

"No."

"I belonged to Roger," she said, blowing smoke toward the curtained window. "Not for money. I'm not like that. I dance, but I never fucked a man for money. I loved being with Roger. Do you know he took me inside the White House? I met Reagan."

I shook my head no.

"And now you're going to have everything that he had . . ." she said, looking directly at me with a small smirk. "You're the one who'll get to vote on the Star Wars bill this fall. You'll have the swing vote on the Appropriations Subcommittee on Highways. They want to redo the interstate bridges between here and Canada. Did you know that? The governor will be calling you on that one and you can get him to come do a fund-raiser for you. There's a real nice bunch around here who'll pay a thousand a head to have lunch with the governor . . .

"Anyway, you'll have me too," she said, sitting back on the couch and placing her arms along its back with her legs crossed and a little arch in her spine. "If you want that . . ."

I glanced at the envelope. The feeling in my legs was beginning to return. The smoke from the cigarette helped. I started to back toward the door.

"I kind of have someone," I said.

"Yeah, that's standard," she said. "A wife?"

"Maybe."

She dashed her cigarette into an ashtray and hopped up off the couch. She came toward me with a bubbling giggle and took hold of my hand, pressing it up against her breast before I could react.

"Yeah, well, this is politics," she said, her voice dropping into a husky whisper, her fingers tracing up the inside of my thigh. "So she'll get used to it. They all do . . ."

I pulled my hand back. Her other hand groped my crotch.

"You'll need a release," she said, her pink lips barely moving. "It's a brutal job. I can keep your mind clear. We all need to clear our minds."

I knocked her hand away and pushed her harder than I meant to. She tripped and fell to the floor, her head thudding up against the wall.

"I'm sorry," I said, reaching out to help her up. "I didn't mean to."

"Asshole," she said, swatting at me, then pushing a long strand of the blonde hair from her face.

I turned, yanked open the door, and jumped down off the porch, skipping the steps. I edged past the wreck of a Honda. My suit pants caught and tore on a wild metal shred protruding from the smashed bumper.

As I climbed into my Supra, I looked around. Halfway up the block was an unmarked police car. In the shadows of the front seat, a nickel-size ember — about the size of a cigar — glowed then faded out. That didn't seem unusual to me. In a neighborhood like this, the police probably knew everybody by their first name.

I never thought much of it back then.

9

I never hated my mother for what she did. Maybe it was because my father refused to blame her.

"I knew what your mother needed," he once said, "and I knew I didn't have it."

My mother was a pretty woman who liked to laugh and read books. She was a Mohawk raised on the Onondaga Indian Reservation. That meant that even among the disenfranchised, she was disenfranchised.

As loving as she was to me and to my father, my mother had an insatiable desire for things. I can still remember the one trip we took to Florida over a winter school break. We stayed at a cheap motel across the street from the beach in St. Petersburg. One day, the three of us took a long walk and found ourselves in an exclusive neighborhood on the bay. I can still see the glimmer in my mother's dark eyes and hear her delicate gasps at the size and intricate architectural detail of the homes. The shiny cars in their driveways. The yachts moored to the docks that jutted out from the swimming pools in their backyards.

When my mother wasn't reading a book, she was studying magazines like *Architectural Digest*, *Vogue*, or *Town & Country*. Every cent my father let her have, she spent on things that were irrelevant to the Native American wife of a quarry man. Irrelevant, but fine. Lalique figurines. A Cartier bracelet. A Chanel evening gown she could never wear.

I was ten when she left to marry a man who drove a black Mercedes coupe. A man who owned a large paving company and who bought crushed stone from my father. A man who smelled like peppermint and wore a gold Rolex. He was for real, though. He even took her to Greece on their honeymoon.

My mother told me then that I was a man already. Ahead of my years and that I would be fine. I was like Running Deer, my namesake, the boy chief who led his people to victory over the Hurons when he was only eleven. I tried to make her words come true, to be a man.

I remember that Christmas, tramping off into the dark winter woods after school and sawing down a tree to surprise my father. Something he had always done for the three of us. I remember the quiver in my lip when I refused to give up my seat on the bus to the eighth grader who regularly taunted me. Him walking away. I remember my fingers going numb around a wrench and the smoke of my breath, lying on the cold concrete floor and looking up at the oil pan of my father's truck as it bled a thick black ribbon into a cut-down Clorox bottle. My first oil change.

But I think I did more than try to be the man my mother said I already was. I think too that I tried to fill the void she left behind. I remember making my father's breakfasts, breaking the yolks like her and peppering them so thick it looked like they fell in the road. Coffee in the tall gurgling percolator. The oily smell of sardines laid out over a bed of tuna salad, capped with a fat slice of onion, wrapped in tinfoil, and lowered carefully into his dented blue lunch pail. Breaking from the math homework spread out over the kitchen table and uncapping two longneck bottles of Budweiser for him and Black Turtle. Setting them down without being asked on the porch railing where the two of them sat rocking in the darkness — the way she had always done.

While my mother said I would be fine,

my father said the marriage wouldn't last long.

They were both right.

My life became a storybook of success — scholarship offers, valedictorian, All-America soccer player — and she moved on to marry one of the heirs to the DuPont fortune before I turned fourteen. Two years later, she and her third husband died when their private jet went down over the Atlantic Ocean. They were on their way to Bermuda for the season.

I tried not to cry. To be a man. But I guess all those eggs and coffees and lunches and beer caps had undermined my efforts at manhood. Sixteen and I bawled hysterically right in front of Black Turtle and my father and ran off into the woods to hide.

I only tell you all this because I want you to understand the significance of the next twenty-four hours I'm going to tell you about. Back then, I didn't stop to think about why I felt that I had experienced some kind of spiritual ascension, I only knew that I had. Everything was right.

I had grown up afraid of being my father. I was happy to have his rugged looks, his strong back, and his quick mind. But I was determined to have more. I was going to be rich and powerful. That was the lesson of my childhood.

When I resisted Celeste Oliver's temptation — my own forty days in the desert — I couldn't help congratulating myself. I felt not just worthy of everything that had been placed at my feet, but entitled. I had worked and planned my whole life to be in the path of some fantastic destiny. Finally, on that summer day, I knew that it was in my grasp.

I had this amazing house that everyone wondered how I got my hands on. One of those deals you only hear about. It belonged to the family of a friend I knew at Princeton. They came to me to help work out the estate after the death of their grandmother. When I saw this place, I told them they wouldn't even have to put it on the market.

It was an old Tudor cottage tucked into a small cove on Skaneateles Lake. You couldn't see it from the road or even very clearly from the water because of the massive oaks and towering spruce that surrounded it. It had a prominent rubblework chimney flanked by stucco walls and brunette half-timbering. Gingerbread gableboards and diamond-pane window casements gave it a fairy-tale quality, and it had a thick slate terrace out back that overlooked the water.

The master bedroom upstairs was my favorite spot. It had a set of arched French doors in the peak of the roof that led out onto a small balcony. In the summer, the moon came up over the eastern ridge beyond the lake like a big pumpkin. From there, I could see all the way to the south end of the lake, into the next county where the tree-lined slopes descend almost a thousand feet from the ridge to the deep green water below.

By the time I got home from delivering the envelope to Roger Williamson's mistress, dusk was on its last breath. I quickly changed my clothes and fished the velvet ring box out of the bottom of my sock drawer. Lexis agreed to meet me at Kabuki, a sushi restaurant in town at the head of the lake. During the drive to my dad's I had called for a nine-thirty reservation at the front table overlooking the water.

My buddy's grandmother had planted a bed of orange daylilies under the front windows and I stopped to cut half a dozen of them to give to Lexis. I got there late, but not enough to subdue the glow in Lexis's eyes when I handed her the flowers.

I drank seltzer water with Lexis, but I felt drunk anyway, and by the time we got our molten chocolate cake with green tea ice cream, I had asked her to marry me. She cried and said yes, then we drove back to my place, where I carried her across the threshold and we giggled like kids.

Upstairs, I opened the French doors and stepped out onto the balcony. Water lapped the smooth shale beach below and a broad swath of moonlight sparkled on the lake's surface. As I turned, Lexis slipped her dress off her shoulder and it fell to the floor. I stepped inside, fumbling with my belt, then the zipper. My jeans hit the wood floor and we twined ourselves together on the four-poster bed.

It was deep in the night when I woke up. The breeze had a bite to it and the moon had either gone down or was clouded over. Beyond the balcony now was only blackness. I got up to use the bathroom and shook two aspirin out of a bottle. My water glass clinked against the tap as I filled it with lake water. I swallowed my medicine, then felt my way back into the bedroom, sliding under the warm tangle of sheets and pulling Lexis's naked body close.

I was suddenly and inexplicably overwhelmed by an irrational fear. One day, we would die. Then we would be apart forever. Insane, I knew, but still my heart pushed up into my throat. The rest of my chest felt empty. I never wanted to be without her. Not then. Not for eternity.

"Lexis," I whispered. "I love you."

She stretched, and I could see her smile even in the darkness.

"I love you too," she said without opening her eyes.

"I just don't ever want to be without you," I said, sick with this crazy fear.

"Go back to sleep," she said, turning toward me and wrapping her arms and legs tight around my body. "That could never happen."

10

In the morning, I took a ten-mile run in the drizzling rain. I was drenched and slick with sweat and sucking in air. I shucked off my sneakers and clothes on the end of the dock and plunged into the cold water. After looking around for any fishermen drifting in from the mist, I climbed naked onto the dock, grabbed a towel from the boat, and wrapped it around my waist.

Halfway up the slate walk to the house, I smelled food. Lexis had cooked up my favorite breakfast: broccoli and cheese omelets. We had buttered toast made from thick-cut Italian bread and coffee made from the beans of an espresso blend. We ate outside on the slate terrace even though the air was still damp from the rain. When I finished eating, I sat back and inhaled the curling steam from my coffee mug. Out on the lake, a fishing boat floated past, appearing and disappearing on the fringe of the morning mist. The laughter of the two fishermen rang out across the still water.

We moved inside and sat on the couch by the empty fireplace, reading our books until noon, then took my nineteen-foot Sea Ray into town for fried fish sandwiches at Doug's. By the time we came out, the clouds had thinned and the sun had begun to boil off the dampness. We stopped at Riddler's for the paper.

Someone had leaked the news of my impending nomination and my picture was on page one. I looked around the store and folded the paper in half before buying it with my head down.

Back at the house, we toweled off the deck chairs on the end of the dock and lay reading in the sun. When it got hot enough, we went in the water and played our usual game. I'd take a deep breath and crouch down on the rocky bottom. She'd fit her insteps into my palms, then I'd stand up fast and push for the sky. Lexis would launch into the air and do a flip. I loved seeing her do that and we'd laugh until we couldn't catch our breath.

Dan Parsons sent a long black limousine for us at five-thirty, and by the time we arrived at the convention center, the crowd converged around us, fawning as if we were a museum exhibit. And, me being a Republican with a Native American mother, I guess in a way we were. Cameras flashed at odd intervals. I saw Lexis stare at a tray of champagne being offered to her by a waiter, but she smiled at me and shook her head no to him. We drifted through the swirl of congratulations. Congratulations when they saw her ring. Congratulations on the Iroquois deal. Congratulations for my nomination. Love. Money. Power.

We sat at the head table with the governor and his wife on one side and the Parsonses on the other. On the opposite side of the dais, Bob Rangle was red-faced and drinking a glass of white wine that seemed to be bottomless. The one time we found ourselves face-to-face during cocktails, he scowled and quickly turned away. I wasn't surprised that he was finally showing his true feelings, but I was disappointed that he had chosen to show them here.

I had only one Budweiser before I switched to Perrier, but I was as light-headed as if I'd kept drinking beer. I took a few bites of my prime rib, then lost my appetite. I had refused to prepare some long-drawn-out speech. That was part of doing it my way. Still, I knew enough to at least jot down some notes for what I was about to say. My stomach felt light and queasy, and I was wiping the sweat from my palms on the legs of my pants, concentrating on taking slow deep breaths when a waiter tapped my shoulder.

"Mr. White?" he said. "Those men asked to speak with you."

Standing at the bottom of the steps that led up onto the dais were two uniformed police and a man with an auburn mustache wearing a navy blazer. On either side of them were the stone-faced state troopers who protected the governor.

Lexis saw me looking at them. When I stood up, she said, "Raymond?"

She touched my arm. At that moment, all of it — the adulation, the glamour, the power — began to melt away, and the only thing that mattered to me was her.

I was suddenly struck by the feeling that I'd done something wrong, even though I hadn't. I should have told Lexis about Roger Williamson and the letter and the girl. Why hadn't I?

It was too late. My legs were numb, but I was already at the steps.

The man in the blazer and the orange mustache took a paper out of his inside pocket. He handed it to me.

"Raymond White?" he said quietly.

"Yes."

"Would you please come with us?"

"Why?"

He looked out at the crowd that was beginning to crane their necks. A murmur rose up.

"Because you're under arrest," he said. "For the murder of Celeste Oliver."

11

For a long time I was blinded by my raging hatred for Frank. I would scream his name in the dark. Shout the things I would do to him. Dream about the pain I would inflict. But over the years that hatred settled into my bones, its ache less sharp, but also more complete.

It was a year and a half before I realized Frank was not the only one responsible. I don't mean that weasel-faced Rangle or even that potato-headed insincere drunk, Russo.

There was also someone else.

Daylight was gone, but Dean Villay could still make out where the expansive canopies of the old chestnut trees ended and the night sky began. He could see better than most in the dark. He could see the small triangular sail of the Laser nearly two miles to the south out in the middle of the lake.

Soon the moon would be up. Until then, his fiancée was taking a ridiculous chance.

As if on cue, the drone of a speedboat passed by, heading to the south. No navigation lights on. Another drunken fool or a kid who didn't know better. Villay clenched his hands. His chubby lip curled.

Allison had no business doing this to him. Taking chances. He understood her need to get away. She was upset about her father, even if she barely knew the man. And the party had been a bore, with her mother droning on about the good old days when their mansion on the lake was the center of society for central New York. Now it needed paint, new window casements, and another bathroom.

He had enough people to prosecute already without having to worry about some errant boater and a criminally negligent homicide. He ground his teeth and turned away, walking up the lawn beneath the chestnuts toward the big house. The last of the cars were pulling away down the gravel drive, their tires crunching. Older people mostly, the kind who still tried to look young. Friends of his mother-in-law-to-be.

He threw his gray blazer over his shoulder and climbed the back steps, careful to avoid the rotted one that was second from the top. The screen door screeched and he stepped into the steamy kitchen. Allison's mother wiped her hands on the sides of her pale green chiffon dress while she bitched at two of the caterer's people.

"In my day, to flaunt yourself like that was a disgrace," she was saying. "People would call you lewd. A hussy. You'll not be paid. Not out of my pocket."

The mother had insisted that the help for the evening wear black dresses with white aprons and matching headpieces. This particular girl hadn't buttoned her collar all the way to the neck. Villay rolled his eyes.

"Dean," Allison's mother barked. "Where were you? There are two police officers looking for you. They're in the salon. I gave them lemonade."

Villay excused himself, thankful for the distraction. The two city cops sat on the big musty couch with their hats on the coffee table. They jumped to their feet and set the tall clear glasses back on the doilies Allison's mother had provided for them.

"She told us to wait here, sir," the older one said, pulling his hat over his iron gray crew cut. The blond one nodded.

"They tried to call," he said. "The chief said you were here."

Villay took the cell phone out of his

pocket and turned it back on.

"My engagement party," he said.

The older cop nodded as if he knew and said, "The chief said he was sorry to bother you, but that you'd want to know. There was a girl murdered on the North Side last night, some stripper, and we just arrested Raymond White . . ."

"Not the one in the paper? The one who's going to be congressman?"

"They're pretty sure," the cop said. "The chief had Detective Simmons pick him up at the governor's fund-raiser."

Villay squinted his eyes. His mouth dropped open and he leaned his face toward the cop.

"Lady across the street has been complaining about this girl running a whorehouse," the cop said. "She's been collecting tag numbers. Anyway, she saw Raymond visit and leave last night. Picked him out of a photo lineup. Looks like they fought for a while. He cut her throat with a fishing knife. They found the knife under the backseat of his car and blood on the steering wheel."

"Raymond White?" Villay said, more to himself.

"The chief thought you'd want to talk to him. We're holding him at the Public

Safety Building. The television stations are all there . . ."

Villay returned to the kitchen to tell Allison's mother that he was being called away on an important murder case.

12

"I'm going," I said, shaking the cop's hand off my arm.

The detective with the orange mustache grabbed my hand and pushed it up behind my back, slapping a cuff around my wrist. One of the uniformed cops pulled my other arm and pushed that back too. I felt the metal bracelet chafing the bone of that wrist as well. They shoved me out onto the sidewalk into the flash of blue lights. Television cameras, already there for the governor, were jostling for a shot, moving in. The white glare of their lights blinded me from every direction.

Someone shoved a microphone into my face. The foam windscreen bumped my nose.

"Get back," the detective said, pushing the reporter away.

I ducked my head and they put me into the back of a car. The cameras bobbed up and down outside my window, following the squad car as it pulled slowly away from the curb. The Public Safety Building was just three blocks away, and the media were moving like a horde up the sidewalk as we entered the newly constructed six-story building. I had to wait to pass through the metal detector and I stood there next to a derelict wearing tattered jeans and a filthy shirt.

He looked up from his own pair of handcuffs and asked, "What'd they get you for?"

His breath stunk from whiskey and decay.

I turned my head away from him, swallowing hard to keep the bile down.

Upstairs, they chained me to a metal bench in a small interrogation room. Blue uniforms with different faces peeked in through the open door.

The cop with the orange mustache came in without his navy blazer. He had a fresh yellow pad and a pen in one hand and a tape recorder in the other. The armpits of his shirt were badly stained. He turned on the tape recorder, read me my Miranda warning for a second time, and started asking questions.

I didn't want a lawyer, didn't want them to think I was guilty, even though I knew the textbooks said not to talk once you got your Miranda. My instincts and my innocence were in control. The urge to convince them overwhelmed the distant lessons from my first-year criminal law class.

I told the cop what happened. I swore it was the truth. I had no idea how there could have been blood on my steering wheel. She had bumped her head. Lightly. I shoved her away. Not hard, no. I never saw blood, but maybe it was possible. Yes, I had a tackle box for fishing. I thought I had a fillet knife, why? No, I didn't know her at all.

"Then why were you there?" he asked.

I opened my mouth and stopped. Outside the room, I could hear a muffled burst of laughter from somewhere over in the detectives' offices. People's lives going on as if mine didn't matter. The detective clicked his pen. Open. Shut. Open. Shut. My face felt hot. My armpits were sweating.

"Can I take off my jacket?" I asked.

"Why were you there?" he asked again.

I closed my eyes. I could see Roger Williamson's blue skin. Smell that hospital room.

You tell no one. Will you promise me that?

"I made a promise," I said, opening my eyes.

The detective cocked his head and partially closed one eye. His lip and the mustache above it quivered slightly.

"I can't," I said. "I have to think. I'd better talk to a lawyer. A criminal lawyer . . ."

"You can't tell me why?" he said.

"*Minnick v. Mississippi,*" I said.

He tilted his head the other way.

"I asked for a lawyer," I said. "You're permanently barred from asking me another question. That's the case law . . ."

"You're gonna need it," he said with half a smile.

I looked away from him. The red eye of the tape recorder stared at me until he clicked it off. He snatched it up and stood, holding it in his freckled fist so that the skin was stretched smooth across his knuckles.

He left and I sat for a long time. I was beginning to think about making some racket. They owed me a phone call. I was combing my brain. I never saw a statute or any case law that told me how long they could make you wait for your phone call. Then someone else walked in.

He was a well-built little man — like a gymnast — with curly blond hair, a tan furrowed brow, and hazel eyes. I'd seen him before somewhere, angry, and not looking quite so elfish. He smiled at me suddenly, as if someone had cued him to do it. When he held out his hand, I shook it.

"I'm Dean Villay," he said. "District attorney."

He turned the chair around and sat down, leaning toward me. He wore a gray double-breasted blazer with brass buttons and gray slacks with grass stains at the cuffs. If he had a tie, it was gone. On the collar of his white shirt was a small chocolate-colored stain.

"I asked for my own lawyer."

He flicked his hand in the air, swatting the notion away.

"They told me you cited *Minnick*," he said, smiling even more broadly now. The pupils of his eyes weren't round, but torn on the edges, giving me the sense I could see deeper into his friendly soul.

I felt a wave of relief. Finally, someone with some sense, some understanding of just how ludicrous this all was. Wasn't the DA an elected official? Yes. Political allies? Even from the other party, we very well could be . . .

I shook my head, smiling now.

"You don't know how crazy this was getting," I said with a laugh.

He laughed too. His round cheeks were flushed and I noticed that his tie was dangling from the side pocket of his blazer. I wanted to hug him.

"Sorry," he said. "Cops are cops. But we've got to get this straightened out. They've got a bloody knife that they're pretty sure was the murder weapon."

"A fishing knife?"

"Yes."

"They asked me about that. I have no idea. I have one in my boat, but . . ."

"Jesus, Raymond," he said, rubbing one hand from his forehead down the length of his face. "This is not good."

"But it wasn't *me*," I said, my hands clenched.

"*I* believe you, but what the hell were you doing there?" he said. "People are going to want to know."

"You can keep this quiet, right?" I said, lowering my voice and leaning toward him. "I mean, if you check this out, you're the DA, you can keep this part quiet, but push the investigation the other way and find out who really did this, right?"

"Of course," he said, leaning still closer.

I looked around, even though the room

was a five-by-ten-foot closet and the door was shut.

"I promised someone I'd give her an envelope," I said, in a low tone. "I have no idea what was in it. It had nothing to do with me getting the nomination. But the girl, she said she was having an affair with Roger Williamson."

When that news hit him, the legs of the chair hit the floor and squeaked. His mouth opened, but he quickly put his top teeth over his lip and leaned back toward me again, although not as close.

"He was the one who asked me to deliver the envelope," I said, whispering. "I saw him the day before he died. He asked me not to say anything to anyone. Just give it to her as soon as I got back from New York."

Villay looked away and slowly nodded his head as he chewed his lower lip. He stood up suddenly and held out his small hand again.

"Okay," he said. "That's it. That's easy. I'll go and find the envelope and that's going to go a long way to help you here. You delivered the envelope and you left. The knife, I don't know, maybe the real killer planted it."

"And you can keep the fact that I told

you about the letter between you and me?"
I asked.

"Absolutely," he said, smiling and tapping the side of his head. "You don't get to where I'm at without keeping a few secrets."

13

Even in special housing, which is the box, they will give you an hour of recreation. Time to breathe fresh air and walk in circles. Off by yourself. On a rooftop surrounded by a high fence crowned with concertina wire.

I don't go there.

I don't want to see the sky. I don't want to feel the wind on the back of my neck or the chill of snowflakes pricking my face. I am like an alcoholic who can't bear to have a single mouthful of drink. I don't want to even think about freedom and so I don't want to taste even the foam from that glass.

During the days before my trial I was out on bail, consumed with proving my innocence and trying to act like everything in my life was going to be just fine. I tried to work on the acquisition of a drugstore chain for a big client, but kept finding myself in the law library scrutinizing every detail of every murder case I could get my hands on. I pestered my own defense lawyer incessantly, pushing to keep the trial date from being moved out. I refinished the hardwood floors in my house to keep my hands busy. And my relationship with Lexis limped along in the no-man's-land between the redemption and total destruction of my life.

The lawyers and private investigators I had hired figured it all wrong. Our focus was on finding out who would have wanted Celeste Oliver dead. Whoever really killed her had obviously taken advantage of my visit to divert the blame for the murder to me. The company she kept left us with an endless selection of possibilities. We tried to track them down. Drug dealers. Bikers. Businessmen cheating on their wives. Even some small-time mobsters. Our leads went nowhere. It wasn't until too late that I realized that it wasn't about Celeste Oliver at all. It was only about me.

I heard things during that time that I didn't bother to process. I was in denial. Because I was innocent, I didn't ever really believe I would be convicted. I kept waiting for that final dramatic moment when everything was explained. That envelope. I just knew it would turn up. Somehow. Some way. Now I know that just wasn't possible.

And I've also figured out why.

This is the way it must have happened.

It was almost midnight before Villay's Volvo coupe slowed down outside 1870 Lodi Street. There was a hush on the block that wasn't unusual in the wake of a major crime. The good people counting their blessings and hoping they weren't next. The bad ones keeping low profiles until the heat subsided.

Villay pulled into the driveway behind the red Honda. He stepped out into the night and listened. Crickets. He didn't know crickets could survive in the scant weedy patches crammed between the North Side's dilapidated buildings and blacktop. He scanned the street, up and down, then climbed the front steps, ducking under the yellow tape. The door was locked, but he had a key for the padlock to the hardware that had been bolted in place. He stepped inside and turned on the lights. The heat from the day still lingered and with it the smell of cooked carpet and cigarette ashes. Dark swatches of dried blood stared up at him from the shaggy gold carpet.

"Hello," he said loudly. The sound of his own voice was intended to calm his nerves, but his hand still trembled as he began rifling through the papers that were

91

crammed into the cubbyhole of an old roll-top desk whose broken top was leaning up against the wall.

Villay had a sense of what it was he was looking for, but began to doubt his instincts as he pulled out his third wad of papers. Then he recognized the wavering scrawl of a man who was ready to die. The fat fold of papers pushing out of the ripped-open envelope made his mouth go dry.

When he saw the scrawled handwritten letters, his breathing grew shallow.

Last Will and Testament

The paper shook so badly in his hands that it was difficult to read. He had trouble separating the pages to turn them.

Roger Williamson's family had a little money to begin with, and he had used his position wisely. He had a beach condo in Florida, a big home in Manlius, partnerships in two trailer parks and a golf course, and a healthy portfolio of stocks and bonds. The man was worth about six million dollars.

It was a complete will, dated two days before Roger died. Written in his own hand from his hospital in New Jersey. A holographic will. Handwritten and signed. No witnesses, but completely valid in New York State.

It left everything to Celeste Oliver.

Roger Williamson had recently divorced for the third time. His only living child, a daughter, was the young woman Villay was about to marry. Under Roger Williamson's old will, Villay's fiancée, Allison, was to get everything. The house. The condo. The partnerships. The portfolio.

When Villay had heard how sick the congressman really was, he even began making up a guest list for a New Year's party at the Florida condo. He had also begun to interview stockbrokers who would manage the stocks and bonds.

A small panicked whine escaped his throat. Nausea swept over him and he sat down in the desk's chair, the air hissing out of the plastic cushion. The will was gripped so tightly in his hand that it curled in a funnel around his fist. He took a deep breath and laid it flat on the desk's narrow ledge, smoothing it and scouring it again.

He was right. The will had no survival clause, so even though the stripper had only outlived the congressman by four days, the probate court would treat the estate as if it passed to her the moment Roger died. Roger Williamson's money, his hard-earned fortune, would belong not to his own daughter, but to the heirs of the dead stripper.

There was another option, and Villay told himself it wasn't just about the money. It was about the great man's reputation and the memory his family would have of him. There was no need to sully all that so some white-trash relative of Celeste Oliver's could become suddenly and undeservedly rich.

Villay stood and stuffed the will into the inside breast pocket of his blazer. He crammed the other papers back into the cubbyholes and looked around for a sign of his presence before he realized that he had every right to be there and that no one would ever question him about it. He took a deep breath and let it out slowly.

He left the house and shut the door. The padlock clicked and rattled against the hardware as Villay turned for the steps. He drove to the end of Lodi Street — near the highway entrance — and pulled into a weedy lot. It was a dark nook amid the glow of the city's lights, and when he touched the cigarette lighter from his car to the edge of the will, its orange glow was hot and bright. Villay blew gently and the paper ignited, bursting into flame. Shadows morphed across his face as he tilted the burning document this way and that so that it would catch evenly.

The flame licked his fingertips and he dropped the burning sheets to the ground. The acrid scent, like smoldering leaves, filled the air. Villay raised his foot and stamped out what embers remained of the burnt paper, scattering black ash and small sparks that were quickly swallowed up by the shadows.

14

It was an early taste of summer. The sun, a stranger through the months of gray, left me squinting. The snow had melted, but piles of grit and filth from a winter of plowing still dirtied the no-man's-land where the sidewalk meets the street. The warm air, the sight of an irregular daffodil, and the smell of soggy grass left me lighthearted and eager. I swung my jacket over my shoulder and bounced along on my toes.

Against the wishes of the man hired to defend me, I had insisted on fast-tracking my trial. Emil Rossi, my lawyer, was old school and he believed in badgering the prosecution on every point. But I was an innocent man, anxious to have my life back. Now we were at the end. Tomorrow morning, both sides would make their closing arguments and then the jury would decide.

My father asked me to join him for a beer at the Dinosaur Bar-B-Que, a biker place that regular people go to. I could smell the slow-cooked ribs and chicken as

I crossed the street and edged between two Harleys. Inside, a waitress in black T-shirt and push-up bra with a biker attitude asked me what did I want. Normally you had to wait an hour for a table, but it was just four o'clock and the place was half empty.

"All set," I told her, unfazed and searching.

My father and Black Turtle looked ridiculous in their poorly cut blue suits, lizardskin boots, and short wide ties. I had seen them in the courtroom, but only nodded. It was like they knew what I was thinking, because as I passed the bar, they wrestled off the ties, shed their jackets, and began rolling up their sleeves. In front of them were three longneck bottles of Bud.

I sat down and raised my bottle before taking a long swig.

"What did you think?" I asked. A question that would have been unthinkable before Emil had begun to build me up. After three days of listening to Villay, the jury must have had a pretty bad impression of who I was and what I had done. Things were much better now.

"Good people," Black Turtle said with a nod curt enough to toss his ponytail briefly into sight.

He meant the impressive list of character witnesses. Today Emil had conducted a parade of university professors, CEOs, and the director of the Red Cross office where I had been a volunteer since age fourteen. We could have had the congressman if we wanted. Bob Rangle magnanimously stepped forward to offer his help. For Rangle, it was a politically dangerous move. Emil voted to accept, but I flatly rejected it without knowing why.

My father finished his beer and leaned forward after wiping his mouth on the back of his hand. At the same time, he reached down under the table, producing a worn leather satchel that he thumped down next to the ketchup.

"You're gonna take this," he said in a whisper, "and go."

"Dad?" I said with a short laugh.

"Run. Scat. Skee-daddle," he said.

"They've got to prove the elements of the crime, Dad. The burden is on them and they haven't done it."

"This isn't final exams, goddamn it," he said. His pupils were wide and nearly swimming. His lips trembling beneath the wavy bristles of his gray mustache. His long gray hair was slicked straight back. "Black Turtle has some Mohawk friends up at the border who can get you across. We got you a Canadian passport and a ticket to Zurich. They don't have no extradition from there."

It was quiet among the three of us for a while. My head was buzzing and I was aware of the clashing sounds of Metallica in the background.

"I didn't do it," I said.

My father's face wrinkled and he quickly swiped at his eyes. His voice was broken.

"You know how many people died in jail that didn't?" he said. "You gotta run."

"Weren't you at the same trial I was today?" I said.

"That's just people talking. People that like you. I'm tellin' you," my father said, his leathery face reddening. "I'm not asking. There's almost seven thousand dollars in here."

"What did you sell, Dad?"

"That don't matter," he said. "You're all I got. Everything . . ."

I reached across the table and grabbed hold of his hand. My father made a fist and I put my other hand on top too. My eyes were wet. I felt a flood of emotions inside me that I didn't want coming out. We would have time to look back on it all.

Soon. We could laugh and cry when it was all behind us.

"I know, Dad," I said. "They're gonna acquit me. He hasn't proven anything beyond a reasonable doubt."

"What the fuck does reasonable mean?" he said. "They got her blood. They got that knife. You see things the way you want to."

"That's what works, Dad," I said. "Except for this: Look at me . . . look at my life."

"This is everything and you don't even see it. You got a charge in your hand. It's gonna kill you and it's gonna kill me too."

"Black Turtle," I said, "talk to him."

But Black Turtle directed his blank look at me, not my father.

"I got two good men," he said, signaling to the waitress. "We'll get you across that river. This white court is a bad thing."

"Dad," I said, looking deep into his eyes. "I put up a two-million-dollar bond and I gave my word . . ."

My father looked back at me for a long time until the waitress brought three more bottles of beer.

He finally shook his head and said, "It don't matter."

"That's all we got, remember?" I said,

my voice frantic. "Your words."

"I don't give a *damn*," he said, banging his fist on the table, rattling the bottles and drawing attention to us.

"Don't you see the way that fat guy in the front row looks at you?" he said, hissing, and spraying flecks of white spit across the checkered tablecloth. "Or that scrawny flat-headed schoolteacher? They don't *believe* you. They're gonna get you. I see it. So does Black Turtle, goddamn it. It's not just me. That jury is people whose cards have always been bad and all you ever did was break the house. They never got a chance to do what you've done or be what you are. They can't wait to see you lose."

"It's not about that, Dad," I said. "Did you see them when the Red Cross lady talked about me saving that little girl? The award they gave me?"

"You goddamned fool," he said. He had my wrist now and he was squeezing it to the bone. "That made it even worse. You just don't see it.

"And now you're holding aces and eights," he said. Card players' talk for a dead man's hand. "And you got to fold. I don't care how big the pot is. You take this money and you get your ass across that river. Black Turtle's takin' you right now. I'm walking out that door and you're going with him, son."

My father stood up and put his hand on my cheek. A tear hung from the corner of his mustache, glimmered, and fell to the floor.

"I'm walking out of here," he said again in a husky voice. He turned his face and wiped it on his shoulder. "You go now, boy. I love you. I'll come and see you over there when this all settles down and you'll have it all again. The royal flush. Now you go."

I closed my eyes and he let his hand fall from my face. When I opened them, all I saw was his bowed legs and his broad back, hunched over and disappearing through the door, swallowed up by the sunlight. Black Turtle's eyes darted from the door to me.

"I'm not going," I said, looking down and pushing the leather satchel toward him.

"I know you ain't," he said in his low rumbling voice. "You're too much like him."

15

I dialed Lexis from a payphone and told her I was waiting on the street. I saw the green door in the alley beyond the Tusk open and she appeared with a small wave. There were no tables on the sidewalk yet, even though it was warm enough so that people would have used them. I brushed away the thought of Rangle and Frank and Russo and the day I could have saved myself by simply staying and drinking with them.

My throat felt tight until I saw the glint of the diamond ring on Lexis's hand. That ring had gone off and on several times over these past months. Rocky times where she talked more and more about taking just one drink to dull the edge. Did she believe me? Didn't she? Finally she did.

I smiled at her as she opened the door and composed a smile of her own. I looked into her blue eyes. Her teeth shone white. The sheen of her hair made me want to touch it. Beauty, with a distinct undercurrent of sadness.

We kissed quickly and I slipped my fingers through that hair, taking it in both hands and kissing it like a vestment before turning the key to my new car. They had impounded my Supra, and in order to forget about it I treated myself to a red RX-7. Instead of taking my usual right at the end of the street, I went left.

"Where are you going?" she asked.

"A surprise."

We listened to the news on NPR. I switched it to music when the local announcer started talking about the trial. I wanted to talk, but I had to choose my words carefully. One of the things we had come to argue about most was the way I talked so freely about the future, as if it were set. For whatever reason, Lexis couldn't stand to do that. So we talked about current events or things that had nothing to do with either of us. Or the past.

That's why I knew she'd like my surprise. There wasn't much about either of our pasts that we hadn't discussed over the last nine months. But there was this place that we went to when I was a kid. It was my dad's uncle's place. The brother of the man I was named after, Raymond Edinger. They called it the Blue Hole. I had forgotten about it, to be honest.

I turned south off Route 20 and drove down into Otisco Valley. I hadn't been to the place in years and wasn't even sure who owned it anymore. I didn't want to tell Lexis about it in case we couldn't get in. But as I turned off the road and drove down through the colonnade of massive spruce, I was heartened by the shaggy edges of the gravel drive. The woods opened up and the old white house came into view. It was empty, and one black shutter hung at an angle, distorting the face of what I had remembered as a fussy, well-kept colonial.

"Do you know these people?" Lexis asked.

"Old relatives," I said, swinging the wheel and driving down past the house and onto an overgrown grass trail.

Brown grass and dead weeds swished beneath us and an occasional branch thumped the undercarriage. We kept going down, and as the rocks and mud rattled in the wheel wells, I knew I'd have to keep my foot on the gas to get us out.

I kept going, though, down to the bend, where I stopped and got out at the head of a footpath. The sun was bright on the naked trees that climbed the far side of the steep ravine. The crashing water nearly drowned out all other sounds.

"What is it?" Lexis asked.

"The Blue Hole," I said. "You gotta see it."

She took my hand and I led her, slipping and catching ourselves on the midriffs of thin saplings, down the path and into the ravine. We pushed through a crowded stand of hemlock, then came out suddenly on a shale ledge that jutted out over the swirling pool of water below the falls. The brunt of the water shot through a narrow groove at the falls' head before plummeting another twelve feet to a whirlpool that had the reputation of being bottomless.

No less than three people had died in that hole during my lifetime and I was barely eight years old before my great-uncle closed it to the curious public. Still, the Blue Hole's reputation tempted trespassers of all kinds, and the last person to disappear into its depths was a high school kid who had failed his final exam in math.

When the stream was high, as it was now, curtains of water spilled off either side of the shoot, hissing across the face of the precipitous shale that was bronzed with mossy slime. The noise reverberated off the steep walls and it sounded like a giant fist pounding the earth.

"My God," Lexis said.

I gripped her hand, lacing my fingers in between hers. Already I could feel the constriction in my chest and the bolts of electric thrill surging up from my core to the spot behind my ears.

"We used to jump from here," I said, above the din.

Lexis wiped a strand of hair from her face and wrinkled the corners of her eyes.

"What?"

I began stripping off my shirt and untying my shoes.

"Raymond?" she said. "What the hell?"

For nine months I had existed in a place between heaven and hell, neither alive nor dead, neither happy nor sad.

"Goddamn," I said, breathing deep the smell of mud and water and broken rock, the heady sound of pounding water filling my brain. "It's like we were here like this before."

I handed her my shoes with the socks stuffed inside them. I stripped off my pants and even my boxers, rolling them up into my shirt, wrapping them in my belt, and handing them to Lexis.

"That water's got to be freezing," she said, her eyes wide, but taking the clothes and clutching them tight to her chest. "Are you crazy?"

I took her hand and gripped it again, pointing to the shale path that did several switchbacks through the steep grass before it ended at the bedrock below at the foot of another pool that belonged to a second and smaller falls.

"I've done it a thousand times," I said. "I'll meet you."

"Raymond, you're out of your fucking mind," she said, yanking me back toward her.

I put my arm around her waist and held her tight to my naked body, kissing her hard, letting my blood rise even higher. Then I pulled away.

"I love you," I said, letting go of her hand.

I turned and leapt from the ledge. It was the same ravine. The same crashing water. The same trees that hung on by their bare roots, fighting to stay upright. The same narrow pool that looked so ridiculously small from up here. It was all familiar to me. A feat I had performed countless times. So why was I scared so bad that my heart froze and my adolescent war cry got jammed up in my throat?

The milky green water came up fast and

it hit me hard enough to jar my breath away. Then everything was cold and black and I was fighting helplessly against the swirl with all my might. My arms were flipped this way and that, out of control, grazing the rough rock walls. My feet kicked insanely and I realized I didn't even know if I was fighting my way up or down. My eyes were wide and full of water. The blackness turned green, then white with swirling bubbles, and just before my lungs burst, I shot clear of the surface, sucking in air and flailing like a drowning cat.

The water spun me some more, and I grabbed desperately for the slick ledge on the far side of the pool away from the sheer rock. Finally, I pulled myself up, where I rested, shivering on my hands and knees, until that war whoop finally busted loose.

I heard Lexis's voice calling my name, small between the great rocky walls. It echoed up from the hissing below. It pierced the thundering roar of the water, and I stood to wave my arms at her. She held out my clothes, and beckoned for me to come down.

That night, after we were tangled together beneath the warm blankets in my bed, she asked me what the hell I did it for.

I wanted to give her a reason that was

bigger than the one I really had, but the best I could come up with was that I had forgotten what it felt like to control my own destiny.

"If you could control it," she said, "it wouldn't be your destiny."

We slept like spoons with her head on one of my arms and my other wrapped around her firm belly. I kept waking up and whispering the promise to her that everything was going to be all right. I told her that she was going to be my wife and that I'd take care of her until the end of time.

The next day we drove to the courthouse through a chill rain. By four-thirty, the jury convicted me of murder. My body went numb. My mind whirled. The bailiffs snapped handcuffs on my wrists and started to lead me away. As I neared the door, I came to my senses and I looked for Lexis. Her eyes were glassy. Her mouth hung open. She slowly raised her fingers to me and then Frank was there with that slab of a hand on her shoulder, his head bowed.

I called out to her and pushed back against the bailiffs, struggling, but they shoved me through the door and someone slammed it shut.

16

It took almost three months of processing before they were ready for me at Attica, the state prison notorious for its deadly riot in the early seventies. During that time, I was in isolation at the Public Safety Building in Syracuse. I saw Dan Parsons several times. He swore he'd fight this thing all the way to the Supreme Court. He had retained the famous Harvard Law professor Alan Dershowitz. But both of us knew enough about the law to realize that the judge hadn't committed any reversible errors and no one could overturn a jury.

My father visited me as often as was allowed. Once a week.

He never mentioned my failure to escape when I could have. But just before they shipped me off, he appeared with his eyes puffy and red to tell me the news. Lexis had married Frank Steffano. She was pregnant with his child.

My father said he didn't want me pining for her.

Because of the way I now live, in total

isolation, and because I returned every one of her letters until they stopped coming, it is likely that I never would have known what happened with Lexis and Frank. Sometimes I think it would have been better not to know. Other times I'm thankful that I do. I don't care what anyone says. I don't care that she loved him for a couple of years. I know him. I know her. And I know this is what happened.

Frank's hands were big, and he was careful to limit their touch to Lexis's arms and shoulders. Nothing intimate. He was a friend she could count on. He guided her outside the courthouse and down the steps. His dark blue unmarked cruiser was parked half on the sidewalk and half off in the fire lane.

"Come on," he said, opening the passenger door. "I'll take you home."

By the time he hurried around and climbed in, she was sobbing hysterically. Frank leaned over and pulled her to him, hugging her like a sister whose parents had died, patting her back, speaking softly.

"It'll be okay," he said. "It'll all be okay."

"It can't," she said, her voice a shattered moan.

"I know," he said, "but it will."

Twice people put their faces up to the window and Frank glared at them until they went away. When she finally cried herself out, he let her go and started the engine.

"Maybe you shouldn't go home," he said. "Maybe you shouldn't be alone."

Lexis said nothing. She just stared straight ahead and Frank drove two blocks, where he pulled the cruiser up onto another sidewalk in front of L'Adours, a French restaurant across the street from the stone sandcastle that is City Hall. Frank helped Lexis out and led her by the arm inside to an intimate booth in the nook beneath the staircase. He sat her down and whispered something to Sebastian, the maître d', before taking the seat opposite her.

It wasn't a minute before she had a glass of Alsatian Riesling in front of her and Frank was wiping the froth off his lip from a mug of beer.

"Take a drink," he said, nudging the glass toward her.

Lexis stared at it. She wet her lips with the tip of her tongue.

"I stopped," she said.

"I know," he said. "This is a little different. After what you've been through I

113

don't think there's anyone who wouldn't give you special dispensation . . ."

Light from above glowed in the pale yellow wine. A small bead of condensation snaked its way down the side of the glass.

"I know I've got my issues," he said with a sigh, "but the one thing you won't get from me is any of this holier-than-thou crap. It's okay, Lexis. One drink. You could use it."

She reached out and touched the cool round glass. She pinched the stem between her fingers and ran them lightly up and down for a moment, then sighed and picked it up. She opened her mouth and filled it before setting the half-empty glass down on the table. She let the wine swish around gently inside her cheeks.

Frank smiled at her. Half a laugh spilled up out from his chest. Lexis looked at him and swallowed. Immediately she brought the glass to her lips again, finishing the glass before replacing it on the table without a sound. Frank upended his beer and pushed both glasses toward the edge of the booth. A grinning waiter quickly replaced them.

This time, Lexis took her time. She didn't look at Frank, but his eyes peeked over the rim of his mug even when he was drinking. After she set down the third empty glass on the table, she cleared her throat.

"See," she said, her face crinkling into a pathetic frown that suddenly darkened, "he promised me this wouldn't happen."

Frank took her hand, holding it tight and patting it softly with his other hand.

"I know," he said, quiet and sad.

"Did he do it?" she said suddenly, her eyes locked onto his.

Frank looked down at the table and shook his head slowly from side to side. The waiter set down fresh drinks. He pushed the wine toward her.

"Three is enough," she said. "It's more than enough."

"What's the difference?" Frank said. "Stop worrying. It's just me. Do you want something to eat? My mother always says it's good for you to eat."

"This isn't a date, Frank," Lexis said, her eyebrows knit together.

"I know," Frank said in his best little-boy voice.

Lexis shook her head, looking down. Just the trace of a smile showed on her lips. She took a deep staggering breath and let it out.

"I'm drunk," she said. "Is that good for me?"

"It's not a cardinal sin," he said. "Even the priests drink wine."

"You eat," she said, her words sloppy. "I'll have just one more and then you can take me home."

"I'll order for both of us," he said.

They talked quietly as they waited for the food. Frank led her into talking about how wonderful the past two years of her life had been. He kept going back and back until finally he got to them.

"You know, my mother still thinks you and I will end up together," he said. "She thinks you're the kind of woman who can forgive a mistake, but I don't know."

"You're just a man, Frank," she said with a crooked smile, taking a swig of wine, "and men lie. All of them . . ."

Frank just stared at her.

The food finally came and he ate it in big mouthfuls, but he was more intent on making sure Lexis's wineglass was refilled. She didn't even pick up her fork. After the waiter cleared the plates, he returned with a small tray of tall thin shot glasses. Smoky steam curled up and away from their frosted surfaces.

Frank took one and raised it toward Lexis.

"To forgetting," he said.

She nodded and picked up a glass, letting it clink against his before she threw it down. They had two more each, and Lexis's eyes were beginning to lose focus.

"I should get you back," Frank said.

"Yes," she said in a murmur.

Frank led her to the car by the arm again, helping her inside and dashing around the front. He pulled away from the curb fast and parked on the back side of the alley, away from the Tusk. As he helped her down the alley, she began to stagger.

"Do you have your keys?" he asked.

She fumbled with her purse and dropped it onto the bricks.

"Dizzy," she muttered.

Frank scooped up the purse and tugged her to the green door. He punched in the code and half carried her up the stairs with one arm around her waist and the other holding her arm. They got to her door and he spilled the purse out on the step under the small carriage lamp. The brass key gleamed up at him. He bent down, holding her still, and scooped it up from the mess — one-handed — without bothering to pick up the rest. He jiggled the key and the door flew open.

Frank caught her over his shoulder and carried her in, where he laid her facedown on the big sleigh bed. He went back to the front door and with trembling fingers scooped up the contents of the purse while he scanned the common area. It was empty. He heard a loud group coming up the stairs as he pulled the door shut tight and bolted the lock.

When he returned to the bedroom, he wore a massive grin. His heart pounded as he stripped off his clothes. Lexis wore a skirt, and she swatted feebly at his hands as he unzipped it and slid it off over her shoes. He liked the shoes, dark high-heeled pumps, and he preferred that they stay on.

From his own pile of clothes, he removed a switchblade knife that snapped open with enough force to leave the knuckles on two fingers numb. He eased the blade up under her silk blouse and slid it up the length of her bony spine, exposing her back and pausing only to slice through the band of her bra.

Her head was sideways with her hair draped over her face. She began to blow it away so she could breathe, and Frank slipped his fingers underneath it, sweeping it aside and earning a smile from her.

"Raymond," she said.

His own smile distorted slightly, but stayed big. He kissed the back of her neck, breathing into her ear, letting the stubble on his chin raise a strawberry on her skin.

"It's me, baby," he said.

"Frank?" she said, her body going rigid. Her breathing quickened and she shook her head no.

"Shh," he said.

His fingers worked their way under the band of her dark red underwear. He slit through the silky material, exposing the round moon of her bottom to his thick probing fingers.

"Everything's going to be okay now, baby," he said in a husky whisper. "It's Frank, and he's gonna take care of you, just like he used to . . ."

BOOK TWO

ESCAPE

But then he recoiled at the idea of such an infamous death and swiftly passed from despair to a burning thirst for life and freedom.

The Count of Monte Cristo

17

Moving day.

I look up at the slate gray sky and blink. Snowflakes spiral down and melt on my cheeks. The sergeant of the Special Housing Unit at Great Meadow steps behind me and whacks his baton across the lower part of my spine. I go down in a heap of rattling chains. The others laugh, glad to finally be rid of me, but they shuffle their feet away from my mouth. I've heard the guards say more than once that a human bite is much more unsanitary than even a dog's.

"So long, asshole," the sergeant says.

Two guards lift me up by the arms and drag me across the icy pavement into the snowcapped blue van bearing a yellow state seal. My wrists are handcuffed. The lock on the cuffs is covered with a metal black box to prevent me from picking it open. The box has a padlock of its own with a chain that has been wrapped around my waist. My legs are manacled together just above the ankles.

The two guards sit behind me where I can't see them. A transportation sergeant sits down in the front next to the driver. They can't chain me to the floor. That would be illegal, and if they roll the van and I die in the burning vehicle, none of them will get their state pensions.

I have been promised a trip straight to the box at wherever it is I'm going, so I don't plan to cause any trouble. They call me crazy, but I'm not so crazy. Isolation, or Special Housing, does more than keep me from fantasizing about the life I once had. I know from stories what it means to be in a maximum-security prison. In the regular prison population, a man doesn't stay a man for very long. I've been in the system for just over eighteen years and that's never happened to me.

The snow keeps coming and I doze off. Somewhere in a crazy dream about my dad and Black Turtle and Frank digging up boxes of gold coins in the quarry, I am awakened by the van coming to a stop. I hear the shriek of a huge metal door grinding open, but by the time I come to my senses, we are inside a chain-link fence topped with razor wire. Out the other window, a forty-foot concrete wall glows under the halogen lamps mounted on the guard tower. The massive steel door slams shut behind us and the chain-link gates in front of the van creak open to let us out of the holding area.

They shove me outside, into the flood of lights and the cold. A raucous screeching fills the air. Thousands of desperate croaking voices in an ocean of agony. I look up and think for a moment that this is hell. The sky is alive, a pulsating flow of black vermin scurrying across an indigo plain. Crows. Thousands upon thousands of them.

Another cackle attracts my attention. It's human. A guard in a wool cap with a face of blue razor stubble and an angry yellow smile pokes me in the stomach with his baton.

"Tough guy, huh?" he says.

I let my face go flat and I look into his eyes.

"Ooh, you're real bad," he says. "I'm scared."

Then he cackles again and shoves me toward the entrance to a five-story stone building. Cellblocks with rectangular windows barred by rusty steel.

The stone above and around the entrance is distinct from the building that reaches into the distance on either side.

Around the entrance, the rough-cut blocks are tall and narrow with popped-out horizontal stones and narrow portals. This bluntly decorative stonework rises above the roofline of the cellblocks. As I pass under the gothic peak of the door, I am struck by its similarity to the tower of a church.

The guard pushes me into an elevator. Now there are two of them, standing opposite me. Glowering. The bluebearded one slaps his baton against the palm of his hand. Long narrow fingers with pointy nails. The skin pale and the knuckles sprouting dark hair. I know his kind. The kid who got spit on in high school. Now he can push around murderers and thugs, the worst of the worst. Now he's a badass. That's what he pretends.

The elevator stops, and I am jabbed in the kidney on my way out. A sergeant looks up from his desk.

"Sit down," he says, and I sit.

"Welcome to Auburn."

I gag on my own saliva.

Auburn Prison. Seven miles from the Tudor cottage on Skaneateles Lake. There is a restaurant outside these walls where I used to eat. Balloons, it's called. Good Italian food in the shadow of the west wall.

A point of conversation for diners. Good for a laugh. There is a Dunkin' Donuts in this town. Veal Francesco at Michael's Restaurant. Dadabos Pizza. A movie theater. Curley's, where the guards all drink after work. Places woven into the fabric on the fringes of my old storybook life.

That explains the crows. Hundreds of thousands descend on the tiny city of Auburn each winter. A plague of biblical proportions. Some say the crows are a curse on the forefathers' greed for choosing to have the state's first prison in 1812 instead of accepting the offer to become the state's capital. Some say they are lured by the warmth of a microclimate created by the unique combination of concrete, lights, and the outlet of Owasco Lake.

I suck in air, the precursor to a sob, but I bottle it up. My head begins to throb.

The sergeant looks hard at me.

"Aww," Bluebeard says, "she's crying, Sarge. She's not happy with her new home."

"You can start over here, White," the sergeant says, ignoring Bluebeard and the fact that my eyes are now on my shoes. "If you can live by the rules, you'll be out of SHU in three months. If you fuck up, you'll stay here. We'll start you out on the regular food. If you fuck up, you'll get the loaf. It's the shittiest-tasting slice of crap ever made, but no one ever died from it. That and water. Fuck up again and, well, sometimes we have trouble with the fuse box for the lights in these cells. You choose . . ."

A chair scrapes the floor, and the sergeant's footsteps move toward the door. It closes and I get a whack from Bluebeard across my shoulder blades.

"Up, asshole," he says.

They put on latex gloves. They strip me down and search my rear. Bluebeard whispers to me, calling me his girl, his razor stubble chafing my ear. My eyes water and I close them tight. This part is worse when you fight it. I know.

They make me shower, then give me a new set of clothes. Forest green.

Bluebeard leads me into the top of D block and the other guard uses his keys to open a box on the wall. Home to five levers. Two of them are covered with a red sleeve that tells the guard they belong to the cells of prisoners without recreation. The other guard pulls down the lever on the end and I hear a cell door begin to hum. I am shoved into a tank, a self-contained unit of five steel cells. My cell door clanks open.

From the darkness beyond the cross-hatched steel bars of the cell next to mine appears the pale shape of a face. An old man with tufts of white hair and a hooked nose that he pokes through the bars. Two glowing blue eyes magnified by owlish glasses. Small growths of crud are attached to their whites, encroaching on the irises. He says nothing, but his lower lip disappears behind a crooked row of teeth. It might be a smile. Maybe he's a bug. A nut. Something about these eyes is very different.

Bluebeard shoves me into my cell. His kick barely grazes my backside, and I don't bother to even look back at him. I stand over the bowl and relieve myself, then I crawl onto the bunk and curl into a ball, trying hard not to think about how close I am to home.

18

It was a sunny spring day, so bright the towering buildings of Manhattan seemed almost clean. Sunday. The streets free from the weekday clutter. Lexis looked out of the long dark glass of the window and saw empty parking spaces along Park Avenue in front of their building. Home for the past ten years, ever since Frank somehow worked his way into a casino partnership in Atlantic City. Allen was hunched over his Game Boy, his dark hair hanging straight down in front of his face, his thumbs working the controls with fevered excitement. Frank was on his cell phone, going over his last-minute bets for the basketball games that afternoon.

Their limousine cruised down Fifth Avenue and eased to a stop in front of Rockefeller Plaza. The party planner was waiting in a tuxedo with narrow shoulders. Frank referred to him as "the fairy," but insisted they use him because he had planned the same kind of confirmation party for the governor's nephew. There were others waiting too. The caterer. The florist. The business manager for the band.

Lexis hustled Allen inside, still bent over his Game Boy, while Frank opened the trunk of their Mercedes limo and began dispersing banded stacks of money. Cash was king. That's what Frank always said, and when Lexis stepped inside the Rainbow Room on the top floor she couldn't help feeling that in a way it was. Gold and silver balloons, bundled into columns, rose to the ceiling. The center of every table bloomed with a four-foot-high flower arrangement of white flowers, lilies, roses, orchids, and gardenias. Over the head table loomed a gold football goalpost. At each place was an NFL football personalized for the guests and signed by Joe Namath, who would be joining them at the head table. Cash was king.

Allen looked up from his Game Boy. "Wow."

He ran to his own place at the head table and rolled the football between his hands.

"It says, 'Congratulations to my good friend Allen Francis,' " he said, looking up at her with his hazel brown eyes and blinking.

"That's exciting," Lexis said.

"Why did Dad have to tell him Allen *Francis?*"

"Your father is very proud of you, Allen. This party cost him a lot of money, so please don't act spoiled."

"I'm not spoiled," he said with a frown. "Here. Catch a pass, Mom."

Allen threw a spiral across the room. Lexis made a breadbasket. The ball hit her in the chest and bounced out to the floor.

"Ha. Never throw a pass to a woman. How about this place?" Frank said in his loud low voice as he stepped into the room, arms spread wide, gut spilling out of his tuxedo jacket. "I had mine in the VFW hall. Throw me that other ball."

Frank had grown steadily bigger over the past fourteen years so that he now weighed close to three hundred pounds. Lexis was pretty certain that the more of himself there was, the more he liked it. He still started every morning with a ten-minute gaze into the bathroom mirror, stretching back his lips to examine his teeth and toying with the thick curly locks that had recently gone gray at the temples. Allen took another ball from the table and threw a whistling spiral across the room to Frank. The ball smacked loudly into Frank's hands but he held on.

"See that?"

Lexis dusted off the front of her dress

and adjusted her two-karat diamond ear-rings. Frank tossed the ball back and took a long velvet box out of his coat pocket.

"I got this for you," he said, handing it to her.

"Thank you," she said. She had stopped telling him that she didn't want any more jewelry years ago. It was a diamond neck-lace highlighted by a five-karat teardrop pendant.

"Thank you, Frank."

"Hey," he said, hugging her to him, then letting her go as she pushed away. "I'm not just a great father, you know."

Lexis forced a smile.

The band began to play and the room soon filled up. Other big men in tuxedos with red ties and cummerbunds. Women with screechy voices, Brooklyn accents, high hair, and high heels. Frank's business associates. Low-level politicians. Bookies. Judges. Some of Lexis's friends from the board of the Guggenheim.

Lexis turned from her friend Marge to hear Frank greeting his old friend Bob Rangle. Rangle wore a perfectly tailored black suit with a gray silk tie. His long hands were clutched together and carefully manicured. He'd grown a neat thin mus-tache, maybe to make up for the gleaming baldness that shone through the long strands of hair swept over the top of his head. His frame was still straight, tall, and angular, and he seemed to have become infected with the same disease that caused his wife to walk with an arch in her back and her chin in the air.

"Sorry Dani couldn't be here," Rangle said, referring to his twelve-year-old daughter. "She had a sleepover. It's hard enough to get Katie to a function on Sunday afternoon, but when I told her the governor was coming . . ."

Beside him stood Katie Vanderhorn, his tall wife. Old-money New York. Still pretty with her long auburn hair despite the heavy makeup, crow's feet, and a nose that was so straight surgery wasn't even a question.

"I just read his book," she said, "otherwise, I *promise* you I wouldn't be that interested."

"Is that friend of yours from Merrill Lynch, Michael Blum, coming, do you know?" Frank asked.

"He said he'd try, Frank," Rangle said, looking at his gold Piaget Emperador.

"You'd think having the governor here says something," Frank said.

"In the world of finance, relationships

are important," Rangle said, squinting his close-set dark eyes at two loud men hugging and slapping each other's back.

"There's Joe Namath over there," Frank said, pointing.

The Rangles' faces went blank.

"You should try the cold lobster," Lexis said, motioning toward the ice sculpture of a football player rising up in the middle of the hors d'oeuvre table.

"Thank you, dear," Katie said, and off they went.

"God, he's a flaming asshole," Frank said. "But if I can get that financing . . .

"Where is he?" he continued, looking at his watch and then the door.

"Isn't he always late?" Lexis asked.

"The troopers should be here by now, though," Frank said, looking around. "Some of his people."

Just then, a tall, professorial-looking man with gray hair and gold-rimmed glasses walked in wearing a blue suit and yellow tie. His name was Cornell Ricks, the deputy director of the Thruway Authority and Frank's liaison to the governor's office. Ricks saw Frank and approached him with open arms, giving Frank an awkward hug and a stiff pat on the back.

"Frank, congratulations," he said. "Lexis, you too. I know you're both very proud. I'm sorry the governor can't make it. He sends his deepest regrets, but his wife isn't feeling well at all."

Ricks took Frank by the arm, lowered his voice, and said, "He's *very* concerned, and he was glad that a family man like you would understand."

Frank's mouth was clamped tight and his face began to turn color. Finally, he took a deep breath and let it out through a small space between his lips.

Lexis stepped back and said, "I'll go tell them we can sit down."

She turned quickly away so she didn't have to hear. The waiters had already filled the glasses at each table with red wine. Lexis stopped at a place by the wall and looked around before she picked up a glass and emptied it.

It warmed her empty stomach and she felt it quickly run up her center and calm her brain. She felt better already, and then she saw her boy across the room. The day she had him it looked like neither of them would make it, but now the photographer was lining him up next to Joe Namath, the two of them with their hands on the same football. Allen's face was radiant. She sighed and emptied another wineglass. Her life wasn't so bad.

Really, it wasn't.

19

When I wake, a thin light is seeping in from the dirty window across from my cell. A new start. As soon as I don't cooperate, they'll cover the front of my cell with a steel partition and I'll live again in the darkness. I listen to the sound of my own breathing. In a way, the darkness is better. Then I can't see how small my world really is. I will wait until tonight, though, before I do anything bad. Bluebeard is on the three to eleven shift and I will save my spit, a thick wad of flaxen goo, for his face especially.

Food comes. Soggy carrots with most of the color boiled out of them. A stiff slice of bread. A cup of powdered milk and an oblong hunk of gray meat — origin unknown. I eat, then push the tray out into the walkway. My calluses don't fit the grooves above this door. I'll need new ones, and chin-ups leave my hands dripping with blood. Katas are next. Now I'm breathing hard, sweat mingling with the blood. Tiny scarlet dots spatter the powder blue section of the bars. My own decor.

I do sit-ups and math, talking quietly out loud to hear the sound of a human voice. Numbers turn to history lessons. I recount as much as I can about Auburn. The Seward House, home to the U.S. secretary of state who purchased Alaska. States and capitals. I know a song and I sing it low. Time passes.

"Rec time," says a guard I can't see.

My cell door rattles and hums open.

"Step out."

I do, along with the old man and a brown-skinned young man with a long black ponytail and a thin mustache. We are led up a set of stairs to the roof. A square of concrete caged in by a ten-foot-high honeycomb of rusted metal bars. Recreation. The guard stands outside and locks us in.

The old man gives me a curious look with those magnified orbs, then he begins to shuffle around the perimeter. He is a small man and stooped, and his gnarled hands, like the broad bald spot on his head, are covered with the spots of age. The young punk stuffs his hands into his pants pockets and begins to kick at the walls of the cage. I can only see up. The walls of the roof block any view of the surrounding city.

The bleached sky is dry and crisp. The sun only a glow behind the flat cover of clouds. The sounds of license plates being stamped and wood cabinets being milled float up from unseen shops below. The air is free from the typical stink of human smells, corroded metal, dust, and paint. I breathe deep, then start to walk too, keeping on opposite sides from the old man, following his tracks in the dusting of snow, giving wide berth to the punk.

I am looking up at the place where a mourning dove flapped across the sky when I hear a cry.

The punk has the old man down and he is swinging a blade. I don't think. I react. My snap kick goes up between the punk's legs. He shrieks and groans, staggers and turns. The blade slashes for my face. I leap back, seeing two razors melted into the end of a toothbrush. He slashes again. I measure the arc of the pendulum. The next time, I block his wrist, kick him again between the legs, and greet his dropping face with the full force of my elbow. His nose pops like a lightbulb. I pivot, break his arm, and crush the blade hand under my heel; I stomp and grind. Stomp and grind until his screams hurt my ears.

The guard is talking into his radio, but

he remains outside the cage. His eyes are calm. The old man is rising, fumbling with the plastic frames of his glasses. I help him. He coughs, but there appears to be no blood. He shuffles for the door, leaning against me.

"Let us out, Clarence," the old man says.

Clarence looks back at us. He has a shock of salt-and-pepper hair. A neatly trimmed mustache and goatee. His eyes are permanently sad and he appears to think for a moment, then nods without a word and rattles his keys. Another guard arrives. He watches the punk while Clarence leads us back to our tank. The doors hum shut and it is quiet. I hear Clarence answering questions amid the rattle of keys. There is some shouting in the stairwell. Then the voices all fade away.

"Thank you," says the old man. His voice is small.

I drop down and begin a set of push-ups.

"I heard them say you've been in the box for almost twenty years," the old man says. His voice is a little louder now.

"Shut the fuck up! Shut the fuck up! Shut the fuck up!" screams one of the prisoners who has been denied the enjoyment of recreation, but the old man keeps on as if it were the wind.

"You don't have to do that to be safe," the old man says. "What you just did for me? You've got protection now."

I snort at this news. A fragile old man, on his back, about to be sliced open unless I'm there. That's my protection.

"You don't know anything," he says.

"It doesn't matter," I say.

"Everything matters," he says.

"Not if you're me," I say, speaking into the empty space as if I'm talking to God. "This is my life. This is my world. I don't want to be out there with those animals."

"Outside the wall?"

"The wall?" I say. A short laugh escapes me. "No, I mean out there. With them. I'm not one of them."

"That's where freedom is," he says.

"Freedom to be someone's punk," I say. "Whose punk are you, old-timer?"

The old man clears his throat. His voice takes on a different cast. It has an edge.

"I survived in here. There are three rules in here if you want to survive," he says. "First rule: Never show fear. Second rule: Never be a rat.

"I came here in 1967," he says. "I was thirty-four years old. The biggest buck in A block took my lunch from me on the first day. He said that night, I was going to give him more than that. At two-thirty, I walked out onto the weight court and smashed his skull in with a fifty-pound dumbbell.

"Exact revenge. That's the third rule. The most important. If you don't do it, you'll be a professional victim. You exact it and it's exact. Not just a reaction, but planned out. Precise. It needs to send a message.

"If someone takes your cigarettes, you smash their hand into jelly in a doorjamb. They push you, you break their knees. Touch your food, you gouge out their eyes. Someone tries to make you his punk? You kill him. Believe me, it's self-defense. Whatever it is they did to you? You exact a revenge that's ten times worse, a hundred times if you can. That, they respect."

It's silent between us for a while. I hear my stomach rumble.

"What did they do to you when you hit that guy?" I ask.

"I got out of the box in 1970, just before the riot. I didn't have to hurt anyone else until 1979. Killed him with antifreeze.

"That punk today? Dumbass Colombians. I poisoned one of them two years ago. That's why I'm here. The other ones sent that kid in here to get me before I get out of SHU. Scared. They'll keep low now, and no one's going to touch you either. That's the game. You don't have to be a mole. You can bunk with me."

I laugh again.

"What are you?" he says. "Some homophobic?"

"I'm fine right here," I say.

"What about books?"

"What about them?" I ask.

"You can't read in the hole."

"I got my own dreams," I say.

"Books are more than just dreams," he says. "Books are like a mirror . . . for your soul. You can see yourself. Keep yourself neat and clean. You need that for when you get out. To fit in."

"There's no sense in getting out," I say.

"No sense?" he says, dropping his voice into an urgent whisper that only I can hear. "What are you, certifiable?"

"In, out," I say. "Jail is jail. I like it okay in my own space. I don't care what my soul looks like."

"I'm not talking about jail, kid," he says. "I'm talking about out. Outside the wall. Freedom."

"Don't even say that," I say, my heart thumping before I know it. I am whispering too. "I can scream louder than that guy next to you."

"Why not say it if it's true?"

"It's not true," I say. "There's no way out."

"Kid," he says, "you have no idea . . ."

I wrap my fingers around the bars. My lips are pressed to the steel and I taste its tang through the chips in the paint.

"You've been here for more than forty years," I say in a hiss. "Don't play with me, you crazy old coot."

It's quiet for a time. My ears start ringing and I wonder if I have imagined it all.

"I'm not playing," the old man says in a whisper that only I can hear.

"Who are you?"

"Lester Cole," he says, still low. "Thief and part-time murderer."

"How?" I ask. "How can you do it?"

"They like me here," he says. "They trust me. I fix everything. They get a jammed-up pipe and they need a man to go down into the catwalk and wade through the shit, Lester will do it. Anytime. Day or night. Just ask Lester.

"According to the warden, the job of the prisoners is to serve their time and maintain these buildings. I'm good at it. Plumbing. Electric. Air ducts. So I have . . . opportunities."

"How?"

145

"Patience," he says. "We have time."

"Forty more years?"

"A lot sooner than that, kid," he says. "Sooner than you think."

20

Centre Street. North of Wall Street. South of Chinatown. A powerful street, but relatively unknown outside the legal profession in New York City. Foley Square, and in the middle of it all, a neoclassical monster. Broad stone steps leading to massive fluted columns and justice. Beyond the façade, nearly two dozen men and women. Federal court judges for the Southern District of the Second Circuit. Appointed for life. The best and brightest, insulated from the political system to ensure their unbiased interpretations.

Villay didn't have the nicest chambers, but he didn't have the worst either. The crown molding needed refinishing, but the ceilings were twelve feet high and he had a high-backed leather chair. His clerk was Harvard. Third in his class. Thin, bookish, and blond like the judge himself had once been. Judge Villay ran the tip of a pocketknife under his thumbnail as he listened to the upcoming docket of cases. His broad forehead furrowed.

"What was that?" he said, putting his

little feet down on the floor and looking up at his clerk over the silver reading glasses perched on his elfin nose.

"An appeal," he said. "*Raymond White v. the State of New York*?"

"On what grounds?"

"Racial discrimination. Native American. Not a representative jury."

"Ha!" Villay said, smiling and wagging his head. "I'll be damned. Can't take it. Total bullshit, though. Who's the attorney? Not Dan Parsons still?"

The clerk looked down and nodded. "Yeah. How'd you know?"

"It was my case," Villay said, straightening his back and widening his eyes so that the clerk would stare into their torn pupils. "Murder one. Life without parole. Guy was about to get the Republican Party nomination for an empty congressional seat. Would have won. Big deal back then, part Native American and all that. But discrimination? Parsons was his partner. Must have run out of good ideas. What a fucking joke. Send it to Kim Mezzalingua. She'll get a kick out of it and send Parsons packing as fast as you can say 'summary judgment.'

"What else?" Villay said, returning to his nails.

148

The clerk cleared his throat and continued to read the upcoming docket until he reached the end.

"Make sure I've got time for that drug trafficking trial," Villay said, opening the cabinet for his coat with one hand and pointing at his clerk with the other. "Schedule a good ten days. I don't want it rushed. I'm sick of those bastards poisoning our kids."

He picked up his briefcase just as his secretary stuck her head inside the door.

"It's Ivan Lindgren," she said in an urgent whisper.

"Shit," Villay said. "Tell him I'm gone. Pain in the ass."

He turned and scuttled out the door that led to the back corridor. The way was longer, but worth it if he didn't have to see Lindgren. Outside, there was a light gray rain in the air, and Villay hurried to the curb with his briefcase over his head. He slid into the back of his Town Car, lifted the *Post* from the seat, and told his driver, Jack, to go.

Jack started, then lurched to a stop. Villay crackled the paper down.

"What the hell?"

Through the swish of the wipers he saw Lindgren, his thick brown mustache dripping, his lined forehead beaded with rain, standing tall directly in front of the car. Villay cursed under his breath.

"Go, Jack. He'll move."

The driver's shoulders were hunched over and he clutched the wheel, trembling.

"I . . . can't."

Villay slapped down his paper, huffed, and rolled down the window several inches.

"Get out of the way, you lunatic!" he shouted.

"You talk to me, damn it!" Lindgren shouted back.

Villay looked up and down the sidewalk. Despite the rain, people were stopping to stare.

"*What?*" he said through his teeth.

Lindgren circled the car, keeping his hands on its shiny waxed surface until his face was in the open space of the window and his fingers were clutching its edge.

"Five years," Lindgren said in a hiss. "They built that case for five years and you ruled that wiretap *inadmissible?*"

Villay stabbed his finger at Lindgren and said, "You be careful. You don't talk to a judge that way. I don't care who your father is. I'm a federal judge. You're a government attorney. I'll blackball you twenty ways to Sunday."

"I'll have you . . ."

"What?" Villay said, moving his face closer to Lindgren, smiling.

Lindgren's face started to crumple at the edges.

"They killed three people," he said, his voice broken and his fingertips white. "They *admitted* it."

"Thugs. Killers themselves. In case you weren't aware," Villay said, "we have a constitution in this country. We have laws. I suggest you go read them."

"You could have ruled either way," Lindgren said, his hands dropping to his sides.

"I'm a judge," Villay said. "I answer to a higher power than my willie. Maybe one day, if you grow up, you will too. Jack. Go."

Jack screeched the tires as he pulled away from the curb, then he jammed on the brakes before cruising away.

"Jesus," Villay said, shaking his head. "Go uptown, Jack. Gino's. And try not to kill anyone."

Gino's was already busy, and Villay pushed through the tiny, crowded bar area to the red half-door at the coat check. He turned, and the maître d' smiled and patted the judge on the shoulders before showing him the way to his table. There were no booths or private areas. Gino's was wide open. Well lit, with people crammed into small tables sitting back to back. The red wallpaper was adorned with zebras on carousel poles.

Villay sat down across from a stocky gray-haired man with pale green eyes and a diamond pinky ring and said, "Could you find a place that's a little more obvious next time? Jesus."

"I'm a lawyer. You're a judge," the man said in a heavy New Jersey accent. He wore a dark brown suit and a yellow tie. "What's the fucking difference? We got nothing to hide. Besides, this is one of the few places where you can sling around a briefcase full of cash without anyone taking notice. Place is a fucking gold mine, and cash only. You believe that?"

The waiter appeared in his gray waistcoat and black tie. He set down some breadsticks and gave them a bow.

"Pellegrino with lime," Villay said.

"You ain't going to eat?" the lawyer said, raising his thick gray eyebrows. "I'm getting a sautéed kidney."

"Just Pellegrino," Villay said to the waiter, before leaning over the table. "Stop playing games. Ivan Lindgren practically attacked me just now. Let's get this over with."

The bullnecked lawyer leaned back with a grin and took something from the outside pocket of his suit coat.

"Nervous. Nervous," he said. "But not too nervous to take a little something for the missus."

On the table he set a six-karat pink diamond engagement ring. Villay covered it quickly with his hand and looked around before slipping it into the pocket of his charcoal gray pants.

The lawyer chuckled. "No, not too nervous for that. A million dollars. That's what it's worth. A rare stone for a rare stone."

Villay narrowed his eyes and said, "What about the cash?"

The lawyer knit his brow and said, "I'm a man of honor. If I say five hundred thousand in cash and the ring, I mean it. I'm just telling you you're getting prime rib for the price of hamburger."

He leaned forward and lowered his voice. "Maybe a little discount will be in order next time, eh?"

The waiter brought the lawyer a glass of red wine, then set Villay's glass with ice and lime down and filled it from a green glass bottle.

When he'd gone, Villay took a sip,

looked at his watch, and said, "Can I go?"

The lawyer swallowed a mouthful of wine, shrugged, and said, "Suit yourself."

"I mean, is it there?" Villay asked, scowling.

The lawyer reached into his coat pocket again and handed him a blue plastic chip with a white number on it.

"There," he said.

Villay took another sip and stood to go.

"You should eat," the lawyer said. "Life is a lot better when you've got a full stomach and a nice glass of wine. Hey, aren't you gonna even say thanks?"

"Aren't you?" Villay said, turning.

"Yeah," the lawyer said, leaning back in his chair. "You did good. Thanks."

Villay gave him a two-finger salute. At the coat check, he took back his raincoat as well as the lawyer's bulging brown leather briefcase without leaving a tip for the girl. He pushed out through the tight crowd and into the rain with the briefcase under his coat. The smoky clouds were teeming now, blurring the river of taillights and yellow cabs. He looked left and right, felt a small stab of panic at the sight of a police car with its lights flashing, but quickly chastised himself when he saw a cop writing out a ticket.

Still, he clutched the briefcase tight and kept his eyes riveted on the rearview mirror the entire way home to make sure Jack wasn't looking at him. By the time the black car rolled through the gates, he'd chewed a crater on the inside of his lower lip that was big enough to bleed.

21

I thought that even the remotest sparks of hope were buried and long cold in the ash heap under my ribs. But at the sound of Lester Cole's words, a phoenix springs up.

I am afraid, but unable to stop it. I do not want to die all over again. I have been comfortably numb, slowly rotting away at my own pace. My life is empty, but the only sharp pain I feel is physical and it pales next to the anguish of being destroyed.

Lester tells me he doesn't want to talk anymore now. He just wants me to know that things are different.

The loaf is the shittiest-tasting slice of crap ever made, but time goes by and I behave. Lester is a genius. He teaches me things I never knew. The way particles are assembled on a picture tube. Why airplanes fly and compressed Freon cools air. How J. J. Thomson used cathode rays to discover electrons. The weather on the day in AD 445 when Attila the Hun murdered his brother Bleda to secure the throne and how much the Eastern Roman emperor Theodosis II paid him to maintain peace. The affair between Gauguin and van Gogh that was the real cause of the great artist's self-mutilation.

He pours it out and I suck it up. We whisper to keep the maniacs at bay. During rec, he diagrams things for me in the snow and then the dust. The battle plans of Alexander the Great. The layout for a particle accelerator. Michelangelo's design for the dome of St. Peter's Cathedral.

Bluebeard is giddy with the power he appears to have over me. He gloats at my docile behavior, taking credit for kicking my ass into line. I am given an additional three months in the box for crushing the Colombian's hand and breaking his nose, but my release now nearly coincides with Lester's. We put in a request to be bunked together, and Lester works it out for us to get an end cell on the ground floor, A block First Company.

There are five blocks in Auburn, A through E. Each block has five floors of cells, forty-five in a row, two rows, front and back. It used to be one man to a cell, but to save money, the governor now allows double bunks on the end cell of each company by request.

Clarence takes me down the elevator from Special Housing and across the yard. I blink at the bright sunlight and shuffle my feet along the faded blacktop, enjoying the scuffing sound of long even strides. The yard is a rectangle of pavement surrounded by the cellblocks. Lester has familiarized me with everything during our hour-long rec sessions on the roof by drawing in the grit. The administration building rises above C block to the east. At the west end is the mess hall and auditorium. Corroding basketball hoops are staggered around the inside of the yard in no apparent order.

It's after breakfast, so only a few inmates are scattered in small groups, sitting at metal picnic tables in the shadow of A and B blocks. The men are mostly black. They wear the faded forest green outfits and stare sullenly at me. My heart begins to pound. There are two guard posts on the roofs and what they call a sergeant's box, a trailer without wheels in the yard, butted up to the wall of D block. All the guns are on the roof and in the towers and I can feel them.

I am light-headed with the sensation of freedom, but scared by the thought that I am sticking my neck out for some wild-ass notion of an old man who might be crazy, even if he is brilliant. I keep my eyes straight ahead as I am escorted up the steps and into A block. I think of the first rule and force a sneer onto my face. I think I hear a low whistle, but I pretend not to. I think of the third rule. Exact revenge. Does that whistle mean I have to punch that man's teeth out?

Clarence passes me off to another guard and says he'll see me around. The guard rattles his keys and opens the box of levers.

"Clear on one," he says, and pulls down on one of the brass levers.

I hear the cell door begin to hum. The guard rattles his keys again and opens the barred door leading into First Company. I step inside. All along the wall, inmates push their faces against the bars to see who the fresh meat is. They look like zoo animals. Some hoot and catcall. Some laugh and holler. Lester is standing in the gloom of the double bunk, his thin white tufts of hair blazing. Those enormous eyes shine and his smile exposes how badly he needed dental work as a kid. I step inside and the door begins to hum shut. It clanks in place, and I feel relief as I take Lester's gnarled hand.

"Welcome," he says, pumping my handshake.

I see now that the walls and ceiling are plastered with museum posters. Reprints of famous works of art from Europe and the United States.

"What's all this?" I ask.

Lester's blue eyes glow and crinkle at their corners. I don't even see the yellow scum of the cataracts any longer.

"A surprise, kid," he says. "I never told you what kind of a thief I was."

I know he killed a man during a job. That's all he's ever said about why he's here.

"You stole this kind of stuff?" I ask.

"Picasso, Miró, Rubens, Dalí, Monet, Cassatt," he says. He is beaming now and has straightened his crooked little form up to its full height. "Even a small van Gogh. Jewels too."

I whistle to make him feel good and lean toward the wall to study the brilliant red flower on a Rembrandt, but I can't say that it matters all that much to me.

"I guess a lot of people would kill for this stuff," I say.

"What the hell makes you say that?" he says, and the tone of his voice makes me turn. I see that his face has clouded over.

"Well . . ."

"I killed a guard because he was going to kill me," Lester says, holding up a single bent finger in the air. "It's wrong to kill, except in self-defense. There is no other justification. None."

"No, I guess not," I say and his eyebrows ease up.

"I was there for Jan van Eyck's panels of *The Crucifixion* and *The Last Judgment*," he says. "I had it. I was in and on my way out. The guy wasn't even on duty. Do you want to know what he died for?

"A pen," he says. "His wife gave him a silver pen for their anniversary. He came back for it and saw me going up a rope. He shot three times and missed. I didn't . . . ."

"The well-placed little things are the ones that can move mountains," I say. "I guess that goes the same for the misplaced little things too. You want me on the top bunk?"

Lester rubs the white stubble on his chin and looks up at me.

"Is that Aristotle?" he asks.

"My dad."

"The top is fine," he says.

I hop up and try it out. The ceiling is twenty inches from my face. I am looking at a print of *The Slave Ship* by Turner from the Museum of Fine Arts in Boston.

"God, Lester. How about something a little more cheerful?" I say. "To look at, I mean."

"Of course," he says. "How about an earlier period?"

"Like from the Renaissance or something?" I ask.

"Too far. I was thinking rococo," Lester says, musing as he holds up the soft colorful print and examines it at arm's length. A broad beam of sunlight filters down through the trees, illuminating an elegantly dressed young woman on a swing. "Fragonard's *The Swing*."

"It's better," I tell him. The colors are pleasing and everyone in the picture seems to be happy. Then I lower my voice. "But I shouldn't bother you about it. We're not going to be here very long anyway, eh?"

Lester drops his voice too and says, "We don't need Einstein to tell us about the relativity of time."

"Meaning," I say, "a week? A month? A year?"

The bunk below me creaks and Lester's face appears beside my ear. His bug eyes are wide. I smell those soft carrots from breakfast.

"Every tool in this prison sits on a

162

shadow board," he says. "Do you know what that is?"

"No."

"A board with the shape of that tool painted in black," he says. "If a tool is missing, any tool at all, the entire prison is locked down. Everyone is searched. Everything is searched. Heads roll . . .

"I was in the shop in 1970 when the riot broke out," he says. "I got a hacksaw blade, a chisel, and a claw hammer. More valuable than a Rembrandt. More valuable than the crown jewels. I will have one chance.

"I know you're different, kid. You're not one of these other animals. You saved my life for no reason, and I could use your strength. So, I'll take you with me if I can, but I will *not* be rushed."

Lester's finger stabs up at the ceiling before he drops down out of sight. His bunk creaks, then he lies still. After a time, he begins to snore quietly.

I close my eyes. He's brilliant, but he's mad. A lonely old man who wants someone to care. I cannot stay here. They will get me before the day is out. I'll have to punch the guard when they let us out for lunch. My eyes pinch tight and I try to slow my breathing.

22

Lester moans and the bunk begins to creak. The girl in the picture above me is laughing. Her dress balloons out, showing her skirts. The bunk complains and Lester's face is back by my ear.

"You need to sleep as much as you can during the day," he says in a whisper. "We work at night."

"What do we do?"

Lester looks around. He takes off his glasses. His naked eyes widen and blink. His fingers twist the plastic stem of the glasses. I roll on my side to get a better look.

"Drill bit," he whispers. "With you, it'll be twice as fast. I don't know how long. Twelve months, maybe. Look, kid."

Lester disappears and I slide off the bunk. He checks the bars, listening, then comes back and bends over the toilet. I lean close.

"Each cell is a steel box. Boilerplate steel," he says, whispering. "But the prison was rebuilt in 1930 after the '29 riot, so it's old. Even the molecular order of steel is in the constant state of decomposition, returning to chaos."

When he sees me looking at him funny, he says, "All matter seeks chaos. When it's hot in the summer the sewage line from the toilet sweats like a bastard. In seventy-five years, even seamless half-inch-thick steel gets weak."

He looks over his shoulder, then smudges his thumb against the metal wall close to the toilet. I detect a small hole, filled with a black substance.

"I fill the holes with shoe polish," he says, "every night. We work at night. After lights-out, they do a walkaround every hour to check. On the end cell, you hear the keys to the box before the guard opens the door to get in. You have plenty of time to get to your bunk."

Lester looks wise again. My fingers shake as I reach out to touch the hole. I'm a basket case. Up. Down. Up. Down.

"What's behind there?" I ask.

"Catwalk," he says. "Access to all the pipes and wires and ductwork. Three times since '77 I've broken drill bits off when I'm working in there and let them drop down. This one took a year to find. Down below is the basement, a holding tank of shit and piss and ten inches of scum. They left me in there to unclog a sewer pipe in '99 and I hopped down into it and got this bit.

"Used to be you put everything up your ass, but they got smart back in '98. Now they got the Boss Chair. It's a metal detector you sit on, but my glasses work like a dream. It's pretty goddamn nice, actually, not having to dig it out every night."

I look at him to see if he's playing with me, but his eyes are fixed on the wet steel. He stands up, fits the bit back into his thick plastic glasses, and puts them on. He adjusts the glasses on his hooked nose and, as if on cue, they announce it's time for lunch.

Lester smiles at me and says, "Let's eat."

I don't like the way we move like cattle out of the block and down through the yard toward the dining hall. I'm jumpy and there's some twittering, but I don't know where it's coming from and no one touches me. I don't look anyone in the eye. I don't want to know them. I don't even want to see them.

I take the boiled meat and the limp vegetables they serve me on a tray and follow Lester to a round seat that juts out from under the table on a metal arm. The tabletop is stainless steel like the tray. Two white men sit across from me. One is doughy with a bald head and a full brown beard.

"This is Carl," Lester says, nodding toward the dough man. "Carl, Raymond. And that's Justin."

Justin is younger than I am — mid-thirties — with dirty blond hair, a ponytail, and a long muscular build. His arms are covered with tattoos. A green-and-orange snake's head pokes out from beneath his collar with its tongue licking at his Adam's apple. Part of a claw extends up toward his ear.

"Justin doesn't talk," Lester says. "But he's okay."

Carl belches and grins like an infant.

"They're still finding bodies from Carl," Lester says as if we were talking Easter eggs. "But he wouldn't hurt a soul in here. He likes it here, don't you, Carl?"

"Food's not bad," Carl says.

"He can't hurt anyone," Lester says. "And he doesn't want to. Makes him feel safe to be locked up, I guess. He's not the only one."

After lunch, we go out on the south yard where the weights are. Half a football field of rusty machines and bars with the steel plates welded on so no one can use the bars as weapons. The weights are arranged in a patchwork of square spaces, and each area is painted a different drab color. Lester explains that the faded red weights belong to the Bloods. The yellow ones are for the Latin Kings, the blue for the Sunni Muslims.

"If you want to use them, kid," he says, "the only ones who might let you are the Dirty White Boys."

"Which ones are those?"

"The green ones," he says, pointing. "I could probably get you in without too much trouble."

I see a crowd of whites, mostly younger men with tattoos. Half of them have long hair. They go to work on the weights like miners. Somber and methodical. Justin is one of them.

"Think I'll pass."

Instead, we walk up and down the gritty pavement just outside the chain-link boundary of the weight yard. I look around me at the different men. No one looks back. I'm beginning to feel that Lester and I really are safe.

Lester says hello to a guard that I haven't seen before. The guard smiles and says hi back. You can tell the man likes Lester.

"What about when you get to the catwalk?" I ask when we're out of earshot. "I heard Clarence talking to another guard about a break in Elmira last month. They were saying that no one ever got out of here since it was rebuilt in '30."

"No one ever did," he says, looking up at the clear blue sky, shading his eyes from the summer sun. "Once you get out of the steel cell, the block is just a solid box of concrete. If you could get out of that, you got the wall. It's four feet thick and buried forty feet into the ground."

"So, we're screwed," I say.

He stops and looks at me. His eyes glimmer and he smiles.

"It's so simple, no one ever thought of it," he says. "Or if they did, they didn't have the patience to do it."

"Do what?"

"Escape backwards," he says, and begins to walk. "They get out of the cell, then they have to figure out how to break the block. Then the wall. The pumpkinheads in this place who do make it out of the cell just wander around down in the tunnels for a few days before they start screaming for someone to help them.

"I did it backwards," he says. "It took almost forty years, yeah, but that's what it

169

takes, kid. When we break this cell, I've got the block and the wall already beat."

"How?"

It's time to go in and we do, following the crowd, milling into the back entrance of A block. I'm trying not to step on anyone's toes when I realize that Lester's white tufts are three deep in front of me. I am in a crowd of blacks and being squeezed. None of them look at me. One has thick glasses. I see a hair net and bare shoulders like cannonballs. I see a cheek with two long scars and dreadlocks. I smell boiled beef and pungent body odor.

I try to push forward, but can't and my heart races. Sweat beads on my brow and my palms are wet. Two big hands grab my ass. Moist lips brush my ear.

"Gonna make you my bitch," he says. "Sweet little white thing."

Fingers probe the seam in my pants. I roar and jump and flail.

"Hey, man."

"The fuck?"

"Yo."

Guards strain their necks and arch up on their toes. Batons are drawn. The press loosens. I push free and stumble in through the sliding steel door to First Company.

"Watch where the fuck you goin,'" a long-haired Dirty White Boy says, shoving me.

I swing a wild fist and scramble into the cell, backing into the corner. My fists are balled. My face is hot.

"What?" Lester asks, his smile fading.

"I'll fucking kill them," I say, pointing toward the cell door as it hums shut. "I don't want this, goddamn it. This is why I can't be here."

"What did they do?" he asks.

I tell him and he shakes his head.

"You've been alone too long, kid," he says. "They're like dogs. You look them in the eye. You stare them down. You walk tall. They won't do a damn thing. You should have heard that Colombian I did howling before he died while the poison ate out his guts and they couldn't stop it. No one wants a taste of that."

"That kid tried to get you in the box," I say.

"A kid too stupid to know better," he says. "You don't see me worried."

"I never let myself think like this," I say, my voice breaking. "And, fuck, now I can't stop. I keep thinking we can do it. That's all I can think of."

"We can, kid."

"I can kill one of those motherfuckers," I say. "Just like you. With a dumbbell."

"Don't," he says. "You'll be in the box for five years. Wait. Twelve months. Maybe fourteen. They won't touch you. They'll play with you if you let them. That's the way.

"Listen, there was a women's prison back in the 1800s. When they rebuilt this, they built right around the women's block, and then built over it in 1934. There was a guard I knew in the seventies. I heard the rumors and I got him to get me the plans. They keep them. All of them. From the beginning. In the powerhouse. That brick smokestack you saw out in the south yard."

Lester puts his hand on my arm.

"There was a cistern," he says, dropping his voice to the faintest whisper, "below this block. There's a tunnel down in this shit in the basement. The tunnel goes west toward the shop. Halfway there, there's a manhole. Welded shut. It took me eight years to break the seal. I've spent ten more clearing out the overflow pipe inside the cistern. It goes through the wall. The end of it's buried under the Owasco Outlet. It runs just the other side of the south wall. It's full of water most of the year, but in late summer the water level drops and you can get in there. I'm almost through.

"I see what you think," he says. "The way you roll your eyes sometimes when I talk. But it's real, kid. It's all real."

23

The slide changed, and Lexis stared hard at the low country cottage surrounded by a brooding sky. A small peat fire, a single splash of brilliant orange in a world of gloom, fought bravely, if hopelessly, against the bold brushstrokes of van Gogh's tempest. The screen went black and the lights went on.

Everyone around the long table clapped and blinked in the direction of the curator, who took a slight bow and thanked them all for coming. He'd see them next month and he hoped they would enjoy the exhibit. Lexis left the room, passing by the others piling up outside the elevator. Important people pushing and jostling like everyone else. Lexis would rather walk.

On the outside, the Guggenheim is like an upside-down wedding cake. Inside, the exhibit space is the walls along a long slow spiraling walkway that climbs from the ground floor to the top. Lexis was halfway down the ramp on the Level 4 Rotunda when she heard her name and stopped.

Hurrying after her was Pablo Truscan, the long-legged art critic from the *New York Times*. Truscan looked more like an undertaker with his gray skin and sunken eyes. He had an old-fashioned, droopy mustache. When he caught her, he touched behind his ear before taking her hand.

"I heard about your paintings," he said. "I'd love to see them."

"Thank you," she said. "I'm flattered but I'm afraid I don't show them."

Lexis turned to go, but Truscan hurried after her.

"I understand," the critic said, touching his ear. "It's just that I've heard about all the pain and emotion in them."

Lexis continued down the museum's broad spiraling walkway, her shoes slapping against the smooth floor. She could hear Truscan breathing hard. At the second level she stopped in front of a Chagall painting, *Around Her.*

Pointing at the face of Chagall's dead wife, she said, "He lived for her. That's pain people want to look at. Not mine."

Lexis began to walk more quickly and Truscan dropped back. Outside, she squinted and made a visor of her hand against the summer sunshine. From the corner of her eye she saw a man in a blue blazer and gray slacks stand up from a bench and approach her. There was something familiar.

"Lexis?" he said, stepping in front of her.

She jumped.

"It's me, Dan Parsons."

Raymond's mentor still had that round red face, but he wore glasses now instead of contacts, thick ones with brown plastic frames that magnified eyes whose sparkle had dimmed. His nose seemed bigger and the curly white hair had receded nearly to the top of his head. He offered her what was left of that once-broad smile and she smiled back.

"Dan, I'm sorry, I just —"

"Don't be sorry," he said. "You were thinking. Are you in a hurry? Could you walk a minute?"

"Sure."

They crossed Fifth Avenue and walked into Central Park, where they took the path that circled the pond.

"Last time I saw you, I was still with my firm," Dan said. Broad green trees towered above them and sunlight scattered the blacktop path.

"And you're not practicing now?"

"Here and there. More money in the

stock market," he said, then gave an abrupt laugh. "Until it tanked, anyway. I was up there pretty good. Rode the bubble. Had my own plane. A Falcon. But you know, easy come —"

"I'm sorry," she said.

"I hate to ask," he said. "I know it's been a long time and people generally don't like to bring up the past, but I'm in a pretty tight spot. I remember what you tried to do for Raymond's dad so I thought, maybe."

"What do you mean *tried* to do?" she asked. She had given Paul Russo twenty thousand dollars in cash to help Raymond's father when she heard from Dan that he was in serious financial trouble.

"Oh?" Dan said. He stuffed his hands in his pant pockets, looked at her, and then quickly away. "I thought you knew."

"What?"

"He . . . well, you know how Raymond's father was."

"Was? He died?"

"That winter. After we spoke. They turned off his heat."

"But Paul Russo was going to give him the money. Anonymously," Lexis said, stopping and gripping Dan's arm.

Dan shrugged. "He was proud, Lexis. Too proud, really."

177

"Russo," Lexis said, "that son of a bitch."

She shook her head and scowled out at the rippled surface of the pond.

"I'm sorry. I don't know what happened," Dan said, leading her along by the arm. "Listen, I've got a deal that's pretty exciting. It's just what I need, but the banks are all scared as hell right now and, well, I know your husband and Bob Rangle are pretty close and I was wondering if you wouldn't mind, Lexis.

"If I could just get a meeting with him. Someone to jar his memory to the fact that I was a pretty decent contributor of his. That's all I need. So that's it. That's where I am. Can I buy you a hot dog?"

They had come to the path's end at an entrance on Fifth Avenue. Lexis shook her head no and said, "Thank you."

"I'll have one," Dan said to the vendor, "and a Coke. You want a Coke?"

"I'm fine," she said. "Of course I'll talk to Frank for you, Dan. Do you have a card or something I could give him to call you?"

"Right here," he said, removing a card along with the ten-dollar bill he gave to the vendor. "Hey, I want you to know, I didn't come here to track you down at your meeting. I had some business and I just figured —"

"No, that's all right," Lexis said. "I'll try. It's just that Frank is so busy."

Dan bit into his hot dog, leaving a streak of mustard on his lip, and shrugged.

"Whatever you can do. I understand completely. The old days are . . . uncomfortable sometimes."

"And gone," she said, offering a weak smile and waving to a cab.

"That too," Dan said, opening the door for her and licking at the mustard.

"But that doesn't mean I don't think about them," she said, getting in. "I do. Every day."

24

Lester quickly shows me how to spin the drill bit using a small block of wood for the handle. It takes us an entire night of drilling to punch one small hole in the steel. When I ask about the hacksaw blade, he explains that he wore it out completely working his way through the welded seal of the manhole. It doesn't take long for me to realize that twelve months is a reasonable goal for an opening big enough to squeeze through.

We sleep in shifts and nap during the day. Every waking minute, I am either reading or Lester is teaching me things. Things he knows and things from books he gets at the library. I feel like a man who has a drink after being too distracted to know he was thirsty. Lester is right about the other inmates. They're dogs and I treat them that way. I ignore their barking and, so far, none of them bite.

I use the time when Lester is working his maintenance job to keep doing my katas and my push-ups and sit-ups. Lester sees me one day and criticizes my training. He says karate without grappling is like a gun without bullets.

"Kid," he says, "if you want to kick the ass of a bad man, you have to get in close."

He is old and bent, but he teaches me anyway. At first, I feel silly with my hands wrapped around his thin bones, twisting against the grain of his knotted joints. But whenever I think I've really got him, he pokes a pressure point that I never knew about and sends me reeling in pain.

Lester also teaches me about poison.

"It has always been the erudite way to kill someone," he says. "In case something goes wrong — not that it will — and you end up back in here, you'll be glad to have it."

The second man Lester killed in prison, he got with antifreeze. The Colombian he got with arsenic. For nearly two hundred years, the prison has stuffed rat poison down its holes. The sediment down in the basement is thick with it. Lester scraped the crust off his work clothes into a small plastic bottle, filled it with water, and spun it like a pinwheel on a string. A homemade centrifuge.

"How do you get it into their drink?" I ask.

"When I did the antifreeze, I was working

the chow line," he says, "but they won't let me in there anymore. With the arsenic, I got a little eyedropper from the hospital, walked up to him, told him a funny joke, and squirted it right in his mouth."

"What was the joke?" I ask.

"If you and your friends don't leave me alone, I'm going to have to kill you."

"Real funny."

"To him it was."

Every day, they give Lester a pill for his heart. He says there's nothing wrong with him. It's standard procedure in this country once you turn seventy to start taking heart medicine. When the hole in our cell is almost ready, he begins to break off small bits of his pills so he'll have enough to get him through the first two weeks of our escape.

"After that," he says, "I'll be in New Zealand."

We are lying in our bunks, waiting for the lockdown before we begin work. It is summertime and the air is hot and heavy, cooked over with the smell of human sweat, stale air, and fresh paint. My brow is beaded with sweat. I am wearing just my undershorts, and my arms are splayed out to my sides so my pits can dry.

Lester drones on about New Zealand. I

am studying Fragonard's eighteenth-century painting, a picture of happiness. The woman is happy, sailing up into the sunlight with her lover below. The lover is happy, he can see her wares beneath the ballooning petticoats. The husband is happy too, because he is ignorant of all this, an aging man with a fashionable and lovely young wife. I was ignorant too.

I am quiet after Lester finishes about New Zealand. He is waiting for me to reveal my own wistful plans. I know this because he's mentioned it to me before, that if we get out we need to catch up on all the good things, put the past and all the bad things behind.

We hear the call of the guards up and down the block, and the lights go out. We are quiet for several minutes as the small bedtime noises of five hundred killers slowly wind down.

"We *will* escape," Lester says, as if he were in the midst of a heated argument.

"I didn't say we wouldn't," I say.

"Then why don't you ever talk about your plans?" he asks.

"A wise man speaks because he has something to say," I say, quoting Plato back at him, "a fool because he has to say something."

"And if you were a fool? What would you say, kid?" he asks. "Are you afraid of what I'd think about your grand plan for revenge?"

"Who said that was my plan?"

"Aristotle said it is the mark of an educated mind to be able to entertain a thought without accepting it," he says. "You're an open book, kid, and even though I am against what you're planning, I love you enough to tell you that if you're going to succeed, you need to become more of a cipher than you are."

"Meaning?"

Lester sighs.

"I had a son," he says. "His name was Seth. Died when he was eight. It was the year I killed the prison guard. I don't know, I think if he hadn't died, I never would have tried a museum."

"I thought you had a small van Gogh?" I ask. My blood rises. Even after all this time, I am afraid of being duped. There is still a small voice inside my head telling me Lester is a fake, a brilliantly colorful fake. That we will get out of this cell and there will be no manhole. No cistern.

He is laughing quietly at me, as if he knows what I'm thinking. He says, "I did. But everything I stole until Seth died was from private collections. The market for stolen masterpieces is every bit as lively and lucrative as the ones auctioned at Sotheby's. Everything I stole was already stolen. Until Seth died . . . I guess I stopped caring.

"But," he says, "my point is this. We would play chess, my kid and I. He was good. Exceptional, really. Had my noggin. Even more. But he was a kid, and so he'd always be looking at the pieces he wanted to move. I'd watch his eyes and know what move he was thinking about before he even did it. Like you, kid. I see it in your eyes. The hatred. The determination. Everyone else is gonna see it too."

"I don't care if they see it," I say. I can feel heat in my veins. My voice is louder than it should be.

"Like Carl. He doesn't care," Lester says, and the image of that doughy mass murderer fills my mind. The ear-to-ear grin when he scoops up a spoonful of corn. The consternation over a plate full of olive-colored peas. An open book.

"You think I want to be here?"

"You're safe here, kid, behind these walls," Lester says. "Just like Carl. For instance, what are you going to do about her?"

The breath goes out of me.

"I . . . you . . ." I say.

"I read all about it," he says. "The whole joint talked about it back then. But you were convicted and then that winter the space shuttle went down and then there was Colonel Ghadafi and Libya and people forgot about Raymond White.

"I did too, but I was interested in the players. To see how the tragedy played out. I saw in the newspaper when the girl married a cop and I watched him become a big shot in the casino world and move to New York City. Every once in a while you'll see him standing behind the governor in some group shot. The DA, Villay, he's a federal judge. Maybe on his way to the Supreme Court.

"Then there was the guy who got the congressional seat after you were arrested. Rangle. He's out of politics now, but he made the most of it. He married one of those fancy society women and moves money around on Wall Street. I always found it . . . interesting how well all three of them did . . .

"The girl too, I suppose."

"And why do you *suppose* that?"

"I just don't know much about her," Lester says. "They don't write about her.

Just him. He's a little shady. Got caught up in a racketeering probe of some real estate development company. She's still there, though. I saw a picture of her next to him in the *New York Post* when he got cleared."

I realize that my hands are clenched around the folds of the bedsheet and my teeth clamped tight. I am breathing through my nose, practically snorting.

"Why didn't you tell me this?" I ask.

"Next Tuesday is a new moon," he says. "We'll be leaving. I didn't want you to dwell on it, but I don't want you to do something stupid either."

"Like walk up to him on the street and blow his fucking head off?"

"I've taught you almost everything I know, kid," he says. "I'd hate to see all that go to waste. You could have a nice life for yourself. Isn't it enough to be free?"

"No," I say, "it's not. You're the one with the rule about exacting revenge."

"That's for in here," he says.

"Not to me," I say.

I get down from the bunk and hold out my hand for the drill bit. Lester gives it to me and I softly pound it into its block handle. I press the bit into the corroding plate next to last night's hole. The toilet bowl is damp and cool against my cheek. I push and grind. Push and grind, letting the sharp steel edge bite into the plate, shaving out thin curly strips a micrometer at a time.

Soon, I hear the rattle of keys. The first walk-by always includes a night count. They do two a night. I climb into my bunk and close my eyes. I hear the footsteps of the guard. My eyelids glow briefly red as he swipes the beam of his flashlight over my face. In minutes, I hear him walking back down the company. Keys rattle again and the door hums and the latch clanks into place. I slip down off the bunk. Lester is asleep and I go back to work.

I was in jail eighteen years before I came here. I spent six months in the box. It's been just over a year since we started to drill. The final week passes like a blink. Lester encourages me not to eat much. The thinner I am, the easier it will be to fit through the hole. That's not a problem. I'm not hungry anyway.

It's time.

25

My heart pounds against my ribs. I glance over my shoulder and up at the window. I see nothing but the faint reflection of bars. The moon is dark. Lester and I always whisper, but tonight our hissing can barely be heard. Our bunks are stuffed with quietly crumpled newspaper. We have saved our own hair clippings and stuck them onto the papier-mâché masks that Lester has painted to look like us. In each of our pockets is a small Ziploc bag that contains some cash Lester has hoarded over the years as well as a detailed road map of central New York.

I hear the quiet snap of metal, Lester twisting our escape hatch free from the thin mooring that held it in place. The other edges we have filed smooth. We have bailed out the toilet, draining it into the sink. The pipe lies on the floor in the corner.

Lester squirms through the hole and waves to me. I am naked, glazed in Vaseline. I pass my clothes through, then slip my head into the hole along with my right arm. My left shoulder gets stuck and I feel the bite of the steel. A bead of sweat falls from my nose. I squirm and a small noise sneaks out of my throat. Lester hushes me quietly and whispers that it will be all right. Relax.

I feel his twisted hands on my head and back. He turns me gently, the way a doctor will deliver a child, easing me through the hole. My hips stick, but only for a moment. I am out. I stand with my bare feet on the narrow iron grid of the catwalk. The stink of sewage rises up on the back of the exhausted heat, but my spirit soars. I stand there, greased and naked in this new world. I want to raise my hands over my head and cry out, but instead, I quickly pull on my clothes.

Lester has a black piece of paper that he tapes over the hole. We are in complete darkness now, but only for a few seconds. In his hand, Lester has a small bulb, taped and wired to a D battery. In this pitch, it sheds just enough light for us to see the twisted labyrinth of pipes and wires and ducts protruding from the cells on either side. The tangle of mechanical veins rises five stories.

Lester starts to lower himself through the space between the narrow catwalk and the cells. I follow him, and he guides my ankles as he said he would so that I will find the footholds that will quietly bear my weight. Even though Lester warned me against it, I look down. It is a long way to the oily filth, and I wonder if I will be able to keep from retching once I lower my feet into its murk.

Soon I hear Lester swishing around. My footing is fine, but with five feet to go, I grab a hot water pipe that burns my hand. I stifle a cry, but drop down, splashing back into the sewage. I jump up with my hands plastered over my mouth, but the vomit finds the seams in my fingers and my quiet retching continues for another ten seconds before I am finally able to subdue it. Lester stares at me with those big eyes magnified under their lenses even more in the thin light. He blinks and I shake my head apologetically. He looks up toward the empty catwalk, shrugs, and begins to wade through the mess toward the other end of the cellblock.

The going is tricky with the sediment below the filth sucking on my shoes. Lester is taking long steps that bring his knees briefly clear of the oily stink. My stomach begins to turn again. Beads of sweat tickle my forehead. I think I cannot hold down another convulsion when I see a brick tunnel at the edge of Lester's homemade light.

Lester stops and dips down into the scum. He comes up with his claw hammer and holds it out for me to see. He is grinning. We climb up into the tunnel and crawl along in the gritty crap that lines its belly. I search for a manhole, but see only the long smooth stretch of sediment. Lester stops suddenly and turns around.

"What are we doing?" I say.

"I must have gone past it," he says.

My head spins with that same familiar fear. My heart thumps even harder. The tunnel walls seem suddenly tighter.

"What do you mean?" I say. "How?"

"It's here," he says. "I missed it."

"I thought you dug it up."

"It's been two years, kid," he says. "The water rises up down here in the winter and leaves fresh sediment. Right behind you, there. Dig."

I spin and start to claw at the soft muck, scrabbling like a dog until my fingers rake the bricks below. The stink presses in on me.

"It's brick," I say, my voice rising in pitch.

"Keep going."

Scraps of mud fly through the tunnel and spatter the crumbling walls.

My fingers are numb. They strike something harder than brick.

"I think I got it," I say.

"Here, use this," Lester says, handing over the hammer.

I claw at the edges of the old steel plate. My heart starts to slow and my breath is coming easier now. In minutes, I have exposed the entire manhole cover. Using the claw on the hammer, I lift it up and shove it aside. Cool air lies beneath us in a vast empty space that echoes with the sound of dripping water.

"There are ladder rungs," Lester says, his voice laced with giddiness as he dips the light into the hole.

I see more black water down below. The stench is richer down there, but not as sharp. I see the corroded metal rungs protruding from the brick wall. As I descend into the cistern, the hairy rust flakes off in my hands, leaving them dusty brown.

The water is cold and comes up to my knees. Lester eases himself slowly down and we wade the length of the aging cavern. The walls are alive with spiders that creep and sway under the glow of our dim light. A rat squeaks and scrabbles along a ledge above us, kicking free a swirl of dust into the halo of light.

When we reach the end of the cistern, there is another set of rungs that lead up to the large dark hole of the overflow pipe. The cistern collected water to be used for the women's bathrooms. When the tank filled up during the wet season, the overflow let the excess water run out into the Owasco Outlet. When the prison was rebuilt in 1930, Lester claims the new wall had to be built around this overflow pipe because the women's prison wasn't razed until 1934.

We climb up and in. The pipe is wooden. Narrow, but smooth with only a small deposit of grit on the bottom. Two feet in diameter. Just enough for me to get through without jamming my shoulders. We crawl for a good ways. The only stench now comes from my clothes. The air is stale, but cool. In the thin light from Lester's bulb, I can see a few feet in front of my face, so I don't bump into the pile of broken brick and dirt, but when I see it, my heart constricts.

"It's blocked," I say in a hiss.

"I told you it was," Lester says. "We have to dig."

"How far?"

"Not far," he says.

I begin to pull at the pieces of brick, pushing them under my belly, then moving the mound back toward Lester with my knees and feet. After a time, the pipe behind us is nearly blocked. Lester moves backward, spreading the refuse beneath him, giving me more room to dig.

A battle rages between panic and hope in my mind. I try to reinforce my will with sweet images of freedom. A walk on the beach, cold sand in my toes. Moonlight dancing on water. The taste of a thick steak, red wine, and a Cuban cigar. But it's hatred that wins the day and propels me on. The bullet I will put into Frank Steffano's head. The sound of Rangle's whimper. Villay's squeal. Exact revenge.

I work on.

We must be twenty feet farther than the original blockage. Our muffled coughs are snuffed out by the pipe and the dirt. My arms and hands are numb from their work.

Lester clears his throat and says, "Kid. We have to go back."

I hear, but it doesn't register.

"Raymond," he says, "we won't make it. It's light outside by now. We'll have to come back."

"We're almost there," I say, still clawing

195

at the dirt and bricks. "We have to be."

Lester grips my ankle. I feel the strength in his old hands, constricting my ligaments and the flow of blood. He shakes my leg and I stop digging.

"No, goddamn it," he says, rupturing the quiet. "We need the night. I waited too long for this, kid. We have to go back."

Lester lets go of my ankle. The light jiggles and begins to fade. I hear him squirming back down the pipe. I continue to dig, but soon it's pitch black and I feel the earth squeezing in on me from all sides. A cry bursts from me and I scramble backward, slithering out.

Lester is waiting in the cistern. When I drop down into the cold water, he nods once and turns to go. When we reach the basement beneath the catwalk outside our cell, Lester shows me a spigot jutting out of a pipe that runs up the concrete wall. He turns it on and we rinse most of the stink and slime from our bodies and clothes.

Since most of the Vaseline was rubbed off, it will be harder for me to get back into the cell, so I go first. Lester is able to push me through without drawing more than a trickle of blood from my shoulder. Daylight seeps into the window outside our bars, but everything is still quiet. Lester fits the steel plate and the sewage pipe from the toilet back into the wall. He complains quietly of a pain in his arm. I help him fill the cracks with shoe polish.

We strip out of our clothes and change into our spare set. Lester rinses the dirty ones in what's left of our hot water bucket from the day, then he stuffs them into the laundry bag and tosses them into the corner. I am climbing up into my bunk when I hear him grunt and collapse on the floor.

I take a panicked look around before I start to yell for help.

There is confusion and shouting.

Lester is taken to the prison hospital.

Later, a guard tells me that he's had a heart attack. They don't know how long he'll be in the hospital. He might not make it at all. After two days of worrying, the company sergeant calls me to his desk. He says that tomorrow I will be moved into a new cell by myself. If Lester survives, we can apply for another double bunk when one opens up. If he dies, I will stay in my new single cell.

Night comes and I lie awake with these thoughts spinning through my head: If Lester dies, it could be ten or twenty years, if ever, before I have the chance to get a drill bit of my own. Even if he lives, when the new prisoners take this cell, they will be sure to find the hole. They will either use it, or report it. If they use it and find the open manhole, the route will be discovered and sealed off forever. If they report the hole in the cell, Lester and I will both spend the next three years back in the box.

Here's what I keep coming back to:

If I wait, both of us are likely to be in Auburn for the rest of our lives.

If I go now, alone, I just might make it.

26

I open my eyes to *The Swing*. When Lester first showed it to me, it meant nothing. A pretty baroque painting with soft colors. A pink dress. A broad beam of sunlight through the blue-green trees. A dainty shoe sailing through the air. A young man in the bushes gazing up with admiration. An older refined gentleman entertaining the beautiful young woman. But as I began to study it, it wasn't long before I knew it for what it was. A picture of betrayal.

I have used this painting over the past year to secretly fuel my hatred for the people who betrayed me. The light coming through the window is proof that at least I have not betrayed my friend, even if it costs me everything. I search within myself for even a flicker of contentment. I don't know why, but there is nothing there. I am an empty grave.

The escape hole behind the toilet is so big it makes me ache.

I reach up and slip my finger between the edge of the paper and the metal ceiling, tearing the print free. The paper shears off at the corners where it has been taped. I spread my fingers and mash the print into a ball, then throw it onto the floor.

All the things in the cell besides my bunk and spare set of clothes belong to Lester. They said someone will take care of his things. I haven't decided whether or not I will earn my way back into the box. I realize that I enjoy the small freedoms I've become accustomed to. The sun. The rain on my face. Long walks around the yard. The books. The question is this: How safe will I be without Lester?

I hop down and roll everything into my mattress. After breakfast, I sling the roll over my shoulder and a guard walks me across the yard to E block. I feel naked without Lester by my side.

When the first officer at the desk looks up, I recognize the shadowy face as Bluebeard's. His hair is longer and slicked back with pomade, but his beady eyes still have their gleam.

"Well, well," he says, "the big bucks were snortin' and a-pawin' in here this morning like they smelled a doe in heat, and I guess they did."

His long hairy fingers slide over the change sheet, a yellow pointed nail comes to a stop halfway down the page. He turns his head and raises his voice to a group of officers standing in the doorway.

"Seventeen ready to go?" he says. "New girl's here."

He leers at me and says, "I know you'll be wanting to bunk up once you decide who your new daddy's gonna be, but for now, I hope you'll like your new home."

A guard marches over and says, "Uh, Marty. Seventeen still ain't ready. Garden Hose says he ain't goin'."

"Well, you tell Garden Hose I'm gonna come in there and tickle his ass with my stick," Bluebeard says, putting his hand on his baton as if to prove he means it.

"Told him that already."

"Well, gas the motherfucker out of there," Bluebeard says.

"You'll have to call the lieutenant."

"And I'll do that," Bluebeard says. With his chin in the air, he picks up the phone and punches in a number.

He glares at the guard who brought me and says, "Take her back to A block while I fumigate that bug."

To me, Bluebeard says, "Don't you worry, little lady. We'll have your room for you real soon. Why don't you go out and have a drink by the pool?"

I walk back across the yard to my cell and unroll my bunk. I lay down and stare at the ceiling, empty except for the four corners of the print. I have decided that my next interview with Bluebeard will send a message to the entire prison. It will be nothing for me to launch myself across his desk. I will roll his head between my hands like a melon, snapping his neck and tearing the spinal cord between the third and fourth vertebrae. If I'm going to go to the box, I might as well go in style. When I do get out — if I get out — I feel pretty confident that after something like that, no one will bother me.

I am reviewing the technique in my mind when I hear Lester's gravelly voice at the end of the hall. I jump down and grab the bars. He shuffles slowly toward our cell, prattling to the guard.

"Clear one," the guard says in a loud voice.

I step back.

"Open one."

The bars vibrate and the door slides open. Lester stands there. His enormous eyes are shiny and brimming with tears.

"Later, Jim," he says to the guard in a choked voice.

He steps inside and the bars hum shut.

He opens his arms and steps toward me, hugging me. The tufts of his hair tickle under my chin.

"You stupid son of a bitch," he says, his voice muffled by my shirt. Then he pushes me away. "You should be gone."

"I . . . couldn't."

Lester shakes his head and sits down on the edge of his bunk, laughing softly, but crying at the same time.

"You're a prince, kid," he says, looking up. "Like my own."

"They tried to move me," I say. My own eyes are watering. "I was gone. E block, but the cell wasn't ready. They said you were going to die."

"They wish," he says. "The state would love to have my bunk, but I'm tougher than that."

"Are you all right?"

Lester swats his hand in the air and says, "A minor episode. I'll outlive the doctor. Happens all the time. Sit."

I sit down next to him, and Lester claps my right hand between both of his.

"Tonight," he says, in a whisper, "we go. We'll make it this time."

"My God, Lester," I say. "I mean, I was gone. Do you get it? They moved me out. Then some bug named Garden Hose decides he won't leave the cell . . ."

"I don't know about God, kid," Lester says, "but destiny . . . That's another story. And what you've done . . . The loyalty?

"We still need to split up when we get out," Lester says, "but not for long."

"What do you mean?"

"I'm talking about unimaginable wealth," Lester says, shaking my hand in his, his eyes glittering at me. "I'm talking about sharing it with you, kid. I . . . I didn't know before. Even after all we've been through. Money does things to people, and we'll be on the outside. Things will be different."

Lester's eyes turn glassy and he looks across the cell as if he were peering out over the ocean. He tells me about an old Adirondack lodge built by Thomas Durant on Lake Kora, a place that burned to the ground at the turn of the nineteenth century. Lester bought the only standing building, a guest cottage, in 1964.

"You can only get there by water and it has a cobblestone foundation like a fortress," he says. "Dry as dust. Perfect temperature. Fifty degrees in the middle of summer or the dead of winter.

"I turned it into a huge vault," Lester says. "Brought a locksmith up from Baltimore and two boilermakers from Peoria. The floor is these two-inch-thick oak planks, and with the hardware, you'd have to use dynamite to get it open."

"What's in it?" I ask.

Lester lowers his voice and leans toward me. His big eyes blink and he peers hard through the gloom.

"Almost everything I ever stole," he says. "I was going to live modestly and work for twenty years. Then I was going to sell it all and retire to New Zealand. I still will, but I don't need all that. Put together, by now it's got to be worth close to a billion."

"A billion?" I say. "As in nine zeros?"

"There was a trainload of stuff from the Louvre that Hitler was having shipped from Paris to Berlin. It never made it," Lester says. "I spent over ten years stealing it and now I'm giving half of it to you . . ."

"What can you do with it?" I ask.

"Sell it," Lester says with a shrug.

"To who?"

"Sotheby's," he says. "Christie's. I'll call the director of fine arts. Happens all the time. He'll be outraged, but in about a week I'll get a call back from someone who'll just happen to be looking for what I've got."

Lester tells me the exact location of the

cottage and how to get into the vault. There are two bank vault tumblers. The combination is derived by assigning a numeric value to each of the letters in his son's name — Seth Cole — and subtracting them from fifty for the first descending to forty-three for the last.

"Not that anything's happening to me, kid," he says, showing me those crooked teeth, "but, who knows? Maybe only one of us gets away, and if it's you, I don't want you going hungry."

My face is warm and I put my other hand on top of his and begin to stammer, not knowing what to say.

"If you want to do something," he says, nodding his head as if he can read my thoughts, "promise me this: that you'll use this treasure for yourself. Go. Start a new life. Leave the past alone, kid. Let it die."

I go rigid.

Lester cocks his head just a tick to one side, as if he's heard a small noise. He looks at me for quite a while before he sighs and says, "No, I guess not.

"It's all right," he says, patting my hands. "I love you like my Seth. It's unconditional, and so is this gift. You do with it what you want. That's not for me to decide."

I tell him what I think, but it comes out in a mutter.

"What?" he says.

"You said destiny," I say. "It's my destiny, Lester. It just is."

When night comes, we climb back down into the tunnel. After only a few minutes, the dirt becomes damp. A slow trickle begins to run back down the pipe. My throat grows tight as I imagine the water bursting in and washing us backward into the cistern. It grows to a steady flow, but rises no more than five inches.

It takes me less than an hour to dig through the last layer of soggy silt. I can hear the river's song and feel the cool air rushing in. In anticipation, Lester puts out his waning bulb, but a large stone is wedged into the opening. Try as I might, I cannot push it aside with my hands and the claw hammer does me no good.

Lester and I crawl back down the length of the overflow pipe, then worm our way back, feet first. I roll splashing onto my stomach and wedge my frame against the walls of the wooden pipe. Then, with all my might, I press my legs against the stone. It moves half an inch at a time, but it moves.

The stone scratches against its sandy

bed. I hear Lester's low chuckle bubbling toward me from deeper in the pipe. My heart swells and my legs burn, and in less than two minutes I've shoved that rock aside enough for us to squirm out.

I don't stop to enjoy it. I don't see the stars or the towers or the vertical plane of the wall aglow and stretching up into the night. Instead, I keep my eyes fixed on the darkness around me and I slide over the rocks and into the swift water of a deep pool.

I am free.

27

I swim across the current, not down. This is the plan. They will look for us downstream. They will close off all the roads around the city and squeeze it until they find us. No one has escaped Auburn since the new wall was constructed back in the thirties. Hell will be raised.

It requires great effort to swim through the current. When I feel the rocky riverbed beneath my feet I turn to look at Lester. Water slips past me, but not without a strong steady shove. I see now that Lester is flailing. The sound of splashing rises above the steady hiss of water over stone, and my eyes go up to the tower. It stares down like a dull monolithic eye in its bed of stars. The shadow of the guard is no-where to be seen. The other towers too — there are three in all — are blind.

Lester is almost to me. I stretch out my arms, digging in at the same time with my heels to keep from being swept back into the pool. Lester is four feet from me when he cries out and goes under.

I dive and bump heads with him. We swirl in the water. I have his waist and I scissor-kick my legs until they're numb. My feet hit the riverbed and the darkness is destroyed by white light. The scream of sirens breaks the night. Bullets zip past, humming like angry bees. The water is shin-deep now and Lester is on my back. I run for the railroad bridge.

The thud of a bullet striking him knocks me facedown into the water, but I scramble up without letting go. I slosh upstream, desperate for the cover of a bridge. Two feet from its protective shadow, another bullet strikes Lester, knocking us both forward and down. This time, my elbow strikes a rock and Lester rolls off my back.

His eyes stare up at the underbelly of the bridge. His mouth hangs open, spilling blood. There is yelling above and the strident ringing of alarms.

"Lester!" I shout, lifting him.

I see now, even in the shadows, that the last bullet struck the back of his head. Blood and matter spill from his skull. I retch and drop his body. Frantically, I search around me. On the upstream side of the rail bridge, someone has dumped a bag of garbage and it lies wedged between two great stones. I strip the shirt from my back without unbuttoning it and jam the black bag of garbage inside.

I tie the sleeve of my shirt to Lester's wrist, then I wade toward the deep flow. When I'm close to the middle, I shove Lester's body and the floating bag into the stiffest part of the current. They swirl and shoot downstream. They are pushed out of the shadows and into the beam of the spot-lights. The lights stay with Lester and my shirt. There is more shouting. Bullets rain down, breaking the water's surface, strik-ing Lester's dead body and the garbage as they rise and fall in the current, spinning madly down along the wall. I return to the bank and move with stealth up under the road bridge.

Shots and yells echo up the riverbed. I leave the cover of the bridge and find my-self in a thick tangle of vegetation. Above me is Curley's Restaurant, and I can hear the people spilling out onto the bridge to see what has happened. I keep sloshing up-stream. Vertical concrete embankments re-place the undergrowth where the river bends through the middle of downtown. I stay close to the shadow of the wall where the water is below my knees.

Up to the left is a stately old brick

building with a white cupola. Black-and-white police cars are lined up along the rail that overlooks the river. The police station. The dark shapes of men are jogging out. Red and blue lights spin and tires squeal as they back out and head for the prison. I am almost to the next bridge when I see one figure approach the rail with a flashlight.

A wide drainpipe opens in the wall and I throw myself inside. A moment later, a beam of light sweeps past the mouth of the pipe. I can feel the hammer of my heart between my ears. I wait another minute, then creep toward the edge. The figure is gone and so is the light. I slip out and wade as quietly as I can upstream. When I reach the darkness of the next bridge, I start to run.

I pass under two more bridges and under the shadow of a stainless steel diner with a red neon sign, then the shambles of some tenement apartments before the concrete wall ends and the shadowy overgrowth of bushes and trees crowds the riverbed. The river widens and the going is easy for a time. Stars wink from above and they give the rippled water a pale glow. As I step carefully between the rocks, my ears are filled with a hissing that soon grows into a roar.

I round a bend and see the misty white sheet of water spilling over a dam. There are darkened brick buildings above harnessing the water flow and turning it into electricity. I leave the water for a rocky service road that climbs the right side of the bank up to the top of the dam. Two streetlights give off a blue glow. The pool above the dam is still and black and I stare around, breathing hard. There are a handful of houses with amber light spilling from random crooked windows. A string of laundry hangs in the backyard of the one closest to me and a small dock juts out into the still pool. Moored to it is a small aluminum skiff with an outboard motor.

Destiny.

I case the house as I wade through the bushes and creep across the grass. I can just make out the sound of a radio above the roar of the dam, but see no signs of life. I strip a man's white dress shirt and a worn-out pair of khaki shorts from the line, tuck them under my arm, and hurry toward the boat. After unmooring the skiff, I use the oars and row quietly up past the houses. When I am completely surrounded again by trees, I pull the starter cord and race off.

The skiff finally runs aground and I hop

out. I can see the next dam, not nearly as dramatic as the first, but when I get to the other side, I see what I've been looking for. The inlet. A marina. Dozens of boats, covered and waiting for their owners to take them out on the lake for a day of fun. Across the inlet from the marina, cottages stand clustered together under the trees. I hear the sounds of laughter and smell the campfires of people on vacation. I strip out of my prison pants and T-shirt in the shadows, then change into my new clothes and roll up the sleeves of the shirt before walking through the yard of the marina like I belong there.

I find a boat similar to the one I used to own, an open-bow Four Winns, and uncover it in plain sight of the people on the other side of the narrow inlet. Hotwiring this boat is easier than with my dad's heavy equipment when I was a kid. Two wires clearly exposed beneath the dash. I flip on the running lights, back the boat out of its slip, and wave to the revelers as I ease up the inlet toward the open lake.

The water's surface is smooth, and I am zipping along like a ghost, skimming the surface, flying through the night. The hillsides are dark except for a sprinkling of lights from the homes on the water. I pull up for a few minutes in the middle to strip and wash the scum from my body. The wind soon whips me dry and I stop again to put the clothes back on. Owasco is fourteen miles long, so in less than half an hour I am idling in toward a lively restaurant and bar tucked into the lake's last cove.

This is no coincidence. Lester learned from an electrician about the place called Cascade Grill on the end of the lake. Our plan all along was for me to get us transportation this way. To be obvious and invisible. I was going to drop Lester at a bus station in Binghamton. Lester, my friend.

There is a long dock sticking out into the water. More than a dozen other boats are moored along its edge, bumping gently up against the car tires looped down over its metal support poles. The stillness of the air gives way to the steady hum of people talking and laughing and the vibrations and thumping of a band called the Works. I know because a huge banner stretches across the back of the one-story pale blue building: CASCADE GRILL WELCOMES THE WORKS.

The narrow dock leads right up a ramp and onto Cascade's deck. Bugs swirl in the halos of the small lanterns nailed to a tall fence that blocks out the neighboring cottages. The orange wood of the deck is new and topped with dark green plastic tables and chairs with matching square canvas umbrellas. It's wall-to-wall people. I ease through the crowd with my head bobbing gently to the beat like everyone else, and slip inside and up to the bar.

From my pocket, I remove Lester's baggie of money and the map and I strip off a twenty from 1973. The bartender is a big teddy bear of a man with a walrus mustache and baggy pale green eyes. Even in the smoke of the bar, I can smell stale cigars on his clothes from behind the taps.

"Got any wheat beer?" I ask.

He scowls and shakes his head as if he doesn't even know what I'm talking about.

"Löwenbräu?" I say.

He gives me a funny smile and says, "And you want to borrow my Foreigner eight-track too, right? Come on, buddy, I've got customers."

I see a Bud tap handle and ask for a bottle of that. He reaches down into the cooler, keys off the top, and sets it down in front of me. I point to the twenty and leave the change on the bar like everyone else. With the bottle tipped up to my mouth, I look around. On my left are two muscleheads in tank tops with crew cuts and big tattoos. To my right is a couple in their fifties wearing leather chaps and vests. The man has long gray hair pulled into a ponytail and his chick's poorly bleached cut is windblown.

In front of them is a pile of small bills and change, two bottles of a brew I've never heard of, and a heavy chain with a set of keys. It takes me only a minute to see that they're fall-down drunk.

I cock myself their way on the stool and buy them a drink. He's a math teacher in Union Springs. She's a psychologist from Seneca Falls. Every nice weekend in the summer, they get on their bikes and ride across the state. He rides a 1953 Indian Chief.

"Rebuilt it myself," he says, throwing back his shoulders. He butts out his Marlboro and his eyes take on a sheen. "One of the ones they made in their last order for the New York City police."

I tell them I'm a lawyer from Syracuse with a summer cottage halfway up the lake. We communicate all this by leaning close and yelling above the sound of the band and the noise of the bar. Through the window, I can see the throng swaying with their hands in the air. People start taking off their shirts.

The math teacher finishes off his Saranac Ale and staggers to his feet.

"Be right back," he says, clasping my shoulder and using it to keep from falling on his face.

He disappears around the corner where the bathrooms are before the girlfriend stretches a smile across her face, blushes, and says, "Me too."

She slips off her stool. I put two more twenties on the bar, ask the bartender for another round and whatever the big guys next to me are drinking too. This keeps him busy while I slip the keychain over the lip of the bar and into the pocket of my baggy shorts.

I wait for them to come back and start working on their fresh drinks before I excuse myself for the bathroom. I push through the bar and around the corner. Left is the bathrooms, right is the front door. I go right. Across a small lane is a two-tiered stone parking lot. The Indian Chief is up in the second lot alongside an orange Honda 650. They're parked between a white van and an old Ford Escort.

I look around quick, then mount up. I had a dirt bike growing up, so I know how to drive, but I've never been on something as big and heavy as this. I take it easy down

Route 38 into Moravia, scanning ahead of me for the flashing lights of a roadblock.

It's too soon for that, though, and instead of making a right in the center of town to keep going south on 38, I pull over under a streetlamp to check my map. Straight through the intersection takes me out of town on 38A. Less than a mile after that, I turn off onto a farm road and weave my way across the bottom of Skaneateles, past Glen Haven, through Otisco, across Interstate 81, and on up the other side of Syracuse on Route 46.

Sometime after I was born, in a brief fit of nostalgia, my mother bundled me up and took me to the reservation to show me off to her older half sister. A week later, my mother received a proud phone call from her sister. Of her own volition, the sister had registered me as a member of the tribe. Because my mother was a Mohawk, I was a Mohawk too. Nothing to be overly proud of in the Onondaga Nation, but still, one of the people.

With that lineage came certain rights. For the same reason my father and Black Turtle had been able to line up some help for me to leave the country at the end of my trial, I zigzag my way up along the Adirondack State Park. Sticking to back

219

roads, I go through towns like Ava, Low-ville, and Colton all the way to the St. Regis Mohawk Indian Reservation.

I ease the big Chief down Route 37 onto the reservation and into the town of Hogansburg. Right there off the highway is a long single-story building, newly built. Longhouse of the twenty-first century. The Akwesasne Casino. The sky is beginning to lighten in the east as I pull into the lot. I am teetering on exhaustion until I see a bundle of newspapers that have been tossed onto the curb. I yank one out from beneath the plastic band and search for news of my escape. There is nothing. Yet. I know by the evening edition, my face will make page three at the least.

Inside, I am greeted by a weary-eyed Mohawk whose nameplate reads: UNCLE BUCK. Behind him a single blackjack table is illuminated in the gloomy cavern. A sluggish set of players take their cards from a big red-lipped blonde who just might be a transvestite.

I step into a small grill for a coffee and some eggs. Real eggs. I devour them and order four more, over easy, sopping up the yolk with buttered whole-wheat toast. I wash it down with the sweetest orange juice I've ever tasted. The coffee too is rich and it energizes me from the inside out. I pay with a hundred-dollar bill from 1977. That kind of bill might raise eyebrows, but this is a casino and I leave a tip that's good, but not crazy enough to draw attention.

I return to the entrance, where Uncle Buck is affable enough and apologetic that the casino has no hotel. He tries to direct me across the border to the Canadian side of the reservation and a Best Western, but I know there will be customs agents at the bridge and, rather than risk it, tell him I want something local.

He shrugs. The only place in town is the Rest Inn Motel.

"People complain sometimes that you can smell the cow pasture," he says, "but there's a good gal that runs it."

"I grew up near cows," I say with a smile. "Will she mind me showing up at this hour? I've been riding all night."

"No," he says, his teeth gleaming beneath his regal nose. "She's used to all kinds of things with the casino here now."

My pride in the nation to which I am officially a member continues to deflate as I pass by sagging and decrepit one- and two-story homes with yard dogs snapping after me without restraint. The road needs repair and the scent of filth wafts up out of the ditch, reminding me of the prison's belly.

The motel owner is a stout middle-aged Mohawk woman. I slip her my last hundred and tell her I'd like to pay for two nights. Her small dark eyes look deep into mine before she smiles and gives me a key. I draw the shades and use the bathroom before I lie down on top of the bed and fall into the pit of sleep.

I don't know what time it is when I wake up, but I know what woke me.

The cold barrel of a revolver is tickling my nose.

28

There are three of them. All Indians. All younger than me. Late twenties, early thirties. Long dark hair, flat angry mouths, and scowling brown eyes.

The smallest one has the gun. The two by the door are goons.

"You came to the wrong place to pass your shit, white man," the little one says with a low growl, flipping a hundred-dollar bill at me with his free hand. "We're gonna send you on your way, but we got a little present for you first. Get up."

I get up off the bed with my hands in the air. The gun is still pressed into my nose. I glance down at the bill on the bed and see that it's my own 1977 Ben Franklin. I need to use the bathroom and I tell them.

"You can piss your pants you got to go that bad," the little one says.

The two goons snicker and they shove me out into the bright daylight. Puffy white clouds on a field of blue. The stout motel owner is scowling at me from the shadow of the porch in front of the office.

Her hands are on her hips. My stolen motorcycle has already been loaded into the back of a big dark green Chevy with an extended cab.

They drive me down Route 37. Another pickup with a bed full of Indian men follows us. We pull over in a field behind a big billboard that welcomes the rest of the world to the St. Regis Indian Reservation. The biggest goon shoves me out of the truck. The other one dumps the bike out of the back and it crashes to the ground. The other truck pulls up. Everyone piles out and they make a loose circle around me. The little one they all call Bonaparte stuffs the pistol into the waist of his jeans, walks over to the bike, and pisses on it.

"I wasn't trying to pass anything off on you," I say for the tenth time, "and I'm not a white man. My mother was a Mohawk."

"We're Akwesasne," the little one, Bonaparte, says, zipping up his fly.

"Her family was from the reservation outside Toronto," I say, remembering now that the northern Mohawks call themselves by their own name.

Bonaparte narrows his eyes and says, "You got a white nose."

"My father," I say. "My mother grew up

in the Onondaga Nation."

"So after George here beats your ass black and blue," he says, "you can go back down there and rediscover your roots, but no one comes up here and passes bad money to us. Not no white man. Not no half-breed. Not no skin.

"Go ahead, George."

The biggest Indian steps for me and swings a big fist from out far. I duck and rabbit-punch him just below the rib cage. The air huffs out of George and he staggers, then kicks at me hard with a gilt-toed cowboy boot. He's quick for a big man, and the metal toe nicks my knee and I tumble. George is on top of me with his fists pummeling. I slip out, twist his arm up and back, and jam his face into the gravel. He roars.

I whip my legs around his abdomen and clamp my arms around his neck. I twist and squeeze at the same time, and after less than ten seconds of struggling, George collapses on his face.

I'm on my feet. Ready.

Bonaparte waves his gun in my direction and says, "Take your goddamn bike and get the fuck off this reservation."

It's a ten-mile walk to Massena, but I'm not sitting in this guy's piss.

"You can keep the bike," I say, turning to go. "It's stolen."

"Hey," Bonaparte says. "You really a skin?"

"Call down to the Nation," I say, stopping to look him in the eyes. "My mother was Martha St. Claire. They named me Running Deer."

One side of Bonaparte's mouth creeps up as if he's either skeptical or amused.

"You want a job, Quick Buck?"

"Doing what?"

"What you just did," he says, angling his face down at George, who is now sitting up and rubbing the back of his neck.

"I need a place to stay," I say, "and I need to stay away from the white law."

"The only law here is me," Bonaparte says. "We're a sovereign nation."

He sticks the pistol back in his jeans, turns, and climbs back into the extended cab. I get in on the other side. George gets into the front seat with the other long-haired goon, whose name is Bert. Bert's big belly is shaking and he's having a hard time not smiling, even under George's evil glare.

A grainy picture of Lester and one of me from twenty years ago runs the next day on page five of the *Watertown Daily Times*. It talks about the attempted escape, how Lester Cole was shot dead, and that they are looking for my body somewhere downstream. Mostly, it's treated as downstate news, separate and apart from the North Country. Anyway, Bonaparte and his men don't seem to read much and my hair is much longer now than in the picture. Even so, I take to wearing a Buffalo Bills cap with the brim pulled low.

The Akwesasne let me share a trailer with Bert, the big man with fat round cheeks and eyes squinted in a permanent smile. He has an old streamliner, a silver-skinned melon buried in a nest of high grass and weeds. It's small but clean, with two tiny bedrooms and its own shower and toilet that drains into a septic tank that has to be pumped once a month. Bert leaves me alone for the most part, except when he's trying to get me to participate in one of his two favorite pastimes: drinking Molson Golden and thumb wrestling.

One day I am reading a *New York Times* account about Judge Villay's ruling for the Second Circuit Court of Appeals on same-sex marriages when Bert walks in with a bottle of Molson Golden. He offers me one and I look up from my paper to say that I would. When Bert sees the paper, his face clouds over and he takes a step toward me.

"You know that man?"

There is a picture of the curly-headed little judge, Dean Villay, in the top corner of the page.

"Long time ago," I say.

"Friend?"

"Enemy."

"Good," Bert says, his face softening a bit, but his voice still bitter. He goes to the refrigerator and returns with a bottle of beer for me.

"If I ever get the chance," he says, flopping down in a worn-down La-Z-Boy recliner, "I'm gonna kill that man, judge or no judge."

Bert tells me the story about his younger brother who lived and worked in Watertown and a trip the two of them took one weekend to visit some friends at the Onondaga Nation so they could watch the ABA bowling championships in Syracuse. They were at a South Side bar after the finals when his brother got into a scuffle with some locals. After the fight, the two of them decided to head north instead of spending the night with their friends on the reservation. They were back at his brother's apartment in Watertown when his brother realized that somehow during the fight he had lost his knife, a nickel-plated switchblade.

The next day, the police showed up at the door to arrest his brother for the murder of the man he got into the fight with. Villay was prosecuting his brother on the theory that after the fight, he ambushed the dead man while he walked home, stabbing him fifteen times with the nickel-plated switchblade that was left at the scene.

Bert was his brother's only alibi and chance to prove his innocence. At the trial, Villay had torn Bert to pieces, but the jury never did get to issue a verdict. The night after Bert's testimony, his brother hanged himself in the Public Safety Building.

"I don't know if I'll ever get that chance," Bert says, getting up for two more bottles of beer, "but if I do . . ."

Bonaparte isn't the chief, but he runs things: the casino, the big-stakes bingo parlors, and a smuggling operation that brings mostly cigarettes across the river from Canada, where the taxes are low enough to make the whole venture extremely profitable. Bonaparte also runs some marijuana to supply the Adirondacks, but it's not a big market and I think he and his men smoke most of the profits.

I get paid every Friday in cash. We drive up to Bonaparte's big white contemporary home overlooking the river, and he laughs as he pays me with hundred-dollar bills that he says might be real, but might not, since I don't know the difference. Most of the men eat, drink, smoke, and gamble away their pay, but they don't seem to resent me for saving my money and spending most of my free time reading under the bare bulb that hangs down over Bert's couch. My name has evolved from Running Deer to Bonaparte's Quick Buck to the men's version of Quick Book.

There is an Akwesasne named Andre who is one of Bonaparte's lieutenants, and after a while Bert and I are the ones who get sent with him to collect drug money. I'm not crazy about these runs since they take us off the reservation, but this isn't a democracy and I don't get a vote.

Andre is a young man, only twenty-five. He is smooth-skinned and handsome, with big round eyes, a straight narrow nose, and shiny black hair cut blunt just above his collar. He's a half-breed like me, and with dark hair on his arms and legs, he looks more like a Caucasian than an Indian, but no one ever talks about it. Andre plays the guitar and his passion is his band, but it's his viciousness that pays the bills. He's the one Bonaparte sends out to collect from the white man.

The rumor is that Andre beat up his own father with a tire iron. It is fact that he's done it to plenty of other white men, and it doesn't take me long to realize that Andre likes his job, that he goes into a place eager for trouble.

One night, we catch up with a pot dealer in his cabin outside of Lake Placid. The guy has this high school cheerleader on his couch stripped down and ready to go when we bust in. He coughs up the cash he owes real fast, but Andre bops him on the head with the butt of his gun anyway and grabs the girl by the wrist and starts dragging her screaming into the bedroom.

I put my hand on Andre's shoulder.

"Come on," I say, and before I can blink, his Colt .45 is cocked and in my face.

"You don't touch me, you fucking bookworm," he says. "Not ever."

"Then come on," I say, not letting go.

The girl wrestles free and scampers into the bedroom, where she slams the door shut. Andre gives me a twisted smile.

"You just get your ass outside and wait

for me to finish up in here," he says, "or Bert's gonna be cleaning your brains up off that wall with a paper towel."

My eyes don't waver and I say, "Go ahead. You'll be saving me and a lot of other people a whole hell of a lot of trouble. We got what we came for."

"Bang!" Andre yells, jerking the gun.

I just stare, and he begins to laugh and pats me on the back. To Bert he says, "You got a real loon here, you know that? I hope you lock loon-man in his room at night."

We leave together with the money and Andre's arm around my shoulder. After that, Bonaparte starts sending Bert and me out alone. Andre seems to behave himself whenever we're together, but I still don't trust him and I can't help the feeling that one day, when my guard is down, he's going to do me some harm.

29

The sun had already gone down. Outside, the muffled sound of taxi horns and truck brakes moved along Park Avenue. Lexis stood in the darkness. Only the vaguest shapes of the painting in front of her could be discerned now. When she first went into her trance there was enough light to see. She heard her name being shouted from somewhere deep inside their apartment. She set her brush down on the palette and placed both on the small table where she kept her paints.

She finished off the half-empty glass of chardonnay before shedding her smock and brushing off the front of her sweater. In the front hall, Frank was waiting, holding open her three-quarter-length mink coat.

"Frank," she said. "It's a football game."

"Will you hurry up?" he said, shaking the coat.

He smelled strongly of Cool Water cologne, and the milky soft black leather of his coat matched the color of his belt and shoes. His silk shirt and wool slacks were also black. On his wrist was a big gold Rolex studded with diamonds. On his pinky was a three-karat gold diamond ring.

"Where's your wedding band?" Frank said with a scowl, lifting her hand as she pushed it through the fur sleeve.

"Here," she said, spreading her fingers so he could see the thin platinum band.

"Go get your good one," he said, pointing his finger. The heavy slabs of his cheeks were turning red. She could see the top of his head as he looked down at her feet, and a small bald spot beneath that curly black-and-white hair.

"Frank," she said. "It's a football game."

"It's our championship game and people will be there, goddamn it," he said, still looking down, his lips pressed tight after the words were out. "I don't buy you that stuff to sit in a drawer."

Lexis turned and hurried down the long hallway. She walked through the broad double doors and into her closet. At the far end was her jewelry drawer. She found the ring quickly, and without bothering to lock the drawer, she hurried out of the bedroom and back down the hall, stopping in the kitchen for a quick glass of wine.

"Got it," she said, splaying her fingers

for Frank as she walked into the rotunda entryway of their apartment.

Frank only huffed and opened the door for her. The white-gloved elevator man was waiting. Outside, their long black limo was idling at the curb. Frank wedged his massive frame into the backseat and the doorman handed Lexis in after him. The glass partition was up. That's the way Frank liked it, and he picked up the phone to tell Duvall to hurry up because Lexis had made them late.

"Again," he said, frowning at her.

"Pour me one of those, would you, Frank?" she said. "You'd think you were playing tonight."

Frank poured two fingers of bourbon from the crystal decanter and handed her the Baccarat glass.

"It is like I am playing," he said, pouring himself a glass. "If he didn't remind me so goddamn much of myself, maybe I wouldn't feel this way. But shit, every scout from Syracuse to Alabama is going to be there."

"He seemed calm enough," Lexis said, feeling the warmth of the liquor spread through her. The car turned onto the West Side Highway. Ships moving up the river appeared in the dark. Lights from New

Jersey twinkled on the other side. Ahead, the George Washington Bridge spanned the night, illuminated by hundreds of blue-white lights and pulsing with the flow of red taillights.

"He hides it," he said. "Like I do. He's nervous, though. I can see it. It's a guy thing."

Frank picked up the phone. "Pass that guy, goddamn it, Duvall. I told you to hurry."

The limo surged ahead, swerving in and out of the traffic. Someone blared his horn. Lexis held out her empty glass. Frank pulled down the corners of his mouth.

"Afraid I'll *embarrass* you?" Lexis said, shaking the glass.

Frank puckered his lips and poured another. "Embarrass" was a hot button. A word she would fire at him from time to time that reminded them both of the day she caught him cheating dead to rights. The day he promised to kill her if she ever tried to leave him and take his son.

Frank loved to pretend to the world that all was well in the Steffano household. He hated to be reminded that it was all a façade. She couldn't always push that button, but on a night like tonight, this close to game time and all the people, she knew she had the upper hand.

She smiled to herself and backed into the corner of the car, sipping from her drink with both hands. Frank took out his cell phone and called one of his friends, confirming a business meeting for later.

Theirs wasn't the only limo pulling up to the big game at Riverdale Country, but it was the only one Lexis saw with chrome tire rims that matched the grille. The air was crisp and a breeze wafted up from the Hudson River and across Bertino Field. The bleachers were already filled and buzzing under the lights. They walked across the grass and along the track. The team was warming up. Frank walked through a small opening in the fence and right up to the edge of the playing field where the referees were conferring.

"Allen Francis," he yelled, cupping his hands. "Go *kick* their goddamn ass, son!"

Allen looked at his father, then dipped his face mask down to his knee, intent on his stretching. Frank strode back toward the track pumping his clenched fist, his face a beaming smile.

A man in a brown suede coat with his arm around his wife walked past looking. Under his breath, he said, "What an asshole."

"That Allen's such a good kid," the wife said, shaking her head.

"Nothing like the old man," said the husband.

Lexis jammed her hands into her coat pockets and turned her head.

Frank returned with a flushed face and said, "He's ready now."

He led Lexis up to the top row and told some older people to squeeze down for the quarterback's parents.

"Frank," Lexis said.

Too loud, he said, "What? These snooty old farts wouldn't even be *in* the championship if it weren't for my boy. They can slide their skinny asses right down."

Lexis clamped her lips tight and angled her face away. Frank began to scour the crowd for college scouts with his binoculars. Lexis was thinking that at the quarter break she could get a quick one back at the car.

"There," Frank said, still loud, grabbing her arm and pointing. "That's the guy from Syracuse. There's the one from Penn State over there."

Lexis glanced and nodded, then quickly focused on Allen as the team broke into small groups after their stretching. Allen began throwing passes down the field to his receivers, licking his fingers between throws.

"Look at that arm," Frank said.

"You didn't play quarterback, did you, Frank?" Lexis asked, feeling light-headed.

Frank glanced at her quickly, then put his binoculars back up to his face.

"I had a hell of an arm," he said. "Just like him. But, you know, with my size they put me on the line. That's the only thing he got from you. Those eyes and that frame."

Lexis just nodded.

30

The third collection run for Bert and me on our own takes us to an old refurbished hotel on Raquette Lake by the name of Bright Side. I study a map before we leave and see that Lake Kora is close by and right on the way. I'm driving Bert's old Ford Bronco, and he's asleep with his face against the window when I pull off Route 28 and down Uncas Road. When I stop the truck, Bert scratches his head and rubs his eyes. It's late afternoon and the sun is shining through a warm breeze, but I slip a flashlight from under the seat into the side pocket of my cargo pants.

"A little lost," I say.

"That's okay," he says. "I gotta piss anyway."

Bert climbs out and makes for the bushes. I walk down a dirt path that leads to the water, the smell of pine needles in my nose. Across the lake, under the shadows of some tall hemlock trees, I think I see the rooflines of the cottage that Lester told me about. Up the shore a ways is a weathered dock and a small skiff. I pick my way along the rocks on the water's edge and check out the new camp that was apparently built over the spot where Durant's lodge used to be. It's a Tuesday and late in the season, so I'm not surprised there are no signs of any people.

I'm halfway across the small lake, rowing, when Bert appears on the shore.

"What the fuck you doing?" he asks with his hands cupped around his mouth.

"I think I know where we are," I say. "I had a friend used to own that place over there. I'm just checking it out."

Bert shrugs and rips a thin branch from a tree. He strips off the leaves and starts to whip the seed heads off the grass growing out of the bank. I know if I offer to thumb wrestle him when I make the turn back onto the main road, he won't even remember this place.

The cottage is sagging and it smells damp in there under the shade of the trees. The front porch is coated with moss and even a few saplings struggle up out of the wood. The key is buried in a plastic bag at the base of a post. I dig it up with a flat rock and unlock the heavy front door. In the back of the kitchen is the pantry. I have a hard time swinging back the shelves. They seem to be fixed and, just as I was in the prison, I am gripped by the fear that I am the victim of a ruse. A film of sweat breaks out on my arms as I strain against the wood frame. Finally, their rusty hinges creak and give way and there behind the wall is the full-size door of a safe.

I spin the knob, marveling at how slick it moves after all these years. It clicks, and I spin the second one until it clicks too. I press my weight against the lever and the door swings open. I flick on the flashlight and walk down into the cool dry space that is lined with narrow wooden boxes stacked upright like books on a shelf. My heart starts to thump when I see the metal strongboxes on a shelf in the corner. When I open them, I suck in my breath.

Refracted light sparkles back at me in a million different hues. There are rubies and emeralds fat as walnuts, but mostly it's diamonds set in rings, strung from neck-laces, or mounted on precious crowns. I slip four of the biggest stones into my pockets.

"Holy shit," I say and sit down on the edge of a shelf that is labeled *Picasso*.

I shine the light all around me. Crate after crate, lining the shelves, stacked three tiers high to the massive beams of the ceiling. If anything, Lester grossly underestimated the worth of his fortune.

I sit for several minutes until the light-headed feeling passes, then I go back across the lake to Bert.

"Find it?" he asks.

"What?"

He shrugs, tosses away his switch, and says, "Whatever you were looking for."

"Yeah," I say, adjusting the brim of my cap down over my face. "I found it."

"My grandmother used to say when you found what you're looking for, it's time to start looking for something new," Bert says.

The sun is going down when I pull over the old Ford Bronco at a place called Byrd's Marina. An old guy rents us a party boat for the rest of the day and gives us a map of the lake. I catch him staring at our hair. Bert's is tied in a long ponytail and mine sweeps down to my shoulders. I'm still not used to the way white men look at Indians and I feel that my lips are tight. He puts an X on the spot where Bright Side is and tells us to watch the buoys.

"There's rocks all over this lake," he says, forcing a smile. "Have fun."

I keep my head down, but take the wheel. Bert clutches a life jacket to his chest, the same way he does every time we cross into Canada by boat. A slight breeze coming from the direction of the sunset ripples the water. Lights begin to go on in random cabins around the lakeshore, but most of the places stay dark.

Bright Side is a dinosaur. Big and old and missing a few pieces. The boathouse has been patched together with bald pressure-treated planks. The dock stretches out from a crumbling concrete pier that is cloaked in green moss. The hotel itself is freshly painted, but looks as if it has shifted from the effects of an earthquake. It's easy to see why whoever runs it supplements their income by selling small bags of weed.

We are docked and halfway up the lawn when someone skips down the front porch steps and jogs up to us. His hands are raised in the air in the act of surrender. I peer through the gloom from beneath the brim of my hat and my heart jerks to a stop.

Grinning stupidly at us is a stooped and wrinkled version of Paul Russo. The bags under his red-rimmed eyes are darker now and his shoulders sag and curl forward at the same time. In an attempt to diminish his baldness, he has grown a long flap of dyed-black hair that he sweeps over the top of his head from one protruding ear to the other. His clothes look like they come from an L.L.Bean catalog.

"Hey, guys," he says with false cheerfulness. The wheezy sound of his voice losing its way in that big nose removes any doubt that this is the man from my past life. "I've got some guests in the lobby. Okay if we talk right here?"

I can see Bert staring at me from the corner of my eye, but I keep my face angled down under the brim of the hat and my mouth shut. Bert starts to shift his feet.

Russo laughs nervously through his nose and says, "I know you guys are here for the money and I've got most of it. Here. It's right here . . ."

He pulls a fat wad out of his pants pocket and begins peeling off bills, counting by twenty. When he's finished, he holds the stack out to me.

My bones ache. That's how bad I want to show him my face. To see his eyes go blank. To smell him wet his pants when he stares back at this ghost. To savor his muffled shrieks as we take him away, out to the middle of the lake where I can choke him to death with my bare hands before we tie the anchor to his neck and sink him forever. I know we could do it. It would be easy.

This is my first test.

31

When I was born from the pipe in that prison wall, my second life began. It is a simple life with a single purpose. The lessons of my past life have stayed with me, but gone is the scattered focus. I am here to bloody my sword with the mess of everyone who destroyed Raymond White. I am no longer him and I am no longer Running Deer, or Quick Buck, or Quick Book. The joke is over.

I will take the name of the son of the man who gave me this second life. I will not be overeager or impulsive. I will have ice in my veins because I have already been dead. I will now become Seth Cole.

This is what I tell myself.

I take the money pinched between Russo's fingers and turn to go. I promise myself the time will soon come.

"Tell Bonaparte the rest is coming," he says after us, then we hear that nervous nasal laugh.

"We're not gonna bust him up some?" Bert says to me in a low tone.

We are standing on the dock and I have

the mooring line of the party boat in my hands. Its aluminum pontoons ring hollow as they bump against the wood. A yellow bulb in a broken fixture on the wall of the boathouse glows dully and insects swirl through its beams.

I tilt my hat back and look up at Bert so he can see my eyes.

"Do you want a job?" I ask.

Bert giggles and looks around.

"What do you mean?" he says. "I got a job."

"You want another? You want to work for me?"

"You're not gonna take that money?" he says, his eyebrows furrowing.

"I'll pay it back," I say. "Don't worry about that. I'll pay it back double by the end of the week. You want a job?"

"Workin' for you?" he says. "Just you?"

"Just me."

"Yeah," Bert says, smiling big, the slits of his eyes nearly invisible above those big round cheeks. "I want that job."

I reach out and squeeze his thick arm and we step onto the boat.

I drive all night to just outside New York City, where we flop down in a motel under the shadow of Bear Mountain. We sleep until midmorning, then go into Manhattan.

Bert waits in the truck while I go into Zegna on Fifth Avenue and buy a dark blue suit, shoes, a shirt, and a tie with Russo's money. I step out onto the sidewalk and see that Bert doesn't recognize me without the Bills hat and frumpy clothes that I carry in a Zegna shopping bag.

I go around the corner to a hairstylist and pay for a hundred-dollar trim, pick up a fake Cartier watch on the street, then have Bert drive me to a 49th Street diamond shop. I deal my stones in the backroom with a Hasidic grandfather who gives me a briefcase half full of crisp hundreds banded together in narrow paper sleeves that read: $10,000.

The old man stares up only briefly from beneath his black felt hat and thick round glasses before he tells me where I can get some fake identification made up. The next stop is Western Union so I can wire Bonaparte notice of our respectful termination along with Russo's money in full plus another equal amount as interest for the day's use.

We eat bulging pastrami sandwiches at Katz's Deli before circling the Bronco back to the garment district, where hopefully they're finished making up my identification. For ten thousand dollars cash, I get a valid Mississippi driver's license, a library card from the Oxford Public Library, and a social security card all bearing the name of Lester's dead and long-forgotten son. I give the guy one of the packets of hundreds from the diamond merchant, then Bert and I leave the city.

We hire some strong young kids from a guy Bert knows at the Turning Stone Casino, the Oneida Indian Reservation casino just west of Utica. I rent a U-Haul with a twenty-four-foot van and buy three sets of handheld radios along with a six-horse Johnson outboard motor. It's ten o'clock, pitch black, with the wind promising rain when we post two of the kids along Uncas Road with radios to keep a lookout.

It takes four hours to empty the cottage vault into the truck. During the last half-hour, it begins to rain. I give the kids each ten one-hundred-dollar bills and they grin all the way back to Turning Stone. After we drop them off, Bert and I get a start on our drive back to New York City, stopping when we get to a motel outside Hamilton and hurrying inside to get out of the spattering rain.

The next day, the sky is clear. We find a stout-looking storage facility in one of the sprawling new suburbs of Bergen County across the line into New Jersey. It takes me three days to sell a Cézanne for three hundred and fifty thousand. I know I'm being taken, but it's just one painting, and I want to get out to Los Angeles to begin my transformation.

I use the two months it takes my face to recover from surgery to enhance the knowledge Lester has already given me about moving rare and missing works of art and jewels. I meet buyers from Japan, Germany, France, England, and Indonesia. I get some credit cards going and some brokerage accounts too.

I send Bert back to New Jersey to rent a modest house close to where my paintings are stored. I have a stop to make that I want to do alone. I get off the plane at Syracuse with my head held high, confident I won't be recognized. My eyes will always be the same liquid brown as Raymond White's, but the skin around them has been tightened. My chin is broader than his was and my nose is smaller and straighter.

To return before my surgery would have been stupid. The same thing goes for trying to contact my father. I'm sure Raymond White is still a wanted man and not enough time has gone by for the authorities not to be keeping an eye on the only person in the world who he was connected to.

As I approach the airport security doors, I look up and see the camera. I swallow my spit and quickly take my wallet from my suit coat pocket and look down at it, pretending fascination with its contents as I pass by the screening station and through the doors. I slide the wallet back inside my coat and look around at the crowd of people waiting for family and friends who have arrived on the same flight I was on. It's a lonely feeling to see their eager faces and have their eyes slip right on past me.

I am downstairs and standing in line at the Hertz counter when I see two uniformed police walking toward me. Their faces are set in concrete and they are scanning the terminal. When the one with the brown crew cut meets my eyes, he taps his partner and they head my way. My heart jumps and my muscles go tense. I look around. There are enough people milling about that I think I could get out of the building, but where I'd go from there, I have no idea. I would have to jack someone's car. It would end in a mad chase, probably with a bullet in my spinning head. Before I can act, they are here.

"Excuse me," the crew cut says, "are you Seth Cole?"

"Yes."

The cop smiles in a knowing way and says, "Thought so. You dropped your wallet upstairs."

He is holding the wallet out to me. I reach out and take it. They stare at me with their smiles fading. When I finally sense the tension, I thank them, and thank them again. Their smiles return. They nod and they walk away.

I rent a Cadillac and drive out to my father's. In the weeds that have grown up around the mailbox is a crooked Realtor's sign. I grip the wheel and speed up the hill with rocks clattering off the undercarriage as I search the trees for the lines of the house. There are no vehicles in the driveway, and a blanket of leaves from last autumn has been piled up into the corners of the porch. A torn window screen wafts gently in the breeze.

It's a warm day for October. Indian summer. My armpits sweat, and I sniff at the unfamiliar scent of mothballs in the stuffy air. I peer through the window and the spiderwebs. None of the furniture is familiar. Broken children's toys are scattered about the dirty floor. My spirits are lifted though when the roar of a blast soars over the treetops from the direction of the quarry. I jump down off the steps and speed around the hill, the Cadillac trailing dust in the heat.

The old office trailer is sunken and buried in a sea of saplings and high grass, but down in the quarry I see men in lime green hard hats moving about. The old payloader lies with its back broken in a rusted heap beside the road, but I see fresh yellow equipment crawling like monstrous beetles up ahead. It's obvious there is money being made here, and it's not at all unlikely that my dad finally moved out of the woods.

I don't see him, or Black Turtle, but there is a man with plans spread out over the hood of a Chevy pickup who is obviously in charge. Yellow foam plugs peek out of his ears. His hair and mustache are powdered with stone dust the way my father's always were. He stares up at me from behind his safety goggles and frowns.

"This is a hard hat area," he says. "Who are you?"

"I'm . . ." I say, frozen and sick at how close I came to calling myself Raymond White, "looking for Kevin White."

"Who?" the foreman says, his powdered eyebrows knitted.

A gray bearded man in overalls and leathery skin comes around to my side of the pickup and says to the foreman, "The guy used to own this place. Remember? Guy who froze to death?"

"You got me," the foreman says, tilting back his lime green hardhat and dabbing at his brow with the back of his hand.

My head feels hollow and I hear a sound like waterfalls. I've lost my sense of standing upright.

"Hey, fella. You okay?"

"You sure?" I ask. "Did you know him?"

"Not really," the older man says. "Just remember it in the papers back in, I don't know, 1990 or something, about him having his power cut off middle of January. Didn't pay his bills, they said. Power company took hell for it anyway . . .

"I remember because guys used to kid each other when we first started working this place," he says, nodding his head toward the rusty hulk on the road above us. "There was an old Indian who used to come around —"

"Black Turtle?"

"Yeah, I think that was it. He died too, not long after. Anyway, he said you could see that Kevin White guy's ghost on that old payloader sometimes after dark. Well, that got them all going. You know how rock guys are."

"Rocks in their heads, half of 'em," the foreman says.

"They say it's not a bad way to go," the older man says. "Say you start feeling real warm and then you just kind of go to sleep."

I hear him, but my eyes are on the payloader, broken and flaky. The air above the seat glimmers and I squint my eyes, looking for his shape. But it's only the heat from the brown metal and the weeds, making tracks for the cooler regions of the blue sky. I wish my hatred had a vent like that.

My father is gone. Even his ghost.

32

The snow in upstate New York is piled high by the time I return. It's taken me that long to turn Lester's stash into a massive portfolio of cash and stocks and bonds. Bert is driving me in a black Lincoln Navigator and he has to use four-wheel drive from the minute we leave the Thruway. The slush from the morning's snow is four inches deep. At my feet is a suitcase with a million dollars in cash as well as a street-bought Smith & Wesson .357 with a silencer attached.

Bert's hair is cut short now and he wears an expensive tan shearling coat that makes him look even bigger than he already is. I wear a black leather trench coat, even though it's not as warm. It matches my driving gloves and looks good with the full black beard and mustache I've grown. My hair is still long, but slicked back tight to my head. Paul Russo will be the first person I'll meet up close, in the light, who really knew Raymond White.

Byrd's, the same place that rented us the party boat last summer, rents snowmobiles in the winter. Bert has called ahead, and two red-and-black machines that look like they came out of *Star Wars* are waiting for us in the middle of the plowed lot. The sky is bitter and bleached and the sun shows through in only a pale yellow wash. The same old guy comes outside with his smoky breath trailing him. He gives us helmets to use, and I see him staring at the Ferragamo shoes on my feet.

"You going like that?" he says, nodding toward the shoes and the pant legs of my suit.

I don't know what he's looking at. He's got a Valvoline cap on his head and his nose and ears are red like beets from the cold. I ease the helmet down over my slick hair and get onto the snowmobile. Bert loads up two overnight bags and my briefcase on the back of his snowmobile, then shells out the cash for the machines. I rev my engine until he's mounted up, then we shoot across the street and out onto the frozen lake.

In the open stretches, I grip the accelerator tight. The machine shakes and swerves, floating, almost out of control. Snow crystals whip up under the edge of my helmet. I look down at the speedometer. The needle pushes past eighty and the sensation of speed gets my heart going.

There are other snow machines lined up on the bank outside the old hotel. Heavy gray smoke pours out from three different chimneys. Inside, it's warm and I can smell cinnamon and burning wood. Russo greets us with a clap of his hands. He wears a green sweater with a line of white reindeers knit across the front. His pale neck sticks out of the collar like a broomstick. The veins in his big nose and even his protruding ears are angry from alcohol and his breath smells like cheap scotch.

"Gentlemen," he says, rubbing his hands together, "we've been expecting you. Good ride over?"

When he sees my Ferragamo shoes crusted with snow, he raises his eyebrows, chuckles, and says, "There's a fire around the corner. If you want to give me your credit card, I'll get you checked in."

Bert takes four one-hundred-dollar-bills out of his wallet and extends them toward Russo. Russo looks up at him and his eyes strain for a moment as if he might have seen Bert before.

"We'll pay cash," I say.

"That's not a problem," Russo says, returning his eyes to me. He blinks under my gaze. "How should I fill out your registration?"

I flip out a business card between my first two fingers and extend it toward him. He takes the card and examines it.

"Ah, Mr. Bell, an attorney," he says with a nod before angling his head toward Bert. "And your friend?"

"Put them both under my name," I say. "I want to talk to you after dinner. About some business."

Russo's eyebrows pop up and he touches his fingertips to the knit reindeers.

"In private," I say. I hand my coat and gloves to Bert, then I turn and walk into the great room whose wainscot walls are shimmering in the firelight.

There is a golden oak bar in the corner opposite the fireplace and a pale scrawny woman stares out at me from behind it with big dark eyes. Her hair is the most animated thing about her, long and frizzy. Dark, but shot through with strands of gray. The other guests, snowmobilers in jeans and sweaters, gaze up at my suit, but return their attention to their drinks as soon as they meet my eyes. I have a drink at the bar, answering the hostess — who is also Russo's wife — in short sentences until she excuses herself to see to the dinner.

Bert and I eat our overcooked pot roast

in silence. The dining room overlooks the frozen lake. In the winter moonlight, we can see it and the naked mountains beyond through the frosted panes of glass. The other guests begin their dinner in a drunken uproar, but by the time Mrs. Russo brings around wedges of store-bought pecan pie, our own solemnity seems to have spread. The loudest sound is the silverware striking the old ceramic plates.

Russo comes out of the kitchen, wiping his hands on an apron and casting a worried glance our way before disappearing in the direction of the great room. Bert presses his lips tight and wags his head and we get up and follow our host. Halfway down the hall, there is an open door and we step into a snug office where a fire crackles and Russo sits at a round oak table smoking a Marlboro Light.

"If you don't mind," Bert rumbles, "Mr. Bell doesn't like smoke."

I stare at Russo until he stabs out the cigarette in a ceramic ashtray, blows the smoke out of the corner of his mouth, and says, "No problem."

I set my briefcase down on the table and sit opposite Russo. Bert quietly closes the door and remains standing there.

"Does . . . he want to sit down?" Russo asks.

"We're fine," I say, flipping the latches and opening the case so that the cover prevents Russo from seeing the money and the gun. "Mr. Russo, I am here for a client who might want to give you some money."

"Money? For what?" he says, his eyes darting to Bert and back.

"For some information," I say. "About a man named Raymond White."

The blood drains from Russo's face. In a whisper, he says, "Raymond was a friend."

"That's what I understand," I say. "My client wants to know more about what happened to Mr. White. They were in prison together and Mr. White saved my client's life. Unfortunately, Mr. White was killed during an attempted escape."

"He's dead?"

"Yes," I say.

"I didn't hear that," he says, with his brow furrowed. "I heard they thought he was, but I never heard that he was."

"And my client would like to do something for the people closest to Mr. White," I say. "Mr. White mentioned you several times . . . as a friend."

"Oh, I was," he says. "Raymond . . ." He shakes his head. "What they did to him . . . goddamn."

"But you knew he was framed," I say. "You knew what Frank Steffano and Bob Rangle did."

"He told you?"

"He told my client."

Russo puts his round flat face into his hand.

"I should have said something," he says. "I know. I was drunk back then. Pretty much all the time. I didn't really think they meant it, and when I . . ."

Russo looks up at me with red eyes and says, "I'm telling you the truth. I was scared. I still am. Of them."

"What about his father?" I ask. "Weren't you supposed to help him? I read that he died. They turned off his power. My client was told that you were supposed to help Raymond's father."

"Oh, I did," he says. "Are you kidding? At least I tried. That old . . . he wasn't easy. He didn't want my help or anyone's."

"How do you know that?"

"There was a girl," he says. "Lexis. I don't know how much you know."

"Go on."

"She was Raymond's girl. Then, after everything, she married Frank."

"The man who —"

"Yeah, well, she had a baby boy," he says. "I just know she came to me with money. A lot. She asked me to give it to the father, but that old crab-ass . . ."

"He wouldn't listen. He wouldn't take anything from anyone. Raymond, he was a stubborn son of a bitch and it wasn't hard to see where it came from."

"Why are you still afraid?" I ask.

"Do you know who those guys are?" he says, tilting his head just a touch.

"A cop who did well in business," I say. "A politician who cashed in on Wall Street."

"Ha, *well* in business?" he says. "That Frank, he cut people's nuts off who got in his way. Got involved with the big boys down in Atlantic City. Owns some casinos and hotels and shit.

"*Well?* He's gotta be worth a hundred million and Rangle's probably worth even more. Some fund manager or something and *he* didn't take any prisoners either, I can promise you that. Two very big men. Dangerous to your health, even a fancy lawyer like you."

"And things haven't gone that good for you," I say, looking around.

"Yeah, well, it's not so bad. Little cold in the winter."

I look into the blaze of the fire and nod slowly.

"Aw, who the fuck am I kidding?" he says. "It sucks. If I don't have like a convention of snowmobilers every day for the next two months, the fucking bank will probably take this shithole. Maybe do me a favor. I'm thinking about starting a rumor of a ghost. Sometimes that draws people in."

"You deal drugs too," I say, locking my eyes onto his.

"Hey, who the fuck are you, coming in here?" he says sitting straight and scowling down his nose, but his eyes flicker nervously up at Bert.

"There was another man," I say, ignoring the flare in his nostrils. "His name was Dan Parsons."

"Yeah, makes me look like King fucking Solomon," he says, fidgeting with his pack of Marlboros.

"Meaning?"

"Got kicked out of his own fucking law firm," Russo says. "Big fucking deal. Parsons & Trout. Dan Parsons this. Dan Parsons that. Oh, they paid him, but they wanted him out. His own firm. Didn't do a damn thing but file appeals for Raymond White. Went a little batshit, I guess. Then he took every fuckin' penny he had and got into that dotcom bullshit. Made a fuckin' fortune, then lost a fuckin' fortune. Uncle Sam — as in IRS — didn't get their cut on the upside and last I heard the barbarians were at the gate."

My eyes are drawn back to the fire. One log sticks up at an angle. On its tip is a fiery brand pulsing orange. I watch until the wood pops and the ember falls and disappears into the ashes beneath the grate.

"How much would it take to get this place into good shape?" I ask. "So you could stop selling pot to kids?"

"Kids? You should see the shit these little bastards do."

I stare at him without comment.

"Well," he says, crossing his arms and frowning all the way into the area where his chin mixes with his neck, "I don't know. If I had, like . . . two hundred thousand. That would put me in pretty good shape. That'd pay down my loan to where I could get down to Daytona for a week in February or something. Shit, the fucking winter here never ends."

"Two hundred thousand dollars?" I say.

"Well, you asked."

I reach into the briefcase and push the gun aside. I take twenty stacks of hundreds out and set them on the table.

"A gift," I say, "from Seth Cole. In memory of Raymond White . . . To turn your life around."

"Hey," he says, reaching for the money. "Are you fucking kidding me?"

"No," I say. "I don't kid. It's yours."

"Do I have to claim it?"

A smile creeps onto my lips and I say, "You can do whatever you want with it. It's yours. No one has to know where it came from."

"Hey," he says, peering around the cover of the case as I close it. "How much is in there?"

"There was a million," I say, rising from my seat and snapping shut the latches on the case.

"What if I said I needed a million?"

"Then I would have given it to you," I say. "But I was authorized to give you only what you needed to get your business on track so you could live an honest, decent life. Now hopefully you'll do that."

"I could use it all," he says, his voice rising with the rest of him. "Really. I just didn't want to be greedy, but I need it."

"If you didn't," I say, "then don't."

"What?"

"Be greedy," I say, and leave.

33

When I awake, it's still dark. I shower and change.

I open the door and Bert — playing guard dog — falls backward into the room. He wakes up in a sputter, grabbing for the handle of the Glock in the waist of his pants.

"It's me," I say. "Let's go."

The boards creak beneath our feet, otherwise there's no sound. The wind is gone. Outside, it's frigid. There is a low ceiling of gray clouds that are lit by the glow in the east. We cross the frozen lake and leave our machines in Byrd's empty lot, and I tell Bert to drive us to Syracuse. After almost three hours, we stop at Cosmo's diner near the university for breakfast and I order a broccoli and cheese omelet. It is a taste from another life.

Bert asks if he can get a burger this early and the waitress with an earring in her nose shrugs and says sure. I lean out of our booth and ask the woman at the cash register for a phone book. She smiles and takes it out from under the counter.

Bert hops up to get the book, but when he sits down, he puts it in his lap instead of giving it to me and says, "Can I ask you something?"

"Sure."

"You got all that money now," he says, "but you don't do nothing that's fun."

"What's the question?"

"Don't you want to?"

"Maybe when I finish doing what I have to do," I say, "I'll go to Disney World."

"My grandmother used to say that even a big chief needs to laugh," he says, "or else it makes his spirit small."

He's wearing a crooked smile and extends his beefy fist across the tabletop and says, "Want to wrestle?"

I take his hand and bait him with a chance for a quick win, but I slip out at the last possible second, pin his thumb down, and quickly count to three.

"Best out of three," he says. "You never win a war with just one battle, and I got the phone book."

He beats me two in a row, mashing my thumb and rumbling with laughter, then slaps the phone book down on the table.

"Thanks," I say, rubbing the joint between my first and second digits and opening the book. "My spirit's now soaring."

Dan Parsons is listed at a new address in Skaneateles. Elizabeth Street. Nice neighborhood, but nothing like his white Georgian mansion on the lake. There is also an office listed on Fennell Street. After breakfast, we drive out to Skaneateles, where the trees in the village are frosted and the homes and buildings wear fresh caps of snow.

Dan's office is in the back of the old Trabold's Garage. Someone has renovated the old stone blacksmith shop and put a restaurant on the ground floor. We park in the municipal lot behind all the stores and buildings. There is a bent old man in a hooded parka and heavy snow boots shoveling the stairs that lead up to the offices.

When we reach the bottom, I notice a tear in the corduroy pants stuck into the top of the man's boots and say, "Excuse me, we're looking for Dan Parsons's office."

The man stops his shoveling and turns. It's Dan. His face is pink, either from the cold or embarrassment. Most of his curly white hair is gone. His nose is even more pronounced. His jowls hang limp from his jawbone and the crow's-feet at the corners of his eyes sag with disappointment. His smile is gone.

"I'm him," he says, glancing at Bert and then turning his attention back to the shovel. "If you wait a minute, I'll finish this. What do you got? A house closing?"

I study the profile of his face for the joke. This is a man who brokered billion-dollar deals. A good house closing can net you five hundred.

"No," I say. "I need to talk with you about the IRS."

His head snaps up and his eyes seem to droop even more. He presses his lips tight.

"You don't look like Feds," he says.

"We're not," I say. "I'm here to help."

"Well, I don't have any money to pay you," he says, "so unless you're with Legal Aid, you might as well not waste your time. When's the last time you saw a lawyer who had to shovel the steps to help pay his rent?"

"Can we go inside?" I ask.

Dan shakes his head and slowly mounts the stairs. He grips the railing tight through his ski gloves to steady himself. He kicks some of the snow off the landing and we go inside and down a narrow hall. His office isn't much more than a closet with a desk and a phone. There are two chairs opposite the desk that are wedged between it and the wall. On the wall are pictures of Dan and his wife — fading, but still pretty and trim — and their son, who is now a good-looking young man.

After Dan hangs his parka on the back of the door, I see that his husky shoulders have gone round and his potbelly has become a barrel of flab. He wears an old herringbone blazer that's too tight around his middle, and beneath the wrapping of his plaid scarf is a yellow paisley tie.

He sits down with a sigh and motions to the chairs. Bert and I sit.

"What do you want?" Dan asks.

"I said I'm here to help."

"How's that?"

"How much do you owe the government?" I ask.

Dan's knuckles are swollen and bent. He rests his forearms on the edge of his desk and raps the knuckles gently on the edges of his blotter. Outside I hear the muted banging of a garbage truck emptying a Dumpster.

"Who the hell are you?"

"I'm sorry," I say, taking a card from my pocket and pushing it across the desk. "My name is Arthur Bell. I'm an attorney and I have a client who wants to help you."

"Bob Rangle?" he says.

I have to swallow before I say, "Rangle?"

Dan shrugs and says, "No, I didn't figure. He was the congressman. I put that son of a bitch in office and I went down to New York a few weeks ago to ask for a loan. He runs a fund now."

"No," I say, "I have nothing to do with him. My client is Seth Cole. He was friends with Raymond White."

"What?" he says. His eyes narrow.

"My client was in prison for a time," I say. "Raymond White saved his life. When he heard that Raymond died, my client wanted to do something for the people who were good to him."

"Raymond died?"

I nod.

Dan's eyes lose their focus and he looks down at his hands. They are clenched tight like his teeth.

"No one told me," he says, as if speaking to himself.

"No," I say, "they probably wouldn't. You weren't actually related to him."

His eyes snap up at me. He scowls and says, "He was —"

Then he drops his eyes again and says, "It doesn't matter, does it?"

"My client wants to pay off your debt," I say. "He thinks Raymond would have wanted that."

272

"I've got this dream, you know," Dan says as he massages the fingers of one hand with the other. "I got this dream of starting it over. Parsons & Parsons. My son's gonna be a lawyer, you know?

"Mister," Dan says, looking up again. "I appreciate your coming here. But I owe them thirteen million dollars . . . I've got an insurance policy for ten, and to be honest I've been thinking about taking a fast drive, maybe hitting a bridge. Problem is, my wife would still owe the bastards three more and you better believe these people don't negotiate."

"Mr. Parsons," I say. "Seth Cole has authorized me to pay the IRS in full."

"Hey. Get the hell out of here," he says, shaking his head in disgust. He rises up out of his chair and draws himself up nearly straight. "Who sent you?"

"Believe me," I say. "Thirteen million dollars to Seth Cole isn't what it is to most people. Who's your bank?"

He stares at me for a long time. I hold his gaze, fearful that he will see me.

Finally, he wags his head and says, "Next door."

"Let's go," I say. "You'll see."

Together we go down the back stairs and into the single-story bank next door. I ask for a wire number and I call Bob Mancini, my contact at Goldman Sachs. The girls at the bank are twittering behind the counter and the manager comes out from his office as well.

"What is it?" Dan asks.

The manager is shaking his head. He looks up with a wide grin.

"Mr. Parsons," he says. "Goldman Sachs just put thirteen million dollars in your account."

"Can they take it back?" he asks, shooting a glance at me.

"No sir," the manager says. "It's there. No one can take it but you."

Dan Parsons utters a cry. He grabs my hand and gives it a quick strong shake, then he races out of the building. Bert and I walk outside. I stand on the sidewalk and watch Dan make his way up the street in a ragged jog while Bert gets the truck. When Bert picks me up, I have him drive to Elizabeth Street.

There is a big bay window in the front of the small saltbox house where Dan lives. We stop out front and I roll down my window. Through the bay window, I can see him hugging his wife and swinging her around. I can see the sparkle of tears running down his face. His mouth is open in wild laughter that I don't have to hear.

I roll up the window and stare straight ahead at the snow-covered street that is lined with four-foot banks.

"Back to New York, Bert," I say.

"What about Mickey Mouse and Space Mountain and all that?"

"No," I say. "You liked when I played God, right? Reward a loyal friend? A kind old man? Make his dreams come true? That's like Disney World. You take the ride, get a little scared, then you get off and have some cotton candy or a turkey drumstick. Take your picture with Snow White. But God's got a night job too. God is a judge. Yeah, he rewards the good guy, right? Supposedly . . . But what about the bad?

"God makes a call. Good, you get Disney World. Bad?"

I look Bert in the eye and say, "You go to hell."

BOOK THREE

ASCENSION

It was time for him to go back among men and take up the rank, influence and power which great wealth gives in this world.

The Count of Monte Cristo

34

I know that someone like Frank Steffano doesn't get to where he is by destroying just one man. People like Frank are tumors. They feed off everything decent within their reach. They are worse than parasites who fatten only themselves. Tumors like Frank grow stronger and stronger until they can metastasize. They create other tumors that also grow and thrive. Villay. Rangle. Russo. I'm sure there are others.

I hire Vance International, a private investigative and protective agency made from the cream of the Secret Service, the FBI, and all four branches of the military. I put up a five-million-dollar retainer, which gets their attention. They are my diagnostic team.

You would be shocked at how easy it is to invade someone's privacy. I'm not talking about getting someone's phone records or financial statements, or hacking into their e-mails. I'm talking about seeing and hearing what goes on in their bedroom and the table where they eat breakfast.

Vance International isn't bound by any laws. They have employees who are welcomed into Frank and Lexis's home, into the Rangles', into the Villays'. It happens to every American on a weekly basis. We open our doors to complete strangers, giving them access to our secret places. Cable TV workers. Appliance repairmen. The guy who delivers the dry cleaning. The more money people have, the more intruders enter their homes.

If that fails, Vance has other ways of getting in. Skeleton keys. Lock picks. Drills and glasscutters. Cameras and microphones the size of a pencil lead are easily inserted into ceilings and walls. Tiny transmitters send microwave digital data to receivers that are connected into fiber lines and fed to monitoring stations that gather everything. Then Vance boils it down to the good stuff.

For six months they chronicle for me not only every symptom of the disease, but its complete pathology.

Am I collecting information because I want to destroy the tumors perfectly, or because I want justification for what I'm going to do? Maybe I'm really not as comfortable filling in for God as I make myself out to be. It makes me sick to be this weak, but I think that's the truth. Even after everything that's happened to me, I need something more. A justification to make my judgment. A rationale to dole out my punishment. As if I didn't already have enough of both.

And, just like I figured, Vance International digs up other ruined lives besides mine. None of them are as bad as what happened to me, though. None of them except one. A girl named Helena. At first, I decide to look for her because she could serve an important role in my plan. But the more I learn, the more I feel as if we are somehow connected through our losses and our pain and I wonder if she might also be able to take the edge off my loneliness.

It's late summer when I track her down in a men's club in Fairbanks, Alaska. She's emotionally battered and bruised and so bitter that she's almost wicked. I don't blame her. She was sold off as a prostitute when she was a child. They used her in some movies and then they just used her. She was fifteen when she escaped a flophouse in West Hollywood. It took her a year to steal her way up to Alaska. Someplace she must have fantasized as being safe.

She dances for the oil workers and fishermen during the week, and in exchange, the owner lets her sing with her clothes on over the weekend. She lives in a small one-room cabin that she built herself. She has electricity, but uses an outhouse. The first time I approach her in the club parking lot, she pulls a little 9mm Chief's Special out of her bag and stabs it into my ribs.

"You ever use that?" I ask.

"You're goddamn right," she tells me.

I buy the men's club and shut it down. It still takes me two weeks to convince her I am for real.

Finally I pack her into my G-V and take her to a flat I have in Knightsbridge in London. It takes four weeks before she realizes that she's really safe.

She starts to take walks with me and look me in the eye, and when I take her to a Nathan Lane show near Piccadilly Circus, I catch her smiling halfway through the first act. After the show, when she gets out of the limousine and we walk through the alley into Shepherd's Market, she holds my hand. We have a drink at Ye Grapes, then go around the corner to a Turkish restaurant called Sofra. We sit in a table by the window and eat hummus and skewers of grilled lamb and vegetables.

Her eyes are dark and liquid and deep, framed by long thick lashes that shadow her cheeks when she looks away. Her nose is narrow and straight, long without being big. Her lips are full. She isn't a tall girl, but her figure is curved and her stomach flat. I lean across the table and let my lips brush gently against hers. She looks down and brushes her dark silky hair back out of her face. A tear falls, spattering the rim of her plate.

"If you could have anything in the world," I say, "what would it be?"

"Like, really anything?"

"Really."

Her eyelids flutter as she looks away and out the window at a passing punk with tall spiked hair, leather, and chains.

She sighs and looks down and says, "A singer. A diva."

"Like Jennifer Lopez?" I ask.

"Like that," she says, looking back at me.

"Okay," I say. "I'll take care of it."

Her eyes stare into mine. One corner of her mouth curls up and in a quiet voice she says, "I think you mean that. I can sing, you know."

I nod that I know and say, "I wasn't just watching your body."

"But it takes more than that," she says,

staring at the small candle that burns in its glass by the salt.

"Just money," I say.

"Yeah," she says. "I love the way you say that."

"I mean it," I say.

"I know you do," she says.

"No one will hurt you again," I tell her, reaching out and holding her hand in mine. "No one will touch you. I swear to God they won't."

That night I am awaked to find her standing beside my bed. She is touching my cheek with the back of her fingers. I draw back the sheets and she slips inside and clings to me tight. I hold her and stroke the back of her head, drifting back into sleep.

In the morning, I lock myself up alone in my wood-paneled study to make some serious phone calls. I raise my voice and the price often enough to get my point across for some immediate results regarding Helena's career. Then we go for a walk.

The sky is bright blue between the tall white clouds. We pass Buckingham Palace with its sea of red and yellow tulips, gold gilt statues, cascading fountains, and high wrought iron fence. We walk under the towering London plane trees along the lake in St. James's Park. Ducks dip and splash in the green grasses poking up out of the dark water. The breeze is warm and cinders crunch under our feet. We cross the gritty Horse Guards Parade, and Helena clings to my arm while we stop to watch the Royal Horse Guards change posts in their blue tunics and red plumed helmets.

Soon we're passing by the bronze lions beneath Nelson's Column in Trafalgar Square. I reach out and run my fingers along a cold metal mane. The big black cabs swirl around us like miniature bread trucks. When we mount the steps of the National Gallery, I hurry through the columns and go right to the room where van Gogh's *A Wheatfield, with Cypresses* takes center stage. I stand in the doorway and freeze. The trees burning like green flames and the brilliant yellow of the wheatfield fill my mind with thoughts of Lester. He would want me to be here, enjoying this painting, helping this girl. I see his smile and the glint in those magnified eyes.

"Are you okay?" Helena asks.

She reaches up and touches the corner of my eye, and I feel the dampness on my skin.

"Just thinking," I say.

"Can I tell you what happened?" she asks.

"With you?"

"How he got me."

"Of course," I say. I take her hand and start to move through the rooms of paintings.

"I was supposed to be with my mother," she says. "She was an actress from Montreal. She left my father when I was eight and we went back to Canada. I didn't see him much, but she got a part in an off-Broadway show, so I was staying with him. I didn't find out until a lot later, after I ran away, but she died in a car accident on that same tour in Tulsa, Oklahoma. I was ten.

"My father was a bookie. I didn't know that when I was a kid, just that he was on the phone all the time talking about games and he always had money around the house and a gun. Actually, when I went to look for my grandmother and found out that she was dead, I also found out about her brother — my dad's uncle. He had something to do with the casinos down in New Jersey."

She looks up at me, and I give her hand a squeeze. We stop in front of Monet's *Houses of Parliament, Sunset,* dark and forbidding.

"Anyway, I was walking home one night from a friend's," she says. "It was winter and raining little pieces of ice. I heard a gunshot half a block from my house and saw people running. By the time I got there, a police car came around the corner and ran into the snowbank. A cop got out and ran into the house.

"At first I couldn't move," she says. "I actually wet myself. The cop, he went in with his gun. He was big and he had on a black leather coat with his badge on his hip. It all happened fast."

We move from the Monet into a room with a special exhibit on Joseph Turner. I see *The Slave Ship* on loan from Boston and move toward it. It's the original of the print Lester had hung over my bunk in A block. Carnage and horror in an angry sea. The sun going out on the horizon like the last tail of a gas flame.

"I think I know who he was," I say.

"I'll never forget his face," she says. "My father was on the floor. He was bleeding and there was a gun. That cop, he picked it up and he and my father started to argue. They knew each other. I knew that because they were talking about being partners. And then they started shouting and he shot him. He just put the gun right up to

287

my father's head. I tried to scream."

I look from the painting to Helena. Her eyes are shiny and brimming. She wipes them with the back of her hand and her voice breaks.

"Then he took me," she says. "I didn't move. I couldn't. He just picked me up under his arm like some ogre. He dumped me into the trunk of that police car. He said, 'Pretty little thing.' Smiling like I was a doll or something, and do you know what I said?"

She laughs. A harsh grating sound like the cries of the ravens at the Tower of London.

She looks at the painting, nods, and says, " 'Policemen are my friends.' That's what I said.

"I learned it in school."

35

I've seen an occasional tear from Helena before, but nothing like this. She starts sobbing loud and hard. People move away from us in ripples. I hug her tight and sit her down on a bench, stroking her hair until she stops shuddering. During it all, a white-haired guard clears his throat and starts toward us, but I back him down with a glare.

She grows quiet and I say, "Better?"

She nods her head and says she's fine.

"Come on," I say, taking her by the hand. "I've got a surprise."

We catch one of those big black London cabs back to my flat.

On our way up the elevator, Helena sniffs and looks up at me without raising her chin. I smile and wink. She smiles back and slaps my thigh.

The flat is decorated in antiques, velvet, rich-grained wood in dark hues, marble tops, and swirling gold gilt. The ceiling is a rococo sky with puffy white clouds and feathery angels. A strange collection of men and women are clustered about the furniture near the white marble fireplace. When we go in, they stop talking and turn to stare.

Several teacups clink as they're put back onto their saucers. A tall thin man with a mustache clears his throat and fiddles with his ascot tie. A round little man in a dark suit with wispy hair and liver lips steps forward with a scowl and in a thick Manchester accent says, "What's this all about?"

"Helena," I say, turning to her, "meet Peter Darwin. He's your manager."

"Is this really *serious?*" Darwin says, snorting and choking at the same time.

"No," I say. "When I said a million up front, I meant two."

Darwin's face relaxes and then blooms into a smile.

"Well, well," he says, opening his arms. "You should have said so. Let me shake your hand."

We both shake his hand and then I lead Helena into the midst of the others. The tall ascot tie is her lawyer. The chunky pink-haired woman with cat glasses is her clothes coordinator. The effeminate wisp of a man in black with the shaved head and tortoiseshell glasses is her hairstylist. The pretty green-eyed woman in the sweatsuit is her choreographer and trainer. The white-haired black man is her voice coach. And the little old lady with the straight back and the napkin laid out on her lap is for etiquette.

Helena shakes their hands and nods her head. The little old lady tells her to look people in the eye, dear, and Helena sticks out her tongue, then grins at me.

"Just money," I say to her, then I turn to them. "Thank you all very much for coming. You're here because you're the best. Everyone's getting the same thing. A three-year contract at ten times your normal fees. From what I know about your talents and hers, Helena will be the biggest star the music industry has seen since, who? J-Lo?"

"Honey," says the hairstylist, "with those cheeks and a few highlights she'll make J-Lo look like the tramp she is."

The old lady sniffs.

"You've got three months," I say. "We need an album and an act. I've already booked a studio at Warner Bros. to shoot the videos with Joe Pytka. I'll make my G-V available, so going back and forth will be easier than getting to Scotland. We'll release the first single in late December."

Someone whistles and I hear the words "fast track."

"That's why you're getting the big money. So, I had lunch brought in for everyone and then you can get right to work," I say, leading them to the dining room, where a buffet in shiny silver service waits for us.

Helena leans into me as we fall into the back of the line and says, "This is a joke, right?"

"If you think working your ass off is funny," I say, kissing her forehead.

"Is that supposed to scare me?"

"I don't think that's possible."

"You're right."

She looks up into my eyes. Hers are burning.

"You'll be on your own, you know," I say. "I have work to do in New York."

"Why not here?" she asks.

I don't think she realizes it, but she's gripping my forearm. I pat her hand and say, "I have a job to do. Besides, I don't want to crowd you."

"You couldn't."

"Maybe not," I say, "but I won't."

"What if I need . . . or want you?"

"Tell you what," I say, giving her hand a squeeze before taking it off my arm. "I'll check in."

"What are you?" she says. "My fairy

fucking godmother?"

"A lot of things are going to change, you know," I say, lowering my voice.

"That's bullshit," she says.

I touch the smooth skin on my face and turn to go.

"What the hell is all this? What about lunch?" she says.

"You need to do this," I tell her. "Without me here every minute. Then you'll decide what you want to do.

"No one owns you, Helena. Remember that."

"You're goddamned right," she says, raising her voice and her chin at the same time. "I can do whatever the hell I want. And if I want to give it away I can do that too."

I nod and step backward and say, "I'd like that very much, but we'll see."

36

I really don't want to interfere with Helena's progress. And I really am busy with my own plans. Still, we speak almost every day and she keeps me up to date. While her version of things and Darwin's aren't quite the same, in a little over two months her first single starts right off at number seven.

Since she's filming a video in Los Angeles when I get the news, I grab my plane and head out there for a visit, promising her dinner at Chez Nous. We land in Burbank earlier than expected, and instead of going to Hotel Bel-Air, where Helena's staying, I have the car take me directly to the studio on the Warner lot where they're already shooting the video for her next single. During the ride, "Love to Hate You" comes on over the radio and the DJ makes the appropriate fuss over the hot new artist named Helena.

I tap my foot as I listen and drum my fingers on my leg. Buildings and the trunks of palm trees glowing orange in the late-day sun whiz by on North Hollywood Way.

The lot is snuggled up next to the back side of the dusty green Hollywood Hills. The limo passes through the gates after only a brief stop. We go by French Street, where Bogart met Ingrid Bergman in *Casablanca* and come to a stop in front of a studio the size of an airplane hangar. The doors are open partway and they're wheeling a helicopter inside on a massive dolly.

Darwin is waiting and opens the car door. His face is flushed and beads of sweat have broken out on his forehead even though the shadows are long and cool.

"She's fucking lost it," he says.

"Easy," I say. "What happened?"

"Money is money, but this is too much," he says, his face pinched. "Put a fucking gun in my ribs. You believe that?"

"What'd you do?"

"Me? She won't fix her hair. Won't wear the costumes put out. Won't stop cursing like a sailor. She's a mean bitch, I'll tell you. Makes Ozzy Osbourne look like he came out of charm school."

"What'd *you* do?" I ask.

"I just told her," he says. "One top ten single isn't shit. You know that. I told her if they can't see her tits, they turn the channel."

"Well, you shouldn't have said that."

"Tits are tits. This is the record business."

I press my lips tight and look at him in his flowery silk shirt. He's much more respectable in a tie.

"I'll talk to her," I say, pushing past him and walking into the dark cave of the studio.

"Not now," he says, catching up. "They're almost ready to shoot."

An enormous man with long stringy blond hair and a face as big as a shovel is down on the floor in the middle of it all with a camera on his shoulder. Joe Pytka. He shouts directions, and every time he barks a ripple passes through the brightly lit set. There are fifty people milling around, some of them in tall canvas chairs clustered around a monitor, servers behind a catering table complete with a roast beef under a heat lamp, but most of the people are hurrying to and fro with lights and electric cords and power tools. The helicopter is suspended from a crane now and its rotors are twirling lazily.

There is a girl with Helena's proportions hanging out of the open door of the helicopter with a wind machine blowing back her long brown hair. A stand-in wearing a low-cut purple dress and lots of cleavage.

After a minute, without removing his eye from the camera, Pytka shouts for Helena. There is a flurry of activity in the back corner of the set. Young men and women wearing headsets and carrying clipboards suddenly part and from behind a curtained area Helena emerges with a makeup woman dusting her face, the hairstylist fussing, and the little old lady glaring up at her and running her mouth.

Helena doesn't see me, but she makes a beeline for Pytka and, standing over him with her legs set apart, says, "I'm wearing this."

She's dressed in faded jeans and a snug purple T-shirt.

"Goddamn it," Pytka says, struggling upright. "We're already two hours behind."

"You said the color had to be right," she says. "Now I've got your goddamned color."

"The hair color certainly isn't right, but that's not *my* fault," the bald hairstylist says with a hand on his hip.

"Who the fuck asked *you?*" Helena says, turning on him.

He wilts. The little old lady presses her lips tight and closes her eyes.

"Darwin!" Pytka bellows.

"See?" Darwin says to me. "See?"

He waddles toward the director with his hands raised.

"Helena," I say.

When she sees me, her face lights up. She runs and jumps and wraps her legs around me, kissing my face until I can't help smiling.

"*What* are you doing?" I ask.

"Shooting a video," she says, kissing my lips and climbing down.

She takes my hand and squeezes it.

"We're at number seven."

"You pulled that gun on Darwin?" I say, making my face stern.

"Oh, he's an ass," she says, tugging at me. "Come look at this trailer. It's a star trailer."

She's smiling, but I can see the water in her eyes. I let her pull me outside the studio. Her trailer is around the corner. She's talking to me fast, telling me about songs and clothes and the people that she's met. I stop her on the steps.

"Helena?"

Her face crumples up and two tears streak down either cheek. She gives her head a quick shake.

"I'm sorry," she says, then turns and runs around the back of the trailer.

By the time I get there, the engine of her yellow Boxster is racing and the car takes off with a screech. I run back to the front and jump into my car.

"Follow her," I tell the driver. My driver is excellent and we keep up. It's after the rush, so the thick flow of traffic is moving steadily. She's not trying to lose us, but she's not stopping to talk either. She takes 134 out to the 405 and all the way down to Manhattan Beach as the sun drops into the Pacific. She parks the car right next to the stairs to the beach, hops out into the hazy dusk, runs out along the wooden walkway, and disappears. My heart hammers inside my chest. A blood-red sun smolders beneath the smoky purple clouds. It's as if she's been swallowed up.

I jump out before the car has even stopped. When I reach the stairs, the warm salty smell of ocean laced with dead sea-things hits my face. Helena is halfway to the water, and when I call her name it's swept away by the breeze. I run through the sand, kicking my shoes off as I go to increase my speed. When Helena reaches the water, she goes straight in.

When she's ankle deep, she drops to her knees.

She starts to splash water up onto her

face. When I reach her, she's crying hard.

"This shit," she says, furiously rubbing her cheeks and eyes, smearing the heavy makeup and making a mess of her face.

The surf rolls and crashes, sloshing water up over the waist of her jeans. I kneel beside her and hold her to me, clutching her head to my chest. She shudders and the red is gone from the sky by the time she stops. A star flickers and an airplane blinks, crawling toward Asia.

"Don't you want this?" I ask after a time.

"I used to come here when I was a girl," she says in a whisper, looking out at the night. "There was this old whore. I hated her. I think she did it to make me feel how small I was, come here at night and see the stars. The ocean.

"She'd stand there with her arms crossed and I could always smell her cigarette, even though the breeze goes the other way."

"I told you," I say. "That's all gone now."

"I'm so dirty," she says.

"You never did anything wrong," I say.

"I did so much."

"They did it, not you," I say. "Stop blaming the victim."

"I know everyone is trying to help," she says, "but I can't stand them telling me what to do. What to wear. My body."

"It's an act," I say. "It won't change *you*. Your voice is beautiful. They said it in *Rolling Stone*, but that's not enough. It's a business. Your look. How they sell the act.

"Come on," I say, lifting her up out of the water.

"You're wet," she says, flicking the water off her fingertips into my face and giggling.

"Can you behave yourself?" I say, holding her arms.

A wave crashes.

"Will you still take me out to dinner to celebrate number seven?"

"After we dry off."

"Okay," she says. "Then I might."

37

Bert calls me from the airport and tells me they're here. I choose a black suit, white shirt, and burgundy tie from the closet, checking myself in the mirror. My hair is short now, a wild mess of gel and dark blades. The fashion in L.A. My skin is bronzed, the result of mixing my mother's Mohawk blood with lots of sun. Dark eyes stare back at me, nearly empty except for a distant glimmer. Water at the bottom of a well.

I might be fifty or I might be twenty-five, and since I'm much closer to the former, the corners of my lips curl up into a smile.

In New Orleans, outside the Omni Royal Hotel, I sit with my legs crossed on a cast-iron bench nestled in a bower of red geraniums. It isn't more than ten minutes before a long black car pulls into the brick-paved circular drive. Out on the river, a freighter blares its horn. Closer by, a carriage horse clops along on the street. The humid Louisiana air is thick with the smells from a nearby bakery tainted by last night's leavings of garbage, spilled beer, and horse dung.

Two young men get out of the limo. Allen Steffano, Lexis's boy, is tall and angular with brown eyes and a face that is so similar to his mother's that my stomach turns cold. His friend Martin Debray is in his mid-twenties. Debray is a friend of the Steffano family and a surrogate older brother to Allen. He is freckle-faced and redheaded. Built lean like Allen, only not as tall or as muscular.

The two stretch and blink up at the bright midday sun, then slap each other high five, excited like the rest of the visitors to be at the Super Bowl. Allen tells the captain that the bags are in the back, then takes out a pair of sunglasses. His black T-shirt is skintight and his jeans are baggy and frayed at the bottoms. His moccasins go for $345 a pair.

The captain takes a twenty and gets back to work, slowly shaking his head.

Allen has wavy dark hair. He's lean, but with wide shoulders and the thick upper arms of an athlete. Up close I see his eyes are shot through with shards of yellow. As if he senses the intensity of my gaze, they meet mine, and I look away.

While they check in, I cross the lobby toward the elevators. When they get on, so do I.

"Excuse me," I say, looking at Debray. "Are you with the NFL?"

"Not me," Debray says, smiling and shaking his head.

"But we've met, right?" I say. "Seth Cole."

"No," Debray says, shaking my hand. "I don't think . . ."

"In London," I say, cocking my head and snapping my fingers. "That's it, Debray, right? Martin Debray. At the Dorchester Hotel. Oh, you were pretty messed up, but I'd lost my wallet somewhere in their bar and you paid my bar tab. I was already checked out. Had to catch the first flight out. God. Small world."

He brightens and says, "That's where I stay."

"Well, thanks again," I say. "Talk about embarrassing."

"Not a problem," Debray says. He sees me looking at Allen. "Oh, I'm sorry, this is Allen Steffano."

I shake Allen's hand and say, "Listen, I've got some passes to the commissioner's private party tonight at House of Blues. Any interest?"

They look at each other and their mouths drop open.

"The NFL commissioner?" Martin says.

I nod and, taking the tickets out of my suit coat pocket, I say, "Lots of players will be there. A few of the owners. How about if I meet you there at ten and buy you back a couple drinks?"

Martin looks at Allen and smiles. He looks back at me and says, "Great."

"Sounds good to me," Allen says.

I make a show of extending my wrist so they can see my gold Cartier watch and say, "Great. Ten, then. I'll find you."

That evening, I have dinner with Woody Johnson — the owner of the New York Jets — at Commander's Palace, where the New York Strip steak is as thick as my fist. The truth is that after the crap I ate for twenty years in jail, I can't get enough of the taste of rare meat and red wine.

It's just past nine-thirty when we stoke up cigars for a short stroll down Prytania Street to close the deal. The air is cool, and the smell of tobacco smoke is refreshing after a day of the swampy New Orleans humidity. When we're finished, I raise my hand and a long black Humvee rolls up to the curb, appearing from nowhere. Bert hops out of the back wearing a tuxedo and opens the door. Woody stares and shakes his head at me, saying he'll

305

walk back when I offer to drop him off.

Five hundred dollars got us a motorcycle escort for the night. Behind the cop's spinning blue light, we slice through a Quarter swollen with traffic and milling with drunken sports fans, making it to House of Blues by ten.

I see the boys standing at the bar drinking and swiveling their chins around like bobblehead dolls at the star players and the girls decked out in tight tops with bare midriffs. I greet them with warm handshakes and order another round. The drinks haven't arrived before the commissioner — who's standing close by — breaks off his conversation with Falcons owner Arthur Blank to introduce me to his wife, Jan.

"It looks like Seth is going to be the new owner of the Jets," he says to his wife.

Allen looks like someone just tossed a drink in his face. The commissioner introduces Arthur Blank and his wife, Stephanie, who grabs Michael Vick. The boys' eyes are wide and they set their drinks down on the bar and stand up to shake hands. Small talk, and then we're alone again.

Allen says, "You're buying the Jets?"

"It's not official, yet," I say, sipping a Heineken.

"He's buying the Jets," Allen says to Martin.

"Allen plays at SU," Martin says, pointing at his friend with a bottle of beer. "He wants to be Chad Pennington."

"I love the Jets," Allen says, his eyes shining.

"To the Jets," I say, raising my glass and touching it to their bottles of beer. I have to force myself not to stare at Allen's face. The nose, the shape of the eyes. All Lexis.

Santana croons from the stage and the crowd hoots and cheers. Music and smoke swirl together, soaking up the beams of flashing colored lights. Red. Blue. Yellow. Green. We talk in shouts above the music.

"You really play?" I say, looking into his eyes and not at his face.

"Quarterback," Allen says, looking right back at me.

"He's got a chance to be the starter this year," Martin says, raising his bottle and clinking it against his friend's.

"What are you studying?" I ask.

"Well, I'm gonna go to law school," he says, "but right now I'm actually studying painting."

"Painting to law school?" I say. "That's different."

"My dad wanted me to study finance,"

he says. "Finance and football. He was pissed when he heard, but my mom calmed him down. Anyway, I get to paint for four years. Then I either make it in the NFL or it's law school. Something useful."

"There are plenty of useless lawyers," I say. "Not enough good painters, though."

Allen cocks his head to one side and says, "You sound like my mom."

I keep the drinks coming fast, and after an hour we're all best friends. The boys are going to join me for the game tomorrow in my box on the fifty-yard line. The drinking becomes a small unspoken contest with me the loser. Finally, Allen is swaying. Martin's eyes go in and out of focus and he looks at his bottle and mouths the words on the Budweiser label to himself.

I look at my watch. Midnight. When I look up, I see her. A woman moving through the crowd attracting the attention of every man within twenty feet. Her hair is long and straight. Brassy blonde. It's hard to decide which is more impressive, her figure or her golden face with its powder blue eyes and red lips. She isn't tall, but wears a pair of white pumps that match her snug satin dress. She stops when she sees Allen, and stares. A smile pulls back her delicate lips to show perfect white teeth.

When the girl turns and disappears into the crowd, Allen grins at me. I nod and he staggers after her. Another girl sits down next to Martin. He raises his head and dives in. Bert appears and I tell him to take Martin and his new friend back to the hotel. I leave by the back, my shoes clanging softly on the wrought iron stair that takes me down into the brick alley. I jog for two blocks before I spot the white dress. Allen is right there with her, stumbling to keep up. His head bobs and his hands dance in the space between them. She laughs at him in a high-pitched chirp, then touches his cheek. He takes her arm and they keep walking. I follow, staying on the other side of the street and half a block back.

They plunge into the mob on Bourbon Street, but the girl's dress is like a beacon. They go up one block then leave the throng, turning down St. Peter. By the time I reach the turn, they are at the dark end of the street, a bad and dangerous place where the blight of the battered Creole cottages is disguised by the star-light. The din of Bourbon Street is almost distant now and what was only a moment ago the sound of celebration has taken on a fiendish quality. Mad laughter. Breaking glass. Trumpets and grating shrieks.

A dull breeze rattles the leaves overhead. Shadows stir and begin to spill from the porches and out into the street. Dark shapes of men materialize and close in a loose ring around Allen and the girl in the white dress. Perfectly orchestrated.

I stop in my tracks to watch.

38

The hall on the top floor is long with red carpet and gold trim around the doors. Laughter floats out from behind a door. A tray of chicken wing bones and an empty beer bottle rests outside another. Allen has a suite of rooms down the hall from me. Debray is passed out in his own room, the girl already gone. Allen lets his arm slip from my shoulder and he falls onto his own bed, rolling face up. He smells like alcohol and his eyes shine up at me.

"My father says, 'I always have to bail you out,'" Allen says in a slurred voice. "But *you* bailed me out this time."

"Happy to do it," I say, grunting as I pull off his shoes.

"That was some stuff," he says, his hands chopping at the air, sound effects squirting through his lips until they roll into a merry chuckle. "Bruce Lee stuff, right?"

"Something like it," I say, backing away from him, feeling for the door.

"And now I owe you a life," he says,

holding a fingertip up in the air, his eyes directed toward the crystal fixture over the bed and losing their focus. "That's how they do it over there in Japan or whatever, you know. A life."

I tell him I know, and then say good night. His eyes are already closed when I let myself out into the hall.

Bert is standing at the bar in my suite with a beer in his hand.

"Everything go well?" he asks.

"Clockwork," I say.

When I ask him what he's doing, he looks across the broad living room at my bedroom door. It's closed and I left it open. Bert shrugs, but he's smiling.

"What?" I say.

"Not telling," he says. "Can't."

I cross through the overstuffed furniture and grab the brass lion head handle, turning it. Inside it's dark, but as my eyes adjust, I see the shape of a woman in front of the open tall glass doors that lead out onto the balcony. I feel my heart tighten. Moonlight spills through and a breeze moves the ghostly curtains, making me think for an instant that it's my imagination. Helena has been in L.A. finishing up another video and wasn't supposed to have arrived until tomorrow. Her first single went to number one in its second week and never came down, so it wasn't a huge surprise when she was asked to sing at halftime of the big game.

I step softly and feel the breeze on my face as I reach out for her bare shoulders. She's straight-backed in a white silk slip. Her hair is different now, wavy and glowing with highlights, even more beautiful than before. Since I've only seen her occasionally over the past few months I've been able to marvel at her rapid evolution since our talk on the beach.

Frilly lace borders the swell of her breasts and the soft upper regions of her legs. I moisten my lips and put them to the groove between her collarbone and neck. The tangy scent of a perfume I told her I liked sends a charge from my nose down through the center of my chest.

Without looking, she finds my fingers and laces her own tight between them. When she sighs, I feel her shudder.

"What's wrong?" I say in a whisper, dragging my lips up her long neck to the bottom of her ear. "Nervous about tomorrow?"

She shakes her head no and says, "You kiss me and you hold me and then it always stops. Don't you want me?"

She even speaks differently now. Her words are soft but clearly enunciated with the timbre of a flute. My hands feel a sudden chill. My muscles tighten. That ache in my chest.

"Is it because of what they did to me?" she asks quietly. "Or is there someone else?"

"What they did is done," I say. "That's another life. A bad dream."

"Someone else?"

"It's not like that."

"But there is someone," she says, turning to me now and clasping her hands around my neck. "Something. It's in New York. I can feel it, but I don't care."

She sniffs. Tears are spilling down her cheeks.

"I'll do whatever you want," I say, holding her close.

"I want this."

She takes my hand and leads me away from the window and the moonlight and under the canopy of the high bronze bed. We kiss and on her tongue I can taste the salt from her tears. Her fingers work quickly to unbutton my shirt and plunge inside, sweeping softly up under my arms, stripping my upper body. Bumps rise on my skin in the small breeze from the open doors, but wherever her hands are I'm warm.

I pluck the straps free from her shoulders and roll the silk slowly down her torso, brushing the curves with my nose and lips, breasts, stomach, hip. The slip falls to her feet in a wavy pile. I kneel, dabbing my tongue so that a small tremor runs through her frame. She clenches my hair close to the scalp and shudders.

When I rise her hands find my belt. Undone, my pants and shorts fall to the floor — partners to her slip — and our naked bodies mesh together, feeding off each other's warmth in the night air. Helena grasps my shoulders and climbs my torso, shimmying up with her long muscular legs. Velvet around my lower back. When I lower her onto the bed, we're already one.

She lets out a small groan and it casts my mind loose to swim in an electric sea.

39

Helena and I don't talk about last night, but the sun seems to shine brighter, the chicory coffee seems to taste less bitter, and the voices of the busy city around us seem to ring. After making love again, we have a late breakfast on the terrace, then spend some time doing tourist things. The streetcar out to Tulane. Antique shopping on Royal. A visit to Faulkner's old apartment. Café Du Monde. All with Helena under a broad-brimmed hat and sunglasses to avoid attention.

At three we're back in the room, making love and taking a short nap before she has to leave to get ready for the show. After she's gone, I sit on the terrace with my feet up on the iron railing and a cup of café au lait on my lap. I'm not really thinking. I'm just feeling the warm air and the close comfort of belonging to someone after all the emptiness. I close my eyes.

How could I describe this to Lester? I think maybe a Renoir. *The Ball at the Moulin de la Galette.*

I draw a deep breath and let it go.

Bert clears his throat behind me and I turn my head slow enough so that I can feel the warmth of the sunshine moving across my face.

"They want to know when we go," he says.

I look at my watch and say, "I lost track. I'll get a shower and change and we'll go in, say, forty minutes."

I see his face and say, "What now?"

Bert shrugs and folds his arms across the barrel of his chest.

"There was this farmer south of the reservation — down by Malone — who raised a bunch of pheasants," he says. "The whites would come up from Utica and Albany and go on hunts. They'd put the birds out and spin them around so when they came back later with the dogs they'd still be there."

I narrow my eyes at him and crimp my lips.

He shrugs and says, "I just never thought it was that much fun. That's all."

"You still have to shoot straight," I say, taking my feet from the railing, the afternoon now gone.

The lobby swarms with beaming chatty

people. A real holiday. Allen and Martin are no exception. They slide into the limo after me, grinning stupidly and scrambling to pull bottles of Abita beer from the ice chest. Bert rides backward facing me. The boys sit sideways on the long seat across from the bar. Their talk is fast and pitched. Who will win and by how much. How much they bet. Overs. Unders. Point spreads. Even Bert takes a fifty out of his wallet and answers Debray's bet on who will be the first team to score.

The only person in the whole city who sees tonight the same as me is Helena. A business opportunity. Her CD is already platinum with two number one music videos. The halftime show will throw gas on the flames. And if I shoot straight, I'll infiltrate the lives of my enemies in a very personal way.

The limo moves slowly along the teeming streets behind a motorcycle cop, and people crane their necks to see inside. Allen offers me a beer and I take it. He's talking to me.

"— much did you bet?"

"I'm not big on it," I say, taking the beer and clinking the mouth of the bottle against his. "When I win, I don't really enjoy it and when I lose it makes me sick."

"Well," he says, "I'm not all that big on it, but it pays the bills in my house."

"How's that?"

"My dad is in the casino business."

"Really?" I say, letting the word hang.

"Yeah," Allen says, then turns to Debray. "I don't know how you think Atlanta won't score first with Michael Vick."

They launch into a debate where words are fired back and forth between big mouthfuls of beer.

Bert is doing a bad job of holding back his smile.

"Missed," he says quietly, cracking open fresh bottles of beer.

When the glowing spaceship form of the Superdome comes into view, even with our escort, the limo is forced to a crawl.

At the first lull in their talk I lean forward and say, "Hey, before I forget, let me get you guys' numbers for when I get to New York."

They both say sure. Debray hands me a card and I jot down Allen's numbers on the back.

"We'll have to get together," I say. "I don't really know anyone."

"Kidding, right?" Allen says.

I force a smile and say, "No. I haven't spent much time there. I bought the team more as an investment."

Allen turns to Debray and says, "Can you imagine him doing funnels with Benny Cohen?"

"I know at least one certain blonde who would be all over him," Debray says, the freckles around his wrinkled nose dancing up and down as he snickers.

"The last people you're going to want to meet is our crew," Allen says.

The two of them laugh and Bert joins in, looking at me from the corners of his eyes. He makes a gun with his fingers and fires it into the air.

"When the Jets sale hits the papers," Debray says, "people are going to be taking numbers and getting in line to meet you."

"We'll be lucky if you remember us," Allen says.

"Of course I will," I say, taking out my Palm Pilot. "You know what? Let's set up a lunch."

"Well, I'm in school," Allen says.

"When do you get back?"

"Middle of May."

I look down and scroll through the calendar.

"How about June tenth?" I say. "It's a Thursday."

Allen shrugs and says, "Sure."

"Le Cirque all right? One o'clock?"

"Okay," Allen says. "We'll be there if you will."

"I will," I say. "It's in the book. And don't underestimate the people you know. It's always better to meet people through someone you know."

"We just don't know that many people," Allen says.

"You already mentioned one important person I'd like to meet," I say.

"Who?"

"Your father."

"That's easy," Allen says. "When big mouth here tells everyone what happened last night, my mom and dad are going to want to meet you anyway."

"Good."

I look over at Bert. His finger gun is out again, but the boys are looking at me, and neither one of them can see it. He points it at the back of Allen's head, closes one eye, and lets his thumb drop.

40

I have a lot to do in four months' time, but money is like industrial grease, and things, even big things, slide into place.

On the tenth of June I check my watch as I step up to the wrought iron gates and into the courtyard outside Le Cirque. It is five minutes to one and I slow my pace and stop to admire the brass poles and the zebras and the bold circus colors so that when I walk through the door on the second floor, the big hand is on twelve.

The room is wood-paneled and trimmed with crown molding carved by hand a hundred years ago. At the long, linen-covered table in the center of the room, Allen and Martin's faces turn toward me in obvious surprise. Even the black-tied waiters look expectantly at me. There is an uncorked bottle of champagne on the table and Martin is filling his glass.

Allen jumps up from his chair and says, "Seth. I told him."

"Unbelievable," says Martin with a dumb smile.

"I told you," Allen says, grasping my hand and looking me in the eye. "Means what he says and says what he means."

To me he says, "I wouldn't let him eat. I said you'd be here."

"I'm not late," I say.

"He always is," Allen says, nodding at his friend. "I told him twelve-thirty so he'd be here on time."

"I'm sitting right here, you know," Martin says, raising his glass. "And who could blame me? I was telling Allen that it wouldn't surprise me if you turned out to be a phantasm that we both imagined."

"No," I say, "I'm very real."

"There was nothing in the papers about the Jets," Martin says. "I told everyone and they said I was crazy. I guess it didn't go through?"

"Actually," I say, looking at my watch, "I sign the papers at four o'clock today. We agreed to keep it confidential until then."

Allen is beaming.

"Told you about that too," he says.

In my pocket, I keep an emerald the size of a walnut. After we eat, I take it out and pop a powerful little mint into my mouth, offering one to Allen and Martin.

"What kind of a case is that?" Allen asks, removing a mint with his fingertips.

"It's one of three identical stones," I tell him. "At one time they were the crown jewels of the grand sultan of the Ottoman Empire. Each one priceless, actually."

"You're kidding," says Martin.

"No," I say.

"What happened to the other two?" he asks.

"One I used to finance the down payment on the Jets," I say, looking straight at him. "The other I used to buy enough shares of EMI to get a seat on their board. And this one?"

I snap it shut, shrug, and turn it over in my hand before slipping it back into my pocket. "I just liked the idea of being able to take something that valuable and turning it into . . . well, really, a piece of junk."

"Junk?" Allen says. "You just said it was priceless."

"Was," I say, taking it back out and holding it up between my finger and thumb. "But it's not a crown jewel anymore. It's empty inside and it has these little hinges. When you take the core out of something, it stops being what it was."

"And it's worthless? That's incredible."

"It's not worthless to me, though," I say. "I like it this way. It's functional."

I look down the table. They are leaning

forward so they can see my face.

"Any interest in the concert tonight?" I ask.

"Helena?" Martin asks, sitting up nearly straight. "No tickets. That thing sold out before it was announced . . . But I see by the look on your face that you've got a box. At the Garden. Am I right?"

"You're both welcome."

"You got any of those same girls from Vegas that you had in the box at the Super Bowl?" Martin asks.

"Jesus," Allen says, rolling his eyes.

"Allen has to be careful," Martin says. "Dani Rangle has a ring through his nose."

I smile at Martin and say, "Not this time, but I might be able to arrange for you to meet her dancers."

"Goddamn," Martin says, his face growing red like his hair. "Talk about fine things. I'd take any one of them."

The five backup singers for Helena are also dancers whose bodies have earned them cover space and photo spreads in magazines like *Maxim* and *FHM*.

"Martin," I say, "speaking of Bob Rangle's daughter, I'd like to meet him. I'm looking for a fund to invest in. I heard you work with him."

"That's easy," he says. "I'll talk to him

and set it up. Soon?"

"Sometime over the next couple weeks," I say, rising from the table. "Something casual."

"How about the Hamptons?" Martin says as we walk down the stairs. "They're out there every weekend. We could have lunch."

I tell him that's good and stop at the door to thank Allen for lunch.

"Are you going uptown or down?" he asks.

"Up," I say, "to the NFL offices. I was going to walk. Do you need my car?"

"No, not this time," he says. "But if you could take one minute, my parents' place is right on the way."

My stomach twists.

"You said you'd meet them," he says, looking at me as he holds open the door.

We step out into the sunlight and the sound of a blaring fire truck. My plan was to meet Frank on my own ground, but I put on my sunglasses, turn my face toward his. Over the sirens I say, "Sure, let's go."

The apartment takes up the entire top floor of an old stone building that faces Park Avenue. In a massive circular foyer, columns of polished black granite rise to the vaulted ceiling. High above, the shadows of trees from a rooftop garden flicker down through a dome of leaded glass. The white marble floor is shot through with veins of red, reminding me of animal fat. Between the radius of columns are either vaulted doorways or recessed alcoves where the broken marble busts stand on four-foot-high Ionic pedestals.

I see a noseless Caesar, then a shadow fills the adjacent doorway. Frank has grown big. His feet look almost dainty in their shiny leather pumps. A fat man in a glossy suit coat. The three-hundred-pound mark looks like a distant memory.

The jowls of his face spill out over the edge of his stiff white collar, and their color matches his blood-red tie. His dark curly hair is swept back and sleek from a gel that disguises much of the white. His eyes seem to have receded into his head like licorice jelly beans sunken in dough. His mouth is the same, still small and fat, and he still holds his chin high. He blinks at me before stepping forward and extending a hand with gleaming manicured nails.

I'm suddenly light-headed. A thin sheen of sweat rises to the surface of my skin. I can see my hands sinking into his fleshy neck and me wringing the life out of him. I feel confused, maybe even afraid. My mind drifts for a second, but my hatred is an anchor.

"Mr. Cole," he says in a gruff tone that has taken on a hint of Brooklyn. "I've been waitin' for the chance to say thanks for helpin' out the kid."

The air fills with a hint of cigar smoke, peppermint, Cool Water cologne, and the inky smell of fresh money. I hesitate before taking his hand, and when I do, my eyes are frozen on his, looking for some sign of recognition.

"My pleasure," I say, gripping his hand and trying to focus the rapid pounding of my heart into the tendons of my forearm. My words come out like an ice machine dumping its cubes. I could cave in his skull with the bronze figurine of a centaur resting on the closest column. "He's a fine young man."

My mouth is dry and my throat tight, but Frank's pale blue eyes relax.

"You got that right," he says with a slight nod. "Best thing I've got going. Plays quarterback for Syracuse. Did he tell you? I guess you know about the game. Buying the Jets, right? My casinos make a mint off the NFL."

"It's an investment," I say, "but I know

every team likes to draft hometown players when they get the chance."

"Good," Frank says with a chuckle, then he slaps Allen hard on the back and grabs him by the upper arm to give him a little shake. "But you'll have to negotiate with me if you want this guy."

"You're an agent?" I ask.

"I am," he says.

Allen's face is flushed and he looks at the floor where the toe of his shoe follows a bloodline in the stone.

"Cool under pressure," Frank says, mussing his hair like he's ten. "Just like his old man . . . All right, gotta go. We'll have to get together."

Allen watches his father leave, then he turns to me and shrugs.

"I'm sorry he's so busy," he says.

"No," I say, "don't apologize. A guy like your dad has important things going on. Believe me."

Allen studies my face and I stare flatly back at him.

"I know you're in a hurry too," he says after a blink. "Come on. I'll let you go, but I promised I'd introduce you to my mom."

Allen leads me through a great room with deep-cushioned couches and chairs and a marble fireplace I could almost stand up in. The walls are hung with oil paintings — copies, but good ones — and heavy velvet drapes. Over the mantel is a full-length portrait of Lexis standing on a cliff overlooking whitecapped water.

Her figure is straight and streamlined, draped in a deep blue dress that matches her eyes. Her dark hair is being blown back. The sky is roiling with sunbeams and charcoal clouds. Her lips are pressed together, unsmiling, and she stares off.

Allen sees me looking and says, "That's her. My dad surprised her with that painting. It's a John Currin. She hates it."

"Very pretty," I say.

"She's quiet," he says, "but she's great."

We leave the big room and walk down a long wide hallway.

"She doesn't usually let anyone in her studio," he says. "But when I told her about you and asked if it was okay, she said yes."

He stops in front of a heavy wood-paneled door, gently raps his knuckles, and then swings it open.

41

Like the rest of the apartment, the ceilings in the studio are twenty feet high. The walls are crowded with framed canvases, reminding me of the Vatican Museum. It must be everything she's ever painted. I see one work that I recognize from my past life. It's finished.

Tall arching windows face Park Avenue on the opposite side of the room. At the far end, Lexis stands just out of the sunlight at an easel. Her back is to us, hair up with the wisps of gray. She's dressed in tan capri slacks, flat shoes, and a man's dress shirt rolled up at the sleeves.

Next to her easel a small table is cluttered with tubes of paint and a wineglass, nearly empty and smudged. She stares at the blank canvas in front of her. In one hand is a brush without any paint. Her other hand hangs limp at her side, and when Allen calls softly to her, she makes no indication that she's heard him.

We cross the room and she is startled by his touch. Allen introduces us. She smiles, but when she takes my hand, the color leaves her cheeks. Her fingers are bony and chilled. Her eyes work their way around my face before she looks into mine.

She drops my hand and says, "Allen says you're new to the city."

"I found a place on Fifth Avenue, not too far from the Met," I say, handing her a card with my home phone number on it. "I'd like to have you and Frank over for dinner sometime. Why don't you let me know when you're free?"

"Of course," she says, clutching the card in her hand and bending it.

She squints her eyes at me and angles her head. Her mouth opens as if she's going to say something. I look away to study her empty canvas.

"Well," I say, holding out my wrist to look at my watch. "It was a pleasure, Mrs. Steffano."

"Just Lexis," she says in a small voice.

"Lexis. Okay."

I touch the skin on my face and feel the smooth texture where surgery has built it up and pulled it taut. Allen sees me out. On the street, he thanks me.

"She appreciates what you did," he says. "I told you she's just quiet."

"Allen," I say with a dismissive wave,

"we're friends, right? She's very nice."

"She is," he says with a broad smile that reminds me more of the Lexis I knew than the one I just saw. "See you tonight."

I turn and concentrate on putting one foot in front of the other. It's as if my legs are asleep and I can barely feel the concrete beneath my feet. She is still beautiful. Older. Sad. But the color of her eyes is the same. Those high cheekbones. And as much as I hate her for what she's become, the urge to just hold her felt so heavy in my chest that I thought I was going to fall over.

I shake my head and breathe deep. There is a Starbucks around the corner and I go inside and sit down. It takes a few minutes before I get back to myself. But I think of my father and Lester and also of Helena and everything is soon clear again.

I march up Park Avenue through the bustle to the NFL offices. It takes hours of signing papers, but Woody Johnson seems relieved to be free from his football team. Even as a non–sports fan I know that the pressure on the owner of a sports franchise in New York is unique.

The home I bought is one of the original Fifth Avenue uptown mansions, built in the late 1800s by the robber barons of the time, like Frick, Morgan, and Vanderbilt. After an interview about the team with Ira Berkow from the *New York Times*, I have dinner by myself in the second-floor dining room. Three stone-faced servants hurry in and out. Helena is already at the Garden.

Outside the French doors, I can see the sun as it drops down behind the trees of Central Park. It grows cool enough outside so that moisture beads up on the edges of the glass. I chew mechanically and swallow my lumps of meat without any real pleasure. After a mouthful of wine, I set down my napkin and step out onto the balcony. The smell of fresh tree bark reminds me of another life, when I would turkey hunt as a boy, sitting motionless in the sea of new green leaves, straining my ears and scanning the gray dawn between the silver and black trunks of the trees for a flicker of movement.

I take a cigar from my pocket, and Bert appears like a genie with a wooden match that he strikes up with his thumbnail.

"Thanks," I say. I can see the ghost of my breath and I put my cigar to the flame.

"My grandmother used to say that winter always breathes its one last breath in June," he says before the match goes out and his face is lost in the shadow of a tall potted arborvitae. "You want a coat?"

I look away from Bert and across Fifth Avenue. Beneath their crown of new leaves the tree branches are an inky web. It's impossible to know where one tree ends and the next one begins.

"I don't get cold," I say.

"You don't get hot either," he says. "Like the water snake."

I exhale a plume of blue smoke with a slow nod.

"My grandmother always said to me that every man has the spirit of an animal," Bert says after a pause. "That when our spirits travel from one life to the next, they remember where they were in the last life."

"I don't know," I say, inhaling so that the end of my cigar glows. "I remember my last life pretty well and I wasn't cold-blooded."

"What, a running deer?" he asks. "Like your totem?"

"No," I say, "a white man."

A cab jams on its brakes and the driver lays on his horn before he roars off down the street, swerving after a black Town Car. After that, I can hear the rattle of Bert's breathing above the splash of the fountain out front. Then the lights change and the next wave of traffic sweeps past. The clouds are heavy and low, their gray bellies lit by the city's amber glow.

"She's an amazing woman," Bert says.

"Who?"

"Are there two?"

"Helena?"

"I mean more than just because she's on those posters all over the bus stops," Bert says.

"I know that," I say.

"Then who's the other one?" he asks.

"I saw Allen's mother today," I say after a pause. "I knew her in that past life."

"You knew all of these people."

"Yes and no," I say. "Now I really know them."

I turn to look at Bert, but he's gone, and for a moment I wonder if he was there at all.

I go up to my bedroom on the third floor and change into slacks and a thin cable-knit black sweater, then take my limousine to the Garden. The boys are in the box and full of themselves. Helena is magnificent. After the show, we worm our way through the concrete tunnels into the vaulted green room, where I introduce them — wide-eyed — to Helena and the five dancers that accompany the show. After turning over my limousine to Allen and Martin and the dancers for the night, I get inside the long black car waiting for Helena and we go back to the Fifth Avenue mansion.

Helena showers and I strip off my clothes and wait in the dark for her on the bed. When she comes back, her long hair is wet and she's wearing a red slip. I gently pull it up over her head and run my hands the length of her lean muscular torso.

"Why do you like to stand up?" she says in an amused whisper.

"So I can get three-dimensional," I say. "I don't want to miss anything."

"Front and back," she says. Her teeth gleam in the dim light spilling out from the bathroom.

She turns away from me, arches her back, and pulls me close, reaching behind her and snaking a naked arm around my neck. She twists her head around and our mouths find each other.

After, when we're slick with sweat, I lay breathing heavy with her cheek on my stomach. When I ask her if she's tired, the only response is a soft snore. I stroke her hair, still damp from the shower but full now and slippery smooth.

I ease out from under her, cross the thick oriental rug to my closet, and pull on a pair of jeans. Wearing a dark T-shirt and driving shoes, I step softly down the sweeping spiral stairs, running my hand along the smooth marble banister. A small table lamp outside the library dimly lights the hall on the first floor. The weight of the bronze door handle is cool and it clanks when I turn it to let myself out into the night.

Past the fountain and the white lights mounted on the stone gateposts, the park across the avenue is like ink. I smell the cigar before I see the orange dot of its glow. The image takes me back to the night I delivered Roger Williamson's letter. My heart skips a beat and the hair rises on the back of my neck. I walk toward whoever is standing there looking at my home.

As I cross the street, I can begin to make out the enormous shape of the smoker standing in front of the low stone wall that marks the edge of the park. When the cigar glows orange again, my foot is on the curb and I see the round cheeks and narrowed eyes of my friend.

I exhale and say, "You're up late."

"There's lots of things going on in there, you know," he says, swinging his chin over his shoulder at the murky park. "Bad things. Good things too. I like to walk in there, but not on the path."

"I bet you scare the hell out of people."

"They don't see me," he says, drawing on his cigar. "I'm an Indian. You're the one who should be sleeping."

"Come on," I say, and turn to walk up the sidewalk toward the Metropolitan Museum of Art. "When you've been where I was, you don't like to waste time sleeping."

"Did you get done what you had to tonight?" he asks, stepping along beside me.

"Allen and his friend were impressed," I say. "Especially when they saw Helena."

"She's impressive," he says. "I'm surprised you let her run around all over the place the way she does."

"She's a star, Bert. That's what they do. Go on tour."

"You ever see the way she looks at you whenever she gets ready to leave?" he asks.

"I see her."

"Like she's waiting for you to stop her."

"Why would I do that?" I say.

He glances at me, then jams his hands into the pockets of his coat. The cigar ember glows, then he exhales.

"Isn't just walking like this wasting time?" he asks.

"This is living," I say. "Especially if you've got another one of those Cubans.

You hear that wind in the trees?"

"Here," he says, digging into the front pocket of his jean jacket.

We stop under a wrought iron streetlamp and he lights me up. I draw in the rich smoke and let it linger in the back of my throat before exhaling and watching it hurry away.

We smoke while we walk, not saying a word until we reach the steps of the massive museum. Bright lights shine down on the towering columns and the colorful banners above, each the size of a tractor-trailer. One announces the contents of an Egyptian tomb, another the czar's Fabergé eggs, and the third a Rembrandt exhibit.

"Can you imagine trying to break into this place to steal a painting?" I say.

Bert looks the building over from end to end, then up and down with a wrinkled brow. The ember of his cigar flares and he exhales a plume of smoke.

"You'd have to think big," he says finally.

I nod and say, "I knew a guy who thought big."

"What happened to him?"

I shake my head and say, "In the end it killed him."

I start back toward the mansion and we

walk for a while before Bert says, "Is it gonna kill you?"

"No," I say, taking the cigar out of my mouth. "I'm not the one you have to worry about. But there are some people out there who'll think just getting killed is a pretty good deal."

42

"I'm going for a jog," Lexis said to her maid. She was dressed in a velour sweatsuit and sneakers with her hair tied into a ponytail.

The girl nodded without looking up from her work. Instead of taking the elevator, Lexis quietly opened the door to the stairs, looked behind her, then started down. She let herself out through the maintenance door in the back and jogged down the alley. When she came to the street, she looked before turning right and heading toward the stench of the Third Avenue subway station.

On the platform, she watched the stairs. When the number five train came, she waited until the last second before getting on, the doors nearly closing on her foot. She stood swaying in the car, scanning the faces until she got off on 77th Street. Traffic was heavy. The last remnants of rush hour. Even the sidewalks were crowded with people, and it was a slow-going jog until she reached the park. She snaked her way south, staying off the main paths, looking over her shoulder from time to time.

Tree leaves rustled overhead in a sweet breeze. A duck quacked on the Pond, taking off into the dusk, and its sound echoed off the stone face of the wall bordering 59th Street. Lexis looked behind her at the shadows that had grown thick. She knew Frank liked to keep an eye on the people who were close to him. When she swung her head back around, a jogger coming the other way startled her.

The Plaza Hotel showed its white face through the trees, illuminated by lights that made its green roof practically glow. Lexis smelled the horses and thought of the times she'd taken Allen for long carriage rides through the park. They'd take one every birthday until he turned fifteen and brought a girl of his own. A tradition between the two of them. She thought of others. Reading before bed at night. Museum exhibits on Saturday afternoons. Early breakfasts at E.J.'s while Frank slept in.

A young carriage driver wearing a stovepipe hat looked down from his white carriage and rattled his leather reins.

Cornell Ricks's long stooped back jumped out at her. He sat at the Oak

Room bar, bent over a martini, stirring it absently with a straw, and glancing to his right and left. In front of him on the dark wood was a bowl of mixed nuts. Like most of the people, he was dressed for business. His suit was gray and the thick burgundy and blue stripes of his tie were punctuated with a Harvard pin.

"Thank you for coming," Lexis said, when she was directly behind him.

His pale cheeks flushed and she felt her stomach knot up.

"I'm sorry for the secrecy," she said.

"Not at all. Please," he said, sliding his stool over her way. "Sit."

Lexis looked around at the crowd and said, "Do you think we could get a booth?"

"Of course," he said. He made his way to the hostess and bent over, speaking into her ear for a moment. She nodded and took two menus, pushing through the crowd and seating them in a leather booth right away. What light there was seemed to be absorbed by the dark wood panel that surrounded them.

"I bring the governor here when he's in town," Cornell said to Lexis with a toothy smile as they slid into the booth. "So I'm good for business."

Lexis forced a smile, but it quickly

faded. Cornell leaned over the dark wood table and she could smell the gin.

"So, what can I do?" he asked in a throaty voice.

"I know Frank is a very big contributor," she said, looking down at her hands and nodding to herself.

He nodded right back and said, "And that's why I'm here."

"Can you help *me,* though?" she said, looking up and lowering her voice. "Without saying anything?"

"Like . . . a favor that Frank doesn't know about?" Cornell said.

"Yes."

He leaned back and, smiling, said, "In politics, when someone wants you to have a cup of coffee it's because they want to ask you something easy. A drink lots of times will mean something shaky. But then you're not in politics, so I wasn't sure."

"Everything with Frank is shaky," she said. Her hands were cold and damp and she slid them between her legs and the leather seat. The murmur of conversation around them was interrupted by a woman's high-pitched cackle.

"Not you, though," he said. "You're not shaky. You're just the mystery."

"There's nothing so mysterious," she

said, biting the inside of her lower lip and raising her chin.

"I didn't mean anything," he said, raising his hands before he took another drink.

"Of course I can help you," he said.

Lexis drew in a breath and let it out slowly. When she was finished, she spoke in a rapid burst of words.

"There was a man we all knew. Frank. Bob Rangle. Me. It was twenty years ago. He got life without parole for killing a woman. A stripper. I want to find out what happened to him. Where he is. If he's still even alive. Can you do that and tell me?"

"That's it?" he said.

"Yes. That's it."

"What was his name?" Ricks said.

"His name was Raymond White," she said. "It was 1984. Up in Syracuse."

Ricks shrugged and said, "That's not even hard. If he got life without parole, he's sitting in a jail somewhere."

Lexis pinched her lips and nodded. "Just make absolutely sure —"

Ricks held up his hand and said, "Please. The governor trusts me for a reason. Any information I get is just for you."

43

Upstate New York in the summer is beautiful in many ways. Its waterfalls and the cool clear water of its lakes. The ancient mountains that make up the tail of the Appalachian chain. Rolling fields of yellow wheat, emerald alfalfa, and rustling stalks of corn. Vineyards. Stone mansions. Lonely farmhouses with ancient shade trees and towering views. But to me, none of it is more impressive than God's view.

As my G-V banks to the north in its approach to the Syracuse airport, I can see the glimmering copper strips of the Finger Lakes stretching west toward Buffalo as they reflect the setting sun. I can see Ontario, the big lake with its oceanlike tides and its icy depths, perfect for cooling the nuclear reactors that pump out plumes of white steam into the blue sky. And from here, through the sleepy orange haze, the quilted farm fields and the carpet of hardwoods in full bloom look like the perfect place for a giant — or God himself — to lie down and nap for a century.

I turn to Bert and see him craning his neck for a view of something outside the window on the other side of the plane.

"What are you looking at?" I ask.

"Home," he says. "I think."

"It's out there," I tell him.

"Like a rabbit pen," he says, shifting his massive frame in the leather seat and wrinkling his nose. "We used to own it all."

"You're talking like a white man," I tell him. "Maybe you shouldn't have cut your hair."

Bert feels the blunt ends of his black hair that now falls no farther than his collar.

"You know what I mean," he says. "I know no one can *own* the land, but if anyone is going to say they own it, it should be the Akwesasne."

"Speaking of our people," I say. "Tell me about our brave friend Andre and the reformed Russo. You said you had news about the two of them, but we never talked about it."

"Because you were busy," he says, slitting his eyes, "like a chief getting ready for war, a chief who keeps no counsel but his own."

"Bert," I say, "I think you're jealous."

Bert scowls and says, "I just liked it better when it was you and me and not all these white men in suits with briefcases and sunglasses and those wires sticking out of their ears.

"That's how we lost all this," he says, stabbing his big nose toward the window. "Our chiefs took counsel with the white man's spies."

Bert talks like this when he gets worked up. Sometimes I think he's playing the part of a culture he only knows through old whispering voices.

"I thought you said I'm keeping no counsel but my own," I say, fighting back my smile.

"Well, you're not keeping mine," he says with a sharp nod, folding his thick arms across his barrel chest.

"Okay, medicine man," I say, "tell me the tale of Andre the dog leg and give me your counsel."

Bert looks at me from the farthest corners of his eyes and says with a note of satisfaction, "Your plan to reform the white snake you call Russo was like a fart in the wind. He took the money you gave him and did he fix his hotel or pay his loan? No, he did just what you asked him not to. He put together a drug deal to get every kid from the Thruway to the Canadian border high for the life of a crow."

"What's the life of a crow?" I ask.

"Seven years," he says. "Don't interrupt my Native American clichés. Anyway, it gets better. He brings Andre into the deal."

I smile.

"Andre?"

"Yeah, and they set up a buy from some downstate Haitians, but the deal goes sour and Andre ends up blowing away both of the Haitians. Well, the police know Russo isn't the shooter because Russo took a bullet from the same gun in the leg himself, but they'd got him for the drug deal and an accessory and he's out on bail until the trial."

"And Andre?"

Bert shrugs and says, "He's up on the reservation. He's fine so long as Russo keeps his mouth shut. The Akwesasne is a sovereign nation. You know that. He won't get sold out by our people. We only sell out when it comes to our mountains and our lakes and streams."

I nod and pour myself a can of seltzer over some lime and ice while I digest this news.

"See," Bert says, "your own counsel. That's all."

"I want to see Andre," I tell him. "I think I have a job for him. See if you can get a hold of him and have him come down to New York."

"I don't know if he'll leave."

"Send him some money and promise more. Andre always wanted to be rich and famous," I say, looking back out the window as we begin to descend. "He wants to be a rock star, remember? Tell him what I did for Helena. Tell him I have a deal for him . . . He'll come."

As we approach the airport, I can't help myself from searching out the quarry my father worked for so many years. It's there. A gaping wound in the earth. Small yellow machines crawl in and out, like maggots except for their trails of billowing dust that glimmer in the late-day sun.

There is a black rental Cadillac waiting for us on the tarmac. I drive to an office building in downtown Syracuse. Instead of going in the front, we walk around back into the shadows of the building by the Dumpsters. Mr. Cooper, the agent from Vance International, is middle-aged with dark wiry hair, a crisp white shirt, and a dark blue suit. He is standing and waiting outside by the door in the glow of a single halogen light. He flips shut his cell phone and shakes our hands.

"He should be —" the agent starts to say, but before he can finish, the door swings open and a wiry old Mexican appears with a bag of trash.

"This is Mr. Orroyo," Cooper says.

I extend my hand. The old man looks up at me and blinks before taking it. His hands are small and gnarled.

"Thank you for talking to us," I say. "Mr. Cooper says you worked for Dean Villay at his lake house."

Orroyo shifts the bag of trash from one hand to the other and nods.

"He knows he's not going to get into any trouble, right?" I ask Cooper.

"He's fine," Cooper says. "I talked to him."

"Mr. Orroyo?"

"Sí," he says looking down at his feet. He lets go in Spanish and Cooper begins to translate.

"He worked for Villay," Cooper says. "And saw him that night."

"The night his wife drowned?"

Orroyo looks at me and nods.

"He hit her?"

Orroyo nods and winces and lets it fly.

"He heard her scream," Cooper says. "He hit her many times. With a baseball bat. Then he put her in the sailboat and dragged it out with the powerboat. When he came back, the sailboat was gone."

"And he wasn't alone?"

Orroyo talks and Cooper says, "No. She was with him."

"His new wife?"

Cooper talks to the old man, listens, and says, "Then she was the girlfriend."

"And you've got the bat?" I say to Cooper.

"It was buried in the garden right where he said," Cooper says. "The blood type matched. We'll have to exhume her body to do a DNA."

I turn to the gardener and say, "I'm not blaming you, Mr. Orroyo, but can you tell me why you didn't tell this to the police?"

Orroyo looks puzzled and Cooper translates.

He nods at Cooper and looks up at me with his small dark eyes and rattles the bag as he talks.

"He told me already," Cooper says. "He wasn't there to talk. He was there to work. Cut grass. Plant flowers. Work, not talk. That's what he does now. He works. He doesn't like this talk . . ."

Orroyo lifts the top off the Dumpster and heaves his bag in, letting the top fall with a crash.

"Does he know we found him because of the ten-thousand-dollar check Villay wrote him after the wife died?"

"Sorry, Mr. Cole," Cooper says with a shrug. "He's sticking to that story. Says it was a bonus for good work. He says it's the American way."

Cooper slips Orroyo an envelope that I know is full of cash, and without looking at me the old man goes back inside.

"Here's the lab report on the bat along with the police report and the coroner's," Cooper says. "Says she was caught up in the rigging. There was a strong south wind that night and it banged the boat and the body up against the stone break wall there in town for quite a while. Could be why they didn't suspect anything if he caved her head in."

I take the envelope from him and pull out the reports, examining them under the bluish light.

"I don't know what kind of a witness he'd make," Cooper says, jerking his head at the door. "I think you'll need him, though, to make the connection to the bat, but it was tough just to get him to do this."

"Don't worry," I say. "He won't have to testify."

"Oh," Cooper says. "The way you had us

put this thing together, I thought you were going to try to have it prosecuted."

"It'll be prosecuted," I say, stuffing the papers back into the envelope. "He'll prosecute himself."

Cooper gives me a funny look. I thank him and we leave.

44

I get onto 690 West and we leave the city, skirting Onondaga Lake. When I was young it was the most polluted body of water in the world. If you stood on top of the soda ash cliffs you could smell the raw sewage swirling in the shallows. The worst part was what you couldn't see. A lakebed festering in a stew of mercury- and PCB-contaminated muck.

I read they're rehabilitating it. Dredging. Capping. Treating the sewage. Sucking out the poison with wells and pumps like it was a big snakebite.

The sun is well gone and the pink-and-burgundy glow in the west reflecting off the choppy water makes it blood red. I roll down my window and sniff the air. Nothing.

Bert looks from the water to me and says, "They say you can fish in it now."

"Not me," I say.

"Me neither," he says. "Not to eat. Hey, you missed it."

We drive under the overpass that leads to Skaneateles.

"There's a place I want to see on the way," I tell him.

We get onto the Thruway and off at Weedsport, then drive into Auburn. The prison glows in a bath of halogen light, and I crane my neck as we roll past. I cross the bridge and pull into the parking lot across from Curley's Restaurant. When I get out, Bert follows me. I walk toward the grim fortress, crossing the bridge where Lester was killed. Below, the water babbles through the rocks. I can smell the weeds growing thick on the banks. Above the sheer forty-foot wall, the shape of a guard shifts from one side of the glass tower to the other. He puts one foot up and leans out over the yard with his arms folded on the railing.

It could easily be the same guard who killed my friend. Lester's words ring out in the warm night.

You could have a nice life for yourself. Isn't it enough to be free?

I listen to the water and feel the open night all around me. I have a beautiful woman who loves me and I'm rich beyond reason. I run my hands along the top of the broken wall, my fingers finding the cool smooth stones pushing up through the irregular concrete.

Lester's words repeat themselves in my brain and in a whisper I say, "Yes. It should be."

"You do some time here or something?" Bert says in his low rumble.

I nod, staring at the wall. Then I look at him and say, "And why would I take the chance of doing more?"

"What are you talking about?"

"You want a drink?"

"Sure."

We cross the street, hustling out of the way of a sagging pickup with a bad muffler, and duck into Curley's. The hostess — a heavy young blonde with Viking braids and thick lips — smiles and nods to us as we push past toward the bar. People are three and four deep, but Bert muscles in and reaches over several heads to take a pair of Molson Golden bottles from the bartender.

The beer fizzes in my mouth. My stomach is empty and it goes straight to my brain, easing the tightness in my chest. I repeat Lester's words to myself and shake my head. When I feel someone's elbow in my back, I move closer to Bert. Whoever is behind me takes up the space I gave and I get another elbow amid an eruption of laughter.

I spin around with my hand up, ready to repel whoever it is with a shove until I see three uniforms. Guards from the prison blowing off steam. The blue stubble on the cheek of the one who elbowed me makes my stomach sick. He turns to glare and my whole body goes numb. Bluebeard.

He says, "You got a problem?"

"You do," Bert rumbles, pushing past me and bellying into Bluebeard, "if you don't get some manners."

When Bluebeard's eyes leave me I realize he doesn't know me and the fear eases. To him I'm just a tourist, someone soft who can be intimidated.

"This guy's shoving me," Bluebeard says, his voice now more of a whine, and he steps back from Bert looking up.

Bert shakes his head and turns away. Under his breath he says, "Asshole."

Even when Bluebeard and his friends melt back into the crowd I can see his dark eyes and feel the stubble of his face against my ear. My sickness turns quickly into hatred, then boils to a rage, and I have to leave. I burst through the doorway into the night and suck in the air and the weedy smell. Lester was wrong. It's not enough to be free. Exact revenge is every bit as valid on the outside as it was on the inside.

By the time Bert and I get to Skaneateles, it's dark. People in shorts with sweaters tied around their necks stroll down the sidewalks. Wrought iron streetlamps glow much the same way they did when this place was a stop on the Pony Express. Ahead is Shotwell Park on the tip of the lake, a narrow green lawn between the street and the water. People have their blankets spread under the big hardwoods so they can listen to an old-fashioned brass band that's set up in the big white gazebo. Boats filled with families bob on the water, anchored up close for the show.

Just before we reach two-hundred-year old Sherwood Inn I slow down and make a right on West Lake Street. Bert shifts in his seat.

"Aren't we staying there?" he asks, nodding at the inn.

"Up here," I say.

Bert goes silent.

Gingerbread houses and tall turn-of-the-century clapboard mansions line the street. Ahead, the road darkens and bends to the right. I slow down and a small groan escapes Bert when I make a left between two stone posts whose wrought iron gates stand open to welcome us. While the other

360

homes on the street are illuminated with accent lighting, we drive up a winding way under the black shadows of soaring maple trees with only the murky hint of a mansion up ahead.

"It's his house, isn't it?" Bert says.

"Whose?" I say calmly as I stop the car and turn out the lights. Its crested mansard roof and Second Empire tower cut a jagged silhouette against the night sky. The ancient trees, gnarled and rustling, lean over us and the windows. Empty pools of darkness stare down. The porch sags at one end, and even in the night you can see the peeling white paint on the trim.

"My grandmother used to tell me about the Wendigo," he says. "You ever hear of that? The bird spirit that swoops down on people at night and carries them off? The Wendigo drags his victims across the tops of trees until their legs are nothing but bloody stumps."

On the side of the house a loose screen door raps its frame in the gentle breeze. Its rusty springs softly groan.

"It's a lake house."

"It's too dark," he says. "If you don't believe in spirits, man, I do."

Bert leans my way in the dark front seat. I can see the big round surfaces of his cheeks in the green glow of the digital clock.

"This is where he killed her, right?" he says.

"So?" I say.

Bert exhales loud and slumps down in his seat. A firefly blinks across the pitch-black space in front of the windshield, and I'm conscious of the smell of new car leather and carpet shampoo.

"I can feel her," Bert says.

Bert is breathing heavy now, and in the clock's glow I can see the growing patch of fog on the windshield. The loose door's hinge continues to squeak.

"Good," I say, opening my car door. "Come on. We're spending the night. You need to get over it."

"Why is that?" Bert asks, his hands braced against the dashboard as if we're going to crash.

"Tomorrow morning, I have a contractor meeting us at seven and another guy to put in some electronic equipment. We're going to fix this place up," I say, "and I want you to stay here and make sure it gets done fast. A month at the most. I want a staff and a good cook."

"Like some plumbing or something?"

"No," I say. "A total renovation. I have the plans."

"Never happen in a month."

"You pay ten times what it usually costs. Twenty. Fifty. A hundred. People do anything if you offer them enough money. You'll get it done."

"What's the hurry?"

"I'm going to have some guests," I say, "and I want everything just right . . . for their homecoming."

45

Being a congressman wasn't enough for Bob Rangle. I suspect he never felt like all the people whose backs he had to scratch ever really respected him. He wanted to be one of the ones being scratched. Now he is.

Rangle turned his connections on Capitol Hill into money on Wall Street. Hedge funds. High-risk. High-profit. Profitable enough to attract a second wife named Katie Vanderhorn. Old-money New York. Lots of invitations to all the right events. High on family name, low on family money.

Katie Vanderhorn — who still goes by her own name — has an unusual fondness for Allen's friend and my new acquaintance Martin Debray. Debray apparently has a good relationship with Rangle as well as the missus, because it's a phone call from Debray that lands me on the Rangles' deck overlooking the ocean in East Hampton.

"Do you work for Rangle?" I ask Debray as I adjust my sunglasses and sit down in a large rattan chair facing the ocean surf. I can taste salt on the morning breeze and it cools my bare legs. Sea grass rustles out over the dunes under sunlight broken and scattered by the puffy white clouds. Beyond them, the sky is the palest blue. It's pleasant here now, but the redwood decking that surrounds the pool and the cedar railings have been baked gray by a brutal summer sun.

"No," he says with a feigned smile. "Not at all. We work *together* sometimes. I actually manage an equity fund for Chase and sometimes Bob will bring investors in."

"So you're introducing me as a professional courtesy," I say.

"As a friend," Debray says, sitting down across from me and crossing his legs with a smile.

"I appreciate it," I say.

"The best business I've ever done was out here in the Hamptons," he says. "You develop relationships out here, and that's what business is all about, isn't it?"

"Sometimes. Sometimes it's about results," I say.

Debray is looking over my shoulder. He bumps his smile up a notch and jumps to his feet.

"Seth," he says, taking an auburn-haired

middle-aged woman by the arm, "this is Bob's wife, Katie Vanderhorn."

I stand and take her hand before looking into her yellow eyes.

"My pleasure," I say. "I've heard so much about you, Ms. Vanderhorn."

"I know a Cole family," she says, "from Boston. Are you a Boston Cole?"

She has the high cheekbones of a fashion model, but the skin has been pulled back tight on her face. It's shiny and smooth, unlike the loose wrinkles in her neck. She keeps her pointed chin in the air and her back straight. Her auburn hair is full and long and she's dressed in a robe that hangs open to expose a fancy gold one-piece bathing suit and an impressive chest that also looks like it's been under the surgeon's knife.

"You wouldn't know my family," I say. "They were originally from Belgium. My great-great-grandfather was a minor noble who found a way to put the family money aside for four generations."

"An unusual way to maintain a family name," she says.

"Yes," I say, "but an interesting and effective way to produce incredible wealth."

"Money, money," she says. "You sound like Bob."

"I think you'll find I have manners too," I say. "I hope so. People say even a sliver of reputation with you will leave me welcome anywhere in New York."

She sniffs at this, splays her fingers, and looks down at her nails.

"Martin tells me you bought the Jets," she says.

"Yes," I say. "I thought that if I was going to live in New York, I should own a team."

"I happen to like tennis," she says with a limp smile. "I understand you and Bob are talking business? I'll let you two go then."

"I hope you'll join me for dinner sometime with your husband?" I say.

"I'm old-fashioned that way," she tells me. "If Bob says we're having dinner, then we're having dinner."

Then with a quick glance at Debray, she slips away and out across their private boardwalk toward the beach where someone has already set up a towering blue-and-white-striped cabana.

Debray's eyes linger on her bare legs and a perfectly tucked bottom before he turns to see me looking at him and goes red. A voice from the direction of the house makes us both turn.

"Ah, you met my wife."

It is Rangle, his face sharper than ever. His big dark eyes, barely separated by that pointed nose; great wealth has made him complacent. He has a little mustache and his hair has been dyed as if he tried to match his wife's, but instead of auburn, it's a strange swirl of orange and black. The top of his head is covered with a flap of the stuff, combed over from his right ear. The long fingers of his left hand are clutched in the right. Next to him is a dish.

"Martin," Rangle says, "introduce your new friend to Dani, will you?"

"Of course," Debray says, then introduces me to the young college girl who I know is Rangle's daughter from his first marriage. She is short with dark hair and a body that's curvy and tight.

The girl looks me up and down as she takes my hand. There is a hungry flicker in her dark eyes and a smile that shows just the tips of the small pointy teeth she inherited from her father. She slips out of her robe, throws a little arch in her back, and struts over to a deck chair. There is a small black spider tattoo poised above the crack in her bottom. She sits and begins to oil her brown stomach.

"She's a sophomore at Penn," Rangle says, grinning so hard in his daughter's direction that the corners of his eyes disappear into a web of wrinkles and his teeth gleam in the sunlight. "All A's, and boys lining up like jets over La Guardia."

"Oh," I say. "I thought Martin said she was going with Allen Steffano."

Rangle's elation fades. He looks at me with half a smile and says, "You know young girls. Engaged to one man one day and marrying another man the next . . ."

I feel my face get tight and I tilt my head, studying Rangle hard. For a moment, I feel more like the mouse than the cat, but that can't be.

"Don't get me wrong, Allen's a good kid. But I think I've raised a girl who knows the importance of reputation. Allen's father has done well, but he's a long way from Katie's Christmas party list."

His good girl looks over at me, smiles, and crushes her lower lip with her teeth.

"I understand the mother is a little odd," I say.

"A painter," he says with a nod. "Very pretty, though. But let's sit down and have a drink before lunch."

"Daddy," says the girl, using her hand as a visor against the sun, "I want a drink. Would you?"

"Of course, kitten," Rangle says.

He asks us to sit and he hurries behind the teak bar to mix her a screwdriver, then he hurries across the deck to deliver it into her hands. His pale thin legs protrude from his khaki shorts and move with the awkward gait of an insect. The daughter rewards him with a kiss on the cheek. Debray is smiling as if this is par for the course.

When Rangle returns with bottles of Chimay Belgian Ale for the men, I swallow a mouthful before saying, "I'm pretty direct, Bob. I know you make money, and I want to invest some with you or I wouldn't be here. I have a hundred million I want to move, but . . . what do you think of the Russian stock market?"

"The Russian?" Rangle says, his bony fingers clenching the beer bottle. "Do you have people there?"

"If I didn't," I say, "I wouldn't want to invest in it."

Rangle's beetle eyes dart to Debray and back.

"Why me?" he says, twisting his fingers.

"I need an American," I say. "Someone with a big fund. Someone respected. Someone who isn't afraid to use the information that's available to him. I see you've done well in U.S. treasuries and I'm assuming that it's no coincidence that Martin has an older brother who works closely with Alan Greenspan at the Fed."

"I trade on instinct," Rangle says with a smile, opening his arms, palms up.

"I prefer to trade on information," I tell him without smiling back. "If you're not interested, neither am I. Thanks for the beer."

I take a sip and get up.

"Seth, Seth, Seth," Rangle says, taking my arm. "Please. Sit. Don't be so damn . . . Of course I'm interested. We just need to talk about it. I'm interested. We're both interested, aren't we, Martin?"

"Yes, we are," says Debray.

At lunch, Katie and Dani join us and I tell them all about Andre Kaskarov, a Russian prince whose family escaped the revolution and survived by guile and ruthlessness in Belgium. The mention of royalty gets even Katie's attention. Andre, I explain, was educated in the American embassy in Brussels from an early age. His father envisioned a new Russia where opportunity between East and West would create incredible wealth to go along with the Kaskarov family's noble lineage, and he returned to Moscow with his family in 1991.

"A real prince?" Rangle asks, his eyes agleam.

"There are lots of them," I say with a shrug. "A prince in Russia isn't like the prince in England, but they're still nobles."

"Of course I'd love to meet him," he says. "I think Katie would too, and Dani. We should have dinner."

Dani forces a smile and raises her glass of chardonnay at me.

"I've got a lake cottage upstate," I tell Rangle. "I understand you're from up that way. Skaneateles, it's called. Bill Clinton told me about it."

"The president?"

"Former president."

"I was in Congress during his first term," Rangle says. "I didn't know you were involved in politics."

"No, just power," I say. "Anyway, I'd like to have a small dinner there and an overnight. It's a beautiful place. I guess you know. We'll fly up and back on my G-V. Andre loves it there. We could mix some business."

"With pleasure," Rangle says, looking across the lunch table from his daughter to his wife. "My motto."

Before the coffee comes, I excuse myself to use the bathroom. I'm directed down a long oak hallway to a small marble temple with gold fixtures. After I wash my hands, I grab the doorknob. It's stuck and I hear a giggle through the wood. The door pushes in suddenly, and there is Dani with her pool robe open and her top off, wearing a peach thong. She closes the door behind her and drapes her hands around my neck, swaying.

"Aren't you seeing someone?" I say.

"I'm a debutante," she says, smirking. Her words are slurred. "We don't have the same rules. I like to play."

"I know someone you'll like to play with," I say. "I'd hate to ruin it for him."

"You won't ruin it," she says. "It likes a lot of attention."

I grip her wrist and tug her toward me, then right past. In a blink she's standing inside the bathroom by herself, scowling and huffing. I pull the door shut and walk away.

46

The top fund-raiser for the president of the United States joins me for breakfast at my home in New York City. We sit in the dining room overlooking the park. He's a fiery congressman from Buffalo who speaks in bursts of words with his hands flying into the air like a fighter throwing a series of uppercuts. When he starts in on the importance of the upcoming elections and of maintaining control of both the House and the Senate, I hold up my hand.

I tell him the deal: five million dollars to the RNC for them and the ability to make recommendations on the upcoming Supreme Court nomination for me. Before he can protest, I assure him that all I want is input. I don't care if my candidate is the ultimate selection or not, just that the president is willing to listen.

Breakfast is over. He tells me he'll need clearance and rises from the table.

I stand too and shake his hand, then I slip a bank check out of the breast pocket of my blazer and hand it over to him. He looks at the number and a small smile creeps onto his face.

"I'll call you," he says.

"By the end of the day, if you don't mind," I say, and see him downstairs to the door. The day outside is warm and bright and the sky is pure blue above the full bloom of the trees in the park.

I look at my watch. There's time for a workout before I see Andre, and I think it will do me good, ease some tension. I don't want to end up choking him. By the time I get into the shower, my limbs are trembling from weight lifting, katas, and the heavy bag.

The peaceful emptiness of physical exhaustion keeps my temper from flaring at the sight of Andre's sneer and his jutting chin. He is sitting in jeans and a T-shirt with his leg slung over the arm of a leather chair in my library. Bert stands off in the corner by the shelves of leather-bound books. His hands are clenched by his sides, his eyes half-lidded and directed at Andre.

"Pretty fucking nice setup you two clowns stumbled into," Andre says, looking around until his eyes come to rest on me. "What happened to your face?"

I ignore him and move into the high-backed chair behind my desk. I fold my hands together and look at him until he snorts.

"So, loon-man, Bert tells me you can get me a recording deal, and the truth is, I ain't got too many options these days, so here I am."

In a low rumble, Bert says, "When the hawk flies, the mouse does well to stay in its hole."

"Hey, fuck you and your grandmother," Andre says.

I hold up my hand and Bert stops in his tracks.

"I have a job for you," I say to Andre. "Helena goes on another tour starting in November. If you do the job, you get to open for her on tour. If you're good, I'll get you a two-CD deal with Virgin."

Andre's big dark eyes are gleaming and he says, "Whose fucking skull do I kick in?"

"It's easier than that," I say. "All you have to do is get a haircut, live like a prince, and be nice to some friends of mine."

"What, some fag stuff? I don't do that shit. What do you mean, prince?"

"No, there's actually a girl involved. It would be very helpful if she were to become interested in you."

"Some dog-face?"

"Believe it or not," I say, taking an eight-by-ten glossy photo of Dani out of the top drawer of my desk and handing it over to him, "I think you'll actually like this. But I'll pay you."

"So what's the fucking catch?" he asks, glancing down at the picture and squinting his eyes at me.

"Part of the deal is that you don't ask questions, Andre," I say. "That should sound familiar enough to you."

"Yeah, well you're not Bonaparte," he says, eyes flashing, teeth clenched tight.

"That's right," I say. "Look around. This is a long way from bingo. This is New York City. Big things can happen here. A record career is something I can create by snapping my fingers. Does that interest you, or do you want to go back to bingo?"

"This is some weird shit, man," he says, running a hand through his hair. "Why me?"

"Because you're perfect for the job," I say, "and I know what makes you tick."

"Yeah, what's that?"

"Money," I say. "Fame. Things I can give you, and I know you'll do a lot for them. Kill if you have to, right? I just want you to play a part. You're Prince Andre Koskarov."

"What the fuck . . ."

I explain his role. I give him some tapes to trump up an accent. I hand him a folder with his history in it. I can tell by his face that this appeals to his creative side. His eyes glow when I push a bankbook and a wallet stuffed with cash and credit cards across my desk along with the keys to a ten-room flat on Central Park West.

"Don't have too much fun," I say. "It's just as easy for me to take it all back, and I want you to do your homework. I've hired an acting coach to work with you for a few weeks. Be good."

"And why should you trust me? I'd sell out my own mamma."

"I like risks," I say. "Besides, I've got friends and you've got a warrant. Don't forget that. Not ever."

Andre is vicious, but he's not dumb. I know it won't be long before he's ready to meet the parents. I send him on his way and pick up the phone to arrange for a significant shift in the price of an oil company that trades on the Russian market. By four-thirty, Rangle's hedge fund is up seventy-eight million.

Also, I can't get Bluebeard out of my mind. The sound of his voice. The feel of that razor stubble on my neck. As a favor on the side, my Russian friends agree to send someone upstate to Auburn. They have a lively heroin trade and a good man to plant enough of it in the trunk of Bluebeard's car to put him away for fifteen years. I think that will help him see the error of his ways.

I get a call just before five. The president would be happy to hear my recommendation and give it the highest consideration as long as I understand he has to do what's in the best interest of the country. I ask one last favor: Someone in the president's office needs to call Judge Villay to let him know that the president is interested in my advice and that he can expect a call from me.

The influence of power on some people still amazes me. I let Villay wait three days — giving him time to whip himself into a frenzy of uncertainty and excitement — before I call. He talks to me like I'm a long-lost friend. I invite him to bring his wife to a small dinner at my lake house upstate in Skaneateles the following week, and he says he can't wait.

"I used to have a place on Skaneateles Lake, gosh, fifteen years ago," he says. "Have you eaten at Krebs?"

"No, but I've heard about it."

"Are you on the east side or the west?"

There is a strain in his voice.

"I think east," I say.

He clears his throat and says, "So you get the sunsets. My place was on the west side. Actually, it belonged to my first wife's family."

"I can't believe more people don't know about it," I say. "The first time I saw it — that aqua green color — it reminded me of the Caribbean."

"We used to drink the water straight out of the lake," he says. "I don't know if they still do."

"They do," I say. "Haven't you been back?"

"No. That's kind of my past life."

"Great," I say. "There's nothing like the old days."

47

When I wake up, I am sweating. My spine is rigid and my fingers are clenched. I open my eyes and realize where I am. Sometimes, in that moment between being asleep and awake, I think I'm still in the box. I turn my head into the feather pillow to wipe away the dampness. The sheet and pillowcases are combed cotton.

I don't like to sleep. Not just because I sometimes forget I'm free, but because I have already lost so much time. I inhale the smell of the tall pines whispering outside my window and wonder if any of my weekend guests will appreciate the smell and sound of those trees as much as I do. I wonder if Lexis still would, or if the cesspool she's chosen to live in has deadened her senses.

I push her from my mind and get out of bed. I do my pull-ups on the doorframe, working my arms until they're numb. Now I'm sweating and ready for a run. As I descend the carved wooden staircase, I run my hand over the smooth shiny railing, admiring the work. The foyer has newly laid tile and a crystal chandelier the size of an armchair that throws bite-size prisms of light across the face of the oil paintings on the paneled wall.

Outside, I stretch for a few minutes. A male bluebird boasts from his treetop and swallows twitter and swoop in the pale light. I start in an easy lope down the curving drive and look back up through the thick old maples at the gleaming yellow house flanked by blue spruce. The white trim around the lancet-arched windows and the new slate mansard roof is crisp and clean.

Out on the blacktop road, a colorful troop of cyclists passes me, drafting one another up the long country hill. To my right, a tractor rumbles across a field, spraying manure. The smell turns my stomach, but at the top of the next rise, the wind from the south brings me a face full of fresh lake air and I can see for twenty miles to the south end. Out on the water a handful of triangular sails glides back and forth in the dawn.

I love to run without stopping. Sweating. Free. Gliding like the boats. Soon the sun turns the sky from red to pink, then white before it rises in a blinding ball. I am numb. The sound of my breathing and the steady stream of sweat seem far away. When I reach Mandana, a small hamlet halfway down the lake, I turn back. Bert has seen to it that the staff has breakfast waiting for me at the small linen-dressed table on the back porch. Even though he is cleanly shaven and neatly dressed, there are bags under Bert's bloodshot eyes.

"Bad night?" I say.

He glares at me and says, "You expect me to sleep good here?"

"What about soaring with the spirit of the night?" I say. "Isn't that what your grandmother used to say?"

"The night sky in this place is too thick with crows," he says. "I'll sleep tomorrow night. If it comes."

I take a sip of coffee and say, "Our guests haven't even arrived and you're ready for it to end."

Bert sits down across from me and puts a napkin in his lap before taking a piece of grilled salmon off the serving plate and eating it with his fingers like a bear.

"I just hope that you don't go so far down this river of darkness that you can't get back," he says, looking steadily at me without blinking his big dark eyes. "Because you know where that river goes."

"I think with the money I have," I say, taking a bite of toast, "that I can buy a boat with a motor."

"Even a boat with a motor can't go up a falls," he says.

"I thought you hated the man," I say.

"I do hate him," he says. "I'd like him dead, but I wouldn't invite him to stay at my house before I killed him. Besides, I don't think you should mess with the spirits, man. Make them angry."

I look at my watch and say, "Speaking of angry spirits, Mr. Lawrence should be here by now."

"You better hope the real spirits don't get mad," Bert says.

"They're okay with it. I checked," I say.

I smell the smoke from a cigarette. A moment later, a man in dark slacks and leather jacket with long red hair rounds the corner of the house. He waves without speaking and tosses what's left of his butt down on the grass, grinding it with his toe. Chuck Lawrence was recommended to me by Vance. He's a former government employee. Very smart. Very connected. Very effective.

Chuck and I go upstairs to the guestroom where the Villays will be staying. Chuck holds out his palm. In his hand is something not much bigger than a pin. He points to a spot high up on the wall.

"I inserted one just like this right here," he says. "It's a projection filament. I took off the baseboard and put the transmission unit in the wall. There's another one over here that's a camera so you can see what's going on. There's a speaker here and a microphone there.

"I'll do the same thing in their house tonight," he says. "I just wanted you to see that you really can't detect it. They'll have no idea. Come on, I'll show you how it works."

He draws the shades in the room and turns out the lights, shutting the door behind us. We go into my master suite, and Chuck sits down at the desk. He opens the laptop that's hooked into the ISDN line and boots it up.

"I can call it up from my computer too. Everything is transmitted digitally," he says. "Like a cell phone. The guy who put the artistic part of it together is a special effects genius out in Hollywood. You said spend whatever it takes. What till you see how good this looks."

He shows me what the images will look and sound like, then gives me two small vials.

"Green is for him," he says, closing up his computer. "Red for her. One drop on each of their toothbrushes. Just one, and remember, green for go, he'll be the one up all night. She gets red. Stop. She'll be out of it."

"And you've got their maid in Hewlett Harbor all set?" I ask.

"Took some doing," he said. "I had to go all the way to a quarter million, but we'll be watching her and she knows it, so we should be fine. Now, they're definitely out of there tonight, right?"

"Yes," I say. "And if something happens, I'll call you right away."

"I'll be in and out in a couple of hours," he says, "so, as long as they're on that airplane this afternoon, we should be fine."

"I like it, Chuck," I say. "I like it all."

He shakes his head and says, "This one's different, I tell you that. Could have had the guy terminated a lot quicker and a lot easier."

"Too easy," I say.

48

I find Bert on the back porch leafing through *Travel & Leisure.*

"Find anything interesting?" I ask.

"Not that you care," he says, "but there's a dude ranch out in Montana that I'd like to visit someday."

"We have to get to the airport."

"You don't want me to get them by myself?" he asks, getting up.

"No," I say. "I want to give them a proper greeting."

Bert purses his lips and slowly shakes his head, looking away from me and down toward the water.

We take the black Suburban to the private airport in Syracuse. The day is warm enough for Bert to put on the AC. The G-V is landing as we pull into the terminal, long and gleaming white with its super-size engines and its upturned wingtips. It streaks past, then taxis quickly around, meeting us out on the tarmac. The pilot hurries out and hands down my guests while one of the ground crew pulls the suitcases out of the plane's cargo hold and places them in the back of my truck.

Rangle's wife, Katie Vanderhorn, is first off in a cloud of perfume. I take her hand and kiss her cheek, then say hello to the former congressman himself. Allen Steffano and Dani Rangle step down to join us. Finally, the Villays appear in the cabin door. His curly blond hair has faded to the color of frozen butter over the last twenty years, but the odd tears in his pupils still give him that faraway look. He steps down and grips my hand firmly, showing his white teeth and introducing his wife, Christina, who is lean and creamy-skinned with lustrous black hair. She looks like a model from Victoria's Secret and stands two inches taller than her little husband. Her big eyes are looking past me when she offers a limp hand. On her face is a small frown.

"Christina swore she'd never come back to Syracuse," Villay says. "Hates it here."

"I like the city," she says, offering a small smile.

"Well, I'm honored that you're willing to indulge me," I say with a slight bow. "I think you'll like it. My lake house has been completely remodeled. You'll think you're at the Four Seasons."

"Until I go outside and smell some farmer spreading manure," she says. "Oh, don't mind me. I'm sorry. I'm almost as excited about this Supreme Court appointment as Dean."

"We're a long way from that," Villay says. "But even the possibility was enough to get her to come."

"You're a lawyer as well, I understand?" I say to her.

"Bankruptcy," she says. "Latham & Watkins."

"Excellent. Well, this is Bert and we should get going."

When we get off the interstate and onto the Thruway, it is Villay who says, "I thought we were going to Skaneateles."

"There's some construction on the bypass," I say, "and it's actually quicker to take the Thruway and get off at Weedsport."

"I think that's a lot longer," Villay says, but he shrugs and closes his mouth and looks out the window.

The drive is pleasant enough. Rangle and Villay don't try to hide the fact that they know of each other and there's no tension between the two of them. If they were co-conspirators, their acting would be brilliant. For a moment, I am swamped

389

with a sensation of uncertainty, as if my mind has been bent by prison, my reality imagined. But I remind myself that although they both are guilty of destroying me, neither knows about the other.

For his part, Bert is quiet. His eyes are blank and his face sags like a glob of dough. The only sign of his hatred for Villay is the way his fingers clench the steering wheel.

From Weedsport, we go south. When we crest the hill of State Street in Auburn, I can see the guard towers. My stomach twists and I can hear a sound like waterfalls in my ears. It isn't until we are right alongside the looming walls that Rangle's wife asks, "What is that thing?"

"Auburn Prison," Villay says, before I can answer. "The worst of the worst. Mass murderers. Rapists. Maximum security."

"It's actually a landmark," I say. "Bert, drive around the wall."

Bert crosses the bridge where Lester lost his life. I look down into the Owasco Outlet at the water glinting in the sunlight. We go right on Route 5, separated from the south wall by the outlet. Everyone looks at the long gray canker rising up from the center of the town.

"Imagine," I say, "we're only seven miles

from the most pristine and exclusive water-front in the state."

"The Hamptons are farther than that," Rangle's wife says.

I look in the back to see Rangle nodding with a smug smile, beaming at his wife's comment.

"Of course," I say.

We pass the powerhouse and turn right again on Washington Street where the road runs right smack beside the west wall.

"How high is it?" Allen asks, craning his neck.

"Forty feet," I say.

"My God," Villay's young wife says in disgust, and no one speaks until we are on our way out of town.

When we get into the village of Skaneateles, Bert turns right on West Lake Street. Villay goes bolt upright and grabs the back of Bert's seat. When I look back at him, his yellow eyes are wide and the skin on his tan face is pulled tight.

"Where are we going?" he asks.

"To the house," I say.

His hand is on his young wife's leg and she is clutching it as if he's not squeezing her hard enough.

"But you're on the east side," he says, forcing a smile. "That's what you said."

"Oh, I don't really know," I say with a shrug, not taking my eyes off of him. "East, west, I don't pay too much attention."

"You said the sunsets. You get the sunsets. I said that and you said you did."

"Did I?" I say, raising my eyebrows and glancing at Bert as if he might know. "I'm sorry. I didn't know it mattered."

"No," he says, eyeing his wife. "I'm just . . ."

As his voice fades, tension fills the truck. No one speaks.

"Pretty homes," Rangle's wife says with a sigh. "I suppose if I've got to be here, this is the right street."

"That place belonged to Teddy Roosevelt's sister," I say, pointing to the classical white monster on the hilltop between the lake and us.

We're almost there now and I wonder if Villay will feel anything close to the shock I experienced on the night I was to be given the party nomination twenty years ago. Bert begins to slow and I hear Christina Villay suck in a mouthful of air as we turn into the two stone gateposts and start up the winding drive. The big yellow Second Empire house appears through the trees, and a small moan escapes Villay. I look back. His and his wife's faces are frozen and their bodies have gone rigid.

"Are you all right, Christina?" I ask.

"I'm . . . I think carsick. The motion."

Bert pulls to a stop in front of the house.

"Let's get you out," I say, jogging around to Villay's side of the truck. I open the door and Villay slides out. I hold out my hand to his wife. But she isn't moving.

"I'll . . . just . . . sit here for a few minutes," she says, staring straight ahead. Her creamy complexion has a green cast and her teeth are clenched.

"Honey, come on," Villay says, wedging in beside me and taking her arm. "You'll be all right."

She snatches her arm free and glares at him. "You let me go!"

Dani gets out on the other side, looking away. She pushes the seat forward. Allen, Rangle, and his wife slip out of the truck and make their way to the front steps, where they pause to look back at the scene.

"She'll be all right," Villay says to me, wide-eyed. "She's not feeling well. Please, you all go on in. I'll stay with her for a minute."

I shrug and turn to the others, pointing up the steps. Bert is unloading the luggage from the back.

"Come on," I say, "I'll show you to your rooms and you can change before lunch if you'd like. Bert will take care of the bags."

"I'll get mine," Allen says. He hurries back, pulls his bag out of Bert's hands, and takes Dani's too.

I apologize for being old-fashioned, but tell them since I didn't know how they normally do things that I've prepared separate rooms for Dani and Allen. I show them to their rooms and ask them to make themselves at home. Lunch will be at one and until then they can either head out on the lake with me for some fishing or relax down on the dock or on the back porch.

"I have a woman, Verna, who'll be down in the boathouse giving massages for anyone who'd like one," I say. "She's the best there is. Hands like an ironworker."

Allen asks if he can do anything to help. I tell him just have a beer down on the dock and that I'll meet him there to go fishing in a few minutes. On my way downstairs, I pass Bert coming up.

"Still there?" I ask.

He looks back and grunts. When I walk out onto the porch, Villay and his wife are shouting at each other. When they see me, they stop and stare. Villay runs a hand through his curly hair and forces a smile.

"Your room is the first one on the left when you go upstairs," I say with a smile that suggests it's perfectly normal for them to be acting this way. "I'll be down at the dock. We'll hold the boat for you, Dean. I think you should join us and throw a line in the water. Christina, just ask one of the girls if you need anything. And I've got a masseuse down at the boathouse if you'd like a massage."

"Thank you," Dean Villay says. "I'm sorry. Christina's feeling better. We'll be there soon."

I nod, then go back into the house. My bedroom suite takes up the entire south end of the house, and from the sitting room, I peer out behind the curtains at the two of them, watching their hands stab the air as they bare their teeth. Finally, ten minutes later, they embrace and then Villay helps his wife down out of the truck.

BOOK FOUR

REVENGE

You're a noble and honorable woman and you disarmed me for a moment with your sorrow, but behind me, invisible, unknown and wrathful, there was God, of whom I was only the agent and who did not choose to prevent my blows from reaching their mark.

The Count of Monte Cristo

49

When people think of upstate New York, they think of winter. Brutal cold and storms that dump four or five feet of snow. But the most vicious weather comes in the summer when a warm placid day is suddenly transformed by violent thunder, lightning, and wind that makes children whimper and smells like the end of the world.

Bert has the TV in the living room on without the sound. He points to the screen as I walk past.

"See that?" he says.

I stop and look at the radar map. A dark green wall with a belly of red, yellow, and orange oozes slowly from west to east across the backside of Ohio toward western New York.

"Looks bad," I say, peering outside at the sun-drenched back lawn.

"It will be," Bert says.

"Turn that off, okay?" I say.

Down on the expansive teak dock, Rangle's wife and daughter are lounging on deck chairs, oiled up, with their faces tilted toward the sun. Allen and Rangle are already on board the twenty-eight-foot party boat. Bert gets behind the wheel and the motor puffs blue smoke into the clean air. Villay hurries down the path, across the dock, and hops on board the boat with another apology for holding things up. Bert casts off and we ease out toward the middle of the lake.

Allen digs into the cooler and passes out bottles of Heineken. We talk about the color of the water and the smattering of new homes that mar the crest of the far hills. When we get to where the fish are, Bert drops the anchor and begins handing out fully rigged poles. I scoop up a shiner out of the bait bucket and hold up the wriggling minnow for everyone to see.

I look at Villay as I speak.

"What you want to do is run your hook through the mouth, like this," I say, punching the hook up through the bottom side of the fish's jaw and out through its tiny snout. "Some people hook them through the back, but it kills them too quickly. If you want to get a big one, something worth having, you have to hook it like this."

"What's the difference?" Rangle asks.

"Panic and agony," I say, then smile.

"The minnow thrashes longer and harder when you hook it through the face. The big ones get excited. It's like an IPO."

Rangle smiles with me. Villay is the last one to get a minnow and he hesitates. I put my hand on his arm.

"Bert will do it," I say, looking down at him.

He looks at me and smiles.

We sit quietly around the edge of the boat on padded benches, our poles dangling in the air. Waves lap against the aluminum pontoons. I close my eyes behind their sunglasses and listen, enjoying the bath of sunlight, the taste of a cold bottle of beer, and the pressure I can actually feel building up behind Dean Villay's face. Rangle and Allen talk football among themselves and Bert keeps glancing to the west while I wait.

Villay stands up and his reel clicks as he brings in his line. I open my eyes to see him inching this way. He sits down beside me and says, "I understand you're interested in my ideas on some constitutional issues."

"The president has asked me to give him a name or two," I say, slowly bringing in my own line. "Your career interests me."

"I like to think I'm as conservative as

Clarence Thomas," he says.

"I've read several of your more important decisions," I say, popping my minnow out of the water and letting it writhe in the air. "But I'm not completely clear on where you sit with the death penalty."

I cast my line out again.

The lines on his face ease. He squints at a boat going by before he says, "It's not a deterrent. We know that. But I think in some cases, it's morally justified."

"What about the innocent ones?" I ask. Everyone is listening now. "Doesn't the state become the criminal when one innocent man, even one in a thousand, is executed, when in fact he is innocent?"

"If a man is found guilty in a jury trial of his peers," Villay says with a small smile, "by definition, he cannot be innocent. Are we talking jurisprudence, or philosophy? Those are two very different conversations."

"Well put," I say, and I can see all his perfect teeth.

We catch ten lake trout between us and Bert promises to have the cook serve them with dinner. Lunch is a pleasant buffet served from silver trays and eaten on a long table on the back porch set with crystal glassware and several arrangements of fresh cut flowers. Afterward, I invite Rangle into my study. We are discussing finances when a red Ferrari roars past the window. A few moments later, Bert shows Andre into the study.

He wears a burgundy Hugo Boss shirt that matches his slacks. On his wrist is a Cartier Panther. His accent is passable and his natural arrogance is enough for Rangle to buy into his identity. We hatch a plan for manipulating the Russian stock market, then join the rest of the party back down on the dock for more drinks and sun. Rangle is twisting his fingers madly and is nearly out of breath as he introduces Andre to his daughter. He pulls a deck chair alongside hers and offers it to him. As an afterthought, he introduces Allen, who takes Andre's hand and coolly looks him up and down. The wind picks up late in the afternoon and a blanket of high mackerel-scale clouds blots out the sun.

Dinner is in the dining room at eight. We are dressed in a way that makes Ms. Vanderhorn feel at home and are seated around the grand mahogany table. Two girls in waitress uniforms hurry in and out, serving dinner. Billy Fitzpatrick and his wife, Diane, have joined us. Billy is the district attorney for Onondaga County,

Villay's old job, and his wife is a judge. Both are highly regarded by everyone, and I figure I may as well put the five million I gave to the party to some good use.

I have them seated facing the Villays at my end of the table. Allen presides over the other end, holding his mouth at an odd angle while Andre sucks down Jack-and-Gingers and boasts to the Rangles. From time to time he touches Dani Rangle's bare arm and she giggles.

After the main course is taken away, there is a lull where the conversation fades to a murmur.

I clear my throat and say, "Billy, question for you. What's the statute of limitations on murder?"

Billy's eyes are pale green and set in a round red Irish face. He looks me over.

"That depends on how well you know the DA," he says with just a hint of a long-lost Brooklyn accent. "Just kidding. There is no time limit on prosecuting a murder. It's the only crime that doesn't have one. Why?"

"Bert thinks this place has a ghost," I say. "And he says that the spirit will be restless until someone is punished. Ridiculous, I know, but I'm in a bind. Bert is the best man I've ever come across and I'm pretty fond of this place."

"What? You got a clairvoyant or something? Tarot cards?" Billy asks, dabbing his lips with the napkin.

"Not far off," I say, looking around the table. The others have stopped talking now and their eyes are on me. Villay tugs at his necktie. His wife is stiff and pale in her black dress.

"I don't believe it, but Bert," I say, nodding toward the dim corner of the dining room where he stands in a suit, watching the help, "comes from a long line of Akwesasne medicine men. He told me the first day I showed him this place that there was a ghost. I had a good laugh, right, Bert?"

Bert steps into the light with half his face covered by the shadow of his nose and his eyes narrow canyons of darkness. He grunts and nods, then like distant thunder, he says, "My grandmother always told me that the wings of the dark spirits brush the lips of the medicine man and his line. And when I came to this place, I felt that on my lips."

"Yeah, I saw a psychic one time on the witness stand," Billy says with a mischievous smile. He takes a sip from his wineglass. "Didn't go over too good, but a medicine man? That might work."

This brings a laugh from everyone, even the Villays, and the tension evaporates. While the moment is calm, I excuse myself and go upstairs. I know from the Hewlett Harbor maid whose toothbrush is whose and I slip quickly into the Villays' bedroom, where I put the right drop on each. Their room has been soundproofed, but for good measure I go through the other rooms, applying more drops from the red vial on other toothbrushes.

By the time I get back, dessert is being served and the first fat drops of rain tap intermittently against the windowpanes.

"Please. A toast," I say, raising my wineglass. "To health, happiness, young love, and the Russian stock market."

This brightens everyone except Allen, who stares passively at me. I make a point to grin at him, until finally, he smiles back. Glasses clink together and everyone drinks. I nod to the girls who wait like Bert in the shadows of the long room. They step out and refill everyone's glasses. Rangle is half in the bag and now he stands up.

"I have a toast," he says, bowing his head toward Andre so that the dark auburn flap of his hair falls sideways off the top of his bald head. "To the czar and all his offspring."

Andre looks at him, puzzled, then smiles, although I don't believe he understands who the czar is. We all drink to the czar and Rangle sits down with a satisfied look on his face that quickly melts under his wife's glare.

When Dani giggles and leans toward Andre, he kisses her ear. Allen slams his fist down on the table, jarring the china and tipping over his half-empty wineglass.

"Keep her," he says, and marches out of the room with his head high.

Andre and Dani burst out in giddy laughter. Rangle shows all his teeth and his wife looks like she ate a bad piece of fish. I signal the girls again and they pour more wine.

"A final toast," I say, rising to my feet. "To domestic felicity."

They all stare at me blankly, but raise their glasses just the same and empty them. I take a sip, look at my watch, and suggest after-dinner drinks on the back porch for those who haven't had enough. I then thank them all again for coming, excuse myself, and wish them all a good night.

50

Allen is down at the lake. I can see his shape lit by the low-voltage lights along the shore. The rain is still falling in random bloated drops. Allen appears not to mind as he casts stones from the beach into the rippling black water.

"I'm sorry," I say, toweling off a lounge chair beside him before I sit down and put up my feet.

Allen is silent. A sliver of the orange moon peers through the trees on top of the far hill before disappearing into the bank of clouds. Over the hissing of the wind in the trees I can hear the crunch of Allen's feet on the beach. He throws half a dozen more rocks into the water before raising his voice above the wind and saying, "What made you invite that asshole anyway?"

"It's really not Andre's fault," I say. "He is what he is and I have a business deal with him and Rangle. To tell you the truth, I think it gives you a good out."

"Who says I want an out?" he says, turning to face me. A drop of rain strikes his cheek and he wipes it away.

I fold my hands together.

"Allen," I say quietly. "That's a rocket ship bound for space. You want to be on it because it's fast and sleek and exciting. But whoever mounts that baby is going to burn up as soon as they leave the launching pad. You know that. I know you know . . ."

"What did you . . . plan it or something?"

"Of course not," I say. "But I'll tell you the truth. I didn't stop it, and that's because you're my friend."

"So what," he says with a small smile, looking up at the dark sky then back at me. "I owe you two lives now?"

"You don't owe me anything," I say.

"I feel like I do," he says, "even though I wanted to punch you in there."

"Violent," I say, skipping a rock of my own without getting up from my seat.

"That's my father's side," he says. "To hear him tell it, I'm practically a clone. It makes my mom and me laugh."

"Pretty crazy about your mom, aren't you?"

"Yeah," he says with a shrug. "Dani Rangle is a long way from her. I'll have to remind myself of that for the next one."

"Well," I say, rising from my seat and

looking up. "Time for bed."

"Good night," Allen says.

"As your mom would say, don't forget to brush your teeth," I tell him, and he laughs.

I watch him from my bedroom as the tempo of the rain picks up. I lose his shape for a moment in the mist rising from the water. Then his rain-soaked shape appears from the gray and the back door slams shut. Thunder begins to crash and the blackness is shattered by white bursts of light. The trees bow down and one of the old spruces cracks like a cannon.

I listen to the storm rage and wait until after midnight before I sit down with a mug of green tea and start up the computer. The Villays are snug in their bed under a blue light occasionally lit bright by flashes of lightning outside. Christina's mouth is open, her arm flung over her forehead. Villay himself is tossing and turning, muttering to himself, whining like a feverish child. His eyes are open, but stare blankly at the ceiling.

I split the screen so I can see the images projected onto the ceiling and Villay at the same time, then I start the sequence, just the way Chuck showed me. The instant Villay sees the image of his first wife's face he shrieks like a sorority girl. His head twists from side to side, but his eyes seem frozen on the image, his body pinned to the bed.

In an eerie voice, the computer-generated image of Villay's first wife begins to moan and shriek and it rises on the back of the howling storm outside, flailing above it then sinking back as if she were drowning all over again.

"You killed me, Dean," she says, wailing. "You killed me. You murdered me. You and she. Murderers, Dean. I won't leave you, Dean. You chose her, but now I'm back. I won't leave you, Dean. You killed me . . ."

On and on she groans. For Villay, it is an unending nightmare. One he cannot escape. The drug in the green vial was perfected by the CIA in the eighties, before the end of the cold war. It opens gaping holes in the mind so that horrible images and sounds can be poured in without filter and slosh around to contaminate without end.

It won't happen tonight. Or tomorrow night. But sooner or later, the drug will do its job.

It will break his mind.

51

"Incredible," Rangle says, tapping an open copy of the *Wall Street Journal* that rests on top of the black onyx slab that makes up his desk. "Russian sweet crude through the roof. That's the fifth perfect trend in two weeks."

I clasp my hands behind my back and walk across the thick rug to the window. I can see New Jersey. The Statue of Liberty gleams, emerald in the last rays of the afternoon sun.

"I'm glad you're pleased," I say.

"Do you know what someone said they're calling me?" Rangle asks. "The wizard of Wall Street. Do you think that's a compliment?"

"Of course," I say.

"It's a jealous town," he says, musing. He strokes his little mustache and then grasps his fingers.

"Pleased?" he says, shaking his head, grinning now. "My little girl's head over heels in love. My wife is happy. No small feat there. Did I tell you that Vance International got me copies of the documents that draw a direct line from our Prince Andre all the way to Alexander III? I'd go out and buy a Powerball ticket if I didn't know we were going to make more with our new Russian prince."

I put my hand against the glass. It's warm from the day.

"God, it's a long way down," I say in a low tone.

"Excuse me?" Rangle says. I hear his desk chair swivel my way.

"Did you ever look down?" I ask, glancing back at him. "It's a weird feeling I get whenever I'm up high. What it would be like to have it all rushing up at you and you can't stop it."

Rangle is beside me now. He raps his knuckle on the window.

"Safety glass," he says.

"That's right. We're safe," I say. "We're on the top. But just look."

He glances at me. His eyes flicker down toward the street and the waterfront below. Cars crawl along like ants. People are specks that barely move. He clears his throat and moves back to his desk. The intercom buzzes and his secretary announces that his lawyer is on the line and says he needs to talk to him.

"Not now," he says. "Tell him I'm with

Seth Cole and I'll get right back to him."

I turn and take a seat facing his desk. I make a steeple of my fingertips and say, "On the twentieth, we'll take a position in the Bank of Moscow. There will be a favorable announcement first thing on the twenty-third and the price will jump hard. It'll happen fast and we'll sell into the surge at four p.m. Moscow time."

Rangle leans toward me. His hands grip the edge of the dark wood desktop.

"How much?" he asks. "I can leverage half a billion after what happened with the oil. Everyone will want in."

"As much as you think is wise," I say. "Just buy into it in ten-million-dollar blocks and make sure you use different brokerage houses."

"Oh, what are you worried about?"

"Safety glass," I say quietly.

"What?"

"Nothing."

"My *God*," Rangle says, exposing half his teeth behind a smile that's close to a sneer. "This is it. The Russian market. I was on top in the late nineties and then I took a huge hit, but I told my wife, I said, 'It will come again. One day, the opportunity will be there and I'll jump on it.'"

He looks hard at me, narrowing his eyes.

His ears seem to flatten and he says, "I want a *billion*."

I nod my head and sigh.

"That sounds reasonable," I say. "And while you're at it, there's something I'd like to do . . . for Allen."

"Of course," Rangle says, "he can get in at whatever level he wants. There's no million-dollar minimum for a friend of yours, Seth. You know you don't even have to ask, just tell me."

"It's not about the fund," I say. "That's too obvious. In fact, I want this entirely between you and me. Charity isn't charity unless it's anonymous. I want to help him indirectly. I understand his father is looking for an investor in his company."

"He's been looking," Rangle says, twisting his lips. "And there's a reason he hasn't found one. That's not for you, Seth. Very sketchy. Casinos. Hotels. In his mind if he can sell his partnerships, he can get into the Friars Club."

"It wouldn't be me," I say. "But I have a friend who represents a group of Native Americans. They've got some casinos upstate and they want to get into Atlantic City. I was thinking I could put him in touch with Frank's partners. Not even go through Frank. Buy his interests out and they all live happily ever after."

"You'll be the first person on the planet who wanted to do a favor for Frank Steffano," Rangle said.

"I thought you were old friends," I say.

"That's a strong word," Rangle says. "Frank is a pompous goombah. All this casino stuff has gone to his head, not to mention his ass. Wears a goddamned diamond pinky ring."

"I'd really do it for Allen," I say with a shrug.

Rangle writes something on a piece of paper and hands it across the desk to me.

"Ramo Capozza?" I say, looking at him.

"He's out on Staten Island. Calls himself a businessman. A casino owner. Frank helped out his nephew when he was in some trouble up in Syracuse. Frank likes to tell everyone they were business partners in a development company, but he was a cop and I heard they ran a book until the nephew got murdered."

"Think Ramo's a football fan?"

"His business is gambling," Rangle says.

"The first preseason game is next Friday," I say.

"There you go."

"So, how do I get in touch with him?"

"Actually," Rangle says, picking up the

phone. "My lawyer that just called me? He knows Capozza's lawyer . . ."

Five minutes later I have a number.

52

I thank Rangle and head uptown. I'm meeting Dean Villay for dinner at Patroon. After a week, I grew weary of watching him suffer every night. Instead, I get a report every morning from Lawrence. Two days ago, he said Villay was very close, so I wanted to see him in person. The maître d' shows me to a round high-backed leather booth. Villay looks up from his glass. I can smell the scotch. I extend my hand and notice that his is trembling, damp, and cold.

"Thank you for meeting with me," I say. I slide into the soft seat and the maître d' puts a linen napkin in my lap.

Villay's curly hair is matted. He is wearing a suit, but the knot on his tie is crooked and has been pulled loose. His eyes are red-rimmed, puffy, and moist, and there are several scabs on the side of his face. He picks at one of them and says, "I still want it."

"I'm sorry?" I say, tilting my head. The sounds of the restaurant are muted.

The waiter appears and I order a spar-

kling water with lime and another scotch
— a double — for the judge. Somewhere
by the darkened windows a table of people
laugh together, then break out in polite
clapping that quickly fades.

The shoulders of Villay's jacket are
sprinkled with flakes of dandruff. He goes
to work on a different scab and leans toward me, whispering.

"The Supreme Court. I don't care about
her," he says. The ragged edges of his pupils gape open. "I care about Oliver
Wendell Holmes. I want that. Think.
Harlan, Rehnquist, Brennan. Great justices
that no one but law students remember.
And Holmes was known for his *dissents*.
Opinions that didn't even become law. The
law is malleable. People don't understand
that. *She* doesn't."

"I felt bad that the weekend didn't turn
out," I say. "And I wanted to check on
you."

Villay finishes his drink and smoothes
out a wrinkle in the heavy linen tablecloth
before clenching his empty hands.

"You know there's nothing they can do?"
he says, looking up at me through the tops
of his eyes. "They complain about me. Say
there's something wrong . . ."

He pounds the table, jarring the silver-

419

ware, and says, "Of *course* there's something wrong. That's everyone. We all have secrets. Don't we? But I am appointed for *life*. No one can touch me. Even *she* can't take it."

As the waiter sets down the drinks, Villay picks at another scab. He winces and examines his finger. A crimson smear. His knee jiggles under the table. His eyes dart from side to side.

"You're having trouble?" I say, squeezing the lime into my glass and taking a sip. Another waiter goes by with plates of steaks still sputtering from the grill, leaving a scented trail of seared meat.

Villay leans forward again, grabbing the new drink, whispering. "There should be a law against the jealousy of women. Now *that* would be jurisprudence. That would be helpful. They're like cats. Bitter. Unforgiving. Relentless. Goddamn fucking demons."

"You have a beautiful wife," I say.

"She sleeps," he says. "Beautiful, but do you think she feels? Do you think it even affects her? We went to that house . . . and she *sleeps* . . . but she caused it all to begin with."

"Dean," I say. "You need to rest."

"Ha!" he shouts, and people turn to

stare. Villay leans close again, lowering his voice. "That's the last thing I need. I need Holmes. I need to write laws that squeeze the hordes into small spaces and cull them like a reaper."

I leave a hundred-dollar bill on the table and get up.

"Where are you going?" Villay shrieks, licking his lips and hugging himself so hard that he rocks forward.

I look down on him, smile, and say, "You've lost your mind, old friend."

"What friend? Are you giving it to me?" he says loudly, then puts a knuckle in his mouth and clamps down. Those oddly torn pupils widen, then contract.

The maître d' appears beside me and says, "Is everything all right, sir?"

"Fine," I say, tossing my napkin down on the seat. "Everything is just right."

53

When my car pulls into the gate of my Fifth Avenue home, I raise my eyebrows at the sight of Andre's red Ferrari. My reports on Andre are that he spends every minute with Dani Rangle. She is showing him Manhattan in a big way. They drink rare champagne, eat gold-covered sushi, dance all night, and snort generous amounts of cocaine. Sometimes an expensive call girl will join them to finish things off at his flat.

Against my advice, Allen didn't give up on Dani entirely and there was a scene at the China Club, where she threw a drink at him and Andre threatened to break his neck. Martin and some other friends dragged Allen out and that was the last of it, but it seemed to fuel the fire between Andre and Dani even more. Still, I know Andre hasn't run out of money, even though he's doing a good job trying, so I can't imagine what would bring him here.

A servant opens my limo door before I can. I straighten the edges of my suit coat and readjust my tie knot as I walk up the broad marble stairs and into the cavernous foyer. Bert is waiting by the stairs, his eyes on the arched doors to the library.

"The dog leg?" I say, angling my head toward the doors.

Bert pinches his lips, nods, and says, "Better than that. Your old friend is with him."

"Russo?"

"The scarecrow-face himself. Birds of a feather."

"Where's the girl?"

Bert shrugs and falls in behind me. I take a deep breath and exhale before opening the door.

Russo is sitting on the couch in front of my desk. Gone is his flap of hair. A shadow of razor stubble extends from his face all around the fringes of his round dome. He is thin and pale, and his shoulders have all but collapsed. He's dressed in ratty jeans, a Rolling Stones T-shirt, and a black knit cap that pushes those ears out even farther. His Adam's apple jerks up and down in his neck and his bulging eyes dart back and forth between Andre and me. The insides of his arms are spotted with tiny bruises.

Andre is dressed in pleated navy slacks and a matching silk shirt open at the collar. A heavy chain hangs down to the smooth crease of his chest muscles. He's treated himself to a Rolex and in his hand is a crystal decanter. He hands Russo a large snifter, fills it with bourbon, and then refills his own.

"Drink?" he asks, raising the decanter.

I sit down behind my desk and say, "No. Have a seat, Prince."

"Yeah," he says, half his mouth pulled up in a smile. He throws himself down sideways in a leather chair with his legs over the arm. "I like that. And we've got some business to discuss."

He glares at me until I nod my head.

"My former partner here is down on his luck. So, he naturally sees how things are going for me and he wonders if he can get in on some of the good fortune. I guess you two know each other anyway, right?"

Russo won't look at me, but he is nodding his head so that his dorsal-fin nose cuts the air. Under his breath, he says, "Yep, that's Arthur Bell."

I slip open the top drawer of my desk and wrap my fingers around a Glock 9mm that has been fitted with a silencer. Everything is too close to happening for my plan to be disrupted by these two. I've got my in to Frank. Villay is on the edge. Rangle's financial empire is about to crash. I expected Andre to run off with Rangle's daughter or at least drag her down into addiction; she is Rangle's brightest jewel, and that would make his ruin complete. But I can't be greedy. I'll have to do without these two.

"You're a lot of people at once, apparently," Andre says, grinning at me and raising his glass before taking a swig. "And that's okay with us. We just want to get paid for the information, same as we would if we sold it to, say, the *Post* or someone. You're becoming an important man, Quick Buck–Seth Cole–Arthur Bell–Running Deer. Owning the Jets and all that."

"I think I have something that will make everyone happy," I say. "Bert, would you get that small suitcase that I keep in the upstairs vault?"

"The . . ."

"The brown alligator suitcase," I say. "In the vault. If you go, you'll find it."

Andre sets down his snifter and shifts in his seat. From his waist, he pulls out a jet black Colt .45 and points it at my head.

"Nothing funny, Bert," he says, curling his lip up away from his teeth. "I'm not here to fuck around."

"You'll like what he's got," I say, letting

go of the Glock and easing back in my chair.

Russo stands up and says, "Andre, we —"

"Sit down! You just sit the fuck down and shut the fuck up. You wanted some payout," Andre says without taking his eyes off me. "I'm getting it for you. With the money this guy's got, you sure as fuck don't need mine."

Bert returns and sets down the suitcase on the coffee table between Andre and Russo.

"Open it," Andre tells his partner.

Russo fumbles with the latch and pops it open. His eyes get wide and shiny. He takes a small knife from his pocket, nicks a bag, and touches his finger to the white powder inside. He puts his finger in his mouth, looks at Andre, and says, "Heroin. It's pure."

"About five million dollars' worth," I say. "A gift from me to you. To help keep your partner from having to sell a story that wouldn't help any of us."

"Yeah," Andre says, nodding his head and getting to his feet. "A gift. We can all still get along. We're having a good time, you and me, aren't we, Seth Cole?"

"Things are going very well," I say.

Russo closes the suitcase. Andre and he

back out of the room.

"No hard feelings," Andre says. "You know I'm working on that guitar."

"No problem. You two are doing me a favor. Our deal still stands," I say, and they're gone.

Bert stands looking at me for a moment, then says, "I thought you were going to kill those snakes."

"I thought about it," I say. "But I think this will work even better. I got the heroin from the Russians who run the market. Under the circumstances, I didn't want to refuse it, and now I've put it to good use."

I pick up the phone and call my contact at Vance International, asking them to put two agents on Andre, twenty-four hours a day.

"Just watch him. If he hurts anyone," I say into the phone, "then just tell your men to point the police his way and stay out of sight."

When I put down the phone, Bert says, "You know they'll be back for more."

"Well, it will take even Andre some time to work through that," I say. "And by then, a lot of things can happen."

54

Bert and I ride in the back of my limousine down the steep ramp and into the dark gut of Giants Stadium. At the head of the tunnel leading out onto the field, we get out and watch as Ramo Capozza's long car pulls to a stop behind ours. An eight-year-old boy wearing a Kevin Mawae jersey gets out, followed by a burly gray-haired man with thick eyeglasses and a stooped, shuffling gait. The boy is Joey Capozza and he holds his great-grandfather's hand without shame. There are three other men in suits who surround the Capozzas, carefully examining the tunnel with their scowling eyes. Their mouths are clenched tight and you can see the muscles rippling in their jaws.

I greet the old man and the boy warmly and introduce Bert as my good friend and business associate Mr. Washington. Capozza eyes him carefully up and down. Bert smiles and winks at the kid and we all walk out of the tunnel together with the three suits creating a perimeter.

As we step out onto the turf, a security

guard in a yellow windbreaker touches my hand and says, "No one on the field."

Another guard grabs him and yanks him away, saying, "That's Mr. Cole."

"Sorry, Mr. Cole," the man says, and I nod to him.

Our little group is the only one on the field besides the Jets players and their opponents, who warm up in their football pants and jerseys without the shoulder pads. The white glow of the stadium lights give the turf a false hue, and you can smell that it's not real. The air is still warm, but a cool breeze makes it pleasant to be outside.

"Pappa," the boy says, tugging his great-grandfather's sleeve. "It's Kevin Mawae and Dave Szott. Look."

"Come on," I say, "let's talk to them."

"Can we?" the boy asks.

"Sure."

The two enormous players are all grins. They sign the boy's shirt and call Chad Pennington over to meet him too. The boy bounces on his toes and makes circles around his great-grandfather as we walk back inside the tunnel to make our way upstairs. Ramo Capozza wears a silent grin. He nods to me and quietly says thank you.

Inside the suite, we sit in the front row of

the box with the Capozza muscle standing behind us drinking cans of diet Coke. The game begins, and Joey informs Bert and me who all the players are and what they do.

"I'm sorry," Ramo Capozza says, his brown eyes large but twinkling behind their thick lenses. "Joey, I'm sure Mr. Cole knows his own team."

"Not as well as some people," I say, ruffling the boy's hair. "It's more of an investment for me."

"I understand you're doing quite well with your investing since you've come to New York," he says.

I nod and say, "I've certainly expanded what I'm involved in. It used to be just art. Bert is interested in diversifying too."

"I understand that from you," Ramo says, "but we weren't able to find out much more about Mr. Washington."

"The Akwesasne are a secretive group by nature," I say with a soft laugh. "But I know that when you see Bert's financials, you'll be comfortable bringing his group in as investors. I understand you have a partner who's looking to get out and I just thought . . . well, that it would be good to put the two of you together, Mr. Capozza."

The older man says nothing more. We

watch the game until the second half. Since it's a preseason game, the first-team players are taken out. The boy's eyelids begin to droop and he puts his head on his great-grandfather's shoulder. Ramo Capozza nods to one of the men in back and he scoops the boy out of the seat, cradling him in his arms.

"I think it's time for us to go," Capozza says, shaking my hand. Then he hands a card to Bert. "Call me, Mr. Washington. I'd like to talk more and maybe you could bring us some of that financial information. I don't know what you're thinking, but Frank's interest is worth around a hundred million dollars."

"That's right around what Bert's group is looking to do," I say, and Bert nods.

We thank Mr. Capozza for his time and see him to the door of the suite. He thanks us for giving him a night his great-grandson won't forget.

"Jesus," Bert says when they're gone. "Did you see those three guys? They make Andre look like a choirboy."

"This is the big leagues, Bert."

"And you're going to send me into a meeting with all those guys without you?"

"You'll do fine," I say, taking a can of Bud Light out of the refrigerator and cracking it open for him. "You did great tonight."

"Yeah," Bert says, "with an old man and a little kid."

"Don't let that 'old man' fool you. His teeth are razor-sharp."

"Exactly," Bert says, "and I just want to make sure it's not us that get bitten."

55

We're riding in the back of the limo, quiet in the darkness, when Bert says, "How about you have a beer with me."

"What do you mean?"

"I mean, you and me. How about we just have a beer, like we used to when you lived in my trailer. Remember that?"

"Yeah. I remember."

"Good days, huh?" he says, and I see his massive shape leaning over and I hear him rattling around in the ice chest.

"Not bad," I say. "A little cramped."

"Yeah, that shower wasn't no marble cathedral like that thing you got now. But sometimes I miss just having a bologna sandwich with ketchup on white bread. You?"

I hear the snip and clink of two bottles being opened. Bert hands me one. A Molson Golden that makes me smile. We touch the lips of glass together and drink.

"I like good food," I say. "Good food and red meat."

"I see how you eat those steaks. That 'cause you got hungry in jail?"

"I did get hungry," I said.

"That go away any?"

I take another swig of beer and think about it. We're crossing the GW Bridge now and I can see all the lights of Manhattan.

"You want to thumb wrestle?" I ask.

"I thought we didn't do that no more," he says. "I thought we're a little too fancy for that."

"I don't think anyone's going to see us back here," I say, and hold out my hand. I pin him quickly and he immediately wants to go best out of three. He beats me once and then I get him again and it becomes best out of five. He gets me the next two and then we're done because by then it was best out of seven.

"You ever notice how you have to keep going until you win?" I ask him.

"That's 'cause thumb wrestling is my thing," he says. "Like fucking these people over is your thing."

"Exact revenge," I say, more to myself than to him.

"What?"

"When someone does something to wrong you," I say, "you exact revenge. You

434

take it. But it's exact too in its precision. It's about respect."

Bert only grunts.

"You're the one who told me one time that you'd kill Villay if you ever had the chance, you remember that?" I say.

"Yeah, that's different," he says. "In the old days, the Akwesasne warriors would tomahawk their enemies who fell on the battlefield. That wasn't the way it was with all the tribes. The Hurons? They'd skin 'em while they were still alive and boil them. That's pretty exact, huh? The white man's like that, but in a sneaky way. I think you get this from your dad's side."

"In a way," I say, thinking of Lester.

The car dips down into a tunnel and we lose sight of the city around us. Bert drinks the next beer on his own, and neither of us says anything until we get out in front of the mansion and we say good night.

When I get to my bedroom, I feel something. A dark figure is tucked into the curtains by the balcony. My heart races and I ease my way over toward the night table. There is a gun in the drawer.

I think of Andre, Russo, Villay, Rangle, and Frank all at once.

"Seth?"

"Helena?" I say, exhaling. I step into the

broad strip of light that falls into the bedroom from between the curtains.

She moves into the same light and throws her arms around my shoulders.

"Don't do that."

"I saw you and Bert come in," she says. "Standing in the curtains is lucky for me."

"I thought you were in Toronto."

"I was."

"I thought tomorrow was Boston."

"It is," she says, putting her nose in my chest. "Did you miss me?"

"I always miss you."

"So, you're glad I'm here?" she asks.

"Always."

"Is there someone else?" She pulls away and looks up at me.

"Is that why you were watching?" I ask quietly.

"You're different since we came here," she says. "There's something."

"Work," I say. "Just work."

I kiss her and we move toward the bed.

In the middle of the night, my eyes shoot open. I am breathing hard. Helena is wrapped around me and I twist free and sit up, dabbing at the dampness on my upper lip. I saw Villay, twisting in his sheets. I heard him moan. And scream.

It is 3:37. I look at the computer on the

desk across the room and I get up and get dressed. I resist the urge to turn on the computer. Instead, I sit out on the balcony, watching the sky above the park change from black to purple to blue while I wait for the day to come.

At 6 a.m., I am in the second-floor dining room, having breakfast with Bert, when my cell phone rings.

"He did it," says Chuck Lawrence. "It'll be on the news if you want to see. I waited until now to call. Didn't want to wake you."

"What did he do?" I ask. Bert is looking at me.

"Killed the wife," Lawrence says. "Strangled her. Then went running through the neighborhood in his boxers crying like a baby. I went in as soon as he left and got our stuff out of there. I've seen some bad stuff, but . . . Jesus."

"Where is he now?"

"They took him straight to Winthrop Hospital," he says, "that's where I am. They got him locked up in a rubber room."

By the time the psychiatrists are finished with their initial assessments and I am able to buy my way into Dean Villay's rubber

437

room it's nearly noon. He is lying in the corner wrapped in a straitjacket, sedated. His breathing is shallow and he stares vacantly at the empty wall. His face is sunken and gray and his forehead gleams with a thin sheen of sweat.

His blood-red eyes widen when I kneel and put my face in front of his. The torn pupils are fully dilated, like black stars. I speak in a whisper.

"Do you know who I am?" I say.

His eyes grow wider yet. He nods that he does.

"Cole," he says in a mutter.

"No," I say, keeping my voice very low. I put my lips next to his ear. "Look close. Look at my eyes. It's me . . . Raymond White. I'm back."

I look at him again, staring until his face crumples in agony, his eyes locked on mine.

"You can't be," he says. "You're dead."

His arms begin to squirm inside the canvas straitjacket, making the buckles clink like small spoons. A choking noise bubbles up from his throat. His head starts to shake and jerk from side to side before he explodes into an unending wail.

I put my fingers in my ears and stand up, looking down on him while he twists and shrieks until his throat is torn and an attendant comes in, nervously taking me by the arm and leading me away.

56

The windshield wipers slapped erratically across the cracked glass, making the dark road ahead barely discernible through the rainbow smudge. Andre rubbed the back of his neck, tired from holding it at an angle so he could see out of the one strip that the blade wiped clear. The play in the wheel of the '72 International Harvester made steering the wet, windy back roads a constant battle.

"Piece of *shit*," he said, stubbing out his Marlboro in the ashtray and slapping the dashboard. In the back was most of the heroin, along with three hundred and sixty thousand dollars in cash. They had dumped some of their smack in Syracuse and gotten rid of a little more outside Utica.

Andre wasn't going to do anything stupid, though. He knew the best places for him to unload it were up at the border where it would go to Montreal. He wasn't going to get caught up with another Haitian deal. He was selling only to people he knew. Then, when he had his money, he could go back to New York and check out Seth Cole again to see what else he might have.

"Should have taken that fancy car of yours," Russo said from the backseat, offering up a nearly empty bottle of Jack Daniel's.

"Shut the fuck up," Andre said, swiping the bottle from him and taking a pull. Dani was asleep, curled up on the seat next to him. Like him, she wore jeans and a white tank top T-shirt. He nudged her.

"Whaaat," she said in a long groan.

"Want some?" he said, nudging her still.

"Fuck off," she said and pulled her jean jacket up off the floor and over her head.

"Bitch," Andre said, nudging her with his elbow hard enough in the head to make her sit up and blink. "Have some."

She took the bottle and tipped it up. Amber liquid dribbled down her chin and she swallowed until it was gone.

"I love a girl that swallows," Andre said, and she cuffed him playfully on the back of the head.

"Where'd you find this piece of shit, anyway?" Andre asked Russo, looking at his ugly mug in the rearview mirror. "The junkyard?"

"Got it for four hundred dollars," Russo said, frowning. "So I don't know what you expect. You better believe I'll be buying myself a Mercedes as soon as we get back to civilization. Hey, what are we gonna drink now? There's no liquor stores open."

Instead of answering, Andre focused on an all-night gas station up ahead. He pulled in and handed Russo a hundred-dollar bill.

"Go get a case of something good. Michelob or something. And ask them if there's a decent place to get some rest around here."

"There ain't no Ritz-Carltons," Russo said, hopping out. "I can tell you that."

"He's an asshole," Dani said in a slurred voice when he was gone. She was staring straight ahead.

Andre looked up through the smeared windshield at the bright green and yellow of the BP sign and in a detached voice said, "I know."

"Why'd we even bring that ugly bastard?" she asked. "He gives me the creeps. Why are we riding in this piece of shit?"

"This is America, honey," he said. "I want to see how the real people live."

"You're talking funny."

"I been talking funny for a month," he said. "Now, why don't you give me a kiss."

"He's coming."

"So what," Andre said, grabbing the soft part of her thigh and squeezing. "Maybe we'll let him watch tonight."

"You're sick," she said, and licked his neck.

"I think you'd like that," he said, and swirled his own tongue in her ear.

The rear door opened. Russo slipped in, brushing the rain off his shoulders, and said, "Hey, hey, cut it out. There's a motel about two miles up Route 12 with HBO, can you save it?"

"We might let you watch tonight," Andre said.

Russo cracked open a can and shifted in his seat.

"You want a beer?" he said. "I got some sandwiches too."

Andre busted out laughing and Dani did too.

"You're both fucked up," Russo said, sniffing the air with that big nose and tugging at the collar of his yellow Polo shirt with its tiny blue horseman.

Andre made Russo go inside the motel office and get two connecting rooms on the end. Inside, they put their bags down and met at the little round veneer table in Russo's room. Russo set out three silver cans of beer and Andre took out some needles, surgical tube, a Bunsen burner, and a spoon. He lit a Marlboro and let it dangle from his mouth while he got to work. Dani slipped her jean jacket off, lit a cigarette of her own, and watched him, the blue flame of the burner reflecting double in her dark eyes.

"Lie on the bed," Andre said when the needle was ready. He inhaled deeply and stubbed out his cigarette.

She stubbed out hers too, then lay down in the sagging middle of the dingy bedspread and held out her arm. Andre wrapped her upper arm with the tube, stuck the needle into her vein, and removed the tube while he shot her up. Dani's eyes rolled up. She began to moan and squirm lazily on the bed.

Andre grinned at Russo and said, "You want to go next?"

"Sure," Russo said, raising his can and drinking some of the beer.

After he set it down, he lit up a Newport before he looked at Andre, exhaled the smoke, and said, "Now that she's in la-la land, I want to ask you something."

"Ask," Andre said, tapping some powder

from the bag into the spoon without taking his eyes off it.

"I heard you say something to her earlier about her cut," Russo said, taking a drag, the ember burning bright.

Andre looked up and noticed that as Russo brought the beer can to his lips it trembled slightly. So did the Newport.

"You giving her some of yours?" Russo asked, taking a gulp and replacing the cigarette.

Andre's grin grew wide and he narrowed his eyes at Russo through the smoke and said, "No. I was talking about *her* cut. She's with us. She gets a cut."

" 'Cause the way I see it," Russo said, opening another can of beer, taking another drag, and studying the table in front of him, "it's you and me are partners. I don't see me giving part of my share to her. It was you and me all along, and now all of a sudden she's here. And I know she's your girl, but that doesn't make her a partner . . ."

Russo looked up to see Andre studying him and said, "Well? That's fair, right?"

"I think the liquor's talking for you," Andre said.

"We're gonna make five million dollars and I want my half!" Russo screamed, banging his fist down on the table.

57

The beer can went over. Beer foamed out of it in a bubbling pool that started to run across the small table toward Andre. He didn't move, even when the river of beer ran over the lip of the table, spattering the leg of his jeans. Andre just stared and smiled. Dani groaned happily from the bed.

With the cigarette hanging from his mouth, Russo jumped up and began to mop the spilled beer away from Andre as if he were hoarding gold. The cigarette fell out of his mouth and hissed out in the mess. Russo used his bare bruised arm to sweep it onto the rug, then dried it on his leg as he sat back down.

"Jesus, I got *shot* in that Haitian deal. You fucking shot me in the leg, man. I could have talked and gotten off and you'd be in jail," Russo said. The corners of his mouth were pulled tight and he ran his hand over the stubble of his scalp, knocking off the black cap. "You don't want that."

"Are you gonna cry?" Andre said.

Russo's face was twisting up, wrinkling that nose and making his eyes squint.

"I want my share, Andre," he said, starting to blubber. "This is all because of me. It isn't fair!"

Andre took a deep breath and sighed through puckered lips. In one quick movement, he reached down, pulled the gun from his waist, snapped home a round, and had it pointing directly in Russo's face.

Russo winced and turned his head away, bringing his hands up as if he could block the bullet. Andre sprang to his feet, sending the chair clattering into the wall.

"You want a share? You want your own big share?" Andre said through gritted teeth. "*Fuck* you!"

The gun blast was deafening in the small space and it even got Dani's attention.

"Wow," she said.

Russo was on his side, rabbit-kicking away at the carpet as if his feet could take him away. But the blood coursing from a dark hole just in front of his ear began to slow to a dribble and his kicking became nothing more than a dying tremble.

"Fuck," Andre said.

He stuffed the gun back in his pants and cracked open the door, peering slowly outside until he was sure no one was around.

He waited there for several minutes. Not even a light went on. He went back inside and began to look around. From the bathroom he grabbed a towel and began rubbing the surfaces of everything he or Dani had touched. Doorknobs. The spoon. The needle. The chair. The faucet in the bathroom.

He loaded their bags back into the old truck, then heaved Dani over his shoulder and slumped her down in the front seat. He made one last check, leaving the bag of heroin, before tossing the towel down in the pouring rain and jumping back into the truck. He turned north onto Route 12 and checked his rearview mirror.

His mind started gnawing over all the things he could have done differently, starting with the shooting and going all the way back to when Russo showed up in the first place. He should have gone to Seth then. He had a good thing going and now he had fucked it up just like everything else. He wondered if it was the curse his old man had put on him when Andre beat the hell out of him with a tire iron. He thought about that bloody mess and his old man's words: *I'll fuck you over from the grave, I swear.*

But in a funny way, beating his old man's

head in was what got him on the road to independence. From that time on, people respected him. He was nobody's fool, not even Bonaparte's. He was the one who got the women and the drugs and the kicks, and that's what money was for anyway. He'd beat this trap same as he had the others. How could he be down when he had the drugs and the girl, and hadn't it been a kick to see the look on Russo's face right before he shot him? Not a lot of people got to see that.

He smiled at Dani and flicked his finger against her ass. She groaned, eyes fluttering, and smiled at him.

Andre sighed deeply and smiled back.

His heart rate had started to even out and he was thinking about where he'd dump the gun when he saw the flashing lights in the rearview mirror.

"Fuck!" he said, punching his foot to the floor.

Dani looked back and slowly said, "Wow. This is so fucked."

There was more than one car now, and even as he accelerated up that dark wet highway, they seemed to be closing in. His mind raced to think of a place where he could turn off. Turn off the highway and run. He could survive in these woods if he had to. He'd done it before.

After the bridge over the Big Moose River, there was a bend at the top of the hill and an old logging road right after it. He was almost there and he would briefly be out of sight of the police cars. He thought about the duffel bag full of cash. He could carry that and Seth Cole's suitcase full of drugs and be gone without a trace in this rain. Dani would have to stay behind, and he indulged himself in a small hit of pity.

Andre saw the bridge and he felt a fresh surge of adrenaline firing up the nerves behind his eyeballs. The road ran down and he was just to the bridge when a cop car pulled up off the side road on the other side with its lights flashing.

"Fuck!" he screamed, slamming the wheel, but not letting up on the gas.

The cop car came straight at him, driving right down the middle of the bridge.

"Die, motherfucker!" Andre screamed, heading dead at him, picking up speed.

At the last second, the cop car tried to swerve, but fishtailed instead. Andre smashed into the rear quarter and the big truck spun, rocked, and plunged through the guardrail. The truck seemed to hang in the air, suspended in space. Silent. Peaceful.

Then it dropped. Andre braced himself, outscreaming Dani as the heavy truck plummeted a hundred feet to the rocky riverbed.

58

Bert is dressed in a new gray pinstriped Zegna suit with four buttons on the jacket. His burgundy tie is in a Windsor knot. Miraculously, we found a pair of Ferragamo fifteen double E wingtips. On his wrist is a big silver-and-gold Rolex Submariner.

Chuck Lawrence is fidgeting with the pin in the tie that is really a camera. He lets go and gets on his tiptoes to peer up into Bert's ear.

"Comfortable?" he asks.

"You can't see it, can you?" Bert asks, fingering his ear.

"Don't touch it," Chuck says, and disappears out the front door.

"I don't know about these stripes," Bert says, looking down.

"They make you look less like a refrigerator," I say. "Don't worry. You'll be fine. You're everything you're saying you are, and I'll be right there in your ear."

"Yeah," he says, putting a breath strip into his mouth and replacing the package in his coat pocket, "I'm an Indian from upstate. But I don't own any casinos or know anything about big business. How's it going to come off when I'm just repeating the stuff you say in my ear? My grandmother used to say that a skunk in a possum's coat still smells like a skunk."

"When they see your bank records," I say, handing him the portfolio, "all they'll smell is money."

"Did you have to call it the Iroquois Group and be so fucking obvious?" he asks.

"It's a sentimental thing with me," I say. We are standing in the foyer of the mansion on Fifth Avenue. I open the front door and follow Chuck down the steps toward the white utility van with a boomerang antenna. In front of it is my limousine. "Let's get going, will you? If you're late, that'll piss them off."

Bert looks down at his watch and shuffles after me. He gets into the limo. In the back of the van are two captain's chairs and a metal desk beneath a bank of electronics with four different TV monitors. I get in the back, sit down next to Chuck, and put on my headset.

I push a red button in front of me on the desk and say, *"Bert, do you hear me?"*

"Jesus, not so fucking loud," Bert says.

453

The camera gives me a fish-eye view of the inside of the limo, and now Bert's scowling face dips down into the top of the picture. Chuck Lawrence adjusts some knobs and says, *"How's that."*

"Better," Bert says, but his tone is surly.

"You'll be fine," I say.

Chuck climbs hunchbacked into the front of the van and gets behind the wheel. We follow the limo across the 59th Street Bridge and down into Long Island City.

I watch and listen. When Bert picks up the *Post* off the seat and begins to go through it, I realize that I'm holding my breath. After I read the papers this morning, they went right in the trash so he wouldn't see. I try to make some small talk, but he keeps on turning the pages, even when I start blabbing about the Jets' upcoming game.

I already know the item on Dani Rangle is on page eleven. Two inches. No picture. The small headline reads, FINANCIER'S DAUGHTER DIES. I think maybe Bert will miss it, but he doesn't. The paper rattles and he pulls the lower corner of the page closer to his face.

After a few seconds he puts the small story right up to the camera lens in his tie, rattles the paper loudly, and says, "Did you know this?"

I sigh and press the red button. *"Let's not worry about that now, okay?"*

"You knew," he says. "Jesus."

I stab the red button and ask, *"What's Jesus got to do with it?"*

"She was just nineteen, that's what," he says, looking down into the camera, his nostrils like two dark caves. "First Villay's wife and now this."

"She was no fucking Girl Scout," I say, stabbing the button and blurting out the words before I realize I'm talking about someone who's dead.

Bert is quiet for a minute, long enough for me to wonder what has happened to my soul.

He folds up the paper and sets it down on the seat. I see him angle his chin out the window. Finally, in a low rumble, he nods his head and says, "Yeah. You're right. She was going down anyway. No problem."

His tone isn't convincing.

When we get to the East River Yacht Club, the limo goes in but we drive past and park on the road where we can see the big modern building, a rectangle of concrete with smoky horizontal windows.

Across the East River are the towering sky-scrapers of Manhattan surrounding the silver jewel of the Chrysler Building. There are other limousines out in front of the Yacht Club and men in dark suits patrolling the perimeter whose jackets are bulging with automatic weapons.

"Bert," I say into my headset, *"you're with me, right?"*

"Right here," Bert says. "Ice in my veins. Skunk in a possum suit."

"Good," I say.

Bert is frisked by the men at the door and led inside. He goes up the stairs and through a lobby. In the back, overlooking the river, is a long room with a conference table. Nearly a dozen men are sitting around with small espresso cups in front of them on saucers with small lemon peel shavings. Frank sits in the middle of the group facing the water. Ramo Capozza is at one end of the table and there is a chair for Bert at the other, where he sits down.

"It's good to see you, Mr. Washington," Capozza says.

"Thanks," Bert says.

Someone sets down a cup of espresso in front of Bert along with a sugar bowl and some cream. Bert lays down the portfolio on the table in front of him, but doesn't touch the coffee.

"Thank you for meeting with me, gentlemen," I whisper.

Bert glances down at his tie and stiffly repeats my words.

"Holy crap," Chuck Lawrence says under his breath.

"Don't look at your tie," I say in an even lower whisper.

"Don't look at —" Bert begins to say, then after an uncomfortable pause he recovers. "I mean, would you like to look at these bank papers?"

All the men are looking down the length of the table at him. It is Frank who smiles and says, "Damn right I would. Hand that stuff down here, would you, Jim?"

The portfolio is passed down by the man on Bert's left, and Frank tears it open and begins to pull out the papers. His eyes are narrowed and his massive jowls shake under the effort it takes him to breathe. The diamond ring on his finger flashes on his fluttering hands.

"In a real hurry, aren't you, Frank?" says a man on the other side of the table with a pocked face, a bulbous nose, and a dark widow's peak of slicked-back hair. "I guess our business isn't clean enough for you and all your Park Avenue friends, huh?"

Frank stops what he's doing and looks from the pit-faced man to Ramo Capozza.

Capozza intertwines his fingers and says, "Dominic, Frank has been a good partner for a long time. He's ready to do other things. That's not a sin. I told you, I like the fact that Mr. Washington's group is a new and legitimate source of financing. They know the industry, so I think this could be a good opportunity for everyone. I don't want bitterness . . ."

The man called Dominic folds his hands and dips his head. The rest of the room is silent. A tugboat going by outside sounds its horn. Finally, Bert clears his throat and shifts in his seat. Ramo Capozza nods at Frank and Frank digs back into the papers. He scans one, then another, and slides them down the table toward Capozza. The man to Capozza's right, thin and angular, wearing a creamy brown suit, puts on a pair of gold reading glasses and examines the papers as well.

I'm pretty sure the most interesting one would be the statement from The Bank of Zurich showing a statement from the Iroquois Group for one hundred thirty-seven million dollars. The other would be the state certificate of incorporation showing

Bert Washington as the president of the Iroquois Group.

The man leans toward Capozza and whispers in his ear. Capozza nods. Bert clears his throat again and this time begins to cough. I lift the headset away from my ears and look over at Chuck, who's doing the same thing. When Bert's done, I put the headset back on to catch a few words of Bert's.

"— over the numbers," Bert is saying.

The men all stare at him. Some start to mutter.

"What did he say?" I say in a hiss to Chuck with my hand over the microphone. Chuck shrugs.

"I think everyone should relax," Capozza said, raising his hand. "Donald has the books. It's nothing the different corporations don't already give to the IRS, so let's not get excited. The fact that Mr. Washington's group is thorough is the sign that they're a good group of businessmen and they'll be good partners."

The man with the reading glasses reaches down and sets a box of three-ring binders on the table. The box is pushed all the way down to Bert. Bert sits silent.

"It shouldn't take our accountants much more than a week to check through these, then,

if you gentlemen are still willing, we'll have a deal," I say into Bert's ear.

He repeats it stiffly. Frank squints at him and rolls his tongue around the inside of his mouth.

Ramo Capozza slaps his aging hands gently on the tabletop and says, "Very good, Mr. Washington. We appreciate your coming by. Now, if you'll excuse us, we have some more business here before I meet my daughter for lunch."

Bert doesn't move.

In his ear I say, *"Go shake his hand."*

"Go sha—" Bert starts to say, then stands up and continues. "I'm going to go. Now. Thank you very much."

He picks up the box, moves down the length of the table, and shakes Ramo's hand, then walks out the door. A man leads him through the hall and down the steps.

Bert is actually out the door when I hear Frank say, "Hey, Bert, do you mind if I call you Bert?"

Bert turns and there he is. Frank. Massive. Greasy. But with manicured hands and a three-thousand-dollar suit. A lump swells in my chest.

"No," Bert says.

"Good," Frank says. "Hey, Ramo told

me it was Seth Cole who introduced you. That right?"

"*Yes,*" I say in Bert's ear. "*Tell him yes.*"

"Yes," Bert says stiffly.

Frank angles his head, still looking at Bert. A small smile creeps on his face.

"Yeah, well . . . tell him from me . . . thanks. Okay?"

"Okay," Bert says. He turns away and steps toward the open door of my limo.

"Hey," Frank says, causing Bert to turn toward him again. "Don't think you're going to pull any funny stuff with those records . . .

"The last Indian war didn't go so well for you guys."

59

Frank rubbed his teeth back and forth against the face of his thumbnail. His eyes were looking out the window, but he wasn't really seeing any of the storefronts on 49th Street, he was just staring. When the car pulled up in front of the Diamond Men's Club, Frank waited for his driver to open the door. A bullnecked bodybuilder dressed in a tuxedo hurried outside to hold open the door to the club.

"Good morning, Mr. Steffano," the kid said.

Frank didn't bother to take the thumbnail away from his teeth when he asked, "Mickey in?"

"Seven a.m., same as always," the kid said, rushing to open the inner door. The girl in the cashier's booth stopped chewing her gum to stare.

It was dark inside and the red lights pulsed with the music. On the main stage a blonde girl who looked like she was about fifteen worked the brass pole at the end of the middle runway. Two guys in cowboy hats offered up creased dollar bills. Five or six other men in rumpled business suits were spread out in the dark, sitting at small round tables drinking twenty-dollar drinks.

Frank snuck up on the bartender and watched carefully as he poured a drink, then walked down the stairs, across the floor to the far wall, where he let himself past another musclehead and into the back. He passed a changing room where two half-naked girls were looking at their faces in the mirror and laughing about something. Mickey's office was in the very back, across the hall from Frank's. Frank knocked five times with a rhythm that was Mickey's special code, and after a minute the bolt lock clicked and the door opened.

"What?" Mickey said in his grouchy nasal wheeze before he peered up through his glasses and saw that it was Frank. "Frank. What are you doing here so early?"

"Why?" Frank asked, pushing the door so the knob rattled against the inside wall. "You doing something you shouldn't be? How come any time I come here during the day everyone acts real nervous?"

The space was cramped, and he kept Mickey there instead of letting him use his own spacious office across the hall even though he rarely used it himself and Mickey was there practically twenty-four seven.

"If someone was gonna try to take you, Frank," Mickey said, "they'd be doing it at night. We don't make enough money during the day to pay the phone bill. You're just intimidating. That's why they're nervous."

"Good," Frank said. He pulled up a chrome and leather chair across from Mickey's desk. On top of it sat an open folder with some account sheets, a computer, and an ashtray piled high with spent cigarettes and snowy ash. Behind the desk were a massive safe and two gray file cabinets. Mickey sat down and lit a cigarette, his small fingers struggling to hold the match steady.

"You're shaking," Frank said.

Mickey nodded toward the wall that was lined with pictures of his wife and their two teenage kids. The boy was a miniature of Mickey, small and sneaky-looking with big ears, except the boy didn't wear glasses and he hadn't lost most of his kinky orange hair.

"She's leaving," he said.

"Your wife?"

Mickey nodded.

"She can't do that. You want me to have someone talk to her?"

"No," Mickey said, exhaling. "Let her go. I got an apartment already and that little blonde thing from Sioux City is moving in."

"The girl out there on the pole?"

"How's *your* wife?" Mickey asked, squinting one eye at Frank through the smoke.

"Mickey," Frank said after a moment's pause, "how's our books?"

"Clean."

"I'm not talking just here. I mean the whole crapshoot. The casinos. The hotels. The clubs."

"Clean," Mickey said with a little less conviction.

"How clean?" Frank said, shifting his bulk toward the desk. "Clean enough so if a bunch of hotshot lawyers and accountants dug in there's nothing doing?"

"The way we got it set, it'd be a real shell game. Someone pretty smart would have to have, like, the books from all the companies, and sit down to compare one to the other and have a pretty quick eye to see what you got going on."

"Fuck," Frank said.

"Why?"

465

"No," Frank said, shaking his head. "Don't worry about that. I need to find some things out about a couple of guys."

"Who?"

"Guy named Seth Cole who bought the Jets and his friend, this Bert Washington guy who says he's with a group of Indians who own some of those casinos upstate."

"How much? How soon?"

"All I can and yesterday," Frank said. "And I want you to use all our cops."

"That much?"

"If you need to empty that fucking safe behind you, you do it, understand?" Frank said, making a fist. "I want to know who these motherfuckers are and what they're doing."

Mickey was sitting up straight now and blinking, looking around the room like he was expecting someone to pop up out of nowhere and kill him.

"Ah, I'm just jumpy. Maybe everything's just fine," Frank said, waving his hand in the air and easing back in his chair so that it gave a little groan. He looked over at a picture of Mickey and his family on a beach somewhere and his eyes lost their focus. "I'm so fucking close, Mick. This deal is so perfect."

"Something wrong?"

"I don't know," Frank said, putting his thumbnail back against his teeth, his eyes still on the photograph. "But if it is, I ain't gonna just sit here and take it. You get the money ready too. In case we got to run."

"Run?" Mickey said. "Hey, I don't see running from those guys, Frank. You don't run from them."

"Oh yeah?" Frank said, pulling his thumb out of his mouth and leaning toward Mickey. "What else you gonna do, talk? You gonna throw me under the bus and save your own ass?"

"They don't have to know about me, Frank," Mickey whined, his eyes pulled down at the corners. "I don't want the money."

"Well you're *taking* the fucking money," Frank said, drawing a Glock 9mm out from under his coat and putting it in Mickey's face. "Ten percent. That's your share. You're rich, you and that little Sioux City bimbo. So you better find out for me real quick who these motherfuckers are so I can deal with it."

467

60

When my father died, they cremated his frozen body and buried the ashes in a cardboard box. I had that box dug up and reburied under some tall pine trees on a windy knob that overlooks the valley of the Onondaga Nation. I know how much he loved my mother and Black Turtle too. The stone that marks his new grave is a towering pillar of limestone cut from his own quarry with a sculpted bust of my father on top with his eyes facing the Nation. I know he would have liked that.

But still, after he froze to death, his body was burned — one of the few things my father ever openly despised about death. And I remember the one time we talked about it that he asked me to never let them burn his body.

Because of all that, I believe I would be justified if I didn't feel any remorse as I watch them lower Dani Rangle's dark walnut casket with its single rose and its silver gilt corners into the ground. But justified or not, there is a knot in my stomach.

I sigh and force my mind away from the young girl. My business is with Rangle and it cuts through sentimentality. It has to.

Rangle is stooped over, and when the priest hands him the silver ornamental shovel to deposit the first scoop of dirt over his daughter's dead body, it glints in the bright sunlight and he staggers away. An attendant from the funeral home catches him and stiffly endures his teary hug.

Katie Vanderhorn is much less affected. She stands in her place next to the grave in a black dress and sunglasses with her long hair gently waving in the breeze and is comforted by the one-armed embrace of Martin Debray. There are maybe two dozen other people there, standing under the pale blue sky, in front of their chairs, and dressed in the finest suits and dresses that can be found on Madison Avenue. One man looks at his watch. Another woman yawns. When the priest finally gives up, dumps the dirt himself, says a last prayer, and excuses them, they turn to leave without bothering to comfort the hysterical Bob Rangle.

It is the white-haired priest who takes Rangle by the arm and slowly leads him toward the waiting limousine, following a few steps behind his wife, who is clutching Martin's strong arm. I walk down the hill with the wind in my face, smelling the fresh loamy dirt. I walk around the grave and down the path of white fabric that leads toward the limo.

When I put my hand on the priest's square trim shoulder, he starts and whips his head around. His pale blue eyes are wide when they see me, almost as if he's afraid.

"I need to talk to him, Father," I say, gently separating the older man from Rangle's sagging frame. "Please. It's all right. I'm an old friend."

I support Rangle by one arm and he looks up at me without focusing. There are gray circles under the dark wet pits of his eyes and his nose drips and seems more pointed than ever. The dyed flap of hair hangs crooked across his bald head. The lines on his face are deep and craggy. The face of an old man. He takes a ragged breath, wiping the drip on his sleeve, and a moan escapes him.

I watch the priest walk toward his own waiting Town Car, his robes full of the breeze. When he turns back to look at us, I nod to him and smile. He continues his walk. On the gravel drive, I see Martin

Debray's face in the dark opening of the limousine. Rangle is still crying, although all his tears seem to have been spent.

"I have some more news for you," I say in a tone that makes Rangle straighten and wipe his eyes.

"He was a royal," he says, blubbering.

"Sometimes they're worse," I say. "I tried to call you this morning."

"I was . . ." Rangle looks back at the grave and pulls his arm away from my grip. "You're hurting me."

"The Russian government announced that it's investigating the Bank of Moscow for fraud."

"What?" Rangle's eyes widen and his mouth opens so that I can see his tongue. "When?"

"Midday," I say, soaking up the expression on his face. "Moscow time."

"After we bought?"

"After *you* bought," I say. "Technically, we're not even having this conversation. I'm just a client, remember? My lawyer advised me against talking to you. With your client list, and the amount of money lost, he expects an FBI probe. But I wanted to tell you in person . . ."

I can't help a small smile. The sound that comes from him is exquisite, a strangled cry of rage and horror. His lip curls up under the thin mustache. He clenches his hands and his weak trembling turns into a violent shake.

"It could be worse," I say. "Believe me when I say that."

"You —" he says in a screech, raising his fist. "You're sick."

My heart is racing. I would love to smash his face and snap his neck with my bare hands, but that would be too easy. This is the man who destroyed my life, not for love or even money, but out of greed for power and adulation. He ruined Raymond White for a seat in the U.S. Congress, and for that, his suffering will be a long-drawn-out affair. So instead of hitting him, I turn and walk away, savoring what waits for him now.

61

Rangle made a few discreet calls with his hand over his mouth and the phone and found out that everything Seth told him was true. He slumped in the corner of the limousine and said nothing else the entire way back to his apartment. When the car stopped, he didn't bother with his wife and Debray, but he told the driver to wait for him. He slipped out of the car, hurried through the lobby, and into the elevator.

Bursting into his apartment, he dismissed the maid and headed directly into his bedroom. There he went right to his wife's jewelry safe.

He filled one of her small handbags with everything valuable, then went into his own walk-in closet and took down a large Louis Vuitton suitcase from a shelf. He threw in the handbag and three of his best suits along with a tuxedo and two pair of shoes, then as much summer-wear as he could fit.

He heard Katie come in, mix a drink, and then ease herself down on the bed

473

with a heavy sigh that ended in a long self-pitying groan. Rangle reached up under his sock drawer and sprung the latch on the wooden panel behind his suits. He pushed the clothes aside and spun the tumbler on his own safe. Inside was a black velvet bag that crunched softly when he lifted it. He opened the top, scooping up a handful of diamonds.

Twenty million dollars' worth of investment-grade stones. Better than a Swiss bank account. Better than cash. He slipped the bag into a leather briefcase and slung the shoulder strap across his body. In his bathroom, next to the toilet, was a phone. He dialed information and got the number for the charter at Teterboro. Yes, there was a G-V available on short notice. He asked them to put together a flight plan for Grand Cayman and hung up.

With the suitcase in hand, he walked back out into the bedroom and stopped at the foot of the bed. Katie was propped up on a mountain of pillows with her arm up over her face. He set the suitcase down.

"I'm leaving, Katie," he said, straightening his back and his hair at the same time, "and I'd like you to come with me."

His wife's body started to shake. First just slightly, then almost convulsively, she sucked in some air and let it out in small spurts. At first he thought she was hysterically crying, but when the sound started to come it was pitched with laughter.

She actually shrieked, then said, "Oh, Bob, what do you mean, *leaving?* You're in mourning, remember?"

"You're sick," he said, spitting the word.

Her arm came down off her face and he saw the glitter in her eyes.

"I am sick," she said. "Sick of *you.*"

"Katie, I don't care about everything. I'll take you with me," Rangle said. "If you stay here, there's not going to be anything. The money's gone. All of it."

"But you're wrong, Bob," she said, still grinning. "Martin and I have plenty of money."

"What do you mean, Martin and you?" he said, choking.

"Doesn't your French notion of marriage include business?"

"You have *money* together?"

"Of course," she said, her lips tight. "Lots. He's very good."

Rangle felt his face twisting. He turned quickly and picked up the suitcase, stopping only to slam the bedroom door on her laughter.

When the limo stopped in front of the

terminal at Teterboro, Rangle got out without a word to his driver. Inside, the girl behind the counter said that everything was ready and he snapped that it damned well better be. The driver delivered his suitcase and a handler scooped it up and said he'd put it into the jet. Rangle dismissed his driver and gave the girl his Platinum Card, enjoying the fact that since no one would be left to pay it, this ride was going to be for free.

The G-V was waiting just outside the hangar, its long white body shining in the sun, its massive engines looking almost too big for the rest of the plane. On board, he nodded to the pilots, who were checking their controls, and stepped through the galley into the main cabin.

One of the pilots came back and offered him a drink. Rangle settled into the leather recliner, fastened up his seat belt, and said, "Scotch and soda with ice. A double."

The pilot nodded, and as he fixed the drink in the galley, he said, "I kept the shades down until we take off and get the air-conditioning going, Mr. Rangle, to keep you as cool as we can."

Rangle took the drink from him and sipped the cool golden liquor, letting it dull his nerves.

"Can I take that briefcase for you?" the pilot asked.

"No," Rangle said, clutching it to his chest. "I have some things in here that I need."

"Okay, we'll be taking off right away."

Rangle nodded and looked at the shaded window. He lifted the shade a little and beyond the upward-bent wing saw a fuel truck drive away. He heard heavy footsteps on the stairs and felt the plane shake, then the sound of the stairs being retracted and the cabin door being secured.

Rangle loosened his tie and reclined the seat a little more. The engines screamed to life, and he angled the vent so that the cool air hit his face. The thought of Dani came on him suddenly and his chest convulsed. He swallowed some of his drink and held the briefcase tight as the plane swung around and headed up the runway.

He shut his eyes. After a brief pause, the plane accelerated, pushing him deep into the seat's cushions. When they began to level off, he took another swig and pulled the shade all the way up. Sunlight streamed in. Below was the Hudson River littered with boats and the small white tails of their wakes.

Rangle sat up straight. He leaned across

the cabin and opened the other shades. Mountains. He looked up the aisle. The cockpit door was closed. He sat back down and folded his arms across the briefcase, his mind spinning. He didn't want to seem ridiculous. He looked out the window again. More river and more green hills. They were definitely going north.

He leaned into the aisle again and directed his voice toward the cockpit door.

"Hello?" he said.

Even when he raised his voice to a shout, nothing happened. Rangle got up and started through the galley. When he got halfway through, he realized one of the pilots was sitting in the front chair. A mountain of a man in a white shirt and dark slacks.

"I know this sounds crazy," he said, putting on a foolish grin and reaching out to touch the pilot's shoulder, "but aren't we going the wrong way?"

When the man shifted his bulk around, Rangle clutched his briefcase and stepped back.

"What are you . . . you're the Indian," he said, his voice pitched.

Bert grinned up at him and pointed to the back of the plane with his thumb. "You better go sit down. We're going right."

"This is my charter," Rangle said in a screech. "I'm going to the Caymans."

"You're going someplace a little chillier than that, old weasel," Bert said, shifting around in his seat. "Now go sit down or I'll make you sit down."

"I can pay you," Rangle said, raising his eyebrows and nodding his head, fumbling to open the briefcase. He loosened the neck of the velvet bag and took out a stone about the size of a half-karat. He held it up in the light so that the rays of its glitter dodged back and forth across Bert's fat cheeks.

"That's ten thousand dollars right there."

Bert reached out and took the stone, then dropped it into his mouth and swallowed. Grinning he said, "You know what your stones mean to me? Shit. It'll be a frozen shitsicle where we're headed . . . I hope you packed warm."

62

My G-V isn't back for more than two days before I use it to head north across Canada, the Hudson Bay, the polar cap, and finally to Uelen on the Chukchi Peninsula in the farthest corner of northeast Russia. A couple hundred miles across the Bering Strait is Point Hope, Alaska, population 794. But for Bob Rangle, those 794 Americans may as well be on another planet.

I'm excited, but partway through the trip I take a pill, pull the shades on the unending sun, and sleep. When I wake up we're in a place where the only person who speaks English is a hunting outfitter, Alexi Fedorovich. He meets us on the abandoned military runway twenty miles outside of town in an old Soviet helicopter. The runway itself is lined with the empty skeletons of the once-proud Soviet air force. Some are twin-prop babies from the Second World War and some are the sleek MiGs they pestered us with during the cold war.

Alexi is a thick-chested Russian with a

full red beard and sharp green eyes. With his ship and his weapons he is a law unto himself in this region. The men who work for him are Chukchi natives, distant relatives to the Eskimos. They are here to take us to his northern base camp, the one they use to hunt polar bears, a hundred and fifty miles to the north. I shake his hand, then zip up my fur-lined parka. The sun is about to dip just below the horizon, so it's colder than it will be in a couple hours, when the sun will reappear for the remainder of the long summer day. I tell my pilots to stay with the jet, and Alexi hands them a loaded Kalashnikov that he takes from one of his men.

"For wolf," he says.

My pilots are both former navy fliers, so they do nothing more than shrug and accept the gun. I know wolves are a problem here, but also that the people in this forgotten corner of the former Soviet Union have become as desperate as the wolves themselves. We board the patchwork helicopter and strap in. Alexi flies the machine himself and soon we're tilting away from the airfield to the deafening sound of the chopper blades. Alexi's three men are grim-faced. They don't smile and they don't talk.

Even though the sun is down, its glow lets me clearly see the landscape below. The evergreens grow shorter and shorter until they give way to the low rocky brush and finally to the snow itself. After a time, a finger of jagged black rock appears up ahead, an island in the frozen plain. Just beyond it is the dark gray roiling Chukchi Sea. In the center of the windblown rock formation is a low cabin with smoke pouring up out of a galvanized pipe stack. We land in front of the rocks on a sheet of ice. The men hop out and make right away for the cabin. Alexi and I follow, in less of a hurry because we are outfitted in better gear.

The big Russian slaps his arm around me and hugs me to him as we walk.

"You make many people live good with this diamonds," he says.

"Does he have any left?"

Alexi shakes his head no. He pats his coat and I hear the distinct crunching sound of a bag of small stones.

"When?"

He looks at the plastic watch on his wrist and says, "In morning. Five hours he no fire."

"Alexi?" I say, grabbing his arm and looking up into his face.

"He no dead," Alexi says, showing me a mouthful of yellow and gold teeth. "I tell my man, he no moving, you giving wood. When he coming here, one hour he no spending diamonds. Then, very very spending. He spending every diamond. Every food and every firewood we having. Big fire that day. Very stupid man."

"Greedy," I say to myself.

"Yes, very greedy like you say."

"That's what got him here."

We reach the path that leads through the spiny rocks and the packed snow squeaks under our feet. The door to the cabin opens and I see Bert's big round face in a halo of fur. His expression is as empty as those worn by Alexi's men, and the only welcome he gives me is a grunt as he raises his heavy mitten. Alexi puts his hand on the door and offers me coffee.

"I'm fine," I say. "Thank you. I want to see him."

Bert grunts again and starts down another path that goes around the back side of the cabin. I follow him. There is a snowdrift piled up in the lee of the towering rock protecting the cabin, but a narrow path has been cut through it. When we round the rock, the wind hits us in the face and we have to lean into it until we come to a switchback path that takes us down into a small bowl in the snow whose lip is a semicircle of squat black rocks. White powder snakes along the ground like fast-moving smoke. In the center of it all is the blackened pit of a burnt-out fire.

Bob Rangle is burrowed down into the ashes as far as he can go. Beside him is the open Louis Vuitton suitcase. Every article of clothing that was inside is either on or somehow wrapped around his body. He looks like a homeless man you might see under a frozen bridge.

Bert stops at the lip of the bowl and looks out over the frozen wasteland. The pale disk of the sun is resting on the horizon like a child's flashlight being shone through a bedsheet.

"I know now what kind of animal I was in my last life," Bert says, his eyes narrowed at the sun.

"A turkey?"

"A bird, anyway," he says without cracking a smile. "Maybe a hawk. Something that flies high and brings death like a lightning bolt. I have no stomach for this."

"I know," I say, patting his back.

But Bert only turns and heads back up the path, saying, "I'll leave you to your game."

I grab the sleeve of Bert's parka and pull him around.

"Let me tell you something," I say, looking up at him with clenched teeth. "That piece of shit down there put me in a place where men live like animals."

"And this is what it taught you?"

"Yes," I say. "Three rules, and the third was the most important. Without it, you were done. Exact revenge. Someone does you wrong, you exact revenge. You make it ten times worse for them. A hundred times. That's what *he* taught me, Bert. He and his friends. And now that's what he's getting."

I let him go and I tramp down the path into the bowl. Rangle can barely move, but when he hears his name, he rolls on his side, rattling the chain that is attached to a post Alexi has driven six feet down into the ice. Rangle looks up at me with empty eyes through a slit in the hat he has made out of six pairs of underwear and three pairs of tennis shorts. His mustache and eyebrows and lashes are white with crystals, and when I yank the clothes off his head I see that the end of his sharp nose, like most of his ears, is black and frosted with ice.

He makes a pitiful low groaning noise and tries to pick up his makeshift hat to replace it on his head. But when his hand appears from the folds of his clothes, I see that its long fingers are also frozen and black. A useless claw.

"Do you know why you're here?" I ask him, checking the bile that has surged up into the middle of my throat.

He shakes his head.

"Do you know who I am?"

He shakes his head no again.

"Look at my eyes," I say, kneeling down and moving close. "It's me, Raymond. Raymond White."

He groans and his eyes roll away.

"Look at me," I say, grabbing his cheeks. "This is how my father died, you piece of shit. He froze to death. While you and Frank and Russo were toasting my life in jail, my father felt what you're feeling now. Do you like it?"

He looks away, and I grab his ear and twist it until he shrieks and flops back and forth.

"Look at me! Do you like it?"

"No," he croaks, his eyes glued to me now, welling up. "Please, no."

"I did nothing wrong," I say, standing up and trying not to choke. "My father did nothing wrong. You killed us both and now that you know how it feels, I'm going to save you. Not because you deserve to live. No, Rangle.

"It's because you don't deserve to die . . ."

I walk back up the path. In a ragged choking voice I hear him call the name of the man I used to be.

Raymond. Raymond White.

Back at the cabin, I sit down with the others around the potbelly stove and soak the heat out of my coffee cup with two hands. When they're warm, I look at Alexi and say, "Your American client needs medical care. You have a hospital in Uelen."

"Ten year was Soviet hospital," he says. "Now maybe ten room. Doctor, yes. Animal doctor. But have army nurse good . . . medical."

"I'd like you to pay them enough for him to live there," I say. "He has no one to care for him in America, so he will stay here."

"How long he stay?" Alexi asks, his eyebrows soaring.

I shrug and say, "I don't know. Ten years? Twenty? As long as he lives."

"He no talk Russian," Alexi says. "Doctor cutting hands and feet and nose. Ears too. They no speaking him. He no walking. He staying bed."

"Yes," I say, getting up from the table

and patting Bert's hunched-over shoulders. "In America we do things in a big way. Isn't that right, Bert?"

"That's what the white men say."

"Come on, chief," I say to him, tugging him toward the door. "We're not done."

63

It's a chilly day for August, and outside the van, the late-afternoon rain hammers down on the metal roof. But I'm warm. I want Frank to live in fear and I know that someone like him fears only one thing.

I listen and watch as the guards frisk Bert outside the Yacht Club, but it isn't until he walks into the meeting room overlooking the misty gray river that my heart starts to race. There is Ramo Capozza at the end of the table with his cappuccino and there in the middle is Frank, leaning back with his hands folded over his big belly.

Bert sets down a briefcase of documents on the table in front of him and sits. Frank's eyes never leave him.

"Well, Mr. Washington," Ramo says, setting down his cup on its saucer with a soft clink, "I trust your group is happy."

Bert clears his throat and recites his line, saying, "We would like to know if since we're buying Frank Steffano's piece of the business that we'll get the same deal with

489

the unreported cash."

Ramo glances at the man with the glasses on his right and smiles. He folds his hands together and puts his elbows on the table, leaning forward. His pale green eyes are big behind the thick lenses. Their lids are half closed.

Frank has his jaw set and he glares at Bert.

"Our disbursements," Capozza says, "are all accounted for as payments to the partners. As you can see, this partnership is very profitable. Everything is legitimate. That lets me sleep at night. I like thinking that my grandchildren can go to college without worrying about wiretaps. You understand that, don't you?"

I push the red button on the audio control board in front of me and say, *"Pass him the documents. Tell him that's how you do business too."*

Bert shifts and pushes the briefcase away from him. The man on his left passes it toward Capozza's end of the table.

"That's how we do business too," Bert says stiffly.

"So why do you think there's an issue with some cash?" Capozza says, still smiling, but with his lips at an odd angle across his capped teeth.

"Tell him, 'If you look at these papers, you'll see that over the last three years Frank's taken almost seventy million dollars in cash out of the casinos,'" I say.

Bert repeats the words. The briefcase gets to Frank. Instead of passing it on, he takes hold of it in both hands and stands up.

"I think before this goes any further," Frank says, "that this partnership needs to know more about who *you* are. Don't you think that would be a good idea?"

He is grinning at Bert now, and Bert shifts in his chair and folds his arms across his chest just below the tiny camera lens.

"Little warm in here, Bert?" Frank says, his eyes still glued. "You should be feeling a little warm, 'cause I know this whole thing is a *scam*. It's a scam by you and it's a scam by Seth Cole."

The men around the table begin to murmur, and Frank raises his voice above them.

"You don't represent a group of casino owners, do you?" Frank says. "The Iroquois Group is nothing but a front, and I have some papers here of my own."

Bert pushes back his seat away from the table.

"*Wait, Bert,*" I say. "*Stay there. Tell them if*

you're a scam then why doesn't he let them look at the papers in the briefcase and decide for themselves. Do it. Now. Be angry, Bert."

Bert clears his throat and repeats my words in a rumbling voice that sounds better than anything he's said so far.

"Why don't you give us those papers, Frank?" the pock-faced Dominic says from across the table. "Pass them down to Ramo. You got nothing to be afraid of, right? You wouldn't steal from the partnership. That'd be too stupid . . ."

"I'll pass *this* down," Frank says, and, reaching down beside his chair, he comes up with some papers that he puts down on the table and slides toward Ramo Capozza. The man to Capozza's right examines them through his glasses.

"This proves what I'm saying," Frank says. "This Indian is some low-level muscle for a guy named Bonaparte. The only thing they got is a juiced-up bingo parlor and a drug racket up on the St. Regis Indian Reservation. There is no casino group. The money in that Iroquois Group account came from a shell corporation owned by Seth Cole. It's all a scam to get at me."

"Shit," I say. I turn to Chuck Lawrence and he lifts his headset. "Get ready. If this gets bad, you'll call 911 and report an armed robbery at the Yacht Club. We might have to break this thing up, but wait till I say."

I turn back to the TV monitor.

"What about the briefcase?" Dominic is asking.

"Whatever's in this," Frank says, patting the briefcase without letting go, "is all lies. This guy and Cole had almost two weeks to cook this shit up. It's nothing."

"If it's nothing, then we can look at it," Dominic says, putting both his hands flat out on the table. He looks down at Ramo Capozza, whose eyes are going back and forth between Bert and Frank.

To Bert I say, *"Tell Capozza Frank's lying. Tell him to look at the briefcase."*

Bert says, "He's lying."

"You son of a bitch," Frank says in a growl, reaching inside his jacket. "I ought to take you out right here."

"Frank!" Capozza shouts.

Everyone falls silent and the older man softly says, "This is a business meeting."

He looks at Bert and says, "Mr. Washington, we run this business like a family. We trust each other. We cover each other's backs. Isn't that right, Dominic?"

"Yeah," Dominic says, looking at the table. "We do."

"If you and Mr. Cole have a problem with Frank, you shouldn't be bringing it to us. We're a very loyal group. Frank treated my nephew — God rest his soul — like his own blood and for that I owe him a debt.

"Now, Frank," he says, turning his cold eyes on Frank. "You shouldn't have any problem letting us see that briefcase. Of course we know you wouldn't steal from us and that's how we'll look at it. But we *will* look, Frank . . .

"If what you say is true, and I have no doubt it is, Frank, then you can deal with Mr. Washington and Mr. Cole how you see fit. But . . . we're businessmen here. Isn't that right?"

"Yes," Frank says, handing the briefcase to the man on his right and watching it until it is in the hands of the man next to Capozza.

"Mr. Washington," Capozza says, standing up to signal an end to the meeting. "I know you and Mr. Cole are friends and I appreciate the hospitality you showed me and my great-grandson, but I do not appreciate any of this and you can tell Mr. Cole I said that."

Bert stands up and says, "Can I go?"

Capozza looks at him with an expression of surprise and says, "Of course, Mr.

Washington. I told you. We're all businessmen here and our business is finished."

Bert is quickly escorted out into the rain and put in my limousine. When the door closes, he holds out his tie and looks down into the camera.

"Jesus Christ," he says.

"You did good," I tell him.

"I thought they were gonna kill me," Bert says.

I signal Chuck to get going. He puts down his headset and climbs into the front of the van and we pull away from the curb.

"I was ready to pull the pin," I say. *"We were going to call the cops if it got any more dicey."*

"Yeah, when they started dicing me up," he says.

"You know what I mean," I tell him. *"Have a Molson Golden. There's a six-pack in the ice chest. Have a couple."*

"Now we'll both have to go to that doctor in L.A. and have our faces changed," he says.

"Maybe not," I say.

"You got a plan?"

"Maybe."

"That's comforting."

I hear the slushy sound of ice and the

hiss of a can. Bert brings the gold can up to his mouth and sucks it all the way down before punctuating it with a belch.

"On that note," I say, *"I'm signing off. I'll see you at the house."*

When I get back, the butler meets me at the car with an umbrella and tells me that Helena just got there a few minutes ago. I find her on the couch in the bedroom with her knees drawn up to her chin and staring out at the rain. She's dressed in jeans and a dark green Jets sweatshirt, barefoot, with her dark silky hair pulled back into a ponytail. She jumps up, startled, and meets me halfway across the room, throwing herself into my arms with a squeal, kissing me, and wrapping her legs around my waist.

"I missed you," she says, then repeats it three times and starts laughing when I bite her neck.

"Me too," I say.

"What's wrong?" She lets go and touches my cheek with the back of her hand.

"Things," I say. "Helena, we need to talk."

We sit down on the couch and I tell her about Frank, the man who killed her father. What he did to me. What I'm trying to do to him. I even mention Lexis. I tell

496

her all about Bert's meeting with Ramo Capozza, the brother of her grandmother, my plan, and how it all came to pass. The point is, I never dreamed I would need her to get involved in this, but we're in trouble.

When I finish, she looks out into the gloom. Silver drops of rain slide down the long pane of glass. Some run into the others and become one. Some twist apart and go their own ways. I have no idea why.

"I thought about it a million times," she says, tracing the pattern on the couch with her fingernail. "I told you. I knew who my father's uncle was. Sometimes, when I was up in Alaska, I'd dream about it. Me going to him, and him sending people after Frank Steffano for what he did. But I was always afraid . . ."

"Why?"

She looks at me with tear-filled eyes and says, "I don't know. Part of me thinks the whole thing is my own fault."

"That's not true. I told you that."

"I know," she says, looking at me. "But it's how I *feel.*"

I put my hand on hers and squeeze.

"It's all right," I say.

She presses her lips tight, looks away, and sighs.

"I'll go see my uncle," she says.

"I don't want you to do this just for me," I say.

"I know," she says. "But I was thinking about how you said it was your job to do this, and I don't know if that's right.

"I get up there and I sing, and people — some of them — even cry. And I think they do because it's like they know that I'm still crying inside. I think people sense that. I don't want to sing only like that for the rest of my life and I think maybe if I did this, it would help."

64

The morning sun gleamed off the surfaces of the puddles from the previous night's rain, giving the air the steamy hint of garbage. At the dock, a towering blue freighter caked with rust with the name *Bella Napoli* creaked and swayed. Cranes worked steadily to remove the truck-size containers from her belly while along the dock, long bladed forklifts moved them around like a small colony of ants carrying food ten times their own size.

A long black Mercedes limousine eased through the chain-link gates with their faded red-and-white sign that read *Absolutely No Trespassing*. On the dock already was another limousine, a Cadillac. Outside it stood a well-built man in a suit. Two others walked on either side of an old man, stooped over and wearing brown wingtip shoes, brown slacks, and a baggy yellow cardigan sweater. His glasses were thick and his thin gray hair was plastered down with some kind of barbershop formula.

The man next to the Cadillac stepped in

front of the Mercedes, preventing the car from driving right up to the old man, who was now bent over a crate that two workers had removed from a red container. The two thugs with the old man approached the Mercedes as well, reaching into their jackets with their eyes scanning not just the car, but the whole dock.

Helena got out and made them stare, even though she wore no makeup and nothing fancier than sandals, a pair of faded jeans, and a man's white V-neck T-shirt.

"Holy shit," one guard said to the other. "That's Helena."

Chuck Lawrence got out right after her, and he and the two big men approached one another like dogs in a vacant lot.

"She needs to talk to Mr. Capozza," Lawrence said.

They looked at their boss, who stood with a tomato in each hand, blinking at them all. He nodded.

"Okay," one of them said.

Helena took slow uneven steps and looked down only once to skirt a deep oily puddle. When she reached the old man, she held out her hand. He put the tomatoes into one hand and took hers with the other. Smiling, he held up the bright red fruit. Their stems were a rich green.

"When I was a boy," he said, "my father used to come here to make sure the tomatoes came from Italy. What they do is, people will take a crate from Mexico and put them in a crate that says Italy. But if you don't get good tomatoes, then the sauce is no good and the whole meal stinks."

"Do you know me?" she said with the beginnings of a smile.

"I've seen you on TV," he said. "I have a couple grandkids who'd be happy to trade places with me right now."

"No," she said. "Do you really know who I am?"

Tears filled up in Helena's eyes and she wiped them on the back of her arm. From her back pocket she took out a birth certificate and unfolded it.

Ramo Capozza looked at his men, searching their faces, smiling, but with his eyes narrowed.

"Who sent you?" he asked.

"No one," she said, offering up the certificate. "I'm Helena. My father was Tony. Tony Romano."

"Tony?" Capozza says. His hand falls to his side and the tomatoes drop to the wet pavement, bursting and spilling their seeds.

"They killed him. My sister tried to find you, but your mother disappeared . . ."

"I wasn't with my mother, Uncle Ramo," she said, her face crumpling. "He took me away. They made me do things —"

Ramo Capozza hugged Helena to him and patted his gnarled hand on her back.

"Shhh," he said, glaring at his men over her shoulder to make them look away.

Softly, he said, "I killed those men."

"No," Helena said, pulling away. "You didn't. There weren't any men. It was one man."

Capozza scowled, his thick eyebrows crunching down on top of his pale green eyes.

"That can't be," he said. "Someone is telling you lies. Tony's partner was there."

"It is, Uncle Ramo," she said. "No one is telling me. I *saw* it. It was his partner who did it. I saw Frank Steffano kill my father. I was only ten, but I could never forget his face or what he did to me —"

Ramo Capozza held his niece tight. She was shaking. He continued to pat her back, until his fists were curled into balls. His teeth were clamped together and the corners of his mouth were pulled tight.

He was shaking too.

And then she told her story.

65

In the bowels of a garage on 79th Street, Frank locked up a dark green Ford Excursion with a beep and a blink of its lights. The truck was loaded up with almost everything he needed. Food. Clothes. Weapons. Passports. They'd cross the Canadian border into Montreal. From there they'd fly to Sydney. The other end of the world. The only thing left was the money — he checked his watch — and by now, Mickey should have that.

He walked up and around the concrete bend. The parking attendant, a dark young black man reading a paperback, had his feet propped up on the glass inside his booth. Frank held up his ticket and winked at the kid, then proceeded up the ramp and into the gritty wind, where he turned right and headed for home.

They were waiting for him in the first narrow alleyway between buildings. He saw them as they sprang and he tried to turn and run, but he hadn't taken a step before they were on him and he felt the sharp point of a knife prick his skin an inch from his windpipe. He froze.

The blade came to rest along the carotid artery, pressing into his skin. The warm flow of blood seeped down into the folds of his neck. Frank swallowed and lost control of his bladder. He quickly squeezed and kept the warm wetness from spreading beyond his underwear. A hand reached around and removed the gun from under his arm.

"Get in, Frank," said a voice in his ear that he recognized.

A navy blue Grand Marquis had pulled up alongside the curb. The driver reached back and over to swing open the rear door. Frank got in, fighting the urge to yank his arm free from the man's grip. He slid into the car and strained his eyes to see. The two men wedged themselves in on either side of him. Ramo's men. He felt a gun barrel pressed to his ribs. They pulled out into the street, and when they got under the first light, he saw the man behind the wheel was the scar-faced Dominic Battaglia.

Frank felt his insides go tight.

He looked at the men on either side of him. They were staring straight ahead. Soldiers following orders. Neither of them knew that he had a fishing knife up his sleeve. Now wasn't the right time, but it might save him later.

"Let me go, Dominic," he said in a croak. "I'll give you all the money."

"You think I'm like you?" Dominic said into the rearview mirror. His lips were pulled clear of his teeth.

"It's a lot."

"I know how much it is," Dominic said. "We all do."

Frank's mind spun with a billion possibilities. The car passed over the 59th Street Bridge, then onto the BQE. When they passed the Atlantic Avenue exit where Ramo Capozza lived, Frank knew he was going to die. He could kill one of them with the knife, but he'd die. His eyes searched for an interested Port Authority officer when they passed through the toll at the Verrazano Bridge. There was none.

As they crossed over onto Staten Island, Frank looked north toward the big city. The galaxy of lights. The dark towers. He bit into his lower lip and narrowed his eyes.

They left the main roads and turned onto an empty street marked by a huge billboard with a sketch of the office buildings soon to come. At the back end of the deep loop, tall piles of dirt and stacks of raw steel girders shone under the car's yellow beams. They left the pavement and jolted along a dirt track, through the dirt piles and steel, coming to rest in a cloud of dust at the edge of a foundation hole.

The men on either side of him got out, and for an instant, he felt almost free.

"Get out, Frank," Dominic said, wagging a snub-nosed .38 into the doorway of the car. "Don't make me tell them you squealed like a pig. Be a man. Ramo said if you were a man, you could go easy. Me? I voted to make it last."

Frank slid his bulk to the edge of the seat and hoisted himself out into the warm night. His armpits had bled all the way through his suit coat and he smelled the sour scent of his own fear. His eyes darted up toward the shadowy form of a machine. One of the men was climbing up its side. He heard a heavy metal door squeak open and closed and then the coughing of a diesel motor as it spun to life. Its rheumy eyes glowed and Frank saw now that it was a concrete mixer.

"Come on," Dominic said, pushing Frank toward the hole with the .38 in his back.

Frank stumbled forward. The other muscle was on his left with his gun out too.

Dominic stayed behind him. The barrel of the mixer clanked into action, spinning with an electric whine.

"Kneel down," Dominic said, pointing to the lip of the black hole.

Frank heard the truck's gears grinding into place and the squeak of the axle as it crept forward. He knelt down and bowed his head. He started to shake and blubber.

"Dominic, *please*," he said, sobbing. "You can have it *all*."

He turned his head back to see Dominic with his legs slightly straddled, moving the pistol toward the back of his head.

"I don't want to die," he said, whining and holding his trembling hands up near his temples.

Dominic's toothy grin shone in the headlights of the cement mixer. Frank spun and grabbed Dominic's hands and gun at the same time. The gun flashed, blasting a hole through Frank's palm, but he hung on, dropped to his shoulder, and flipped the smaller man over his back into the hole. Frank rolled, his ears ringing. The second man's gun fired, licking with orange flames, and he felt the bullets humming past his head. Something struck his leg as he came out of his roll with the .38 leveled.

One shot to the head and the man went down like a puppet.

Frank ran limping at the cement mixer. The third man was bursting out of the door, jumping for the ground with the knife in his hand. Frank shot him in the chest in midair and he fell in a heap.

Frank turned and bolted back to the lip of the hole. He stuffed the .38 in his pocket, scooped up the second man's Glock, and checked the load, calmly standing over the deep dark trench, listening. As his eyes adjusted, he saw a shape moving slowly along the bottom. He fired three quick shots and heard Dominic screaming in pain and fear.

Frank moved closer, limping on down the length of the foundation hole, his feet scuffing up little clouds of dust in the headlights. His left hand was throbbing now and he balled it into a fist to try and stop the bleeding. Dominic still screamed.

"Hey, Dominic!" he shouted above the noise. "Fuck you!"

Frank unloaded the Glock into the hole, careful to shoot only below his business partner's waist. Dominic's squealing continued now at a heightened pitch. Frank tossed the empty gun down in the hole. His own gun was in the second man's waist and he took it out before dragging his body to the edge of the hole and kicking the gun into the bottom of the trench with Dominic. The third man went in too, along with the .38 before Frank climbed into the cab of the mixer. He eased the truck to the edge and dumped its load, filling the bottom of the footer with four feet of concrete.

66

Lexis came out of Lincoln Center in high heels, clutching Allen's arm to steady herself.

"Thank you," she said, looking up at him, burying her nose in the sleeve of his tuxedo jacket. "I know that's not your favorite thing."

"That's 'cause you are," he said, opening the door of the limousine for her.

Lexis bit her lip.

"What's wrong?" Allen said. "I thought that was nice."

"Very nice," she said, smiling and touching his arm.

"Man, it's late," Allen said, looking at his watch. "You gotta be tired, huh?"

Lexis yawned and nodded her head.

"I'll drop you off," he said, his voice suddenly upbeat. "I'm shot too, but a bunch of guys are meeting in the Village. You know, since it's my last night."

"You want to have some tea?" she asked. "Or a coffee?"

That's how she saw the night ending. His

last night in the city before going back to school. Just the two of them at the kitchen table. But Allen looked at his watch again and winced.

"You don't mind, right, Mom?"

"Of course not," she said, forcing a smile.

Allen took out his cell phone, turned it on, and called Martin to find out where everyone was going. Lexis sighed, then took her own cell phone out of her purse and turned it on. She had a new message. It was Cornell Ricks, the governor's man. He'd left a package at their building. His voice cold and clipped. Not saying anything else. No hint. Nothing.

Michael, their doorman, had given personal things of hers before to Frank. She dialed the apartment and looked at her watch. There was no answer. She looked at her son, forced a smile, and leaned forward to fill a glass from the crystal decanter of bourbon.

When she looked back at Allen, he was still talking, but watching her. He immediately looked away. Lexis sighed, but still brought the glass to her lips. She took two small sips, watching her son, then swallowed the whole thing and fumbled with the decanter again, refilling her glass with her eyes on him the whole time.

The second one she enjoyed a little more, and by the time the car pulled to a stop in front of their building, she was feeling much better. She replaced the empty glass in its holder and let Allen help her out. Michael held the door for them with a slight bow.

"Mrs. Steffano," he said in his Brooklyn accent. "Your husband just came in. He doesn't look good. He said he took a spill at one of his construction sites, but I'm worried. There was a lot of blood."

She asked about the package.

He rubbed the side of his face and showed her his crooked yellow teeth.

"Mr. Steffano took it up for you about fifteen minutes ago when he came in."

Lexis gripped Allen's arm and walked unevenly to the elevator.

"What's wrong, Mom?" he asked.

They got on the elevator.

"Nothing," she said, forcing a smile. "Maybe you should just go like you are."

"In a tux?" he said with a brief laugh. "Right, Mom. What's wrong?"

"Everything's fine," she said.

They arrived at the top floor.

"Mom," Allen said, stepping out into the hall.

He followed Lexis into the apartment.

"Dad?" he called.

She shut the door behind them. When Frank didn't respond, she took a deep breath. Maybe he was gone. Maybe he didn't read what Cornell Ricks brought her. Maybe there was nothing much inside the envelope besides an account of how Raymond White had died in jail or was living out his life in a cell somewhere.

Allen was looking at her.

"I'm just tired," she said. "Your father probably got a Band-Aid and went right back out."

When she reached up to kiss his cheek, she heard Frank's muffled voice calling her name from deep inside their master bedroom.

Allen looked that way.

"Allen," she said, following him down the hall.

Allen disappeared into the bedroom and she heard him cry out.

She went in. Frank was sitting on the bed, a gun in one hand, the other in a fist jammed into his coat pocket. His suit, like his face, was covered with dirt. The collar of his shirt was red with blood, and when he took the other hand out of his pocket, she saw the bloody bandage. There was a hole in his pants and a dark stain. Behind him was a manila envelope, opened with the papers spilling out. On it was her name.

"Allen," Frank said in a growl, "listen. We've got trouble."

"What happened?"

Frank held up his bloody hand and pressed his lips tight. He raised his voice.

"Allen Francis. Listen, goddamn it," Frank said. "I've got a plan. It'll all work. Go change your clothes and pack some things for a few days. I'll meet you on the back stairs."

He looked at his watch and said, "Hurry up. We've got to meet Mickey at the Rockefeller Outlook at midnight."

"Dad, we start practice —"

"Goddamn it! Look at this!" Frank shouted, holding up his hand clenched around the bloody white rag. "Go get your *fucking* things!"

Allen left. Lexis moved toward her husband, reaching for his hand.

"Frank, let me —"

"You get back," he said, waving the gun at her and grinning. "You're not coming. I'm getting the money from Mickey and you'll have *nothing*."

"Frank, what are you talking about?"

"Bitch," he said, standing up and raising the gun as if to strike her.

Lexis flinched and backed away.

"Get in the closet."

"Frank, tell me."

"Shut the *fuck* up," he said, limping toward her, herding her back. "I know."

Frank pointed his bloody hand back at the papers on the bed.

"That fucking Raymond White is behind all this. Him and that Seth Cole," Frank said in a harsh whisper, "and you *knew*. He escaped and he's out there. Who do you think ruined Rangle? *His* daughter's dead. That fucking Raymond White wants to kill *me*. He wants to kill my son, and you *knew*."

"Allen won't leave me," she said, feeling the doorframe of her closet and stepping inside.

"You think he'll know?" Frank said, grinning even wider, moving into the doorway and steadying himself on the door handle. "Just that we had to split up. To be safe. That we'll meet you. But don't you *ever* let me see you again."

Frank had her backed into the corner. He raised the pistol and struck her in the side of the head. Lexis crumpled to the floor. She tried to raise her hands, but

Frank brought the gun down again and again. Blood spilled down her face. One eye went dark. Her teeth were shattered and she gagged on the bony fragments and the blood.

Frank stopped and stepped back. He was breathing hard, holding himself up by the bar that held a row of dresses, smearing their collars with his own blood.

"You *can't* take him," she sobbed, spitting blood and teeth onto the carpet, her head hanging. "You can't, Frank."

Frank was bent over, huffing from his efforts. He tilted his head up, his pale blue eyes burning beneath his thick dark eyebrows.

"The only reason I'm not going to kill you," he said, "is because of that boy."

Frank turned to go, staggering toward the closet door.

"You *can't*, Frank!" she shouted, sobbing now, her face already puffy from the swelling. "He's *not* yours!"

Frank whipped around, pointing the gun at her, his hand shaking.

"He's *mine*," she moaned, looking away.

"Not anymore," Frank said. He slammed the door shut and left her in the emptiness.

67

Helena and I lie in the dark, the sweat cooling our naked bodies. My fingers are interlaced with hers and I squeeze them, compressing the bones between the second and third knuckles with my own. I used to do this to Lexis and I wonder if I should feel ashamed, thinking of her when I'm lying here like this.

I can't help what I think. It was another life, but some parts of it are still vivid, no matter how hard I try to forget.

Helena rolls my way, puts her fingertip against my Adam's apple, and starts drawing a straight line down when the phone rings.

Helena groans and says, "Don't answer it. It'll be Darwin. He's the only person I gave your home number to that would call this late."

"You should talk to him if it is," I say, picking up the phone.

"It's eleven o'clock," Helena says, arching her neck so she can see the clock by the bedside.

When I hear Chuck Lawrence's voice on the line, my body goes rigid.

"I know you said not to interfere," he says, "but you better come over here."

"Why?"

"She's in pretty bad shape," he says.

"Lexis?" I say, and now Helena's body goes rigid too.

"She needs a doctor," he says, "but she wants you first."

"I'm coming," I say, and swing my legs out of bed.

I look down at Helena. She grabs my hand.

"What's wrong?" she asks. "Where are you going?"

"An old friend," I say, pulling away from her and putting on my dark blue slacks. I pull on a matching short-sleeved collared shirt, button it up without tucking it in, and slip on my shoes.

"That's his wife," she says, tilting her head and raising one eyebrow.

"She *is* an old friend," I say, putting on my watch. "Please, Helena. This is almost over."

"Then what?" she asks.

I shake my head that I don't know.

"And us?" she says, raising her voice. "Am I part of your *plan?*"

I bend down to kiss her.

"Don't," I say, running my fingers through her long silky hair. "I'll be back."

I don't make any noise leaving my room, but when I get to the bottom of the stairs, Bert is hustling after me, pulling on his shirt.

"Working?" he asks.

"Maybe."

"Forget me?"

"Figured you'd make it."

"You know me," he says with a thin smile. "Never like to miss any fun."

In the garage next to my limousine is a boxy black Mercedes G55. I get in and drive toward Lexis's address on Park Avenue. At 54th Street, I run through a yellow light turning red. The car behind me makes it too. Maybe it's following me, but I don't have time to worry about that. I leave the SUV right there on the street. The doorman seems flustered — purple-faced with a crooked hat — but he sends us right up. The heavy wooden door is open. We go in and I call Chuck's name. My voice rebounds off the glass dome far above. The Caesar without a nose stares from his pedestal. I walk through the rotunda entry, my heels clicking on the marble until they reach the deep rug of the great room. I stop short and Bert bumps into me.

She stares down at me from that painting and then I hear Chuck's voice coming from the vaulted passageway on the opposite side from where Lexis has her studio.

I jog down the hall, past a doorway that leads into the kitchen, and into a bedroom of long drapes and marble columns. Chuck is sitting on the bed with his arm around Lexis. Her hands cover the top of her head. When she looks up at me, I stop, sickened.

"Jesus," I say.

"Frank," Chuck says, getting up and moving away from the bed.

Her hair is crimson and matted. One eye is a bluish slit. That side of her face has grown red and swollen. She's been crying and holds a knotted towel in her hand.

"Raymond," she says.

I hear Bert grunt behind me.

"You're thinking of someone else," I say, frozen in front of her.

"I know who you are," she says.

I shake my head and feel my plastic face.

"The Blue Hole," she says, angling her head. "I think of it every day."

Behind her is a painting on the wall.

Thundering water, foamy green. Three figures in the mist. Faceless parents holding hands with a child. My face is stern. I can feel it heat and my eyes filling.

"You said it couldn't happen," I say, sitting beside her on the bed, staring at my hands. "That we couldn't be apart."

I can smell the hint of Frank's Cool Water cologne. The demon that haunts even my memories. She reaches out and takes my hand, stroking my palm with her fingertips.

"In a way, we weren't," she says, looking into my eyes and tilting her head. "Part of you has been with me all the time. We made love that day, remember?"

I squint at the painting and see, now, my totem — the stick figure of a running deer — faintly etched in the mist above the father. A smaller totem floats over the child in the middle.

"You're a liar," I say, the words coming out before I can think about them. I stand.

She looks down, quiet for a moment. Then, without looking up, she says, "You've *seen* him. His eyes."

"He's not mine," I say. "If he was, you stole him. He belongs to you now, you and your husband.

"Chuck, call an ambulance," I say, then turn to go.

Lexis doesn't speak but I hear a wail as I put my hand on the door.

I stop.

"You loved me," she says.

I turn and glare at her. "I did."

"This mess," she says. Shaking her head, she drops off the edge of the bed and onto her knees. "It's all a mist. All these years. It can change. I'm begging you. He's your *son*."

I drop my head and close my eyes. I take a deep breath, fighting back a tide of emotions.

Suddenly Chuck steps forward.

"Frank said something to Allen about getting his money from Mickey and meeting him at the Rockefeller Outlook," he says. "It's a rest area on the Palisades Parkway, just north of the George Washington Bridge."

"Give me your gun," I say to Chuck.

I feel the heft of his HK self-loading .45 and close my fingers around it. Without looking back, I turn and go.

68

On our way up the Hudson Parkway, I call Ramo Capozza and tell him I think I've got a package for him. I ask him to have a couple guys meet me at the outlook. We cross the GW and head north on the Palisades. A few miles up, Bert points at the blue-and-white sign glowing in our headlights. The Rockefeller Outlook. There are no headlights in my rearview mirror. Ahead a pair of taillights disappear around a bend. I slow and pull off the parkway.

Under a row of streetlights, faded yellow diagonal lines mark two dozen parking spots along the river's side of the narrow parking area. It's empty except for a dark green Excursion and a small Mercedes sedan. Nothing moves. Beyond them is a line of trees, ghostlike in the glow of light. I turn off my headlights and coast to a stop behind the Excursion. Small stones and grit crunch under the tires, and I hold my finger to my lips signaling Bert to be quiet.

We slip out of the black G55 and stand together surveying the area. The trees that line the sharp edge of the Palisades are broken by a sidewalk lined with lollipop telescopes where you can see the sights of the Hudson up close for fifty cents. Beyond the walk is a jagged line of black rocks separating the outlook from the plunging drop that leads to the river hundreds of feet below. On the far side of the Hudson, the distant lights from the Bronx twinkle around the mouth of the Harlem River.

But there is no sign of Frank.

I lean close to Bert and in a whisper say, "Stay here. I'll take a look."

"I should go too," Bert says in a low rumble.

"No," I say. "If they come back, don't let them get away. Be careful."

I leave Bert in the shadow of the Excursion. Crouching low, I hurry up onto the sidewalk. Now I can see the city to the south.

I hear nothing except the rustle of leaves in the breeze until the horn of a freighter moving upriver sounds from deep below. There is a sign I see now planted between the big toothy rocks. do not climb on the bluff. As I move closer to the edge of the darkness, a light flashes at the same time a pop sounds from below. They are swallowed almost instantly by the darkness, and for a moment I wonder if I imagined it. Then I hear a shriek, and voices.

Frank.

Nothing mattered to Frank anymore but his boy and the money. When he saw Mickey's car resting under the lights, his face stretched taut with a grin. Things were working so well that the pain in his leg and hand and neck seemed distant, unimportant. He pulled up the truck alongside the small Mercedes and looked around only briefly before climbing out.

Allen got out too. Frank turned to tell him to stay, but the throb in the meat of his leg and the sharp stabbing pain in his hand made him think again. A car whooshed past on the parkway, its taillights a blur.

"Come on," Frank said, and limped toward the darkness.

He stepped up onto the curb, kicking a pinecone and crushing some broken glass. The loose edge of a garbage bag snapped against its metal can. Frank sniffed again. No sign of Mickey. The cut in his neck began to burn. Then he heard his name being called and the smell of a cigarette floated up and swirled away.

The muted sound came again from the blackness beyond the outlook's lip and was quickly swept away on the breeze. Frank steadied himself against a metal telescope and slid the Glock out from under his arm before creeping toward the edge. When he got to the rock barrier he eased down onto the rough cool stone and leaned over into the dark, looking and aiming at the same time.

The dim figure of a man with the ember of a cigarette glowing in his mouth waved his arms.

"Frank," he said. "Down here."

It was Mickey, his rat face lit by the sudden orange flare of the cigarette.

Frank sat down on the top of one of the big rocks and swung his legs over the side. As his eyes adjusted, he saw that a steep grassy bank descended about twelve feet to another outcropping of flat rock. Beyond that was a darkness deeper yet. Even from where he was, Frank could feel the void and it chilled his spine.

"Come on," he said to Allen, and struggled down to the outcrop below, letting his bottom slide along, matting the grass for the last four feet.

Allen's feet struck the rock and he bent over to help. Frank stood breathing hard, wincing from the pain. Mickey was grinning at them in the dim glow from the big city ten miles away. He stood on the very edge between two enormous duffel bags, the canvas kind used for carrying hockey equipment. In front of Mickey was a small suitcase.

Mickey pitched his butt over the edge, opened his arms, and said, "It's not that I don't trust you, Frank. But this is a lot of money and it'll take you a few minutes to get it back up that hill. Time for me to get my little Sioux City girl and get going. Nothing personal. Just the way you taught me."

"Where's the passports?" Frank asked, hobbling slowly toward the edge.

Mickey smiled and said, "You'll get those when I get up on that ledge and you're down here."

"But you've got them?" Frank said, his voice rising to expose the panic he was beginning to feel.

"Sure I do," Mickey said. He picked up the suitcase and started to circle away from the edge.

Frank raised the Glock and shot him in the knee.

Mickey dropped and writhed on the rock ledge, mewling. Frank closed the gap, reached into Mickey's coat, and came up with a sleek new Smith & Wesson Model 66. He held it out to Allen.

"You might need this."

Allen looked at him blankly.

"Take it!" Frank shouted.

"Dad, Jesus," Allen said, shaking his head and grabbing a handful of his own hair.

Frank frowned at his son, the silence and the stupid expression on his face.

"Be a man, goddamn it," Frank said. "You're my son, now act like it."

"I don't want that," he said, pushing away the gun, his eyes fixed on Mickey.

"You will if you need it," Frank said, opening his hand and slapping it in there. "You think you just get a Platinum Card and a Land Cruiser on your sixteenth birthday? You gotta do things to get that stuff."

Frank bent back down. He dug deeper into Mickey's coat and came up with a thick brown envelope. Mickey continued to whimper.

"Shut up," Frank snarled.

He tore open the envelope to examine the papers in the dim light. Passports with his and Lexis's and Allen's pictures in them along with phony birth certificates, credit cards, driver's licenses, and social security cards. The whole package had cost him a hundred thousand dollars, but the names and the social security numbers were real, so they could get through any airport or customs agent in the world without raising an alarm. The ones for Lexis he slipped back into the envelope and tossed over the edge of the bluff.

By daybreak, Capozza's men would be hunting for him with everything they had, but he and Allen would be long gone.

"What do you think about seventy million dollars?" he said, looking from the bags to his son. "You think we can get by on that? Huh?"

Allen looked at him blankly.

"Dad," he said, "are you kidding?"

Frank pulled his collar away from his neck, exposing a thin red line of flesh.

"Is this a joke?" he said.

"Jesus, Dad," Allen said, stepping away from him.

Frank stuck his Glock in Mickey's face. The smaller man winced and started scrabbling away.

"Get over there," Frank said, wagging his gun toward the bags, prodding Mickey with the barrel.

"Frank," Mickey said in a whine,

clutching his mangled knee, "what are you gonna do?"

Mickey was cowering there at the lip. Frank raised the gun as if to strike. When Mickey turned his face away, Frank put the bottom of his shoe against the accountant's rump and shoved. Mickey screamed and flailed, his arms grasping air. He hung for a moment in the empty space, then disappeared into the darkness with a fading howl.

"Jesus," Allen said, his voice breaking, his eyes leaking tears. He stood there, arms by his sides with the wind whipping at his dark hair. One fist was clenched. In the other hand, he held the Model 66 by the barrel. Frank felt his face grow hot.

"Take one of these," he said. He put his Glock into its shoulder holster, hoisted one of the big heavy bags, and lifted the small suitcase of Mickey's money with his hurt hand.

"Take it!" Frank yelled, limping toward the bank with his hands full.

Allen nodded, but didn't move.

Frank sensed something coming at him from above, but he had no time to think and react. He heard a cry and felt the jolt. Everything went black and he fell backward, dropping the money and splitting the back of his scalp open on the stone.

69

The sound of Frank's raised voice makes my heart beat faster and my shoulders tense. I dart down behind one of the rocks with the .45 raised and listen.

I hear Frank shout again over the wind. The murmur of Allen's response. A growl and the whining stops. I ease into the space between two of the rocks and look down.

Frank looking at papers. Allen with a gun. Frank tosses an envelope away, then prods the man he shot toward the edge. When he kicks him over, my gut twists, but I hold tight. He's still got that gun and I'll be an easy target if I show myself with the glow of the rest area lights behind me.

Allen is crying, and then Frank's greed takes over. Instead of leaving one of the bags and keeping the gun in his hand, he holsters it, picks up one bag and the suitcase, and heads snarling toward the grassy slope.

I could kill him now, but that wouldn't do. Not after all I've been through.

Capozza's men — the thing that really terrifies Frank — are on their way. He needs to suffer. I stick the .45 into the waist of my pants. When he's close, I jump up onto the rock I'm hiding behind and launch myself down on top of him. In midair, I am illuminated by headlight beams that swing over the top of me from behind.

I strike him and roll to the side, rising to my feet and drawing my gun.

Frank crabs his fat frame backward toward the ledge, leaving the money behind. The lights from whatever car has just arrived stream over the top of us, broad blue beams that stab into the darkness above the pitchy river.

"Stop!" I yell.

Allen stands off to the side, between us. He has a revolver in his hands, pointed my way now, wagging it back and forth. My gun is aimed steady at Frank's head. His shoulders heave up and down from the effort to breathe. His hands go in the air and he gets up on one knee. He glares at me, blinking, those empty blue eyes piercing beneath the eaves of his heavy brow.

"Seth," he says, the name slipping from his bared teeth. "Where's Raymond?"

"You're looking at him," I say with a tight smile.

Frank looks at Allen and screams, "Shoot him!"

My eyes never waver from the snake.

"Allen," I say, "I came to take you back to your mother."

"Do what I say!" Frank screams. His face is red and flecks of white spittle fly from his small chubby lips.

"He's not your father, Allen," I say slowly, relishing the shade of purple that blooms in Frank's face. "That's why you're nothing like him. You're my son."

"You *fucking* liar," Frank snarls. "I'll kill you . . ."

He starts to lower his hands. I shake the gun at him.

"Move, Frank, and you'll die right now."

"*Kill* him!" Frank shouts at Allen. "Pull the fucking trigger!"

"Genetics, Allen," I say. "You took biology. Two blue-eyed parents can only have blue-eyed kids. You have brown eyes . . . like mine."

I hear Bert call my name from behind. That low rumble. His giant shadow confuses the headlight beams. I see Allen spin and the flash of his gun. The shadow disappears and Bert cries out.

My eyes flicker. Frank dives. Allen goes down with him. My gun follows Frank, but

I can't pull the trigger. His head is behind Allen's.

I see the glint of metal. Long and thin. From his sleeve, Frank has drawn a blade that now rests against Allen's throat. A fishing fillet knife. Like the one used to frame me in another lifetime.

"If he's yours, then you don't want me slittin' his throat," Frank says in a growl. He raises himself up behind Allen, pulling him up too, using him as a shield.

Allen's eyes are wide. He gropes for his neck.

The knife licks his skin and his limbs freeze.

I see those deep brown eyes. I see myself.

"Seth," he says, begging me.

"See?" Frank says, sneering from behind Allen's dark head of hair.

"He's mine, Frank," I say. "The whole game is mine. They'll find you."

"They'll find you dead first," Frank snarls. "Put the fucking gun down, or they'll find him too."

My hand lowers and my fingers go loose. The .45 clatters to the rock floor.

"Get down," Frank says. "Put your hands on your head. Now! Him or you."

I feel the energy drain quickly from my

body. I kneel and lace my fingers over the top of my head, but I'm watching.

"Good," Frank says. He pushes Allen aside and draws his Glock.

He limps over to me and touches the pistol to my forehead. I can hear his ragged breath. I can smell his cologne and garlic wrapped in mint. He moves behind me where I can't see him, dragging the metal barrel across my scalp and up over my fingers until it comes to rest in the soft tissue beneath the back of my skull.

Allen's face is white, his hair a tangle from the wind. Behind him the big city blazes, floating.

"I'm gonna do what that jury shoulda done," Frank says in a husky whisper. "The death sentence."

I close my eyes and the gunshot explodes in my ears.

Frank crashes down on top of me and I see a burst of lights. When he rolls off, I am covered in blood.

Helena is standing in the beams of the headlights, her shadow like a dark angel, hair pulled back, faded jeans, the smoking three-inch Chief's Special in her hands. She crouches, hops over the edge of the rocks, and slides down the grassy bank with her gun raised.

I pull my legs out from under Frank's bulk and step back. Allen is on his knees, shaking, his head in his hands. Frank's gut protrudes up out of his dirty jacket, stretching the buttons of the white shirt that is now crimson with blood on the left side. His chest heaves up and down and as he wheezes blood foams at his lips. His eyes are wide with fear and he stares up at Helena. His fingers twitch and claw around the rocky ledge in search of his gun.

Helena's eyes are glassy and narrowed, and when I call her name, she doesn't react. The Chief's Special is trembling, but well aimed at Frank's face.

"Helena!" I shout. "Don't."

"Do you remember me?" she says to Frank.

She drops the gun from his face to his crotch and fires three quick 9mm rounds.

The only thing I can hear through the hot smell of powder and the smoke and the ringing in my ears is the symphony of Frank's piercing screams.

Another car shrieks to a stop above us and I hear the slamming of doors. Capozza's men are soon beside me with their guns drawn. They grin like jackals as they haul Frank up the hillside by his ankles. His agony is mixed with fear now. Sobs punctuate his shrill moaning as his head bumps along the stony ground.

Allen's face is blank. I tell him to come on. I take Helena's hand and tug her up the hill. Bert is dusting himself off, bleeding from a nick in the upper arm from Allen's gun. Under the glow of the streetlights I can see Frank twisting and hysterical in the trunk of an old Lincoln Town Car. Capozza's men slam it shut and go back over the edge for the money. They heave the heavy duffel bags into the backseat and then climb into the front. The doors slam.

Inside the trunk, Frank's muffled squealing pitches even higher. The car's gears clank. The tires yip. Off they go.

EPILOGUE

On the front steps of my Fifth Avenue mansion I stop to inhale the smell of fallen leaves. Orange, yellow, and red light up the treetops in the park. It's cloudy in the city, but the TV says the weather upstate is beautiful. My limousine takes me to Teterboro airport. When I climb on board my plane, Bert is sitting there in the main cabin, grinning up at me.

"Hey," I say. "When did you get back?"

"This morning," he says. "You gotta go next time. Here, look at this."

He hands me a small cardboard folder with a photo inside. Bert taking up a two-person seat on a giant log ride, plummeting, hands in the air, mouth wide in a happy scream.

"Splash Mountain," he says.

I give him a smile, hand his photo back, and sit down in the leather seat across the aisle. I recline my seat, close my eyes, and say, "Syracuse plays Louisville today. Allen's starting at quarterback. You coming with me?"

"He's doing all right?" Bert says.

"He's finally sleeping at night," I say, "so they think he may have started to put it behind him. They say it was harder with Frank just disappearing. No closure, I guess."

"What about you?" Bert says. "Is it behind you?"

"I guess."

The jet takes off and the rumble of the engines puts me to sleep until we're ready to land and I sit up. Below, the trees are on fire with the colors of autumn. When we get off, the blue sky is crisp. I tell the pilots to leave my bags. Bert and I drive to the Dome and watch the game from my box. Lexis is there. She has some guests from the fine arts department, where it's been arranged for her to teach next semester.

Syracuse wins the game and Allen makes his share of good plays. Afterward, we wait outside the players' entrance with Lexis, but when Allen appears limping slightly and his head wet from the showers, Bert and I hang back. I watch her nod and smile at him. She kisses his cheek and off he goes with his friends.

In the truck, Lexis says, "I got Dinosaur Bar-B-Que for dinner. I know you like it."

"My dad sure did."

"Allen's coming."

I raise an eyebrow.

"What did the counselor say about that?"

"He lost his father, Raymond."

"I'm his father," I say.

"Be patient," she says. "It will all work out."

Lexis insisted on something modest. A four-bedroom Queen Anne row house on a hill adjacent to campus so she can walk to classes. Bert and I have a beer on the front porch while Lexis gets it ready.

Dinner is nice. Barbecue with mashed potatoes, greens, gravy, and corn bread on fancy china plates. A round table with a linen cloth in the modest high-ceilinged dining room. Candles flickering down on us from an antique silver candelabra. Allen brings a friend from the team who's as big as Bert, and I have to stop them from thumb wrestling so I can make a toast with the port.

I raise my glass and say, "To family."

Bert clears his throat. Allen and Lexis look at the table, then Allen looks up at me and says, "Family."

Allen and his friend tell us they're already late to the bars on Marshall Street. I'm glad to see him kiss his mom and give her a big hug in front of the friend. I'm even happier when he shakes my hand and looks me in the eye. When they're gone, we move to the living room. The floorboards creak under our feet.

Bert brings in some wood and starts a fire before lowering himself into a big mission oak chair with leather padding. The walls are covered with a light blue paper that goes nicely with the white trim. Prints, mostly Monet and Mary Cassatt, hang in simple frames, and the window sashes are crowded with small green plants growing in jam jars behind the thin white curtains. Against one wall is a big bookcase filled to the top.

Lexis sets a tray of coffee on the table in front of the couch and sits down next to me. The fireplace is brick with a carved golden oak mantel. Above it rests the painting of the Blue Hole with its family in the mist. The wood pops and I stare at the flames. We talk football for a few minutes, then our voices trail off. Bert gets up to take a walk. He invites us to come, but we just sit.

When the front door closes, Lexis leans her head into my shoulder and says, "Will you ever just stay?"

I take a deep breath and exhale slowly through my nose.

"I'll always be here for you, Lexis, but Raymond's gone. I told you that," I say quietly.

"What about Seth?" she says, touching my cheek with the back of her fingernails. Her eyes are moist.

"Didn't you say if you could control it, then it wasn't your destiny?" I say, taking her fingers in my hand and squeezing them before I set them back into her lap.

When I stand up, I try to look at her, but can't.

"I'm sorry," I say in a whisper.

As I come down the front steps, Bert appears on the sidewalk out of the darkness. His hands are jammed deep into the pockets of his leather coat.

"What are you doing?" I ask him.

He shrugs and says, "What are you?"

"Got a trip," I say. "A long one."

"Need me?" he says.

"You can take me to the airport."

We get into the truck. I start the engine and say, "You can do anything you want, you know."

"Yeah," Bert says, nodding. "Twenty million dollars is a lot. I don't know if I ever said thanks. I could buy some of this land back."

I smile at him and hold out my fist with

my thumb raised. I pin him quick and we play while I drive one-handed until he gets the edge on me at best out of twenty. When we pull out onto the tarmac, I shut off the engine and we sit listening to it click.

A big 727 rolls down toward the end of the runway, its lights flashing in the dark. It sits for a moment, then its engines begin to whine then scream and it starts off. We can hear the thumping of its tires, the pace quickening until the wheels leave the earth. It seems to hang for a moment and I hold my breath. Then it noses up and soars off with a roar.

"I still don't get that," Bert says.

A ground handler appears in a gray jumpsuit and knocks on the window to ask if he should get the pilots. I tell him yes and he walks inside.

"So," Bert says. "Am I going?"

"No," I say, shaking my head. "I've got to do this alone."

The pilots come out of the hangar, look my way, then board the plane.

"You'll miss me," Bert says.

"I know."

"You'll call me, though?" he says. "If you got anyone else you want to kill or destroy or something?"

I laugh and Bert grins. I get out of the truck and he steps around and walks me to the plane.

"What would your grandmother say?" I ask.

"My grandmother would do this," he says, and he wraps his arms around me and lifts me up off the ground, squeezing the breath out of me before setting me down. "And then she'd say fly with the eagles my friend and look sharp."

I clap a hand on his shoulder and press my lips tight, widening my eyes so they won't spill their tears.

When I wake, I sit up and look out the window. The sun is breaching the green mountains and the Mediterranean shines up at me like stained glass. In Naples, a car and driver are waiting on the tarmac. He takes me south along the Amalfi coast, a winding road that snakes in and out of tunnels and along the lips of sheer cliffs.

The car passes through Positano, whose houses and shops are as colorful as a palette. A mile outside of town, on a hairpin bend, we drive through a set of gates and straight into the brick-paved entrance of the San Pietro Hotel. Inside is an elevator that takes me down through the rock. I walk out into a dank cave that is suddenly filled with a breath of salty air, cooled by the sea. Ahead is a sliver of beach. Shells. Pebbles. Cool black sand.

Up some stone steps and I'm standing at one end of a broad terrace whose lip drops ten feet to the surf. Concrete poured over the rocks. Thick padded lounge chairs covered with orange terrycloth. At the bar are three men in white polo shirts. One is behind the bar, cleaning glasses; the other two lean against it, talking.

Half a dozen patrons are already stretched out in the sunshine that has just cleared the cliffs above. At the far end of the terrace, off by itself, one of the orange lounge chairs faces the open sea to the north. All that is visible is the back of a woman's head and one long bronze arm as it replaces a glass of ice and lime onto a small cocktail table. I step into the sunlight, weave through the chairs, and step out into the open space. The two men from the bar are suddenly by my side.

One touches my sleeve. In heavily accented English, he says, "I'm sorry. You cannot go there. This is private."

"I know her," I say, removing his hand.

"I'm sorry, sir," he says. "No one can disturb her."

"How long has she been here like this?" I ask. "With no one talking to her?"

The man scowls at me and says, "Three weeks. Maybe four. Please."

"No," I say, starting her way and shrugging them aside. "She'll want to see me."

"Sir," he says, raising his voice.

I keep going. Helena is stretched out in a white two-piece bathing suit. She must have her eyes closed behind the sunglasses because she doesn't get up when I block out the light.

"Please go away," she says. "Nothing personal, but as soon as I sign one thing, I'll get hounded for the rest of the day."

Her voice is tired and irritated.

"What if I don't ask you to sign anything?" I ask, and her body stiffens.

She takes off her sunglasses and blinks up at me.

"Why are you here?" she asks, scowling.

"Because you are," I say, "and I'm finished with everything that had to be done."

"With her?"

I nod, but say, "Yes and no. She's the mother of my son. Part of me cares about her."

"And the other part?" she asks, her lip trembling.

I kneel down beside her chair.

"Everything else," I say, "is for you. If you'll take it."

She presses her lips tight and says, "You'll never leave?"

"You saved my life," I say. "The new one."

"Meaning?"

"I owe you a life," I say. "I want to pay it back to you. Ten times. A hundred if I can."

"Show me," she says.

"I will."

She reaches up and touches my face, guiding me to her until our lips touch . . . From the corner of my eye I see the waiters gawking, wishing they were me, and then I shut my eyes.

ABOUT THE AUTHOR

Tim Green is the bestselling author of nine previous thrillers, as well as the nonfiction *New York Times* bestseller *The Dark Side of the Game*. In 1986 he graduated from Syracuse University at the top of his class with an English degree before playing eight years in the NFL and becoming a member of the New York State Bar. Today he is the host of Fox TV's *A Current Affair* and a featured commentator on *Good Morning America*, NPR, *The Bob Edwards Show*, and FOX Sports. He lives with his wife and four children in upstate New York, where he's working on his next book and practicing law.